John Campbell was born in 1936 in Belfast's York Street district. After leaving school, he worked at Belfast Docks until 1985. He now works for the Queen's University, Belfast, and is a senior shop steward for the Transport & General Workers' Union. A well-known writer and commentator on Belfast working-class life, he has published three individual collections of poetry: *Saturday Night in York Street* (1982), *An Oul Jobbin' Poet* (1989) and *Memories of York Street* (1991). *The Rose and The Blade: New & Selected Poems 1957-1997* was published recently by Lagan Press.

CORNER KINGDOM

CORNER KINGDOM

JOHN CAMPBELL

LAGAN PRESS
BELFAST

Published by
Lagan Press
7 Lower Crescent, Belfast BT7 1NR

ISBN: 1 873687 65 6
Author: Campbell, John
Title: Corner Kingdom
Format: Paperback
1999

Cover Photograph: Belfast Street Scene early 1950s
(*photographer and area unknown*)
Cover Design: December
Set in New Baskerville
Printed by Noel Murphy Printing, Belfast

for Barbara—
who lived through the nightmare

A Dedication

To all who slung the Rosies
or sunk the China clay.
Who drove a winch in winter,
or shovelled grain all day.
To those who signed the dockets
or drew the stowage plan.
For those who loaded yella meal
up a screeching Iron-Man.
To the expert on the bull-rope
who worked with skill and speed.
For those who topped the 'tween-decks
or followed down the lead.
For the watchmen and the hatchmen,
the truckers and the sweepers,
for the men who worked the Slag boat,
or stacked the railway sleepers.
To those who toiled on ship or shore
and fed the hungry hook.
To this all but vanished species,
I dedicate this book.

ONE

A thin, almost invisible, sheet of drizzle sprayed the grey square-setts that formed the surface of the Clarendon Dock. It brought curses and exclamations of disgust from the dock labourers and casuals who had been pouring into the schooling pen since the early hours of Wednesday morning when the Belfast Harbour police had opened the large wooden gates to allow them to report for work. The rain was also damned by the newspaper-seller who struggled hard to keep his copies of the early morning dailies dry and sellable.

He leaned against his bicycle and watched with a detached air as the stream of men filed past him and positioned themselves in the area where the foremen and gangers of the various stevedores would school labour for the vessels that needed loading or unloading. Heavy overcoats stretching almost to ground level were in abundance. Flat caps clung to heads in various positions of fashion. Some were pulled low across the wearer's eyes whilst others hung precariously to the side of its owner's head. Business was not good as the men seldom bought newspapers when it was raining. The schooling pen was an open berth and the newspapers would be reduced to an unreadable pulp in no time at all.

"Givus a *Mirror*, Bucky," said a voice to his left. Without looking up, he produced a paper from below the rubber ground sheet that covered the canvas bag in the carrier of the bike and passed it to the stockily-built middle-aged man. He counted the coins passed into his half-gloved hand and reached over to select the change from a satchel around his waist. "Keep it," said the man

11

as he folded the newspaper carefully and put it into his overcoat pocket.

"Thanks, Jack," sighed Bucky as his numb fingers dragged the bottom of his pullover down to hide the money-bag. He nodded at the youth standing at Jack's side. "That's Aggie's eldest, isn't it?" he inquired, as if the boy wasn't there. "Yer surely not bringing him down here for a day's work?" Jack was a small man with a boxer's flat face and thick short grey hair which looked like the bristles on a scrubbing brush.

"Me ma asked me to bring him down. Since our Billy dropped dead in the shipyard Aggie's had it hard."

"What age is he?" continued Bucky.

"He's just over fifteen, but he's big for his age. Does a bit of boxin' amateur for Roly Briggs," he continued, mentioning a local youth club instructor. "Gonna be an Ulster champion, aren't ya Jim?" he said turning to the boy and throwing a playful punch which the lad easily deflected as he said "Yis Uncle Jack," with a bashful smile.

"Is that his da's overcoat he's wearin'?" whispered Bucky, not wishing to offend the lad. "Aye," replied Jack, "It's kinda big for him but he hadn't one of his own an' anybody who'd come out a day like that without one, hasn't got one."

Somewhat ashamed and embarrased by the men talking about him as if he wasn't there, Jim found himself half moving and half pushed forward into the dense pack of men forging their way into the square. He moved on aimlessly and found himself at the opposite end of the schooling pen. The men were beginning to form themselves into semi-circles and he became immersed in one.

The gable end of a large wooden transit shed formed the radius of the circle. It was painted grey and bore the graffitti of tired and idle hands. The men's eyes rested on a huge paunchy ganger. His back was pressed hard against the wooden wall for support and his feet were planted firmly on the glistening square-setts.

12

He swayed gently back and forth whilst drumming a fistful of job-checks from one hand to the other. These objects were circular metal discs similar to a large silver coin and stamped with the initials of the stevedore for whom the ganger employed the men.

His face was expressionless as he took a pocket watch from his overcoat and squinted at it for a second or two, before averting his eyes upward into the drizzle. He readjusted the storm collars to cover his exposed neck and then punched the hand holding the watch back into the pocket in a bad-tempered gesture.

"Big Ned mustn't have got a curer yet," whispered a pale-faced scarecrow of a man to Jim's right. They were so close that Jim could feel the wet spittle on his cheek as the man continued: "He was in the Bunch last night ... blutered. Two of his cronies had to carry him out to his car."

"Aye," growled another voice, "an' I bet he niver bought a drink."

"Why change the habit of a lifetime?" tittered another.

All around them similar semi-circles formed. Each school watched each ganger apprehensively whilst droplets of rain fell from the peaks of their caps onto the tips of their noses or trickled down the back of their necks as they moved and fidgeted like a herd of hobbled horses.

Almost every inch of the compound was covered by a sweating, soaking carpet of humanity as almost two thousand casual workers swamped the square going through their daily soul-destroying ritual of seeking work. Ned continued to sway as he viewed the restless men beyond his own school and listened to their raucous voices as they bantered each other. He allowed himself a tight smile of pride as he brought his eyes back to the men facing him.

There was no talking, laughing, or shuffling horseplay. Each individual's eyes were firmly fixed on the ganger's fleshy features, and each knew he didn't like talkers, laughers, jokers, pushers or fly men. His expert gaze sought workers. Tough, experienced, obedient men who would sweat under his gaze and take his insults in silence as he drove them harder and faster than any other ganger on Belfast's cross-channel dock.

Jim Harvey gazed with absolute awe that stopped on the other side of fright. He had never stood as close to a figure which commanded so much respect and instilled so much fear. Ned was about six feet tall and seemed almost as wide. He looked to weigh in the region of seventeen stone. His many-chinned unshaven features harboured small pig-like eyes the colour of ebony and seemed capable of biting chunks of flesh from any face he looked upon. Jim thought him to be in his late forties.

He was clad in a dark navy surplus overcoat which buttoned double across his well-fed stomach. The hem of this garment stopped a foot from the ground and umbrellowed over his wide-legged blue denim overalls. His size twelve handmade brown boots were long-legged and upturned at the toes by the constant rocking of his body.

The semi-circle stiffened as one man when a piercing scream from a steam-driven klaxon horn on the roof of the nearby Gallaher's tobacco factory cut through the mizzle at exactly four minutes to eight o'clock.

Jim felt the crowd tighten as each man intensified his efforts to catch the ganger's eye. When he shifted his feet and drew the hand containing the silver discs from the warmth of his roomy pocket the youth suddenly remembered his uncle's advice not to stray from his side. He was caught in the tightly-packed mass and was unable to dislodge himself.

When the crowd edged forward a fraction in anticipation, the ganger snarled obscenities that cracked on the damp air like a lion-tamer's whip. The men fell back sheepishly, shuffling until they were behind a line marked only by his angry glare.

He grunted with satisfaction when a suitable distance between himself and the mass was established and at that moment, on the first stroke of the Albert Clock as it chimed the hour of eight, he began selecting his men.

His wintery gaze fell on one of the few men who didn't wilt

under it. The man was a registered dock labourer and as such was almost Ned's equal. He and his colleagues did not often seek the dirty and dangerous hard work associated with a cement boat but when they did their union membership of the Belfast dockers' branch entitled them to receive the cleanest and safest jobs in the gang. Ned's eyes flickered impatiently as another man wearing the same conspicious lapel badge also stepped forward with his hand outstretched.

"Hatch an' spell yer mate on the winch, an' no booze or I'll have ye up before the green table," were the terse instructions the man received as he moved to join his companion. The ganger fingered the remaining discs pensively as his eyes locked with a non-union casual who had spent most of the previous night filling him with Black Bush whiskey in order to get a winch driving job. That position had gone to the first man schooled. The casual was a very competent winch-driver and ordinarily would have been Ned's choice. Unfortunately he was unable for any other physical work and Ned's eyes quickly passed over him.

Jim, trapped like a sardine in the middle of the crowd, had given up trying to escape. He watched as the ganger's gaze moved slowly around the human semi-circle with the same menace as the turret gun of a Churchill tank. His head stabbed the air as he nodded four times, deftly and quickly at four men each wearing the distinctive lapel badge who walked forward to receive a job-check from the pudgy hands.

"Back-jag number one hatch," ordered the ganger, his eyes fixed on the men he would choose next. "Back-jag my arse," whispered someone behind Jim. "That's just another name for scratchin' yer clinkers whilst mugs like us do the heavy graft."

"Aye, if yer lucky till git it," hissed another.

The ganger heard the remarks and scowled in the general direction. "Fuck off if yis don't like it. First preference means first preference." Ned took no nonsense. Like it or not, the men wearing the distinct blue buttons in their coat lapels were his brothers in union—as for the others, he regarded them as dirt

15

beneath his feet. Just so many bodies to be employed and exploited. Any man who stepped out of line or in any other way incurred the wrath of the big ganger would find the following morning that the steely glare would ignore him and nod out another man in his place.

This procedure would persist until the man had served his penance. If the offence was serious, then his chance of employment was as dead as if the big man had read his obituary in the *Belfast Telegraph*. Ned was judge, jury and hatchet man if need be, consequently the shoremen remained tight-lipped and didn't ask for help from the back-jaggers who were employed to aid them throw dusty sacks, each weighing one hundredweight from the truck beds into tiers that rose head-high.

As he gazed into the sea of anxious faces, Ned noticed with satisfaction the departure of the remaining first preference men in the direction of other schools. He smiled thinly. He didn't like them around when there was work to be done. They insisted in sticking to union rules and worse than that some of them couldn't be bullied.

He much preferred the second preference men. They were also unionised but not members of the dockers' union and therefore with little or no rights. Their pecking order was recognised by a lapel badge which was coloured red. It carried the letters SP, denoting second preference.

He grinned without mirth as some of the reds broke from his school and scattered towards the other gangers, leaving their places to be filled instantly by pinched-faced non-union casuals. These men had no preference and no rights. Both sets of preference men openly despised this group whom they saw as parasites.

Ned neither acknowledged nor cared about the hurried exodus. He waited until they settled down and then started looking for six holdsmen. These were the workers who toiled in the hatch of the vessels stacking the bags into rope slings. This dirty and extremely dangerous duty was performed at high speed, sometimes in intolerable conditions. The hatchman would watch their progress then signal the winch-driver to hoist the sling carrying the bags out of the ship's hold and onto the breast of the quay where the shoremen would be waiting to receive it. The ship's winches were mostly steam-driven and superior in speed to the slow-moving harbour-owned cranes which were also costly for the stevedores to hire.

The hatchmen toiled in pairs and had to be strong and experienced. Each man tried to retain his own mate, becoming quiet and withdrawn if forced to work with a stranger.

"There's no room in a cement houl for beginners," Ned would often say to men who approached him for such a job. He would take nothing but experts. This morning he needed six such men and smiled smugly as he noted more than twenty men who fitted the bill. Moreover he knew the men he was hiring, having chosen them almost twenty minutes earlier.

The checks jumped deftly from his hand as his head dipped rapidly back and forth like a man with a nervous tic. "Right ... you ... you. Here Billy ... C'mon Mack" and the six chosen slingers melted backwards to join the previously selected men. Those remaining were tense knowing only nine jobs were left. They prayed he'd dispose of them quickly and allow them to be maybe successful elsewhere.

Sensing their desperation, he took a perverse satisfaction in moving the checks from hand to hand. They had obviously diminished in number and some of the men stared intently at them as if hypnotised. Showing no signs of haste, he swayed gently and studied each concerned face intently.

He noted a few men casting backward glances at other gangers who had employed many more men in the same space of time. They proceeded quickly, treating the dockers and casuals with equal dignity. He sniggered sardonically, knowing he could get more work done in a day than they could in a week.

"C'mon," he growled, cocking his head at a tall rangy man with long legs and a raw-boned complexion. The casual, who sported a long flowing moustache, grinned with delight as he took the check. "You ... You ... Right ... C'mon ... " The chosen men exploded from the circle, each wearing expressions of relief. Quickly turning his back on the disappointed remainder, he held out his hands for the men's white cards.

These postcard-sized pieces of cardboard were the casual's only proof of work obtained at the quay. One side bore the worker's name, address and insurance number. The reverse side was cut into seven boxed segments denoting each day of the week. On the first day the casual received work, his insurance cards would be taken from him and stamped for the week and he would receive a white card. At the end of a spell the stevedore concerned would stamp his recognised letter in the appropriate box. The Central Wages Office would then pay out the following Thursday whatever money the casual had earned that week. The reds and blues carried paybooks which were also stamped and their holiday pay was calculated on the amount of stamps gathered over the year. The casuals were not entitled to holiday pay. The white cards served one purpose. Unscruplous stevedores would only take men who had the white card as it saved them the expense of an insurance stamp.

As the men handed back the checks and dug out their white cards the ganger singled out three of the shoremen. "Williams, Thompson, Reilly, git the truck and ropes from the store."

The men groaned inwardly, but nodded servile agreement. Jim was moving away to look for his Uncle Jack when he heard Ned explode with anger. "You're not stamped," he snarled with a venom that made Jim tremble. The tirade was directed at a man who had sheepishly handed a set of insurance cards to him. "Bloody hell, I can't take them on a Wednesday—the boss would flay me." He hurled the insurance cards into the air and roughly grabbed the check from the man's outstretched hand. The others watched silently as the shamefaced man bent to pick up the cards.

Ned turned and glared at the men who had hurriedly

reassembled. He had lost all interest for toying. His head was aching from last night's whiskey and he needed a quick cure which would not be enjoyed until the first heave was out and the boat was fully operational. Only then would he be able to slip into the backroom of the Bunch Of Grapes and sip some Black Bush in comfort.

Thrusting the check into the nearest hand, he shouldered his way through the crowd and squeezed into the driving seat of a blue-coloured Austin parked a few feet from where he stood.

"Don't be all bloody day gittin' to the boat," he snarled before driving off.

Jim Harvey looked with astonishment at the silver job-check nestling in the palm of his hand. The men around him dispersed bitterly. "Wudn't it be a great day for humanity if that bastard drove into the dock an' niver cum up again?" said one man wheeling a bicycle. "No chance," muttered his mate, adding, "Shite floats."

Jim watched as the car weaved through the departing men who were wending their way to the street corners where they would wile away the hours until the time came for their daily trip to the dole office. He was about to reach the check to one of them when he was pushed forward roughly and turned to see his Uncle Jack's angry face.

"Where'd ya go? I wus lukin' for ye, but cudn't leave the school I was in ta find ye," he growled harshly, all in one breath. Jim felt a nervous tension rising from the pit of his stomach. It was the same feeling he got when entering the boxing ring to fight. "I was just stannin'," he began.

"Niver mind," interupted Jack impatiently, "Yill havta go down there an' do yer best. Yer big for yer age an' strong enough." His tone softened. "Do ye know where she's lyin'?"

"Yis," replied the boy, "She's at the Herdman Channel."

"Go on down anyway," said Jack feeling somewhat guilty at neglecting the boy. "Big Ned'll probably chase ye, but go on—give it a dig."

Jim nodded mutely and quickened his pace. He caught up with the work gang and stayed slightly behind listening to their good-natured banter. They were in for a spell of work that would last a day or two and be as rough as an excursion to hell, but the money was better than most jobs.

Entering the harbour gates at Whitla Street he drew level with a small man wearing large hobnailed boots. The bottom of his threadbare trousers were tucked into his khaki-coloured socks. He was between the shafts of a red painted wooden handtruck and strutted across the square-setts like an aggressive banty-cock.

"Hi kid," he yelled at Jim. "Givus us a wee han' wi this truck." Recognising him as one of the men the ganger had ordered to go for equipment, Jim ran forward eagerly. The little casual was pulling the truck like a horse pulls a cart. Jim grabbed the shaft and added his weight. The truck was covered with what he assumed to be cement dust.

"Are ye at the cement?" he shouted to make himself heard over the clatter of the two steel wheels. The trucker glanced at him without disguising his scorn. "Naw, I'm shiftin' furniture for the man next door. Are you at it?"

Jim nodded and the man shook his head in disbelief. "Hell's gates son, them begs is heavier 'n you are." The lad looked at his unsympathetic and unshaven face and felt his stomach turn over. He wanted to let go of the truck, drop back and fade out of sight. But he held on, knowing his mother was in need of the money the spell might bring. He plodded on, head down as the rain worked its way through his long lank dark hair, soaking the collar of his tartan working shirt as it trickled down his back.

Following the steel tracks of the goods trains which moved cargo from the nearby railway station to the harbour sheds, they eventually sighted the bleak sheds of the Gotto Wharf, having covered almost half-a-mile in silence. The cement shed was a large hollow shell built with corrugated steel. It perched on the side of the Herdman Channel and was dwarfed by Rank's Flour Mill. Everything inside it was coated with the same dust that caked the truck. The small grey brick that formed the uneven floor glinted wetly as Jim and his companion hauled the truck in through one of the large open doorways.

"Thanks kid, an' beat it," snarled the little man, pushing Jim to the side and forcing him to loosen his grip on the shaft. The boy stopped breathless, as the trucker galloped by the ganger who was bellowing orders at the oncoming men. The inside of the cement shed was cold with blobs of condensation dripping from the roof to the floor, making the surface wet and slippery.

The ganger continued to bellow as the men ran to execute his every command. "Shoremen ... Git them waterside dours open. Youse hatchmen—git aboard an' stan' by ta strip the hatches when that rain dies. Weather forecast says it'll stop shortly an' I want this bloody boat finished the marra."

The shore-gang raced to the massive sliding doors and began prising them open.

"Hi you!" Jim froze when he realised the foreman was shouting at him. "Bring them rope slings up here," yelled Ned. The boy ran forward and lifted one neatly folded sling. He was numbed by the ganger's sarcastic bark. "Them all ... Them all ... Lift them all ... We'll be here all day if you lift them one at a time." Trying not to panic, Jim lifted the awkwardly-shaped bundle and proceeded to entangle them around his feet.

"For fuck's sake help him," snarled the foreman. Two shoremen left the doors and pushed Jim aside. "The people that git these childer jobs shud be made to work with thim," complained one man whose damp cap was pushed to the back of his carrot-coloured hair. Despite the cold, his shirt sleeves were rolled up to reveal thick, heavily tattooed arms. Lifting the bundle with ease he carried them up to the open door.

Jim was desperate to get from under the ganger's feet and ran towards the men forcing the doors along the runners which were blocked in places by hardened cement. He jumped in front of a casual wearing a red-coloured checkered shirt. Seconds later the checkered arm grabbed his shirt collar and flung him aside.

"More strength in an Oxo," laughed the man as Jim rose quickly to his feet, bewildered and embarrassed. He turned his head and saw the ganger bearing down on him, gesturing wildly. "Who are you anyway?" he screamed, "How in the name of Hell's gates did you git a check from me? This is a cement boat, not bloody Duffy's Circus." He scowled at Jim's light frame and added, "I've a pair of boots heavier than you. This is man's work, son, an' I've seen better men than you in the children's hospital."

Jim stood head bowed and silent under the onslaught. "Who's gonna work with ye? Shure there's not a man here strong enough to carry a wee shite like you. Givus that check an' go home and play hide an' seek or somethin."

Jim continued to look at his boots, trying to hide a deep flush of embarrassment, whilst searching his pockets for the check. He didn't see the slim, lightly-built man with a cap pulled low over amused eyes who walked from the shore gang to stand between him and Ned.

"He kin wurk with me ... I kin carry him," he said evenly, smiling coldly at the scowling ganger. "What for?" argued the ganger, "Shure ten minutes 'ill take me to the corner of Jack Mallen's pub. There'll be a few of the boys hingin' about there."

"He'll do me," insisted the other, moving Jim gently away from the ganger.

"Alright, alright," roared the ganger. The rain had stopped and he was anxious to get started. "But if he doesn't pull his weight, I'm chasin' him." He turned and stormed towards the waterside. "Get that bloody derrick topped—I want outa this tub the marra," he bellowed at the men on the ship's deck.

"Nigh kid," said Jim's saviour, "My name's Billy Kelly an' you an' me will be teamin' with Sammy Reilly here. He's the best trucker this side of the Pollock Dock." He gestured to the little man Jim had entered the shed with. Reilly was two or three yards away pouring oil from a milk bottle over the wheels of his truck. "Just do what I tell ye an' you an' me 'ill git along alright." He added, "C'mon, let's help Reilly git the truck in workin' order."

Reilly looked up when they arrived beside him. "She's a good 'un Billy," he said, gazing at Jim without recognition. Kelly looked past him and through the open doors. "We'd better git ready, it's clearin' up."

"Aye," replied Reilly, casting a sideways glance at the inexperienced Jim. "Whist I seen the last beg out," he added darkly.

The hatches and hatch-beams were speedily removed. Jim stood pensively and watched as the first slingful of cement bags were lifted from the hatch by the ship's winch. He counted four stacks of fawn-coloured paper sacks piled six high in the groaning rope sling. The winchman whipped it deftly across the ship's deck and down to the handtruck positioned on the narrow breast of the quay.

Acting on the hand-signals of the hatchman, he braked when the heave was about a foot above the truck. The load swung gently as the three man crew steadied it until it was directly over the truck. When satisfied with its position, the shoremen yelled at the hatchman whose hand signal told the winch-driver to lower. Almost before the load landed with a thud on the wooden body, the man between the shafts turned his back to the load, bent his knees and lifted the shafts waist high with a grimace. The men behind him shoved their shoulders into the bags, and quickly unhooked the eye of the sling whilst pushing the truck off the breast of the quay and into the shed.

Jim marvelled at the speed and efficiency of the team and prayed he wouldn't let Kelly down.

He watched as Reilly took a small grey pebble and popped it into his mouth before whispering, "It's us." Picking up the shafts of the truck he moved towards the open door. "Twenty-four begs," he noted glumly. "Big Ned must be on a bonus."

Kelly spoke with an urgency to Jim. "You stay to the right an' keep the heave straight. Reilly 'ill luk after the front. Don't push or pull 'er. Reilly 'ill do the rest. When yer man lowers, I'll grab the bight an' you hook off ... Okay?" Jim nodded mutely.

23

The loaded sling screamed over the ship's side and hovered above the truck for a split second.

"Lower," yelled Reilly and the stack of cement crashed heavily onto the truck, causing the two steel wheels on either side to fall back into a rut. Jim reached over and quickly unhooked the rope, as Kelly's left hand shot out and pulled the released rope's end over to his side of the truck and tucked in it between the bags.

"Houl the hook till it starts risin', in case it hits some of us," advised Kelly.

"Nigh," snarled Reilly, hoisting the shafts. Jim grabbed the fourth bag down on the back row and pulled with all his might. He almost cried with relief as the wheels rose out of the rut and the truck clattered into the shed. The first truck was still unloading as Reilly steered skilfully to the other side of it. Kelly had the sling cleared from the heave when Reilly stopped and sat down on one of the shafts.

"Right kid, speedo," hissed Kelly. Their hands were a blur as between them they lifted one sack at a time and threw them to the floor, one on top of another until they reached ten high.

"Deck," ordered Kelly, as Reilly moved the truck back a foot. Jim obeyed and they dropped the bag to the floor to begin another tier.

In less than a minute the truck was empty. "Grab that sheet," commanded Kelly as he pulled the empty sling from the already moving truck. Jim nodded silently and grabbed the strip of canvas that was placed over the rope by the holdsmen to stop the sling cutting into the bottom bags when the heave was hoisted ashore.

"Watch the dust don't get in yer eyes," puffed Reilly as Jim broke into a run to keep up with the trucker. Cement caked to the sweat streaming down his face as he worked steadily until the first tea-break.

The cups were stained grey like everything else in sight, but Jim gulped the sweet strong beverage as if it were the most delicious drink on earth. His hands shook slightly as he sipped from the cracked mug. He grinned warmly at Kelly's reassuring nod. "Yer doin' okay, kid," he said.

He knew he was doing alright when the ganger, fresh from the backroom of the Bunch of Grapes, came over to where they were seated.

"You're learnin' fast kid," he said with what passed for a reassuring smile flitting across his whiskey-flushed features.

"What's yer name anyway?"

"Jim Harvey, sor."

"Is Henry Harvey yer uncle an' Sam Harvey?"

"Yis, sor."

"What's yer ma's name?"

"Agnes, sor," replied the boy.

"Aggie Fennel?" laughed the ganger, using her maiden name. "I used to take her to the Alhambra an' court her in the back seat." He smiled at Jim slyly. "Shure I cud be yer da," he added craftily.

Again Jim nodded dumbly, not fully appreciating what was being said. "Right," snarled the ganger, tiring of the game, "Tea-break's over." The men dropped their cups into a bucket sitting on a wooden table and shuffled back to the trucks, looking forward to the longer lunch-break at twelve o'clock.

"First day on the quay an' yer talkin' man till man with Big Ned. Tuk me five months to get that honour. An' kid, don't be takin' that crap about yer ma serious, 'cause he tole the same story till all of us. It's his idea of a joke."

They walked warily through the burst bags accumulated during the unloading. The dust rose from the dunnage and circled around the work gang, floating to the roof of the building and cutting down the grey autumn light that filtered through the stained and cracked glass panels in the shed roof.

They worked ceaselessly with a minimum of talk under the baleful eye of the ganger. Jim watched as a truck in front of them was hit by a fast-falling heave. The hatchman had misjudged the speed and distance and the load, weighing over a ton, hit the back end of the truck. The force of the impact caused the front of the truck to rise into the air. The unfortunate trucker was hurled up along with it and crashed into the top of the heave before falling to the ground.

The ganger ran to the side of the ship nearest the accident and leaned over the rail. "Every time I luk at you Hagan yer sittin' on yer arse. Get the fuck up outa there or I'll go down the road an' git a man in yer place," he screamed at the bemused trucker who had landed heavily on the quay.

Hagan rose shakily to his feet and grasped the shafts of the truck as the heave was refloated and landed properly. The man's face was lined with agony as he steered the load towards the pile. The back-jaggers watched with arms folded as the men fought manfully to keep the load on the truck as it moved toward the pile.

"Why don't they help?" asked Jim.

"They might git their han's dirty," grinned Kelly.

"Everybody luks after themselves. It's hard enough to do your own work without doin' somebody else's," added Reilly coldly.

"Anyway, if Hagan had been watchin' the heave instead of dreamin', his mates wudn't a lost that time. This is no place for dreamers, kid." Lifting the shafts he returned to sucking the little grey pebble that kept his mouth from drying up.

Jim looked longingly at a galvanised steel bucket half-filled with drinking water. It had a perpetual skin of dust on its surface. A cracked finger-marked cup hung at its side, attached by a piece of rusty wire. The men drank from it occasionally to replace lost fluid and clear the cement from their mouths and throats.

Kelly noticed Jim eyeing the bucket. "Run over an' git a mouthful, or yill be spitting concrete blocks," he shouted above the noise of the trucks.

"Is it clean?" asked the boy anxiously.

"Clean enough if yer thirsty," retorted Reilly sarcastically.

"It's okay," said Kelly. "The back-jaggers are supposed to replace it with fresh water when it gets dusty, but it looks like they've got better things to do." He looked grimly at the group of men standing to the side of the pile or resting on the bags.

Jim felt as if all the moisture in his body had dried up. Running to the bucket between heaves he took a hurried gulp, pausing only to brush away the thin skin of scum on the surface. He had never tasted champagne but guessed it must have been similar to the warm tepid liquid that coursed down his parched throat and into his dried-out stomach.

He was tempted to take another cupful when the ganger's voice rose above the roar of the steam winch and the clatter of the truck wheels. "Hurry up Aggie—leave some for the others." Jim dropped the cup and raced to the pile where the men worked engulfed in a grey mist that was growing thicker by the hour.

Kelly grinned at his embarrassed features. "He'll continue to call you Aggie to demoralise and degrade you. He's sayin' you're a boy in a man's world an' that's the next thing to a woman in a man's world. Yill just havta grin an' bear it."

Reassured by Kelly's tight grin, he allowed himself a mischievous smile in return, and set about unloading the truck with a venom that caused Reilly to crack his cement-lined face with a laugh of relief. He knew for all the talk about him being a number one trucker he was only as good as the men behind him. Kelly seemed to possess the strength of two men and the lad hadn't flagged all morning.

"That's the last heave for the mornin'," said Kelly, breaking his thoughts. "Nip home an' git yer lunch kid, an' be back for one."

Jim needed no second bidding—he dropped the canvas sheet close to the waterside and almost ran from the shed. Reilly sat down wearily on the truck shaft and pulled a crumpled bag containing sandwiches from his jacket pocket and prayed Kelly wouldn't go to the pub for a liquid lunch.

Reaching Whitla Street Jim hopped on the back of a horse-drawn cart loaded with bags of bran flakes. The carter nodded civilly at him as he turned the horse into Nelson Street. As they moved along the narrow street lined with kitchen houses, he kept looking at his reflection in the windows and felt a boyish enjoyment at seeing himself coated with cement.

Eventually he reached the large parlour house he lived in with his younger sister and mother. Mrs. Harvey, a petite widow in her early fifties, rose in alarm when he opened the kitchen door.

"God take care of us son, what happened till ye?"

"I'm at the cement, ma," he answered proudly. "Yid better git some papers down in case I dirty the sofa."

The woman became a hive of activity. "When Jack an' you didn't come back I knew ye musta got somethin'," she called over her shoulder as she rushed into the scullery. "Do ye want a fry?" she shouted from the little room.

Jim realised he was still out of breath. "Naw, ma. Just givus a boul of cornflakes with plenty a milk 'cause I'm dead thirsty." He hung his coat on a hook behind the kitchen door as his mother spread newspaper pages all over the sofa. Walking out to the backyard he eased off his boots and left them just inside the door.

He stood beside his mother at the cold water tap, dwarfing her as she poured a bottle of milk into a basin sitting in the sink. "Wash yer face an' hans in that son, it's better than water. An' ye went without yer cap," she added admonishingly.

"Aye," he laughed, "The boys say if I don't wash my hair the night, I'll havta comb it with a hammer an' chisel tomarra."

Mrs. Harvey watched her only son as he placed his hands gingerly into the milk and threw it up over his face. She looked at his thin gaunt frame and fresh boyish features. She had worried when he had taken up amateur boxing, but his excursion into the cruel, dangerous dockwork had caused her greater concern.

Jim opened his soft dark eyes and noted her fear. "Don't worry ma," he said with a smile, as he reached for the towel on the back of the yard door.

28

Still covered from head to toe in dust and minus his jacket, Kelly sauntered into the Terminus Bar on York Street. His cap was down over his eyes as he walked straight-backed toward the counter.

The public house was large and roomy and did a passing trade from railway commuters who used the nearby LMS station. He raised his hands in the air, acknowledging with a grin the many shouts of welcome from casuals and dockers.

Hooking his thumbs into a broad, well-worn leather belt tied tightly around his slim waist, he rocked gently back and forth on his heels until the barman nodded in his direction.

"Pint an' a Bush, Hector, an' tramp the pint well down," he yelled over the hum of conversation. "Givus a shout when its ready," he added, walking slowly to a table occupied by four casuals.

"How's it goin', Willie?" asked one as he eased himself into a vacant chair.

"Cement," he grimaced. His grimy face cracked into a smile when he saw Jack Harvey.

"Got yer nephew with me, Jack. He's a good lad. Reilly an' me have no complaints."

Harvey was visibly relieved. "So he's with you—I was worried about him," he confessed. Kelly's pint of porter was sat down beside him and he took a long contented draught, before downing the whiskey in one gulp. "Stout lad, good pedigree," he murmured, licking his lips.

"I thought the animal wuda chased him," replied Jack, using the nickname the casuals utilized when referring to the ganger. He went to the bar and shoved a Black Bush in front of Kelly. His voice was soft and low. "Appreciate yer help in the matter, Billy. Jimmy's da died of a heart attack a while back an' Aggie's gittin' it hard."

Kelly smiled knowingly and tilted the whiskey in Jack's direction. "Aye," he replied soberly. "I wus at the funeral. Good men are missed," he added an instant before planting the empty glass

29

back on the table. He looked around him for the barman.

"Set 'em up Hector, it's Kelly's hook on," he bawled.

Three or four streets away, Jim's mother fussed over him as he lifted his cap and coat. "Need any money?" she asked. "It's alright mum," he said with a gentle smile. "I've got a few bob left from the buroo money."

"Ack, but yill maybe be goin' for a shandy," she said in a worried tone. The thought of him drinking with grown men gave her concern. She was relieved when he shook his head.

"Just git an extra coupla bottles of milk, ma."

He walked quickly down the hall and turned towards York Street. Gallaher's tobacco factory dwarfed the rows of two-storey shops on the opposite side of the street. He mingled with the workers, easily identified by their smart emerald green overalls, out on their lunch-break. A heady aroma of tobacco came through the open factory gates as he strode proudly by the Ulster Bank and Adair's fish shop and paused at the door of Wellwood's chemist shop. The owner was a kindly bald-headed man who wore spectacles and a white coat. He was well-known and respected by the locals. Jim wondered if he could do anything with the blisters, but cast the thought away thinking Kelly would laugh at him if he turned up wearing plasters on his wounds.

He strolled on, nodding shyly at people he knew. McCormick's fruit shop had a spread of shiny apples on display and he bought three. He began to eat one, placing the other two in his pocket for Kelly and Reilly. The thirst never left him and he bought a small bottle of white lemonade in the Maypole which he drank in one go.

Moving on purposefully he almost collided with a young girl hurrying back to the tobacco factory. She smiled shyly in response to his nod. He walked on before taking a quick look back to see her watching him. Her uncles were all registered dockers and she knew the prestige that went with the dust-covered clothes. He gathered from the blush that rose on her face that she was glad to see him.

A wave of noisy laughter erupted from the Terminus Bar as he passed by its wide open doors. The smell of stale drink mingled with the tobacco aroma and almost made him sick. Crossing Whitla Street at the entrance of Earl Lane he stopped at the public water fountain and took a drink from the steel cup that was chained to the wall above the tap.

Moving at a brisk pace he reached the Gotto Wharf at five minutes to one. Reilly had the truck on its back and was pouring oil between the wheels and the axle.

"Is Kelly not with ye?" he asked fearfully. Jim shook his head.

"God help us," wailed the little trucker hoarsly. "There's the first heave out an' we're next." He stooped quickly and threw the truck back onto its wheels before carefully hiding the half-filled bottle behind one of the shed doors.

All his new-found confidence ebbed as Jim stared helplessly at Reilly. "We're lost without him, kid," said Reilly's unspoken look. As they moved tentatively toward the narrow breast of quay Kelly walked with a slight swagger through the waterside doors.

"S'alright kid," he said thickly, "let's go." He was coatless and capless. The tail of his shirt was hanging out and two long furry objects were dangling from the buckle of his belt.

"A pair of bloody rabbits," croaked Reilly, rolling his eyes at Jim.

Amid cheers from the rest of the gang Kelly took his place at the side of the truck pausing only to smile and wink at Jim. The hatchman stood silently as the men approached the gently swinging heave. He knew better than to cross words with Kelly. The winch-driver's face arrived at the side of the ship and he was about to let loose with a mouthful but Kelly's steely stare struck him dumb.

"How'd you git there, Crozier?" he asked adding, "Where's Dinky?"

"Ned sent him to another job an' brought me down from the corner," growled the heavily-built Crozier. He'd heard of Kelly's reputation but was more afraid of falling out of favour with the ganger. "Let's git a move on or I'll git the sack," he added, walking back to the winch.

The heave landed with a thud onto the truck and they pushed it into the shed. Although intoxicated, Kelly worked as effortlessly as he had done that morning.

A short time later a Bedford lorry from a nearby builder's yard drove into the shed for a load of cement. In the absence of the ganger the men prepared to load it from the ship's cargo thus saving the trouble of pulling the cement into the pile. Kelly nodded to Jim to follow him and they both clambered onto the lorry-bed. Reilly stayed on the ground with a wheelbarrow to take away any burst bags.

"Roll in below the hook," Kelly told the driver. "An' move out when I stamp the floor twice." Jim took a quick glance at the rabbits. Both were tied by their ears to the belt and completely covered in cement.

"Right, kid," said Kelly, his arm around Jim's waist and his legs spaced to keep himself steady. "When the heave comes ashore we'll land it here." He tapped the spot with his foot. "That'll allow us room to stow. Not too near and not too far from the headboard, savvy?" He patted Jim reassuringly on the head as the lad nodded.

The roaring donkey engine and the groaning of the single derrick's guy ropes warned them that a heave was being hauled quickly from the bowels of the ship. During the dinner break the tide had ebbed considerably and the ship's rail was almost level with the lorry bed. As the load cleared the hatch coamings the bull-rope man holding the heave in the centre of the hatch released the taut rope from the clamp jammed on the side of the hatch, allowing the derrick to swing shorewards and twenty-four hundredweight dropped with frightening speed to stop with a screech six inches from the floor of the lorry. Jim and Kelly grabbed it and pushed forward towards their mark. Crozier had other ideas. Having been told by Ned to speed things up, he dropped the heave immediately.

"Hook off, kid," he screamed. Jim's willing hand was grabbed and held by Kelly. The heave was six feet away from where he'd made the mark.

"Float it, Crozier," yelled Kelly. The winchman hurled a mouthful of obscenites and raced across the narrow deck to the ship's rail. As he leaned forward his unshaven chin was level with the floor of the lorry.

"Hook the fuckin' thing off, kid," he screamed. His voice was reduced to a gurgle as Kelly's boot thudded into his open mouth. It withdrew as quickly as it entered and seconds later blood seeped from Crozier's mouth onto his chin. After spitting out some teeth he became enraged and moved to retaliate. The hatchman wrapped his arms around him and turned him toward the winch.

"Big Ned'll sack ye if yer not at that winch when he comes back," he screamed. Glaring with hatred at Kelly's defiant grin, he pushed a dirty pocket handkerchief into his ruptured mouth and skulked back to the winch.

Jim's stomach nerves tightened as the winch growled to life and the heave was floated. He strained with Kelly as they pushed the load further up the lorry, relaxing only when Kelly yelled to the hatchman to lower the heave. His hands were trembling as he undid the rope. Kelly's brutal act had frightened him and he found himself unable to look at the face of the man working beside him.

Soon he had other problems. Large water blisters were forming and breaking on his palms and fingers. Each time he gripped a bag, the open sores were being tormented by the loose cement on the sharp-cornered paper sacks. Gritting his teeth against the agony, he worked in silence until the afternoon tea-break.

Kelly eyed Crozier warily as the winchman came ashore. Blood seeped from the corners of his mouth which he rinsed with a cup of tea. He avoided Kelly's gaze but stared hatefully at Jim who was trying, unsuccessfully, to soothe his aching hands. Kelly knew Crozier to be a useful street brawler and thought he would bide his time in an effort to salvage his reputation. What he didn't know was the winchman was already aware of his ruthless ability and would not be seeking a return engagement. He would reserve his venom for Jim.

He shifted his gaze to the lad. It was agony for anyone with soft hands. The paper sacks were warm to the touch with sharp corners containing small steel staples. They needed to be gripped forcibly and in the process the soft skin would be blistered by the heat and eventually burst.

He spoke to Jim quietly. "Only one cure kid," he whispered, "piss on 'em." He lowered his hands between his legs in demonstration. Jim half-smiled. "I'm serious," continued Kelly. "We all do it—it hardens the skin." He showed his own palms, unmarked except for a faint film of dust. He rose from the truck he was sitting on and threw the remains of his tea onto the floor.

"Right kid, next break we'll be sippin' somethin cool in the wee bar." At this remark Reilly who'd been pouring more oil into the wheels of the truck rolled his eyes skyward.

"He's too young for to drink," he scolded.

Kelly gazed at him grimly. "He'll be oul enuff before this boat is finished. He mightr't luk it, but he'll feel it."

The wee bar was an apt discription for the public house. No bigger than an ordinary dwelling house, it sat on the corner of Dock Street and Earl Lane. Ships tied up a few hundred yards further down the street and the bar catered for many nationalities. During the Second World War it had been the favourite haunt of the American forces who'd roamed the blacked-out streets in their hundreds packing the dancehalls and the pubs, often fighting pitched battles with the embittered local men.

A small number of jaded females still sold their favours at a reasonable price. They answered to nicknames laid on them by the scornful neighbourhood women who despised the ladies of easy virtue. Diamond Lil, Tugboat Annie and the Duchess still plied their doubtful wares to any interested party.

Jim entered the establishment warily. He had quite a few relatives in the immediate area who would be angry at seeing him enter or leave such an unsavoury establishment. He felt he owed Kelly a few drinks for carrying him through the day and secretly looked forward to being seen in the company of a man who could be charming and courteous one moment and brutal and savage the next. He decided to risk it and walked through the narrow doorway ahead of Kelly who seemed to have sobered up completely.

The older man noted the boy's uncertainty and smiled understandingly at Reilly as the lad took the lead into the bar. It was packed to capacity with loudly talking men and a smattering of women. Jim edged gingerly towards the bar, trying not to brush up against anyone.

One of the team of hard-working fast-moving barmen noticed him. He was a wiry middle-aged man wearing a beer-stained striped shirt with no collar. His sleeves were rolled up to his armpits. "What's it to be, kid?" he asked quickly, throwing an empty Guinness bottle into a crate. The clatter was barely audible over the din of the customers.

"Three whiskeys and three pints, mister," stammered the boy, looking nervously around him to see if any of his uncles were on the premises. He knew if they saw him first his only warning would be an open-handed slap across the head. The barman studied him for a moment, then shrugged. "If he's oul enough till order it, he's oul enuff till drink it," he muttered.

The drinks were almost thrown at him by the fast-moving barman. He squinted through the swirling smoke for some aid and was grateful when Kelly stepped forward to help him carry the drinks to a nearby table. Cradling the remaining drinks and his change, he inched his way through the crowd.

35

"There ye are, kid," said Kelly, more in the tone of a toast than a greeting as he threw the contents of the whiskey glass to the back of his throat. Scorning the porter he rose quickly to his feet. "Right—my shout," he said walking to the bar.

Reilly lowered his pint in one go with hands that were as shaky as Jim's. He looked after Kelly. "I'm still dyin of thirst an' he's throwin' firewater down him." He looked at the whiskey beside Jim. "I thought yid more sense. That stuff 'ill ruin ya," he scowled.

"I'll just drink the one. I tole me ma I'd go straight home," mumbled the boy. Reilly nodded understandingly. He knew the boy was impressed by Kelly and felt he should try to explain Kelly's behaviour. Checking first that the docker was still out of hearing range, he whispered, "Do ye know Billy Kelly, son?"

"No," said Jim defensively, "But only for him I'd have been sacked." He suddenly remembered Reilly's rejection of him earlier that morning and glared fiercely at the older man.

Reilly took a reflective sip and settled back. "Yis, son—Billy Kelly's a good lad when he's away from this." He jiggled the whiskey glass. "He's really a first preference man, but he's under suspension. That's why he's workin' like you an' me as an Arab with no rights worth talkin' about. He got mad drunk three weeks ago an' bate up the boss at the Bristol boat. He served all through the war as an airborne commando and he's a real roughhouse when he starts."

Reilly was speaking faster and lower with each sentence. As he continued to speak to Jim he never took his eyes of the man in question as he clowned around at the bar with a few pint-drinking casuals. "He's lethal with all that ju-jitsy stuff an' he's easy provoked with a wild temper. That's why he booted Crozier. So watch 'im, kid," finished Reilly rolling his eyes, "An' don't try to match drinks with 'im."

Jim felt a sudden stab of depression. He had forgotten the savage act of brutality against Crozier. Reilly's eyes told the boy to say nothing more on the subject as Kelly approached the table and put down three whiskeys. Someone close by began to sing in a faltering drunken voice and Jim watched self-consciously as a middle-aged woman unwrapped herself from a man who was embracing her and began to dance between the tables. Others clapped their hands in time with the singer and Jim was about to do the same, when he remembered his blisters.

He found himself looking at Billy Kelly closely for the first time. He was about thirty years old, of average height with nothing about him to denote his fierceness except a deep barrel of a chest and thick muscled arms. His hair was dark brown beneath the cement dust and his eyes were a cannonball grey with what seemed like a permanent twinkle, which Jim imagined would dull to a dangerous glint if he was angered. Despite Reilly's stories of physical violence, his features were finely chiselled and unmarked.

He seemed as sober as ever when he rose with a grin and wandered off towards the bar. Although he had barely spoken to Jim since they had entered the lad was flattered to be in his company and the heady atmosphere caused him to grow more confident as the time passed. After a while he began to gaze around the small bar-room with its stone floor and faded wallpaper. He glanced guardedly at the women who vied for the attention of the men. Eventually one middle-aged matron, noticing his youthful vulnerability sat down in the seat vacated by Reilly who had rushed out the door during one of the moments Kelly's back was turned.

She looked squarely into Jim's face. "Y'know son, I'm a terrible bad woman," she said with a sigh.

"Shure I know that, missus," he countered helpfully, "My ma says only bad wimmin comes in here. But she says yis are more unfortunate than anything else."

The woman flashed him a baffled smile. Her wrinkled features were a kaleidoscope of flaming red rouge, blue eyeshade and pink lipstick that looked like it had been put on by a drunken house painter. She reminded him of the red Indians he had seen in the Saturday matinees in the Duncairn. Wearing a frayed fur coat over a green jumper and a frock that rose to her knees, her body was bloated and lumpy in the wrong places and her sparse frizzled hair was cut short and bleached white.

"Can I tell you a wee story, son?" she asked softly, recognising him to be nothing like the hard-headed regulars. "My wee boy," she continued, stifling a sob, "He's somethin' of the age of yerself, was to go to London tonight to join a ship as a cabin boy. It wuda bin his first trip, but he can't go because he sent me to git his boat-train ticket an' I went an' spent it on drink." She rubbed her face tiredly before grabbing Jim's hands in her own. "Ach son, yer ma's right—I am a desperate bad woman."

The boy experienced a huge wave of drunken compassion and remembered how he himself had been helped. He leaned forward. "Missus, I wudn't have the boat fare on me, but I've about two shillin' left. Ye kin have that," he offered grandly.

"Ack, yer a good lad," she sobbed as her hand shot out and pocketed the coins. "Yer mother must be proud of ye—at least I'll be able to buy somethin' for his supper an' he'll have a full stummik when I break the bad news till him."

Her face took on a look of strange intent as her hands moved deftly under the table and began to unbutton the fly of his jeans. "Aw missus," he stammered with shock and embarrassment as she delved into his private parts and began to fondle him.

"There now," she said a few moments later, expertly rearranging his trousers. "Fair exchange, no robbery," she added, rising quickly and moving towards the bar, pausing only to wipe her hands on the sleeve of his jacket.

Grabbing a whiskey he downed it immediately and almost choked as the hard liquor burned its way down his throat. He felt excited, exhilarated and ashamed. He knew without looking that his jeans were now covered with more than cement. Casually lifting his overcoat he placed it on his lap and let his eyes wander innocently around the room. No one seemed to notice his fading embarrassment or returned his glance. The action had all taken place beneath the table and no one seemed to have cared.

He looked again at the clock and groaned inwardly. "Half-nine ... almost closin' time," he slurred to himself. Lifting his whiskey glass he peered drunkenly over its rim in an effort to locate Kelly. Rising abruptly and lurching unsteadily on his feet he staggered towards the bar, finding it extremely hard to keep his eyes open. "Where's Kelly?" he mumbled to the first person he collided with. The man turned his head slowly and Jim almost froze with terror as he recognised the winchman Kelly had booted in the mouth.

He tried to move away but was grabbed roughly by his shirt front. "Fuck you and Kelly," snarled Crozier emphasising the point with a punch that Jim could have easily evaded had he been sober. However he stood stupified as Crozier's fist exploded against the side of his head. The force of the blow sent him crashing to the floor and rolling backwards. He collided with a table and sent its contents to the gaudy well-worn tiles. Fired by anger and instinct he rose dazedly. The rest of the clientele moved aside swiftly and silently leaving a small square vacant for the combatants to do battle in.

The older man moved into the space grinning wickedly. He grabbed Jim by the shoulder and was about to floor him again when Kelly slipped roughly between them. Crozier's smile left him as their bodies touched. He averted his gaze from the baleful glare of Kelly's eyes. "What about givin' me this dance?" grinned Kelly before head-butting him viciously between the eyes. The bridge of his nose broke with a dry crack that was heard by everyone in the bar except Crozier. Bowling backwards at breakneck speed he collided with the front of the bar and slid slowly to the floor. Kelly waited for a moment to see if he would rise again. When he didn't, the docker moved forward and placed the two rabbits around Crozier's neck.

"Billy, you shudn't have interfered," gasped Jim shaking with nervous fury. Kelly eyed the fast-rising lump on the side of the lad's head with some concern. "His fight was with me, now sit down till I look at that bump." He moved the bewildered lad onto a chair and showed no concern as a group of men dragged the unfortunate Crozier into a nearby room.

"Last orders," shouted the sparse-haired barman as he headed towards Kelly. "I've phoned for the peelers," he said sternly, but with no animosity in his voice.

"That's great," beamed Kelly with a warmth that washed away all the hostilities within the boy. "I'll git ye home an' then I'll come back an' git ye a peeler's baton for yer birthday." He coaxed the boy to his feet and shuffled him slowly out the side door and into Earl Lane. "Don't breathe deeply," he said quickly as Jim's eyes glazed and his legs began to buckle. Shaking his head sadly Kelly hoisted the limp form of the boy onto his shoulders as vomit drooled from Jim's lips and down the back of the docker's shirt.

TWO

J IM Harvey woke up in his mother's kitchen with the chimes
of midnight ringing from a clock on the mantlepiece and was
horrified to discover he had vision in only one eye. Putting a
hand fearfully to the unseeing side of his face, he was immensely
relieved when he found a lump of raw steak covering it. The
family cat on his stomach stirred and looked at him sleepily. He
stroked it gratefully, knowing it would keep cockroaches and
other insects that infested the house at night away from him.
Lifting the steak off, he looked at it dumbly for a moment before
replacing it and promptly falling asleep again.

He awoke to the sound of steam hammers which seemed to be
tapping away inside his head. Daylight seeped in through the
large window that looked out into the backyard and he realised
it was morning. He remembered nothing of the previous night
and wondered why he felt physically sick. His tongue felt as if it
was glued to the roof of his mouth and his head was being assailed
by a monotonous and measured thump that seemed to grow
louder.

As the hammering continued he lurched into the dark scullery.
The piece of steak dropped unnoticed to the floor and the cat
leapt on it as Jim staggered to the enamel sink and turned on the
tap of the gas-controlled geyser. He put his mouth below the pipe
gasping and choking as the cold water gouged its way down a
throat lined with sandpaper. He felt a terrible pain as he tried to
open his hands. Placing them into the water to cool them he
shrieked out loud as it touched the raw open blisters.

41

He vaguely heard the front door slamming and the sound of hurried footsteps in the hall. Looking up he saw his Uncle Henry framed in the doorway of the scullery. A strikingly handsome man in his early forties, Henry sported a pencil-line moustache beneath a large and fleshy nose and dark, piercing eyes. An eight piece tweed cap was perched on the side of his head at an angle that defied gravity. His dark, but grey-tinted hair was thick and wavy. It was pushed forward in a kiss-curl which lay across his unlined forehead and looked ridiculous in proportion to his bull-like build.

The dark eyes were contemptous as they glared at Jim.

"Wurk!" he snarled harshly, "Have ye forgot yiv got wurk to go til?"

Jim held onto the kitchen sink for support. He felt weak and drained. "What happened, Uncle Henry?" he sobbed childlike as he looked pleadingly him. His mind was in a turmoil and refused to provide him with the violent events of the previous night.

"Niver mind, we'll go inta that later. Give him a cuppa tea, Aggie—he luks like a bloody ghost."

He saw his mother behind the large bulk of his uncle. She was in her nightdress and weeping quietly.

"I'd rather he didn't go back to the docks, Henry. I toul Jack ! didn't want him there in the first place. He'll learn nothin' but drinkin' an' fightin' ... If yid a seen the state of him last night when that fella Kelly brought him home after ten. Somebody musta give him a diggin'."

"Git 'im a cuppa tea," repeated Henry irritably, "An' hurry up or we'll be late." Mrs. Harvey hesitated for a moment, then obeyed. Her hands trembled as she put the teapot on the stove and ignited the gas.

"I'll havta go to the yard," moaned Jim lurching towards the back door. As he stood in the unlit whitewashed toilet, he vaguely remembered Kelly's advice. Closing his eyes tightly he held his hands in front of him and allowed the warm liquid to flow over them.

He found it difficult to stand still and used the flaking wall to steady himself. Stumbling back through the latched door he saw his Uncle Jack had joined Henry and was sitting sullenly on the arm of the settee.

"Mornin' Uncle Jack," he mumbled politely.

"Git that tea down ye an' c'mon," was the curt reply.

He could sense both men were angry with him and felt flashes of recognition as unclear pictures ran through his brain. Gradually the events of the previous night began to emerge.

"I didn't start it, Uncle Henry. Crozier hit me for nuthin ... I wus only ... " The words poured out in a nervous torrent before Henry interupted. "Stop whimperin' an' drink that tea or yill go without it," he bellowed, rising and moving toward the kitchen door. Jim followed meekly, unable to face the tea or his mother.

They walked in silence, the boy between the two men, until they reached the cement shed. The ganger had just arrived and both men stepped forward and spoke to him. They conversed in whispers, their tones inaudible. Suddenly they broke off and Jack and Henry walked quickly out of the shed without even a backward glance at the lad.

The foreman waited until they were out of sight before beckoning Jim to him. "Yer a lucky man," he said thoughtfully, "to have uncles like that." Jim nodded vaguely, still in a state of shock. The ganger fumbled at his fly buttons and turning the top of his body slightly away from the boy, he began to urinate noisily against the shed door.

"At least yer early, but remember, any fightin at my boat an' yill niver wurk on the quay again," he sternly warned over his shoulder. Jim nodded dumbly. His head was still throbbing fiercely and his mouth was parched and dry. He moved listlessly towards a cast-iron drinking fountain that sat outside the shed. The bulk of the gang were beginning to filter into the shed and bantered him unmercifully about his bruised face. He ignored them and stuck his head beneath the water tap, shivering as the cold liquid ran through his hair and down his face. He cupped his hands and caught some, using it to rinse his mouth. Shaking his head like a dog he moved slowly back to the boat.

Reilly had arrived and was oiling the truck wheels. He flashed Jim an 'I told you so' look before returning to his maintenance.

Kelly walked throught the shed door a few moments later and examined Jim's face with childish exaggeration. "I've cut meself worse shavin'," he laughed. They walked out to the breast of the quay and were met by the ganger. "I want this boat cleared for lunchtime," he growled, his black eyes biting into Jim's face, "an' I don't want no return bouts here. Crozier's up there with his busted gub an' you're down here with yours. That's the way I want it. When the boat's finished yis kin kick yerselves till death."

He walked to the gangplank and hauled himself onto the deck. The guy ropes screeched and a heave was dragged ashore. The tobbacco factory horn blared as twenty-four bags of cement crashed onto Reilly's truck with a heavy thud.

Reilly waited until the rope was free of the ship's hook then gritted his teeth and raised the shafts waist high. Pushing the pebble to the side of his mouth he muttered, "Lie intil it," and felt the weight of the men behind him as he headed for the pile.

Despite his heavy hangover Jim did not falter. Every hour that passed saw him gain unspoken admiration from the rest of the squad all of whom knew of his run-in with Crozier. Kelly kept his thoughts to himself as they worked ceaselessly through the morning.

At fifteen minutes to noon Jim felt absolutely drained. Drawing on every ounce of will power he possessed he forced his body to go through the motions. He knew a few more heaves would see the lunch-break and he kept himself going by thinking about the bottles of milk, submerged in cold water in the sink, he knew his mother would have waiting on him.

Ned had other ideas. Leaning over the ship's rail he addressed the shore-gang. "We're workin' through!" he growled. "If we don't take a meal break I reckon we'll be out of here before two o'clock. Most of the gang welcomed the news. Jim felt faint and hoped he could see in the next two hours without collapsing. His body was on fire and he ached from head to toe. He silently thanked providence for the three nights a week he spent in the White City boxing club knowing the fitness and stamina gained from his training was the only thing keeping him up.

Kelly's strength never wavered. He was still fresh when the ganger called 'ropes up' signifying three heaves would finish the job.

Jim received his first white card along with his insurance cards and a grumpy assertion from the ganger that he would never again receive a mid-week check if his cards weren't stamped.

Summoning the dregs of his strength, he helped Reilly pull the truck loaded with slings and sheets down through the narrow streets and into the stevedore's yard. Tired as he was, he didn't protest as boys from the nearby Mariner's school jumped aboard for a free ride, remembering fondly doing the same thing himself.

He staggered painfully the short distance to his home. Excessive sweat had caused the skin between his legs to become raw and he walked the final few yards with difficulty. His last thoughts as he lay down on the small sofa was Crozier's hateful glare which his two swollen eyes could not hide.

As he slept fitfully, his mother carefully unlaced his boots and gently took the cap from his head. She rubbed butter on his calloused, blistered hands and sobbed silently as she watched his young cement-lined face contort with pain. He looked so much like his late father that she was tempted to lean over and kiss him on the forehead.

Kelly had followed him at a discreet distance. Making sure he had made it through the door, he wended his way to the wee bar where he had coaxed Reilly to meet him for one drink.

"Well," asked Reilly. "Did he make it?"

"Under his own steam," laughed Kelly as he ordered a Bush.

Reilly nodded almost proudly. "Got to admit the kid's got guts but he's too young in the tooth for work like that."

45

Kelly tossed the drink down his throat as Reilly watched dumbly. The little man was relaxed to the point of insensibility, glad beyond belief that the job was finished and knowing within his heart the same thing would happen again.

He looked guardedly at Kelly whose eyes always seemed to be laughing at some private joke. The man's body and arms were as hard to the touch as granite under the denim shirt and jacket he always wore. He flinched as the amused eyes flashed at him— "Don't be fallin' asleep on me, Sammy—the hook's hingin' an' its your call."

He turned with a quizzical grin as a tall sunbronzed man wearing a brown leather jacket leaned over his shoulder and ordered a round of drinks in a broad American accent. His face was the colour of wrinkled parchment. Kelly nodded courteously as the seaman bid him the time of day politely before moving away.

"Bloody Americans," huffed Reilly, "Spoilin' the brass—I cud a got my ashes hauled by oul Nelly for a half-crown but now them lads is in she wouldn't wear me."

"Aye," laughed Kelly, "half-a-crown wudn't even git ye a luk at it the day. The ladies 'ill be swimmin' in dough when them fellas git a lotta likker intil them," he added before calling the barman over.

"What do I owe ye for last week's strap drink, Ernie?" he asked. The barman walked to his account book and studied it for a moment. "Seven pounds, fourteen an' fourpence an' I'll not charge ye for the damage ye did last night when ye stretched Crozier."

Kelly looked at him with mock surprise. "Are ye sure it was me?" he laughed as he counted out the money. "I'm not barred though, shure I'm not?" he asked seriously.

The barman scooped up the cash and looked at him squarely with affection. "When I kin find someone who kin handle ye, yill be barred."

He grabbed Reilly's shoulder as the little man edged to the

door. "Have another one," he roared, "an' then we'll go roun' to the Terminus."

Reilly groaned. Crozier had headed in that direction and he knew Kelly, although appearing buoyant and relaxed, wanted the matter settled once and for all. Unable to speak to the winchman at the boat, he wanted to warn him against taking reprisal against the lad.

Crozier was not in the bar when they arrived. "Saw ye comin' three streets away," quipped the barman. "He jumped on a green bus for Carrick, so he kin git a drink in peace."

Kelly grinned, but Reilly noted the grimness in his eyes and wondered why he had taken such an interest in the lad's welfare.

Three streets away the Harvey brothers were about to sort out their wages. Henry, a bachelor, lived there with his widowed mother and Sam and Jack dined there every day although they were both married. Jack lived a few streets away and Sam a few doors. The kitchen house had two small upstairs bedrooms in which ten children, five of whom were girls, were reared to adulthood. The diminutive sitting room had been enlarged by removing the pantry wall. A gas-fuelled stove was close to a large black enamelled range in which burned a coal fire. It was bordered by a large brass fender bearing in scroll in its centre, a large replica of a cap badge worn by the regiment of the Royal Irish Rifles in which the late Mr. Harvey had served with distinction during the First World War, rising to the rank of sergeant.

The brothers sat facing each other at a large table which took up most of the floor space in the room. Henry's cap was in the centre of the table filled with pound notes and coins. A large deep dish sat in front of each man and Mrs. Harvey's elderly hands were shaking as she ladled delicious stew into each dish.

She dreaded pay days and cried many times when utensils and food flew across the narrow room as the three men fought bitterly over every penny. She studied each one closely as they spooned the food into their mouths whilst staring intently at the cap.

Sam was the oldest. A white-haired father of eleven childen who drank and gambled heavily. "Och, they all drank and gambled heavily," she sighed sadly. Like his brothers he was known in the area as a useful street brawler with somewhat more street cunning than the other two. Henry was the middle brother, separated from Sam by two elder sisters. His heavy running-to-fat frame disguised a fast-moving hard puncher with colossal strength gained by carrying hundred-weight bags of potatoes all day long in the transit shed where he worked. Jack, the youngest brother, had equal credentials. He was smaller and softer in nature than his brothers, but when provoked became a formidable opponent. All three were dressed in heavy shirts stained with potato dust. Silk scarves to keep the dust from going down their necks were wrapped around their throats. Henry sported a leather waistcoat with a large hole worn through the right shoulder.

"Aggie was roun' here the day cryin'," said Mrs. Harvey conversationally as she put a match to the gas ring beneath a large teapot. "She says wee Jim's han's are in a terrible state an' that pig Crozier give him a terrible face ... I don't know what yis were thinkin' of lettin' a chile drink in that dirty whore house round the corner. Are yis gonna let that fella Crozier git away with it?" she asked sternly.

"Luk ma," replied Sam between mouthfuls of stew. "If we interfered the wee lad wudn't be able to stick the sleggin'. Besides Billy Kelly thumped Crozier. The wee buck's too soft for the docks. Aggie should send him to the mill," he added, his eyes fixed rigidly on the money.

"Cud yis not wurk him in with youse?" persisted the old woman. "Ye cud give him a week's wages an' help our Aggie out. Ack, if ye seen his wee han's ..." Her voice trailed off to a whimper as she dabbed her eyes with the corner of her apron.

Henry threw his spoon down in exasperation. He was rushing through his supper in order to share out the money and have a good wash. "Ma, he's too light to work wid us. Jack an' me had ta take him down till the boat this mornin' or he'd niver have made it. I had ta slip that big bastard Ned a poun' to keep him on, an' ye know I have no love for that shitbag."

"After what ye done for his boss?" screeched Mrs. Harvey.

Henry exploded. "That's over an' done with, ma. Johnny Jackson got me a red button for takin' that rap for him. He doesn't owe me nothin'."

"C'mon jailbird," snorted Sam, "Git the dough sorted, I wanta few drinks."

"Right," agreed Henry, ignoring the jibe. He pulled the cap toward him and began to separate the money into three piles.

Sam watched as the last silver coins were set in place. "Is that it?" he asked, a dangerous tone in his voice.

"Yis," replied Henry guardedly, looking him straight in the face.

Sam heaved an injured sigh. "What about the cargo in York Dock one?" he asked quietly, putting his half-smoked Park Drive carefully on the edge of the table.

Henry coloured slightly. "That's storage for a cargo I hope we'll git next week."

"Storage my balls," snarled his brother. "You got paid for it, so decorate the middle." The little room vibrated as he banged the table heavily sending his cigarette and Henry's cap to the floor.

Henry rose angrily. "I'm tellin ye the truth. Ye know if a load comes up from the country a day or two early we havta store it without pay to guarantee us the rest of the cargo."

Sam was unconvinced. "I still say ye got paid for it an' I want my share," he snarled.

"Yis are scarin' m' ma," scolded Jack

"Luk Sam," said Henry, adopting a persecuted manner and thinking quickly, "Why don't ye search me if you think I've got any more." Mrs. Harvey cringed in a darkened corner with her hand across her mouth. Jack said nothing, happy with his share.

Sam's eyes bored into Henry for a solid minute then he

stepped forward and received a stinging slap across his face from Henry. Jack dived quickly between the two men as the table went flying and Mrs. Harvey screamed.

He walked straight into Sam's returning right hook and fell without a sound. Both men closed in on each other. They froze momentarily when they heard another thud and turned to see their mother lying on the linoleum.

"I'm away," muttered Sam backing out of the room.

As the front door slammed shut, Mrs. Harvey rose from the floor with a smug smile and dusted her apron.

Henry reached down, pulled up his trouser leg and pulled a bulky envelope from out of his sock. He placed it in his hip pocket, smacked it triumphantly and winked at his mother. "Thanks ma—yer on an extra quid this week." He looked at the prostrate form of his younger brother snoring peacefully on the floor. "When are ye goin' till catch yerself on?" he growled as he lifted the body and placed him on the sofa.

Crozier walked unsteadily into the fish and chip shop at the corner of Nelson Street. His eyes took a moment to adjust to the bright lights. He stood awhile inside the door relishing the heat before joining the row of people queuing Indian-file. He caught sight of his reflection in the large mirror behind the counter. His face was swollen and a large bruise between his eyes was turning black. He was angry at allowing Kelly to take him out so quickly, but did not relish a return bout. There was something about the lean docker that made him shiver in the warmth of the supper saloon. He remembered the look on Kelly's face just before he struck, and it was the look of a man enjoying his work. He had been told later by one of the men who dragged him in to the backroom of the bar that Kelly's viciousness far outstripped that of any other man on the quay. They warned him to go home and forget the attack. 'He's a bin lid' was how one man put it.

He rubbed his head ruefully. Had he known Kelly was so formidable he wouldn't have got on his wrong side. The crowd fidgeted a few paces and he shuffled forward deep in thought. "It was all that wee bastard's fault," he concluded silently, "Oh, if I ever meet up with him ... "

At that moment a young lad clad in dust-covered jeans walked in through the door. His black hair was uncombed and the eyes in his pale face blinked as they tried to accustom themselves to the bright lights. Crozier stared idly at him, thinking there was something familiar about him. Only when he saw the wide-eyed look of panic on the lad's face did he realise it was Jim Harvey.

Jim sprang to life as Crozier lunged drunkenly at him, scattering the orderly queue. He ran out into the street and heard the harsh breathing that told him Crozier was hard on his heels. Because of the chaffing on his upper legs he found it difficult to run at full speed. The street was pitch black except for the intermittent light that glowed in the windows. He cursed himself for leaving the comfort of his home. His mouth had been parched and his mother had suggested some ice-cream. He looked over his shoulder and saw Crozier labouring about ten feet behind him with a look of hatred on his features that caused Jim to step up the pace. Despite his blind panic, he headed for his Granny Harvey's house in the hope that some of his uncles would be there.

He looked again at his pursuer and two men lurched drunkenly into his path. "Stop that wee bastard," panted Crozier from the darkness. Rough hands grabbed and held him. "Let me alone," he screamed in terror.

"What have ye done on Crozier?" slurred the man who held him tightest as he dragged and pulled both men until he reached his Granny's door. Crozier arrived snarling hatefully and grabbed a handful of Jim's shirt front. The lad almost cried with relief as his grandmother's front door creaked open. She peered for a moment at the melee outside her door. Recognising her grandson, she screamed loudly for Henry. "C'mon, c'mon quick ... " She screamed. "They're killin' wee Jim."

"Git back in yer cage, ye oul buzzard," roared Crozier, pushing hard at the front door and causing the old woman to fall behind it. Henry had just washed his hair which he intended to curl later and had a large towel wrapped tightly around his head. Hearing his mother's cry he walked blindly into the dark hall. Thinking his mother had fallen he stooped to pick her up. Crozier, now totally out of control, forgot about Jim as he attacked Henry's muffled head with all his might. Roaring like a castrated bull Henry tore the towel from his head to get a look at his attacker.

It was Crozier's turn to experience fear. He backed slowly down the hall, his offending hands spread in anguish. "Ach Henry," he whined, "I din't know it was you." He almost stepped on Mrs. Harvey. "Here, Missus," he whimpered, "Let me—"

The sentence was left hanging as Henry's right fist crashed into his face. The ferocity of the blow propelled him backwards up the remainder of the hall and into the narrow street where his speeding body was halted by the brick wall of a house on the opposite side of the street. He dropped to a sitting position and took no further part in the proceedings.

Leaping over his mother, Henry charged snarling at the two men who were loudly protesting their innocence. As he closed with the nearest one, the other leapt onto his back in an effort to restrain him.

"We didn't know he was one of usin's," cried the man as Henry plucked him from his back like an offending insect and crashed him to the ground like a bag of potatoes. He looked sideways at Jim who was standing petrified by the raw violence. "Run for yer Uncle Sam," he roared as the man below him fought for survival.

Sam was already aware of the situation and was charging down the street. He was wearing nothing but trousers and heavy unlaced boots that clattered with every step he took.

"Ajapers," sobbed the man Henry had tossed from his back. He had just regained his feet when one of Sam's boots ploughed into the side of his head. He squealed with the pain and screamed even louder as his tormentor continued to kick him, moving his body half a yard across the square-setts with every rib-crunching thud.

"What happened?" Sam shouted between kicks.

"Crozier," grunted Henry nodding at the inert body at the opposite wall. "He hit mi ma!"

"Did he now?" frowned Sam, his eyes blazing furiously. "Well he won't do that again," he added strolling purposefully towards the unconscious man.

Henry restrained him forcibly. "Leave him. He's out of it." He nodded at the other two stretched out on the road. "So are they. Jim," he scowled, "Go tell the barman in the Stalingrad to ring three nines ... tell him there's an ambulance needed."

Jim obeyed mutely feeling his stomach heave as he raced past the inert Crozier. The street was beginning to fill up with women who had left their homes when they heard the noise of the battle. Gathering around the shaken Mrs. Harvey, they fussed over her, scowling in the direction of the fallen men.

Moments later an ambulance cut its way through the darkness and picked up the casualties. A police officer passed around the onlookers searching for eye witnesses. Henry and Sam had disappeared. Some of Mrs. Harvey's daughters had arrived and were visibly angry. The policeman was berated by the women.

"Whoever done it shud git a medal," snarled one. "Them blirts deserve everything they got," she continued, glaring at the men being stretchered into the ambulance.

Jim tried to feel some pity for Crozier, but could not forget the look in the man's eyes when he had grabbed him by the throat. He knew had it not been for the intervention of his uncles that it would have been him being taken away to hospital.

Feeling weary and frightened, he trudged the short distance to his home. His mother was asleep, clad in her nightdress, in a chair in front of a roaring fire. With a bitter laugh he realised he had forgotten all about the ice-cream. Moving quietly he walked out into the yard to the toilet where he dutifully urinated on his blistered, shaking hands.

Stiff and wracked with pain he lifted a bottle of milk from a pail of water and climbed the narrow stairs to his bedroom, calling the cat to come with him. It was eight o'clock and he set his alarm for seven. He knew there'd be no sleep for him until he cleared the spectre of Crozier's battered features from his mind. The cat settled on the bottom of his bed and he fell into a listless sleep knowing Tabby would keep the mice away.

Henry put the rubber hosepipe he had used to sluice the potato dust from his body onto the hook on the yard wall. As he dried his naked body he heard the clock in the kitchen chiming eight times. Throwing the towel from him he lifted a set of snow white linen drawers from the top of the mangle. He lifted his feet carefully, making sure he didn't step into any of the little puddles that lay in the hollows of the cracked tiles. Donning an equally white vest, he checked that he was decent before pressing the latch on the yard door and stooping through its low headbeam into the kitchen.

He moved irritably and almost unnoticed through the neighbourhood women who were fussing over his mother stretched out on the settee and enjoying every moment of the attention she was receiving. His face bore no marks of the vicious punch delivered by Crozier as the thick towel had absorbed most of the impact. He patted his mother's head affectionately as he passed her and opened a small cupboard by the kitchen window. Lifting his shaving equipment he walked through the crowd to a small square shaped mirror hanging above the fireplace. Opening the cut-throat razor that had belonged to his father, he stropped the open blade three or four times across the surface of a broad leather belt which hung on a nail on the side of the chimney breast ever since he could remember.

Soaping his face he looked expectantly at his mother who cautioned the women to be quiet. "Wheesh," she whispered, "in case he cuts hisself." The room fell quiet and remained so until he cleaned the razor and put the gear back in the cupboard.

Pushing through the women he foraged beneath the settee and produced a pair of brown handmade brogues which he buffed briskly with a dry cloth until they shone brightly. Lowering his head, he climbed the staircase to his room and returned clad in a brown diagonal-striped, double-breasted lounge suit. He wore an open necked coffee coloured shirt with long spear-pointed collars spread out over the lapels of his coat.

Checking his reflection in the fly-specked mirror he flipped the top of his Dublin-bought cigarette lighter and puffed a Park Drive. His brown eyes shone with anticipation as he left the room.

"I'm away for a drink, ma," he called cheerily, checking carefully that the brown envelope was nestling safely in the inside pocket of his suit. He thought about Sam as he walked up the narrow street to the bar. He knew there'd be no trouble from Jack whom he'd woken up and sent home just before the fight erupted, but Sam had been as venomous as ever after the ambulance had departed.

He giggled suddenly, rubbing his hands together with glee.

"Ack, shure I'll worry about that the marra," he laughed.

Reaching the public house, he entered by the narrow back door and was immediately assailed by the strong smell of alcohol and thick swirling clouds of tobbacco smoke. A steady hum of conversation mingled with song and laughter as he moved slowly through the packed throng, nodding and joking with the people he knew.

One of the assorted ladies present, who answered to the name of Diamond Lil, grinned when she saw him.

"Ack, big man," she roared throwing her arms wide open in welcome, "Clark Gable 'ill niver be dead while yer alive."

"Is Clark Gable dead?" asked Henry with mock sincerity.

"Not as far as I know but shure ye know what I mane," she replied in genuine delight.

Henry smiled gently. "Here girl—git yerself a wee drink an'

mebbe I'll see ye later." He slipped her two half-crowns with a mischievous wink.

Taking the money appreciatively she lowered her voice. "One of them big Yanks over there wants to pin me, but I'm houlin' out for as much money an' drink as I kin git." He smiled knowingly as she continued. "When I git rid of him ye kin take me over home an' git it in comfort, free of charge." She lived alone in Great George's Street since her husband had been reported missing in the Normandy landings. Her three children had long been taken into care.

She walked back to the crowded table rolling her hips shamelessly. Henry turned to the bar and ordered a Black Bush and a bottle of Guinness. The drinks were banged down in front of him and he poured half of the stout into his whiskey glass before taking a deep draught. Smacking his lips contentedly, he leaned an elbow on the bar-top and let his eyes drift slowly around the crowded pub.

He noticed Ned Semple, the cement boat ganger, sitting at a drink-laden table close to the toilet door. His mind went back to earlier that morning when he'd bribed Ned to keep Jim in the gang. He decided grudgingly that he owed the man a drink and moved to the table. "What are ye havin?" he asked tonelessly.

"Me usual," smiled the ganger with the laconic assurance of a man who seldom bought his own liquor. He relied on the men seated with him to do that. It was their way of buying their work and making it almost certain, but not quite, that they got preferential treatment after the blues and reds, before men who were too proud, too principled or too poor to play his game.

Henry returned with a glass of Black Bush, pointedly ignoring the other men at the table. Gazing straight into the ganger's dark piggish eyes, he placed the drink in front of him. "That's for the favour," he said truthfully.

Ned took a pensive sip. "He done his wurk or he wudn't a bin there. But I'd keep him away from that nutcase Kelly, if I was you."

His guarded friendship with Henry stemmed from the fact

that his employer treated Harvey like a son. A few years earlier a cart filled with stolen goods had been found in the stevedore's yard. Pilfering charges were levelled against the stevedore by another shipping company, when Harvey, who had been a carter at the time, stepped forward and accepted responsibility.

The authorities had been embarrassed at bringing charges against the respected stevedore who was also a justice of the peace. The stolen goods were luxuries meant for American bases in the Province and the military police were also involved.

The harbour detectives were overjoyed at Harvey's confession and speedily arraigned him for trial a few days later when he received an four-month sentence. The magistrate said the sentence would have been more severe had he been convinced the carter was the only person involved in the crime. The case was quickly concluded and Henry did his time without a murmur.

Mrs. Harvey never ceased to declare his innocence and rumour abounded that Henry had taken the rap for Jackson. From the first week of his incarceration, his mother received by registered post a sum of money in the region of what he would have earned had he been still at his work. This secret was kept between her son and herself and, of course, the anonymous subscriber. When he left prison he was awarded a second preference button and assigned his own workforce of non-union men. This gang included his brothers and other relatives. The work was hard, dirty and unwanted by the first or second preference men.

Ned knew, rumour or not, that Harvey carried more weight with Jackson than he did, and but for his intervention he would have sacked the lad immediately. The situation rankled the ganger making him even more spiteful.

"I may not be able to take him tomorrow," He said half-apologetically, returning his empty tumbler to the table with bang. Henry knew he was looking for not only another drink but capitulation and surrender. The young lad's continued employment depended on him toeing the line and buying the boy's work.

"Yill be at least three men short from yer regular gang," he replied quickly in an effort to buy more thinking time.

Ned's eyes narrowed. "Me short? Niver. I've always got men to spare," he mumbled.

"Well, ye kin fergit about Crozier, Billy Smith and Alex Bell, for me an' our Sam sent 'em to the Mater a few hours ago." He moved away, then turned again. "An' by the way, don't be lukin' for the wee fella the marra ... I'm takin' him wid me to the spuds."

"He's too light for the taties," scowled the ganger.

"If he kin wurk the cement he kin wurk anywhere," yelled Henry.

"Shure Kelly and Reilly carried him," sneered Ned, flustered.

"An' I kin carry him too, wid Kelly an' Reilly on his back for that matter," retorted Henry, turning from the ganger and ordering himself another Black Bush.

The bar had fallen silent during the exchange and Henry wondered if he had gone too far. He knew he was outside the ganger's power, but had a few friends and relatives Ned could make thing hard for. Being a man who liked the easy way in all matters, he regretted the outburst and began wondering how he would break the news to Sam that the lad was joining them.

"Ach," he muttered, lowering the drink in one gulp, "After a day at the spuds, he'll be glad to go inta the mill as a doffer."

He turned to see Diamond Lil beside him. "C'mon an' have a drink, girl," he grinned grabbing her playfully by the waist.

She waved a five-pound note in front of him. "Shure, the Yanks are buying this one. I'll git ye a Bush as well—slip it up there an' they'll niver notice."

Henry didn't argue—he leaned back on the bar and watched as the Yanks chatted and joked with the two woman remaining at the table. "Bin tryin' till git me inta the backroom all day," said Lil with a superior grin.

"Cover me till I git rid of this," she giggled, opening her blouse and placing some of the change from the fiver into a wad of notes already there, wedged between her breasts and her brassiere.

"Their boat's berthed at the Pollock," she continued as she waited on the barman setting up the drinks. "Yer man wanted me down on an all-night basis."

"Are ye goin'?" asked Henry.

"Are ye jokin'?" she howled, "Them fella's 'ud leave me black an' blue. 'Sides," she reflected grimly. "Last time I went down there with two sailors they got what they wanted in the doorway of the American Bar an' then ran off without payin' me. Men like that are real bastards."

"The lowest of the low," agreed Henry.

She winked before grabbing the tray of drinks and the silver from the change and returning to the table. "I'm keepin' my legs crossed till the last minute. See ye later," she winked.

The floor waiter stood beside Henry and watched her peevishly. "Won't even let me near the table," he complained.

"Aw mebbe they'll give ye a few bob later on," said Henry consolingly.

Piper Brolly was a squat, pot-bellied pensioner with a wino's florid complexion and two cauliflower ears, souvenirs of his time as a bare-fisted bar-room fighter. He took orders to tables and returned empty bottles and glasses to the bar. He was paid a mere pittance and relied on the generosity of the clientele to boost his income.

When the American sailors had arrived earlier he had been chased from the table by the women who had descended on them like vultures. Plying their wares with experience gained over many years with many nationalities the women had conned the seamen most of the day until the Yanks knew they would have to succeed or lose face with the sneering locals. They too were tough durable men with experiences of many waterfront bars all over the world. They knew the women would hold out until the last minute.

"Last night she was sellin' it for two half-crowns an' no takers, today she'll coin about thirty quid," fumed Piper.

As they watched, one of the seamen rose drunkenly and began

to embrace the woman next to him. She was stout and lumpy with a middle-aged spread. Her face was covered in powder and garish red lipstick. Bleached yellow hair was piled high on her head like a pompadour. The hands which held the man tightly to her were covered with cheap rings. She wore a knee-length fur coat which she was never seen without and an artificial smile that never left her face. The locals scathingly referred to her as the Duchess.

"I need a woman," bellowed the sailor desperately.

Patiently unwinding herself from his embrace, she took his hand like a little boy and slowly led him through the customers to the small backroom which Crozier had been dragged into the previous night. It contained a large wooden table surrounded by half-a-dozen folding chairs, and was used mainly by card players and the women. A large drink-stained mirror covered most of the rear wall. Before closing the door from the inside, the Duchess handed Piper a shilling. "Don't let anyone in till we're finished," she muttered harshly.

He looked at the coin in his hand with contempt. His pride was injured but he didn't show it. He nodded curtly closing the door tightly until he heard harsh and heavy breathing. Then, with a stealth befitting a peeping Tom, he gently turned the grimy door handle and let the heavy door slide backwards of its own volition.

It made no sound because he oiled the large hinges every night after closing time. It was a game played only on visitors and locals who liked an audience. Stepping back with a tight grin he signalled the men closest to him to be quiet. As they looked through the doorway, the huge mirror reflected the Duchess and the American beginning to get to grips with each other. Through nudges and winks the rest of the drinkers became aware of the free show. The woman lay stoically beneath the sailor. Her fleshy legs were bent over one end of the table and her huge bundle of yellow hair cascaded over the other end. At first glance it looked as if the American was making love to a rag-doll. If she was aware of the voyeurs she did not show it, but lay impassively chewing gum until the sailor recorded his climax with a long shrill yell.

Piper closed the door as gently as he had opened it. The pair emerged moments later and the Duchess bowed to the ripple of applause that echoed around the bar. The Yank had given her a crisp white five pound note which was now wedged securely between her suspender belt and stocking top.

She noticed Henry and squealed with delight. "Ack, man," she whispered, "them big brown eyes of yours gives me goose pimples. You remind me of my oul fella. He was a big man like you, when he was at himself."

Her husband had been a prisoner of war in Japan for four years and had returned more dead than alive. Wheelchair-bound and unable to fend for himself, she earned their survival money the only way she could. Unable to leave the house, her husband had no say in the matter.

Henry kissed her sincerely on the cheek and she responded with a warmth that caused the Yank to step forward menacingly.

"That's my woman, mister," he said guardedly

She turned her head angrily. "Piss off. I owe you nuthin'."

The American pushed back the peak of his forage cap and squared his feet. Although middle-aged he was a big man with wide shoulders and a broken nose. Henry disengaged himself quickly.

"No offence sailor," he said quickly.

The Duchess looked sadly at Henry for a split second, then flashed her artificial smile at the Yank and linked him back to their table.

"Good man Henry," said the bar manager approvingly. The Americans were buying well and would use the bar and the women until their ship sailed, if there was no trouble.

"Aye," agreed Henry, "Not much point in rockin' the boat."

He looked across the smokey haze at Diamond who was still holding out. He caught her eyes and she winked slyly, as she slid a handful of change off the table and into her handbag lying on her lap.

As Kelly left the Terminus, a wave of cold air almost knocked him down. He leaned heavily against the pub door and looked blankly out into York Street in an effort to gather his thoughts. Pushing his cap to the back of his head he rubbed a hand slowly across his eyes as if trying to wipe them clean.

He noticed his shirt was hanging out of the front of his trousers and tried valiantly to tuck it, blissfully unaware that his shirt tail was billowing freely in the breeze. Suddenly it all came back to him. He took a deep indignant breath and clenched his teeth. Crozier had got to the kid.

"What was it the oul fella said?" he asked himself as he tried to remember. Stopping, he put his elbow against the rough brick of a darkened shop doorway and leaned his head in his hand. "Crozier hit oul Mrs. Harvey," he slurred, "an' he's in York Street Barracks for his own safety ... an' he's gonna be charged wid assault in the mornin'."

Straightening resolutely, he turned himself in the general direction of the police station and lurched slowly along the street. Hearing the soft clip-clop of hooves directly behind him he turned to see two young lads in short trousers astride two large chestnut horses.

They stopped obediently as he stepped onto the road in front of them. Grabbing a home-made bridle he steadied himself against the horse's head before speaking.

"What's yer names boys?" he croaked.

"Jim Nickle, Billy Robb," came the obedient replies.

"Where yis goin'?"

"Pithead." The sullen voice became a frightened whisper. "We didn't do nuthin', mister."

"S'alright, son," murmured Kelly, soothingly. He knew most of the local carters grazed their horses and ponies in open fields on the nearby Duncrue Road. The carter's sons and their friends rode the animals to the fields from the little backstreet stables, and brought them back the next morning. The law turned a blind eye if the riders behaved responsibly.

"Are yis takin' these yokes back till the slab?" he queried.

"Yis, mister."

"Here," he said, pulling the bridle, "Here's five bob. Leave this one for me, an' help me onto it. I'll take it down when I'm finished."

The boy dismounted gladly and soon Kelly was hunched over the horse's neck like a drunken Indian as he rode bareback throught the streets to York Street barrack. Eventually reaching his destination, he pulled heavily on the rope halter and the horse stopped obediently.

"McKinstry," he roared loudly, almost falling from his mount as it shied at the ferociousness of his voice. "McKinstry," he repeated, "git that bloody woman an' child bater out here or I'll go down an' git 'im meself."

A double-decker trolley-bus whirred silently by with all its lights blazing, almost colliding with the horse's rear quarters. The station's heavily fortified door swung open and revealed a tall erect figure dressed in the uniform of a member of the Royal Ulster Constabulary, standing in the half light of the hallway.

"Who's that looking for McKinstry?" he called in a strong Scottish accent.

"Willie Kelly. Wud ye bring out that piece of dog shit before I git this yoke to clim' them steps and bring 'im out meself."

McKinstry's tunic buttons glinted in the muted street light as he stepped briskly down the stone steps that led to the station door. His peaked cap was pulled down over his expressionless eyes and his thin lips were twisted in a sardonic grin. A gleaming blackthorn walking stick was tucked under his left arm like a sergeant major's baton. He stood six foot four in his black laced boots with spit polish toes that reflected the glare of the street light. He was fifty years old, straight as a ramrod and as hard as the granite steps he had just walked down. A large Webley forty-five calibre revolver set in a black holster high on his waist and was attached to his body by a corded lanyard. He looked with restrained amusement at the figure astride the horse.

"Willie Kelly, is that animal yours?" he barked as if addressing a squad.

"Naw, McKinstry," he grinned, "I borrowed it from Gene Autry."

"Head McKinstry to you!" shouted the policeman as his arm flashed upwards and down again. The blackthorn cracked wickedly against the horse's rump. It rose on its hind legs with a frightened whinny causing Kelly to slide from its back. He was knocked unconscious when his head hit a lamp standard.

"Station guard!" shrilled McKinstry, in the direction of the barrack door. Immediately a constable ran down the steps and stood over the senseless docker. "Throw him in a cell for the night. Not the same one as Crozier," he ordered.

"Right, sor," replied the constable smartly, adding, "What about the horse?"

McKinstry rubbed the toe of his boot with the silver tip of the blackthorn and watched the horse disappearing in the general direction of the Duncrue fields. Traffic was light and he was relieved to see it came to no harm as it galloped into Whitla Street. He looked at the constable. "If a woman called Jean Audry reports the loss of a horse charge this ruffian with theft," he ordered before sauntering off in the direction of the docks.

The police station sat in a Georgian house close to the corner of Little George's Street and Head Constable McKinstry was the custodian of law and order in the area. Every night when on duty he could be seen walking stiffly along the main road as far as the railway station.

Feared and respected by the local community, he kept the hard men and easy ladies in their place. He believed in corporal punishment and was not above dealing it out himself. The Webley never left its holster even in the direst of circumstances. Neither did he resort to the long truncheon favoured by his constables. The blackthorn stick was a formidable weapon in itself, and had been replaced many times, having been broken over the heads of wrongdoers from all over the world.

He knew Henry Harvey as well as he knew most of the roughnecks of York Street. None of them held any dread for him. Passing the White Lion at the corner of Henry Street he noticed with smug satisfaction that the doors were shut and the lights were out. A group of passing men spoke respectfully to him as he crossed York Street to give the Bowling Green passing attention. He continued in this manner until he reached the White Hart Bar at the corner of Dock Street. As he stood at the corner he could see the the clock on the railway steeple glowing like a huge yellow moon.

"Six minutes past ten." He checked his watch by the light of a torch attached to his belt and clucked approvingly. From where he stood the road curved inward like a banana for about one thousand yards and in his present position he could see the front doors of ten public houses. All were closed with darkened windows.

He turned and peered down Dock Street towards the York branch dock. As his eyes grew accustomed to the gloom he recognised the outline of a ship high in the water. His features wrinkled with distaste. "Where there are ships, there are sex-starved men and that means trouble" was the first thing he told each new recruit to his station.

Placing his hands behind his back he walked slowly in the direction of the public house on the corner of Earl Lane. He slowed a little as he came to Dock Street Mews. There was the sound of muted giggles and heavy breathing coming from the gloom. He proceeded the next few yards on his tip-toes and flattened himself against the brick wall of the barber shop inching his head slowly around the corner until he was looking directly into the gloom. Bringing his torch up silently he pointed it in the direction of the sound and switched it on.

In the beam of light he saw a man and a woman writhing drunkenly in a sexual embrace. The woman was seated on a galvanised rubbish bin with the hem of her skirt tucked into its waistband. Her legs were draped over the man's shoulders and the sight of her large white thighs caused McKinstry to abandon his usual procedure. He charged indignantly down the alley and smashed the torch against the man's head.

"Name," he screamed, "What is your name?" as the man fell to the ground.

"Arthur," he moaned in an accent McKinstry recognised as foreign. He picked the man up by his hair and held him close to his body. The sailor looked fearfully at the Webley.

"Git back to your ship you scumbag. If I ever see you ashore on my patch again, you'll spend the next six months cleaning out the shit houses in the Crumlin Road jail." He released him and the sailor took to his heels.

He turned his attention to the woman who was frozen in her position on top of the bin. "I only went with him 'cause Jackie needs the money—he's up in court for fightin'." Her pancake coloured face was tear streaked and full of fright.

The Head seemed about to have a seizure as he looked at her. She had managed to pull her skirt down but her pink knickers hung precariously onto one shapely ankle.

He grabbed her roughly by the bleached hair and dragged her from the top of the bin causing it to topple over, spreading rubbish around his feet. Still holding onto her hair, he put his back to the wall and slid into a sitting position and pulled her down across his knees.

Turning her head she looked fearfully at him as he raised the blackthorn over his head and brought it down across her bare buttocks twice, causing her to yelp with pain.

Rising quickly he stood her on her feet and grabbed her roughly by the shoulders. "Next time I catch you plying your filthy wares you'll be up in front of the Beak. Fix your clothes and get away home, you shameless hussy."

As she tearfully departed, he noticed a gathering of men had congregated at the mouth of the Mews, drawn by the squeals of the prostitute. Placing both hands and the stick behind his back he sauntered towards them. As he walked out of the gloom, they parted obediently to let him pass. He stopped and searched each man's face.

Only Henry Harvey met his gaze.

"Thought somebody was beatin' up Mina," he said lamely.

McKinstry ignored the statement. "Still behaving youself, Harvey?" he asked.

"Aye, sor," replied Henry, hating himself.

"Working away?" said McKinstry, cocking his head.

"Yis, Head."

McKinsty nodded approvingly. "Are you going to prosecute Crozier?" he continued.

Harvey shook his head vaguely.

"Honour among thieves, eh?" smirked McKinstry. "No matter—he's in cells and I'll have him up tomorrow. A man who hits a women is the lowest scum on earth," he added as he moved off into Dock Street. "Don't congregate, boys," he advised over his shoulder. "Remember, three's a crowd."

Brushing the front of his uniform and straightening his cap he moved slowly off in the direction of the railway station. The men watched silently as he disappeared around a corner.

Henry said his goodbyes and headed off in the direction of Great George's Street. He patted the half-bottle of Bush in his inside pocket and hoped Diamond wouldn't be too drunk to enjoy his company.

67

THREE

A T seven-thirty the next morning he was in Jim's bedroom shaking the lad awake.

"Git away down to the Chapel Shed an' tell the boys yiv to start with them. It's only a trial, mind. If yer nat able, I can't carry ye."

As he clattered down the stairs and out the door, Jim rose wearily. His body was still wracked with the exertion of the cement cargo. He sighed heavily and reached for his jeans.

York branch A and B were two large forwarding and receiving depots and were commonly known as the Chapel Sheds because they backed off into the street which housed a chapel that catered for the needs of visiting seamen of the Catholic persuasion.

The buildings were similar in construction to the cement sheds except that the massive sliding doors were made of wood. Jim entered the large open door at the harbour gate close to the American Bar. His nostrils were assailed by a pleasant country lane aroma as he walked pensively yet cockily down the narrow passage that separated the various cargoes. Stark wintery sunlight beamed weakly through pigeon-stained plate-glass windows in the high sloped roof and damp straw littered the wetly glistening square-setts which studded the floor.

The earthy smell came from bags of neatly-tiered potatoes each in different piles according to their brand names. He could hear pigeons cooing on the steel struts overhead and the floor and cargo were liberally dotted with droppings. As he continued walking he saw crates of oranges, grapefruits and melons stacked among and between the piles of potatoes.

As he breathed in the farmyard atmosphere, the factory horn blasted to inform all within hearing distance that it was now four minutes to eight. He turned a corner and saw a man bent worriedly over a pile of ledgers and sheaves of paper. The potatoes were stacked around his desk and the piles formed a wall around him affording some protection from the wind coming through the open doors that would have blown his papers off the desk. He wore a long burberry overcoat that reached almost to his ankles and a flat cloth cap. His features were sharp and pointed yet kindly and his hands were covered with gloves that had the fingers ripped out to enable him to write in the ledgers that lay before him.

Jim approached him warily. He recognised the man as Tom Flynn, a second preference cargo checker who now and again drank with his Uncle Henry. He waited courteously until Flynn looked up from his papers.

"Mr. Flynn, me Uncle Henry said I wus to report here for wurk," he said shyly.

The checker grinned warmly. "Just hing aroun'. The carriers 'ill be here shortly."

He returned to his papers and his worried look as Jim wandered out of the makeshift redoubt and sat down on a bag of potatoes.

He noticed men coming in through doors at the far end of the shed. He watched as some approached the huge waterside doors and slid them open whilst others lifted rope slings and placed them across their shoulders.

"Hi kid, are you here?" called a familiar voice. Jim turned and saw the diminutive Reilly on his knees pouring oil into a green coloured handtruck. Glad to see a familiar face he moved forward to help.

"Naw," he replied, holding the truck steady whilst Reilly poured the thick black oil between the wheel bearings and the axle. He noticed the trucks were made of tubular steel and much lighter to handle than the wooden ones used at the cement boat.

"Oh," replied Reilly sarcastically, "Are ye jist down slummin'?"

69

"Naw," repeated the boy self-consciously. "I'm gonna be workin' wid me Uncle Henry."

"Yer goin' to be a humper then," he replied, tossing the truck onto its back. Jim gazed quizzically at him and Reilly continued.

"Carryin' spuds off the lorries that come in here. That's what yer uncles do. We call it humpin' ... " He gazed at Jim seriously. "It's rough work son an' I think yer a bit light for it."

Jim was about to answer when a large burly man came running towards them bellowing obsenities. His cap sat on the back of his head revealing thick white hair and his chubby features were contorted in an angry scowl. He was dressed in an airforce blue duffel coat and a pair of brown corduroy trousers.

"Has anybody seen that bastard Hairy Ham?" he roared at the kneeling men.

"Aye, thonder he is," pointed Reilly. The big man glared shortsightedly in the direction of Reilly's finger, then raced forward unleashing a string of swearwords with every stride.

"Who's that?" whispered Jim, feeling the pangs of insecurity begin to rise in his stomach.

"That's Uncle, the ganger. That's his nickname. He's good to the Arabs, so they all call him Uncle," explained the trucker. "He's lukin' for the winchman who shuda bin on board waitin' to lift the first heave. The derricks must be topped and the winch runnin' with the first heave on the hook and stowed before seven minutes past eight or we're all entitled to extra money," he grinned, adding "I've yet to see it. Only the blues wud ask for it an' they don't cum here offen."

Jim watched fearfully as the ganger located the winchman and pushed and shoved the hapless man up the narrow gangplank.

"Git that bloody winch goin' an' git a heave intil her, ye useless oul ballocks," he roared. He turned to the shoremen, who had loaded up and were watching the proceedings with undisguised mirth.

"Is there no cargo net for this hatch?" he asked, scowling as the men looked around before shaking their heads. "Work away will an' I'll go an' see if I kin dig up one." Two loaded trucks moved out obediently onto the narrow breast. The other truck's occupant, small and weasel-faced with a bad limp looked apologetically at Uncle.

"We're a man short. There's only the two of us," he whimpered.

"What about the other gang. Is he in it?" scowled the ganger impatiently.

"Naw, they're all made up," whinged the trucker.

The ganger let forth another stream of obscenities. Grasping his cap he threw it to the floor and began to leap up and down on it. When his rage subsided, he stooped to pick it up. Rising breathlessly, his glance fell on Jim.

"Are ye not wid me?" he asked with a suspicious glare that frightened the boy.

"He's wid Henry," volunteered Reilly.

"Niver mind that," countered Uncle. "Git behin' that truck wid Snowy an' his mate. I'll talk till Henry when he comes in."

Quickly dismissing the lad, he turned to the shoremen waiting patiently on the ship's hook being lowered for the first heave.

"Has he not got a heave in yet?" he snarled. No one answered. Uncle's eyes searched the quay for a weapon. Lifting a large wooden wedge he placed the hand carrying it back into a hurling position. "Where is the dopey bastard?" he screamed.

"Tyin' up the guy ropes," said a shoreman, moving hastily out of range.

The cap on the winchman's head was just visible above the ship's rail as he knelt on the deck to adjust the waterside guy rope. Uncle flecked the air with spit as he roared again and hurled the wedge at the bobbing cap.

"Git that winch motorin'," he bellowed as the missile struck the ship's rail inches away from the winch-driver's head. He scurried across the deck on his hands and knees and roared the donkey engine into life.

Jim moved in behind Snowy's truck and began helping to load bags onto it. Reilly caught the other man's eye and putting his

71

thumbs up, pointed at the boy. "Good lad," he shouted, "Henry Harvey's nephew."

"Good pedigree," grunted the man, as he threw the sling over the top of the heave which consisted of ten bags. When the rope was securely around the bags the trucker lifted the shafts and began to pull the cart over the slippery uneven surface, limping badly as he went.

He glared darkly at the men behind him to make sure they were pulling their weight. "Don't worry about Snowy," grinned Jim's new partner, "He has no favourites, he hates everybody." Jim nodded but didn't answer. He was too busy pushing the loaded truck towards the ship's side. Snowy turned expertly as Jim held the loop of the rope in the air and the third man reached for the quickly descending hook. Grasping it, he swung it towards Jim who hooked the loop into the eye of the hook.

"Up," roared his companion to the ganger who was doubling as hatchman. He signalled the winch-driver and the heave was lifted into the air and whipped over the ship's rail before descending into the hold of the ship where the rest of the gang unloaded it and tossed the empty sling out of the hatch onto the breast.

His companion picked up a sling and they ran back to the pile and loaded up to repeat the performance. Jim hooked on and the heave began to lift.

"Whoa ... Whoa," howled Uncle as the truck also began to lift. Snowy had placed one end of the sling under the truckshaft instead of over it, tying the truck in with the heave. The winchman lowered the truck to the ground and the ganger moved along the rail.

"Git that fuckin' rope fixed pronto," he yelled.

Snowy's hand's trembled as he rearranged the rope. The heave lifted cleanly this time and Snowy, red-faced and angry turned the truck and pushed it back into the shed.

"Hey, Bob," he growled at the man working with Jim, "if that oul ballocks shouts at me again, I'm gonna heel-up."

72

"Yer not concentrating, Snowy. Ye cud a sent them spuds inta the drink an' Uncle wuda left us for a day or two," replied Bob.

Snowy replied by throwing the truck down angrily when they arrived at the pile. He sat on a shaft and began to untangle his end of the rope.

"How can I concentrate when I've got thirty-five thousand pounds worth of stocks and shares to worry about?" He glared at Jim who reacted with a nervous laugh. Snowy ignored him and continued mumbling.

Bob prodded the young lad. "Can you lay a rope?" he asked.

Jim shook his head. "Okay," replied his companion, "I'll do it this mornin', you watch, then you kin do it in the afternoon." Jim nodded tersely and soon they were pulling noisily alongside the ship as the hook was taking the heave from the truck before them.

"Good," smiled Bob, "that'll git us a breather."

Jim grinned back. He knew he was being accepted because of his connections but also because he was strong, willing and obedient.

His pleasure was shortlived. Once again as the hook lifted the heave, the truck went with it. This time the ganger's frantic warning was not heard. The truck was ten feet in the air before it fell free and crashed into the water between the ship and the quay. The sling emptied and the ten bags fell to the ground.

Tearing his cap from his head, the ganger threw it to the deck and proceeded to dance on it. He stooped to search for a missile and Snowy ran for cover as a steel shackle pin bounced across the square-setts.

"Git a grapplin' iron," screamed the ganger, "an' git that truck outa the water before the boss comes round." The ship was moved a few feet from the quay to allow the men to lower the grappling iron into the water. Snowy's face was ashen and jumping with nervous tension as the ganger verbally abused him.

Eventually the truck, dripping with mud and seaweed was hauled ashore. Uncle pointed a trembling finger at the cringing trucker. "No more ... No more! Next time an' yi'll go with it," threatened the foreman.

Snowy mumbled under his breath as he pushed the truck back to the pile, moving slowly with an exaggerated limp.

"Oul bastard," he muttered as Jim and Bob laboured to load the truck. He looked directly at Jim. "I don't havta work here," he stated seriously, "I've got thousands tied up in stocks an' shares." He looked over his shoulder threateningly. "But I'll fix him!" he added mysteriously. "I'm havin supper wid Sir Basil Brooke." He grinned at Jim. "He'll not have a job this time next week."

Jim gulped and worked on as Bob winked at him and touched his head meaningfully before pointing at Snowy who was now pulling the laden truck towards the ship's side. Another set of men passed on their way back to the pile. "Don't be washin' her again," laughed one condescendingly. A string of oaths caused him to laugh even harder.

Jim watched horrified as the truck was lifted again and tumbled into the water. This time the potatoes went with it. The ganger looked to the heavens and screamed before taking a run to the gangplank. Snowy stood, rooted by terror, as the big man bore down on him and pushed him to the ground.

"I've a good mind till throw ye in along wid it, ye stupid ballocks ye," he roared. He fumed as they went through the grappling procedure until the truck was successfully located and hoisted onto the jetty.

"Try an' git it right, Snowy," said Bob nervously as they moved back again after loading up. "Aye," scowled another man nearby, "we don't wanta be here all week."

"Shut yer yap," snarled the trucker.

They inched out onto the breast and Jim was about to hook on when the ganger roared, "Hold it." He raced down the gangplank with a piece of light rope in his hand and Jim watched horrified as the ganger tied one end of the rope tightly around the trucker's waist before fastening the other end to the body of the truck.

74

"Nigh," snarled the big man, "if it goes in again, you go wid it, an' this time we won't be in a hurry ta git the grapplin' iron."

Jim waited with baited breath and sighed with relief as the heave lifted cleanly and the truck remained firmly on the ground. Snowy trudged sullenly back to the pile. "Wait till I talk till Sir Basil," he muttered darkly. Only at lunchtime did he put a hand to the offending rope and remove it from his waist.

Jim resisted the urge to go to the pub and settled for a good dinner and two bottles of milk. He returned to the shed and took the rope from Bob. Moving to the pile, he lowered the rope to the floor and allowed two feet of it to go under Snowy's truck. He threw the other end to Snowy who spread it into the spaces on the truck board just as Bob had showed him. He received a dark glare from the trucker and a nod of approval from Bob. The truck-board held four bags, three were then put on top of them and then two with one on the top to make up the ten. The finished heave resembled a triangle.

They stopped again at three o'clock and Bob asked him if he wanted a shandy. The pub, at the back of the shed, was packed with dockers working in the immediate area.

Jim hesitated at the narrow doorway when he saw Henry seated at the bar. His waistcoat was unbuttoned and his shirt was covered with a fine soil from the potato sacks he was carrying.

"Yill be alright," coaxed Bob pushing him gently towards a table. "We're only havin' one or two." Soon he was nursing a pint of shandy which he poured down his grateful throat.

Reilly, complete with beer, ambled towards them and smiled warmly. "I tole ye he wus a good 'un."

"Aye," said Bob, "Snowy's name droppin' as usual."

"Does he really know Sir Basil Brooke?" asked Jim innocently.

"Shure he does," replied Reilly winking at Bob. "Did ye see yer Uncle Henry at the bar," he continued, "him an' Bilson's bin there all mornin'. They've a bet on. First man to leave his stool an' go for a pump owes the other a fiver. They've bin at it since half-eight this mornin', I'll bet they're ready to burst."

He looked quizzically at Jim. "Have ye heard about Kelly?" The lad shook his head.

"He's in the cooler, charged wid rustlin'," retorted Reilly with a grin.

"Yer jokin'," said Bob.

"No kiddin'," guffawed Reilly. "He wus lookin' for Crozier for thumpin' Jim. Crozier is in too, but they're in different cells. McKinstry's doin' Crozier for disorderly behaviour and assault."

"But where does the rustlin' come in?" asked Bob.

"Kelly wus so drunk he rode over to the barrack on a horse. McKinstry says he stole it." As the two men burst into laughter, Jim rose to buy a drink.

Henry scowled as he saw the boy at the bar.

"Make that yer last," he ordered. "Yill be with me the marra," he added closing his eyes dismissively. Jim nodded obediently and returned to his seat. He turned as the bar door was thrown open and his Uncle Sam stormed in to search the sea of faces before striding purposefully towards Henry.

"Hi boy," he snarled. "There's two hundred ton on wheels over there, it's about time ye came over an' done a bit!"

Henry gazed disdainfully at him for a moment before turning away. Sam grabbed him angrily by the shoulder and spun him around.

"Don't think I'm gonna do it all," he thundered as specks of spittle sprayed into Henry's face. As Henry eyed the fist clutching his waistcoat, his voice took on subued tone: "Cool down, Sam. Sit down an' have a wee drink. The drivers an' helpers are big an' ugly enough to empty their own lorries."

Sam lifted the drink grudgingly and looked around for a place to sit. His eyes fell on his nephew. "I see yer pickin' up all the good habits," he teased.

"I wus just goin'," stammered the boy, rising from his seat.

"Sit where ye are," replied Sam warmly. "Don't let that big lump of shit run yer life." He had large laughing eyes which looked deeply into his nephew's face. As Sam grinned and joked,

Jim was amazed at how his mood had changed. His affectionate laugh helped him to relax.

"I hear Snowy's gittin' up Uncle's nose," he laughed.

"Aye," sighed Bob, "I wus left with him this mornin'. Luckily the wee lad came along to pull me out."

Sam nodded. "Snowy's a fifty ton penalty ... I don't know why the big man gives him a job."

"Uncle's not as hard as he lets on to," broke in Reilly. "Shure luk at the stick he gives Hairy Ham yet he always takes him if there's no preference men."

Sam finished his pint with a flourish. "They're all a lot of bastards," he contended. "They wudn't give you an' me daylight if they cud help it." His dark eyes probed Reilly's face. "When did you ever git a job that wusn't hard 'n dirty an' low paid compared to what they git. An' they'd keep that from ye if they could. Like I said, a parcel of bastards."

He loosened his belt and tucked his shirt-tail into his pants and glared at Henry. "Don't be all bloody day, boy," he snarled as he barged out the door.

Bob emptied his glass and wiped his lips. "Time we were outa here," he muttered. They passed Henry and Bilson on the way out. Both men were lowering pints whilst glaring at each other.

The potato boat finished at four o'clock. Jim helped bring the slings back to the checker's redoubt where he received his white card from the ganger. He fell into step with some of the gang as they walked towards the shed exit. Bob stopped at the American Bar. "Fancy a drink?" he asked. Jim declined, mindful of his last drinking bout. Going straight home he drank two bottles of milk straight from the pail of cold water his mother had left them in. His body was dehydrated and his throat felt dry and constricted. The milk tasted deliciously cool. When he finished them, he refused something solid and promptly fell asleep.

Henry looked at Bilson's sweating features whilst he forced the remains of a pint down his own throat. His body felt as if it was about to burst. The Guinness was creeping back up his throat and the pressure on his bladder was unbearable. He felt urine trickle from his penis and crossed his legs in an effort to stem it. His one consolation was that Bilson was in a similar condition.

He finished the pint with a show of confidence and nodded at Bilson. "Same again?" he queried, adding, "Are ye sure ye don't wanta visit the bogs?"

"After you," growled Bilson eyeing the two crisp white fivers lying on top of the cash register.

The rest of the patrons listened to every word. They had followed the saga from early morning, and knew the end was near. Both men feigned confidence as the barman pulled two pints. As they were reached across the bar Henry slyly slid an empty pint tumbler and placed it between his legs. Before anyone could warn Bilson, he opened his flies and began to urinate into the glass.

Bilson was furious as Henry filled the tumbler and set it up on the bar. He looked around for an empty glass to perform the same act but the horrified barman pulled them from his reach. Henry smiled smugly as he buttoned his flies.

Bilson pointed at him. "You went to the toilet," he snarled.

Henry shook his head defensively. "Niver left this stool." He smiled at the audience. "Wasn't that the bet boys?"

The men roared agreement and Bilson conceded. "Give 'im the money, John," he yelled, "I need to go for a piss." He vacated his stool at speed and ran down the room and out the back door. He returned just as suddenly, hopping from one leg to another.

"Some bastard's blocked the yard door with full Guinness barrels. I'll piss myself before I git out," he wailed.

As the men guffawed at his plight, he looked around in desperation. His eyes fell on the open fire blazing at the other end of the room. Within a moment the bar was filled with the stench of boiling urine as he emptied his bladder into the flames.

His face was a picture of contentment. "An' ye needn't phone the peelers," he shouted over his shoulder to the outraged barman. "A man's gotta relieve hisself an' anyway, ye can't houl what's not in yer han'," he cried before striding red-faced and unsteadily out into the street.

Henry folded the two fivers and pocketed them. He looked at the freshly drawn pints. "Put them behin' the bar till tamarra John," he ordered before striding out and over to the potato shed.

He moved in beside Sam and waited until the driver who was standing on the bed of the vehicle brought a bag to the chime. Henry got it onto his shoulder and tossed it effortlessy in to the pile. Sam moved off for a break and Henry worked silently and quickly until the last load was on the floor.

Henry signed the man's docket and put his coat on as the grateful driver reached him five shillings.

"Fancy a pint before we go home?" queried Sam as his brother reached him half-a-crown. "Why not?" answered Henry as they walked from the light of the shed into the darkness of Princes' Dock Street.

They crossed Dock Street in silence and turned in to the warmth of the Majestic.

Jim was woken at six o'clock by the sound of his mother setting the supper dishes. The skin on his palms felt tight and painful. The butter his mother had rubbed on had left them sticky and wet. He was glad he'd come straight home and looked around the room at the familiar objects that made him feel comfortable. He smiled warmly at his late father's photograph placed side by side with a picture of one of the ships he had sailed in during the war. The fireboard over the glowing fire was laden with knick-knacks gathered over a lifetime. Brass candlesticks adorned each end and a small chiming clock set in the middle. Over at the window that looked out into the yard sat a large walnut-coloured wireless. His father had bought it with some of his demob pay and it never seemed to be turned off. Even as he gazed at it music flowed softly around the room.

"Okay son?" smiled his mother coming in from the scullery.

He answered warmly and stretched. His body felt weak and listless. He lifted the evening paper and flipped through the pages until he reached the entertainments guide.

"Think I'll go to the pitchers tonight. There's a good one on at the Troxy.

"Aye son," replied his mother. "There's yer supper an' a plate of ice-cream till cool ye down." He rose stiffly, pulled a chair to the table and ate the ice-cream.

"Turn the radio up a bit mum," he called between mouthfuls as he heard someone push the front door open and walk up the hall.

"That's our Lizzie," cried his mother rushing into the scullery and emerging with her daughter's dinner as the girl entered the room and threw off her coat.

"Saw me Uncle Henry an' me Uncle Sam rollin' down York Street, singin' away at the top of their voices. All my mates were laughin' at them. Bloody disgraces," she huffed sitting down at the table.

Jim didn't answer. He finished his dinner and went down the long backyard into the darkened toilet and dutifully urinated over his aching hands. The swelling on his face had subsided slightly, but his head still ached where Crozier had punched him.

He returned wearily to the scullery and switched on the gas operated water geyser over the sink.

"I'm gonna have a wash," he declared gruffily, pulling across the curtain that served as a door. Stripping completely, he half-filled a small galvanised bath with warm soapy water and stood in it before turning on the geyser. The pilot light ignited the ring beneath the boiler and almost immediately hot water poured into the sink which he had blocked. Using a large face cloth he sluiced his body freely, working the suds into the regions that were aching. When he reached the red and angry blotches beween his legs, he daubed lightly, fearful of breaking the chafed skin.

He dried himself and liberally patted his sister's talcum powder between his thighs and around his rear. His mother had left him a change of underwear, clean denims and a freshly ironed shirt. A popular song wafted from the radio and he began to sing in tune with the melody. After cleaning his teeth he rubbed the toothbrush over his tongue in an effort to wipe out the taste of cement that remained in his mouth despite numerous attempts to remove it. He took a tin of vaseline out of a drawer and plastered some of it on his freshly washed hair and combed it forward into a fashionable peak.

He thought for a moment of putting some of the vaseline on his chafed skin but dismissed the idea. He tidied up behind him and pulled back the curtain. His sister smiled up at him from the book she was reading. She was still wearing her emerald green smock and the smell of tobbaco hung around her.

He lifted his best coat from behind the kitchen door and checked that his money was in the butt pocket of his jeans.

"See yis," he called, making his way into the street.

He reached the corner and mingled with some lads who had been waiting on him. After a bit of high-spirited ribbing about his marked features they started off to the bus stop at Gallahers.

"Heard yer Uncle Henry give Crozier an awful lacing," declared one boy as they crossed the road.

"Aye, John," nodded Jim sagely. "One blatter he hit him. Shure Crozier musta thought a Greencastle trolley-bus had come down North Thomas Street and run over him. It wus like a cowboy pitcher. Bodies all over the place ... I hadda fly for an ambulance." He conveniently forgot his fright and fear at the raw violence.

He was interupted by another of his cronies who cut in excitedly: "There's yer Uncle Henry nigh ... " he stammered pointing excitedly towards the top of Dock Street. Jim looked in the direction and saw his Uncle Henry, dressed to kill, weave drunkenly across the road. He paused for a moment to support himself on a keep-left sign before moving off again.

"Hell's gates!" shouted Jim, "He's headin' for his motorbike!"

The boys watched with bated breath as Henry lurched toward the powerful Norton motor cycle parked below a window of McCormick's fruit shop. After two futile attempts he managed to mount it.

"He kin hardly stan' let alone drive that thing," gasped his nephew as Henry tried vainly to kick-start the heavy machine to life.

Jim ran quickly across the deserted road and tapped his uncle politely on the shoulder. Henry turned, wild-eyed and unseeing.

"Uncle Henry, yill kill yerself," cried the boy.

"Fuck off," snarled Henry. Jim stood back shocked at the reaction. He was relieved to see his Uncle Sam emerge from the pub across the road. His relief turned to horror as Sam kicked the pedal until the powerful engine roared angrily.

Henry let out the clutch with a flourish and flew across the kerb and into the street. He was unable to make the turn into Brougham Street and the boys watched stunned as the bike left the road and crashed through the front door of the Gibraltar Bar.

Rushing to the bar they entered through the mangled doors. The motor-bike, its wheels still turning lay on top of a shattered table at the far end of the room. Men wandered shocked and dazed among upturned tables and chairs and fragments of glass lay all over the carpeted floor.

Henry was under a table and being viciously kicked by the frail grey-haired old woman who owned the house.

"Git the peelers. Git the peelers," she screamed insanely at the barman who was dialling frantically on the telephone behind the bar.

Jim ran forward and tried to shield his uncle from the woman's atttack. "Leave him alone," he cried.

"Leave him alone!" echoed the woman incredously. "Luk at the state of this bar. It's a wonder no one was killed." She aimed another kick at the dazed Henry. "Luk at ye, ye drunkin' bastard ye ... I'll make sure ye git six months for this."

The barman came to the end of the counter. "The peelers 'ill be here in five minutes," he called.

Henry raised himself painfully on one elbow and looked imploringly at the woman.

"Cud ye see yer way till givin' me a bottle an' a halfin, while we're waitin' on the peelers, Hetty?" he asked dolefully.

The bar-owner screamed indignantly and began to kick savagely at Henry's unprotected head. Jim moved to physically restrain her.

"Beat it, Jim," snarled Henry irritably. "Go on. Git away out of it before the cops come," he commanded.

The boy obeyed mutely. Picking his way through the wreckage he moved into the street and caught a glimpse of his Uncle Sam standing outside the bar Henry had left earlier.

"Is the bastard dead?" he called to Jim through cupped hands.

Jim shook his head.

"More's the pity," scowled Sam to himself, as he returned to his drink.

Jim and his pals boarded the trolley-bus that took them to the Troxy cinema, a mile further down on the Shore Road. As they joined the queue Jim was the centre of attraction telling them of his episode with Crozier and Kelly.

"My da says Kelly's the best scrapper in this town," said one boy seriously, as the queue began to move forward slowly.

"My da says he's a nutcase," replied another.

"Kelly kin fight," stated Jim, from experience as Crozier's bruised face floated into his mind.

"Cud he bate yer Uncle Henry?" inquired another.

Jim screwed up his face in thought. He remembered his father saying with a laugh that Henry would rather talk than fight because he was vain about his looks. But he would never allow anyone to intimidate him. Torn between the two men Jim answered truthfully. "Ack, I don't know."

When they eventually entered the cinema, the film had already started and there were no seats available. The usher had earlier approached the queue shouting 'Standing Room Only.' Later, as he moved with the jostling crowd down the long corridor to the exit doors, Jim looked for the young girl he had spoken to in York Street during the lunch-break of his first day at the cement boat.

The effort was fruitless and the walk home, during which he purchased a fish supper for himself and a fish for his mother, took his mind off the incident at the Gibraltar Bar.

Henry, Kelly and Crozier sat in separate rows in Courtroom A of the Belfast Court of Petty Sessions in Victoria Street. Head McKinstry had placed a constable on each side of Crozier to avoid an attack from either of the two defendants. He was not unduly worried, but could have done without Henry Harvey being tried by the same courtroom as the other two.

Harvey sat resplendant in a tailor-made brown houndstooth single breasted suit with a matching waistcoat. He wore a cream-coloured shirt with the top button undone and a silk sea-green neckerchief adorned with large brown horseshoes was tied loosely in a carter's knot around his neck.

Kelly, grinning impishly, was wearing the cement-crusted clothes he was arrested in, as was Crozier who was staring dejectedly out of two very black eyes. McKinstry had meant to produce the luckless winchman at an earlier court, but lack of witnesses to the assault had presented problems. The two men injured along with Crozier had received serious bruising but had left the hospital before the police arrived.

The officer who had escorted Kelly to the cells had neglected to search him properly and an empty half-bottle of Black Bush was found when the officer unlocked his cell the next morning.

Kelly was unable to stand and the luckless officer was suspended from duty on the spot by an enraged Head Constable.

"It's your duty to look in on any prisoner every fifteen minutes. We could have had a bloody corpse on our hands," he snarled at the unfortunate officer.

Harvey had been arrested in the wrecked bar and released on his own bail to appear the next morning after a group of women from the street had picketed the police station demanding his release. He left the barracks to resounding cheers.

The court stood as the magistrate entered and took his seat. Henry nodded at a few casuals who, unable to find work, had come to the courtroom to pass a few hours. He nodded to Kelly, who smiled vacantly, then glared at Crozier who averted his eyes.

After the represented cases had been listened to and dealt with, the charge of driving a motor cycle in a public place whilst under the influence of alcohol was read to Harvey.

He stood smartly to attention in the dock. "Guilty as charged your worship," he stated in a loud clear voice whilst looking directly at the magistrate.

Mr. Edmond Jeffries stared over the rims of his spectacles at the paragon of sartorial splendour before him. He checked Harvey's occupation on the charge sheet before lifting his head.

"Looks more like an out-of-work film star than a docker!" he said anticipating the titter of laughter that swept the courtroom. His face was haggard after a night of brandy and cigars and he hoped he could keep his breakfast where it was until the recess.

He had been hunting to hounds the previous day in the County Down and felt depressed having to return to Belfast to hear the cases of drunkenness and violence that seemed to be the main occupations of the people who lived in the filthy ghettos close to the docks.

He forced his mind back to the proceedings. Leaning an elbow on the bench he lolled his head into the palm of his hand and looked at Harvey sternly.

"This is a very serious matter," he droned. "You could very well have killed someone—as it is the landlady of this particular establishment suffered a nervous breakdown and is at this moment under heavy sedation for shock. Consequently she is unable to attend this court to describe how you managed to propel a motor-driven cycle into a crowded saloon bar. And it seems," he continued in a bored voice that suggested he had heard it all before, "no one else can be persuaded to give evidence which seems to me to induce the fact that everyone else in the place must have been at the toilet or asleep."

He waited for the predictable laughter to subside before continuing. "Therefore, in the interest of the law, I can only remand the defendant on bail until the lady is well enough ... "

The shocked police prosecutor broke in politely but firmly.

"Your worship, the defendant has pleaded guilty," he said tactfully.

Mr. Edmond Jefferies snapped to attention. "Er yes ... of course, of course," he stuttered.

"That's right, sor," agreed Harvey grandly. "I plead guilty and place myself in your merciful and capable hands, sor."

The magistrate smiled benignly and studied his notes. "Very good Mr. Harvey, we do appreciate your co-operation." He was impressed by Harvey's stature and obedience and wished all the riff-raff who stood before him day and daily were possessed of the good manners and dress-sense of the man in front of him.

"Any previous?" he asked.

"Four months jail for possessing stolen property five years ago," answered the police officer.

"Hmm," sniffed the magistrate, shuffling his papers, "Your alcohol count was amazingly high, so I'm afraid I'll have to suspend your driving licence for ten years. As no one was seriously hurt I will fine you twenty pounds and twenty-five pounds damages, and, of course, the cost of the court."

Henry stood to attention and clicked his heels. "Thank you, sor. Could I ask for time to pay?"

"Very well," coughed the magistrate, throughly enjoying the

calculated bootlicking. "Five pounds per month for the fine and perhaps you can come to some arrangement with this unfortunate lady who seems to be somewhat highly strung." He looked over his glasses at Harvey. "I would suggest you sell your motor-bike and pay the lady from the proceeds."

Henry nodded and stepped down and went to the body of the court where he paid the first instalment of his fine before moving to the back of the court and listening to the disorderly charge against Crozier. Despite McKinstry's pleadings Mrs. Harvey wouldn't make a statement.

"What happened to your face?" asked the magistrate, as Crozier stood in the dock.

"I fell, yer worship," he replied sheepishly.

"Aye, fell like Nelson from a fusillade of shot," shouted a woman at the back of the court. The room was filled with laughter as McKinstry and his constables tried to regain order.

"Fined thirty shillings," said the magistrate when the courtroom fell silent.

Kelly was next. Mr. Edmonds studied the file long and hard before levelling narrowed eyes at the man in the dock. "It's difficult to believe that you were once a non-commissioned officer in the very regiment which I myself served in during the last war. I also see you were decorated for bravery. Twelve years a regular soldier and now look at you!" he barked. "Where is the dignity and bearing that goes with such a record! How can you stand before me like a bag of dirty washing?" he roared, genuinely outraged at what he saw as an insult to his regiment.

He stabbed at the offence sheet with a leg of his spectacles. "And what is this charge? Some kind of joke ... Rustling a carthorse! And drunk in charge! What possessed you to ride a horse without lights through a built-up area after lighting-up time?" he finished, glaring at Kelly with unconcealed fury.

Kelly looked at the floor for a moment then raised his eyes to the bench. "I wus tryin' to enlist in the Mounties," he grinned.

"This is a courtroom, not a music hall," snarled the magistrate, jealous of the applause which erupted for a full minute. "Another remark like that and I will jail you immediately for contempt of court."

Waiting until the mirth subsided, he addressed the defendant sternly. "I should make an example of you but in view of your excellent war record which Head McKinstry has furnished me with and in view of the fact that the animal concerned is with its rightful owner and he has preferred no charges against you I can only fine you for disorderly behaviour." He gavelled the bench. "Thirty shillings and costs."

Henry rose quickly and paid the amount, receiving a curious glance from Mr. Edmonds as he bowed and scraped his way back to his seat.

Jim walked stiffly home. His legs and arms ached with every step and his face and clothes were covered with potato dust. Dry soil from the jute sacks had found its way down the neck of his shirt and was irritating a wound on his right shoulder caused by the heavy sacks biting into his skin.

He entered the kitchen and blinked at the bright light that shone from the middle of the ceiling. A fire was blazing in the middle of the hearth and he sat down thankfully in front of it. Removing his jacket slowly and deliberately, he unbuttoned his shirt. Easing it carefully from his body, he stepped to a long mirror and examined his back and shoulders. The skin on the top of his back was marked, but the sorest part seemed to be on his shoulder-blade and try as he might he couldn't see it in the mirror.

"Ma," he called. His mother shuffled from the kitchen. He looked through the mirror at her.

"Is the skin on me back broke?" he asked.

"Yis son," she whispered, trembling, "it's terrible raw lukin'. Ye musta bin wurkin' very hard."

"Not half," he grimaced. "Niver seen as many lorry loads of spuds in me life."

"Sit yerself down," she murmured, "I've a big fry for ye. After yev ate it I'll put somethin' on that back to ease it. The boys usually cover it with the white of an egg or a drop of methylated spirits till the skin hardens." She gently brushed away potato soil that was sticking to the sweat on his back.

"I'll be alright," he muttered, taking the plate onto his knee and tucking into its contents. "Uncle Henry wus at court this mornin' so we're a man short. It'll be easier after dinner when he returns."

"Don't bank on it," whispered his mother under her breath. She reached up to the shelf beside the window and switched on the radio. It took a moment or two to warm up before the music blared all over the house.

He returned to the Chapel Shed and was soon off-loading sacks of potatoes from the lorries and on to the floor of the shed. His shoulder was level with the chime of the lorry and each time the driver let the bag go Jim caught it by one lug and hauled it onto his back. When the sack crashed onto his bruised shoulder he stifled a moan and kept on going. As one lorry emptied he moved to another as did the others he was teamed with.

Henry didn't return and, at six-thirty, Jim left the Chapel Shed with blood seeping through the shoulder of his shirt and coat. The grateful lorrymen had given him money varying from two shillings to five shillings. He accepted an invite to the American Bar by the other potato carriers who laughed uproariously when he couldn't raise his right arm to the level of the bar-top to lift his pint of shandy.

He sat down and had it reached to him. Holding the tumbler in both hands he almost finished the cool drink in one long draught. After buying the squad a drink he excused himself and walked slowly like an old man until he reached his front door. The pain made him cry out as he took off his jacket. He tried to remove his shirt and found it had stuck to the wound on his back.

Hearing him gasp, his sister rose from the book she was reading. Her pretty face was concerned. "How'd ye do that till yerself?" she cried.

He turned his face away from her as the pain made him sob.

"They say it goes like that for a week or two until it heals"

"A week or two! Jimmy, yill be dead in a week or two if ye continue at that. Where are ye wurkin' anyway? In a torture chamber?" she replied.

She bathed the shirt and wound gently with a hot cloth until she was able to remove the garment.

"Man that's wicked lukin'," she sighed. "C'mon inta the sink till I clean it up. It's as well mum's in me Granny's. She'd a fainted at the sight a that."

"There nigh," she said some minutes later, "That's all the soil cleaned from it. Wait till I put somethin' on it."

"Ack no, it'll be alright in the mornin'," he muttered.

"That's raw flesh, Jimmy. It'll niver heal if ye go back there in the mornin' ... "

"I'll be alright," he repeated, shuffling her to the curtained doorway. "I want to git a good wash, so go back to yer book an' switch on the wireless for me, love." She gave him an affectionate hug and moved obediently out of the little room, pulling the curtain over as she left.

He ran hot water from the geyser until the basin was full. Taking a deep breath he plunged his hands into it, clenching his teeth as the water stung the broken blisters. Forcing himself to ignore the pain he washed the rest of his body and dressed in fresh clothes.

He sat down to his supper and groaned with mock agony as Lizzie brought a plate filled with steak, peas and potatoes from the oven. "After carryin' them all day, now I've got ta eat 'em."

"Here's yer milk," laughed his sister.

Half-an-hour later, ignoring Lizzie's protests he joined his mates at the street corner. He steered clear of the horseplay and kept his back to the wall, content to watch the throngs of people walking along the pavements as they made their way to the pubs and picture houses.

Henry and Kelly roared loudly at a shared joke with the driver as they left his taxi and entered Dubarry's. The bar sat in the shadow of the Albert Clock and had a dubious reputation. Kelly hesitated at the entrance. "Mebbe we shud go elsewhere Harvey—this place is fulla whores."

"Yill be alright," replied his companion soothingly, taking his arm and leading him to a space at the bar. "Two Black Bush an' two pints a Guinness," he growled over the counter. Lifting the drinks they chose a table close to the door and sat down contentedly. The bar looked no different from any other pub on the Belfast waterfront except that most of the customers were lone females with bored expressions.

Henry sipped pensively and watched as some sailors made contact with the women.

"Fancy any of 'em?" he queried slyly.

"Natatall," replied Kelly curtly as he lowered a Black Bush.

Harvey didn't answer. His attention was taken by a woman who had just come out of the ladies' toilet and sat down at a table across from them.

"Man dear, wud ye luk at the poop deck on that!" he leered.

Kelly ignored the remark and sipped at his pint. Harvey looked at him with mock concern.

"I hope I'm not drinkin' wid a fruit."

Kelly grinned. "They way you're dressed ye luk more like a pig's ear than I do."

Both men roared with laughter. Harvey watched the woman until he caught her eye. "Hi girl, c'mon an' tell me yer life story."

She lifted her drink and swept across the room. The pillar-box red sweater struggled valiantly to control her massive mammaries as they bounced in rhythm to her hip-swinging walk.

91

Henry was impressed. "Last time I saw anythin' like that was when a cargo of melons broke from their moorin' on the Nellie Bywater," he quipped.

The woman sat down heavily, almost upsetting the table. Slightly the worse for drink she crossed her nyloned legs in a flurry of abandonment that caused Henry to lick his lips appreciatively. Her face was a ploughed field of pancake powder, rouge and lipstick. Her eyes were a sad sky blue and her full mouth was fixed in a permanent smile.

A broad band of red ribbon kept her strawberry coloured hair back from her face and cheap heavy jewelled earrings had lengthened her earlobes by half an inch.

"What's yer pleasure girl?" grinned Harvey, tearing his eyes from her heaving bosom.

"A double gin an' tonic, chicken, an' my friends 'ill have the same." Henry glanced at the table she'd left. It was vacant with only one empty glass on it.

"We're yer friends now, big girl," he growled.

He turned in his chair and waved at an old man standing at the bar. "Hi son," he called, "Bring me two Black Bush an' a gin an' tonic."

The man was thin and bent slightly forward at the waist. He wore a long faded dexter and a cloth cap pulled down to one side of his face. He approached the table apologetically—"I don't wurk here," he ventured.

Henry smiled pleasantly. "That's alright, son. Git yerself one as well." He crumpled a white five pound note into the man's hand.

"Now luv," he smiled, turning his attention to the mountains of flesh facing him across the table, "Is them real?"

The blond grinned proudly and lifted the hem of her sweater up to her chin. Henry gasped as the naked breasts fell free.

"Ye wudn't git many of them in a pound," he mused admiringly. The old man had returned with the drinks and was leaning across the table when Henry grabbed his head playfully and pushed his face into the woman's cleavage.

"Git a mouthful of them oul-timer an' tell me if they're genuine," he roared.

"Well, are ye interested big fella?" asked the blond, totally ignoring the old man as he reluctantly withdrew his face.

Henry flashed her a wide smile. "I am luv, but me mate's a prude an' ... "

Kelly's eyes rose dangerously from the whiskey glass he'd been nursing. "Don't push yer luck, Harvey," he growled. "I've had my filla loose wimmin. One of 'em give me a dose in France an' I don't wanna go through that again."

The woman bristled. "Y'cuda got that anywhere."

"I know," scowled Kelly, a dangerous sneer invading his features, "the bint I got it from had just left a guy whose last touch was a peroxided blond from Dubarry's."

"Big joke," snapped the woman taking a quick draw from her cigarette and exhaling into Kelly's face. Her tone softened.

"Was that during the war?" she asked.

"No! I wus over on a day trip," he replied sarcastically.

Henry found himself ignored. "What outfit were ye in?" asked the woman.

"Rifles," replied Kelly proudly, in spite of himself.

"Oh," she smiled, crushing her cigarette into an ashtray and opening her legs to allow Henry's hand to explore further.

"My husband was a Skin—did ye know any of 'em?" she queried.

"Wudn't go near 'em with a barge pole," sneered Kelly. He nodded at Henry by way of explanation. "Half of 'em were queer an' the other half slept wid them."

She rose with an insulted scream. "That's a rotten thing to say. My hubby's buried in El Aleamein."

"Bum up in hope, I presume," continued Kelly relentlessly.

The prostitute lost control. "Bastard ... Bastard ... Bastard," she chanted and leapt clumsily onto the drink-filled table splitting the knees of her nylons in the process.

Crouching on all fours on the table, she swung her heavy box handbag at Kelly's grinning features. The docker easily evaded her attack and she was almost out of breath when a giant of a barman ran forward and used the woman's vital statistics to drag her from the table and propel her out into the street.

He returned to the table and towered over Kelly and Henry. He was at least three inches over six foot tall and weighed about sixteen stones. His chest and stomach bulged out of a white beer-stained tee-shirt. A checkered apron stretched to his boots and his thick hairy arms were riddled with faded tattooes.

The blond had left without her handbag. It had fallen to the floor, opening itself in the process. Kelly lifted it casually as the barman stood at the table.

"What's in that beg?" he snarled suspiciously.

Kelly looked up thoughtfully, his face wreathed in a choirboy smile: "It's fulla whores ... C'mon an' pick yer ma out."

Henry said a silent prayer as the full impact of the coldly delivered insult slowly registered with the bartender.

"Bastard," he screamed, lunging forward, his beefy hands reaching for Kelly's throat. The docker rose quickly. He was still smiling but his eyes were hard and merciless as he easily evaded the searching fingers. The barman's weight forced the table forward pinning Kelly's lower body to the wall behind him. Henry watched as Kelly casually measured the shortest distance between two points and hit the big man twice on the chin with two of the fastest punches Harvey had ever seen delivered.

The bartender's head jerked to the left and then sharply to the right. His eyes were closed as he crashed to the floor.

Kelly nodded mockingly as he pushed the table away from him. "The bum's gotta glass chin," he stated softly.

"We better move," yelled Harvey "or we'll be making another court appearance." He quickly bundled the still smiling Kelly through the door and soon they were weaving down Tomb Street. Reaching Great George's Street, they stopped at the Bear's Paw. Henry looked sideways at Kelly who wasn't even out of breath. "What about one in here?" he asked. Kelly nodded and both men entered the public bar. They looked reasonably sober to the fussy owner and she served up two Black Bush without comment.

"Is that right what you said about the Enniskillen regiment?"

"Naw," grinned Kelly, "I just said it for badness. I don't like forward wimmin."

Henry thought of the blank look on the bartender's face as he crashed to the floor. "Remind me niver to fall out with ye," he said soberly.

FOUR

THE Orange Hall sat at the top of Alexander Park Avenue. The boys made their way slowly towards it, stopping now and then to sample some of the Mundies wine each one carried in a half-bottle in his jacket pocket. Eventually they climbed the steep hill enjoying the brassy dance music that filtered from the open windows of the building.

Entering the brightly lit doorway, they timidly paid the admission fee then made their way to the toilets to hide their wine. At the cloakroom they handed over their overcoats and then returned to the gents' to be united with their bottles.

Climbing the backstairs they entered the ballroom. The dance floor was packed with dancing youngsters. Within a moment Jim was jiving with a girl who worked with his sister, but his eyes were constantly searching the room for the girl he had spoken to in York Street the previous day.

"Have ye seen Maureen McGivern here, Nora?" he asked as she ducked in below his arm and whirled so quickly that her skirt billowed up exposing her shapely legs and a brief glimpse of her stocking tops.

Her pretty face froze in a perplexed frown: "Hor," she grimaced. "Madam's in the corner at the stage wid all the boys who fancy her because her ma's a money-lender."

Jim grinned at her petulance and pulled her ample body to him. She was a small pretty girl with soft brown eyes and black hair that stretched to the small of her back. They danced well together and he was fond of her. They both enjoyed jiving and he

96

delighted in whirling her all around the floor. The drink had dulled the pain between his legs and on his shoulder and the urine seemed to be helping his palms. Now and then his hand would drop to her rounded hip and she would let it remain there for a moment before pushing it away with a smug smile.

Steering her towards the bandstand he looked over her head and searched the sea of faces until he saw Maureen sitting on the edge of the bandstand. She was wearing a pink off-the-shoulder party dress with a matching silk scarf tied like a cowboy's bandana around her neck. Her short hair was natural blond and curly. She wore a mildly amused expression as she talked to a tall thin faced boy beside her.

The set finished but Jim remained on the floor with Nora holding her to him protectively as the band began to play a slow waltz. "Fancy a moody?" he grinned closing his arms around her waist. The saxophone player pushed the mouthpiece away from him and wet his lips before looking down with melting eyes on the dancers. He embraced the microphone and began to sing:

Some enchanted evening,
You may see a stranger,
You may see a stranger,
Across a crowded room.

Nora buried her head in Jim's chest and wrapped her arms around his slim waist. As they danced closer to the bandstand, Maureen threw her head back and laughed at a remark made by her companion. She turned her head slightly and Jim was able to see her white even teeth. Her eyes caught his and she returned his smile with a wide-eyed grin.

Once you have found her
Never let her go ...
Once you have found her
Never let her go!

A group of dancers had stopped before the rostrum to listen appreciatively as the singer crooned into the mike. Jim continued dancing and the second time around he received a searching glance which he construed as a challenge. He lowered his face into Nora's hair and breathed in the beautiful aroma of perfume that wafted from her scented tresses.

When the dance ended, he thanked her and escorted her back to the wooden chair she occupied beside her friends. She sat down, stony-faced and silent. Pushing his way gently through the crowd, he positioned himself close to Maureen and waited. As the band struck up a slow foxtrot, he strode purposely forward and from a distance of six paces reached out his hand to her.

She looked slowly over him, taking in his cream shirt with its long buttoned down collars. A slim black knitted tie hung from his neck reaching the first button of his single breasted suit which was smoke blue window pane check and looked as if it was tailor made. The jacket, although not a drape, was quite long and his trousers were narrow enough to be drainpipes. Yellow socks peeped out above his black laced sponge-soled shoes.

She rose from the bandstand and took his hand. Her three inch stilletto heels only raised her head to his shoulder. They began to dance instinctively before they reached the floor. He pulled her to him and found she fitted like a soft glove against his body. Her waist was tiny and his arm easily encircled it.

Lowering his head, he put his cheek on hers and closed his eyes, content to breath the headiness of her perfume. His contentment was short-lived as a woman screamed and he heard his name called. The dancers at the other end of the room split rapidly and bodies in a blur of movement rolled punching and kicking across the floor.

Jim tried to disengage but found Maureen's hands holding tightly to his wrists. "No," she whispered pleadingly, her eyes wide and apprehensive. He broke free and without a word ran to the fracas. Fighting his way through the onlookers, he challenged two young men who were punching viciously at his friend John.

The men were strangers to him and the tallest one turned and smiled dangerously. "Beat it!" he ordered, grabbing Jim viciously and digging his fingers into his injured back. Jim let out a cry of pain and brought his right hand up in a sweeping arc. His knuckles caught the man below the chin. He watched somewhat amazed as his attacker fell to the floor like a puppet with its strings cut.

He hadn't time to contemplate. Another youth ran towards him screaming profanities, and Jim felled him with a clubbing right hook. He shifted his feet and was attacked again, this time by a scrub-haired girl who tried to put his eyes out with the heel of her stilletto shoe which she was brandishing like a hammer.

He laughed with nervous relief as Nora jumped on the girl's back and pulled her to the floor by her hair. Another man squared up to him and he dropped into a crouch as his boxing skills took over.

At that moment the band struck up the National Anthem and everybody immediately stood to attention.

With the last note the fighting resumed and by the time a breathless policeman arrived Jim was escorting Nora along North Queen Street towards her home.

"Tole ye she was stuck-up!" declared the girl as they sat in the Moyola Cafe, sipping coffee and listening to the jukebox. Jim made no reply.

"When are ye boxin' again?" she asked with a grin.

"Dunno," he replied, "Haven't much time for trainin'."

"I saw yer last fight in the Ulster Hall!" she replied shyly.

"How'd I do?" he grinned. She rubbed his bruised knuckles lovingly.

"Don't know," she laughed, "I was too busy hidin' my eyes."

He joined in her laughter as he rose to get two more coffees.

Moments later she was groaning with real or exaggerated passion as she pressed her lower body into his. She had allowed him to open the buttons on her dress and fondle her breast, but despite his pleadings, she refused to allow him to go any further.

99

She thought his gasps of pain was his inability to conceal his passion as she dug her long nails into the wound in his back and teased him beyond endurance. After an hour of wrestling in the darkened entry behind her home he decided to call it a day and left her to the door.

Reaching home he climbed the stairs to his bedroom and removed his jacket. He found his shirt had again stuck to the wound. Weary from the day's work and the drink taken he removed the rest of his garments and fell into bed still wearing the blood-stained shirt.

It seemed like moments later when his mother's constant shouts awoke him. Rising groggily, he noticed the bed linen was smeared with blood. Mrs. Harvey entered the room and gasped with horror. "Ack son, yill bleed till death."

Jim smiled despite his pain. "It's nat that bad, but I'm sure me shirt's ruined," he grimaced

"I thought it was healed up," said his mother, inching the shirt away from the wound. "It's all broke out again," she whimpered, "Ye musta hit it again somethin'."

"Aye ma," he agreed, remembering Nora's long nails.

"Wait till I git a clean cloth," she shouted, literally running down the two flights of stairs to the kitchen. Returning breathless, she daubed tenderly at the wound.

"There," she replied moments later, "the bleedin's stopped, but yer nat goin' back till that job," she added savagely.

"Ack ma, I'll havta ... " he whimpered, feeling as if someone had gouged a lump from his shoulder. Anyway it's Saturday an' I think we only work till one o'clock."

He was distressed to hear her begin to weep. "At least son, give it time to heal. Take a day off," she advised through her tears.

"Aye alright," he muttered with some relief and climbed back into bed. Half-an-hour later he was awakened from a peaceful doze by the banging of doors. He cringed in terror as someone bounded up the stairs two at a time. His bedroom door crashed against the wall as Henry stormed through it knocking the alarm clock off its shelf with the force of his entry.

"What the hell's gates are ye doin' lyin' there?" he thundered. "Git ta fuck outa yer pit an' git down till the Chapel Sheds. Lyin' there like a hospital case girnin' about a wee bruise on yer back. If ye listen till oul dolls like yer ma, yill finish up bein' one."

He turned to the bedroom door before continuing, "There's men down there, real men doin' yer wurk so git down there as fast as ye can an' stap behavin' like a wee chile still crappin' yella."

Jim nodded mutely and rose wearily. Downstairs he found his boots, clean socks and a shirt sitting in their usual place on top of the fender in front of the fire.

He mother reached him a bowl of porridge and watched silently as he tried to eat it. She wasn't to know his sickness was due to excessive drink taken the night before.

When he was about to put his jacket on, she attempted to push a cushion up the back of it to protect his broken skin.

"Ack ma," he yelled in protest, "I can't go out like that. They'd be callin' me Quasimodo." He hugged her tightly as her eyes began to fill up, and reluctantly settled for some ointment and a pillow slip over his shoulder under his shirt.

It fell off during the first load, but he kept at it doggedly, refusing to give in to the pain knowing his courage and stamina was again being tested. The other carriers told him it would eventually seal over and heal itself. The jovial countrymen who brought the loads in from all over Ireland worked along with him and were very generous with their tips when he finished each load.

At ten, Henry stepped up to the lorry Jim was helping to unload. He pushed Jim aside. "Is yer back any easier?" he scowled tossing hundredweight bags from his shoulders into the air in the direction of the pile a few feet in front of him.

The boy watched fascinated as each bag flew and fell deftly

into the tier he aimed it at, just like a dart thrower placing darts into a board.

"Are ye deaf as well as stupid?" roared his uncle.

"It's a bit better," he stammered.

"Away over till the Yankee Bar an' git yerself a couple a hot whiskeys. They'll dull the pain. Only a couple nigh," he warned with a narrowing of his eyes, "An' if ye see those other two lazy bastards ... tell them to leave me a glass of whiskey over the bar an' ta git ta fuck over here."

"Yis," cried the lad with great relief, anxious to get away from his uncle and the loads of potatoes that never seemed to stop coming into the shed.

He walked over to the American Bar and peered through a solid sheet of tobbaco smoke until he picked out his two workmates sitting close to a small one bar electric fire. Both were much older than he was with many years of potato handling behind them.

"What are yis havin'?" he said tentatively, rattling the half-crowns in his pocket.

"Two whiskeys, kid," answered the smaller one immediately. He was wearing a brown tweed overcoat that had seen better days. Its skirts had been cut off and it only stretched to his waist. A crumpled brown eight-piece cap sat on his head, and like all the other carriers he wore a silk scarf around his neck. His face was florid and an open snuff box sat on the table beside him.

His companion was taller by a head and wore a suit jacket with the stuffing from the right shoulder pad sticking out like a ball of fluff. His cheerful face and his shirt front were covered with potato dust. A khaki forage cap with a greasy peak sat on the back of his head. His silk scarf was polka-dotted and tied cowboy fashion in a thin band around his neck. His eyes were bright and friendly as he waved Jim to a chair.

"Sit down kid an' niver min' that miserable ballocks. What's yer pleasure?"

Jim gulped at his kindness. "Uncle Henry says a hot whiskey 'ill help my back," he said.

102

"It won't be long till yer an alcoholic like the rest of us if ye start drinkin' whiskey at this hour of the mornin'," he replied before shouting the order to a white-haired bespectacled bartender who folded his morning paper and turned on the water geyser.

Jim looked absently round the small bar. The U-shaped counter was waist-high to a normal sized man and ran from the side door to the gents'. Two large spacious windows looked into Princes' Dock Street, whilst another two were situated at the Shortt Street entrance, throwing a lot of light into the bar-room. The bar-top was also spotlessly clean and large ornamental mirrors advertising various brands of alcohol shone brightly on the wallpapered walls. Although it was early morning, the pub was reasonably crowded and had been since half-past-seven when the barman had arrived to open up.

Most of the clientele were on tea-breaks from the various ships in the area, although some had been known to walk quite a bit as the barman had a reputation for drawing a good pint of porter.

"Zis a new recruit, Harry?" asked a beefy-faced man as he took a pinch from Harry's snuff-box.

"Aye," came the reply, "He's Jim Harvey's lad. His back's in raw flesh an' I don't think he'll stick the pace," he added matter of factly, as if Jim wasn't there.

"Shure yill be alright," smiled the man comfortingly. He was wearing a navy blue crombie overcoat and a dark soft hat. "My name's Bob Dell. I'm a checker in York Dock. I sailed with yer father ... He was a good man," he added kindly.

A hot whiskey was set down in front of Jim and he sipped at it pensively.

"Did Clarke Gable say for us to go over?" asked Harry, with a scowl on his face.

"Aye, he did," gulped Jim, "Do yis want a drink before yis go?" he asked.

"That's what I like Andy," smiled Harry "a man who persists in buyin' drink."

"Aye," replied Andy sarcastically, "'cause it's a cert you don't."

He looked at Jim seriously. "Lissen, we'll have a drink wid ye at dinner-hour or whenever we finish, an' fill ye in on the do an' don't of being a spud-humper."

Jim nodded eagerly. As they rose to leave Andy turned back and whispered in his ear. "See when yer gittin' yer other hot whiskey, ask for it wid a stutter an' oul Joe 'ill give ye a double measure. He's a sucker for anybody wid a handicap." He squeezed Jim's arm knowingly. "See ya later."

They left the bar shouting good-natured abuse at the other drinkers. Eventually the men quietened down and Jim sat self-consciously holding his drink.

"Aren't you the lad who was involved in the fight wid Crozier the other day?" Bob Dell asked softly.

"Aye," retorted Jim.

"I can see some of the marks still on yer face. He's a nasty bastard. He hasn't been seen since yesterday. Suppose ye heard about yer Uncle Henry an' Kelly an' him bein' at court yisterday?" he continued.

Jim shook his head—"I knew he wus there, but didn't hear what happened ... I wus at a dance last night."

"Henry an' Kelly teamed up after the court an' wrecked Dubarry's an' then ended up fighting the entire crew of a German coaster outside the chip shop in Earl Street," guffawed his new found friend.

"Aye," reflected Jim grimly, "He pulled me outa bed this mornin, or I wud nat have bin here."

"Cud ye not carry on yer other shouder?" asked Dell.

"Naw. I tried it but the begs won't fall properly an' I havta fix 'em an' that takes time an' Henry shouts at me," he answered childishly.

The elderly checker shrugged, feeling sorry for the lad.

"Ack, yill soon git the hang of it," he whispered as he emptied his pint.

"Cud I git ye a drink?" offered Jim, not wanting to be left alone.

"No thanks," smiled Dell, as he rose tiredly.

Jim waited until he'd left before hobbling up to the bar. He was about to order when he remembered Andy's advice. He put on his best 'poor' face and ordered: "Cu ... Cu ... Cud ... Y' ... Y' ... Y' ... Y'... Ye ... Gi ... Gi ... Giv ... M' ... M' ... Me ... "

The barman's warm smile melted to a glare of indignation. His face turned crimson and his mouth puckered angrily as he tried to reply.

"A ... A ... A ... A ... Are Y ... Y ... Y ... You ...T ... T ... T... Tryin' ... T ... Ta... Ah M ... M ... Make ... A ... A ... A ... Cu ... Cu ... Cu ... Cunt ... A ... A ... Me?"

Jim stood rooted. It was the worst stoppage he had ever heard.

He felt shame and embarrassment which quickly turned to terror as the furious bartender lifted a huge bung-starter and ran to the opening in the counter, screaming "G ... G ... Gittt ... Ou ... Ou ... Out ... "

Jim fled for his life. Reaching the Chapel Sheds, he looked over his shoulder and saw the irate barman flounder for breath at the dock gate. His white apron fluttered in the breeze as he waved the bung-starter angrily in his direction.

"Parcel of bastards," he muttered as he thought of Andy and Harry. He buttoned the top button of his shirt and walked quickly towards a lorry stacked high with potatoes. The driver moved a bag to the chime of the lorry and Jim put his back under it. The driver was grateful for the help and gave him a half-a-crown when the load was on the floor.

They worked ceaselessly through the remainder of the morning until just one lorry remained. The driver had arrived with no helper and Harry informed him that according to union rules he had to give whoever helped him a payment of one shilling per ton. In the absence of Henry, the three carriers gathered around the ten ton load and emptied it in record time, receiving a pound note as their reward.

Harry took command of the paper money and dug deep into his coat pocket. "Here kid ... Here's yer wack," he said reaching Jim three florins.

"But I'm not in the union," replied the youngster haltingly.

"Neither are we," grinned Andy as he received his share. Brushing the dirt and straw from their clothes they sauntered the length of the shed towards the American Bar.

Jim suddenly remembered the barman's anger and looked at Andy accusingly. "Ye nearly got me brained."

"C'mon," smiled Andy reassuringly. "I wus just kiddin' ye. By the way did ye git any other tips the day?" he asked.

"Aye," muttered Jim guardedly.

"Hide most of it down yer stockin', 'cos the big fella 'ill be lukin' his share."

"Why?" asked the boy, dumbfounded. "Shure he gits his own."

Andy continued slowly as if addressing an infant. "He believes he's entitled to half of what ye git seein' as he got ye the job in the first place. Salt most of it away an' keep two or three shillin's in case he asks ye for somethin'." He smiled gently at Jim's crestfallen features.

"Seein' as it's yer first week he mightn't ask."

The conversation had caused Jim to forget about the stuttering barman, who immediately on seeing him raced from the back of the bar. He threw his arms around the lad and roared with laughter. "Y... Y ... Ye ... S ... S ... Shudaaaaa ... S ... S ... See... Seen ... T ... T ... Th ... a ... Wa ... Wa ... Wee ...B ...B ... Bugger ...R ... R ... Run ... " he guffawed. "A ... Aw ... SSSon ... I ... I ... Kne ... Knew ... TTThey ... PPPPut ... YYYe ... UUUp ... TTTil IIIt ... "

Laughing with nervous relief Jim moved on to sit down with his workmates, glad to be a part of the team.

A familiar voice cut through the noise. "Have ye anythin' for me?" He looked around the bar and saw Henry hunched over a table with a challenging look on his features.

Jim felt his heart sink. "Aye," he nodded sadly as he realised he had forgotten to follow Andy's advice. Taking the half-crowns and florins from his pocket he threw them onto the table and watched sullenly as Henry counted them quickly.

"Two quid," he muttered, somewhat surprised. "Ye musta

worked hard the day. But them two bastards 'ill nat be long teachin' ye how ta dodge the column." He reached Jim a handful of coins and put the rest in his pocket. "There ye are," he grinned, "Half an' Half ...

"Aren't ye glad I got ye outa yer pit this mornin'?"

Jim nodded mutely and began to move away.

"Are ye nat buyin' me a drink ... ?" asked his uncle with a smirk at the man seated beside him.

Jim looked at him glumly. "Aye, what 'ill it be?" he replied.

"A half a whiskey for me an' a half for my frien' here," ordered his uncle.

Controlling the anger that had risen in him he walked to the bar and returned with the drinks. He felt deflated. He had planned to give his mother half of the tips to prove he could provide for the home.

"I tole ye to plank it," whispered Andy fiercely as the boy sat down dejectedly.

"I forgot," muttered Jim staring at the floor.

"Well, don't fergit the next time or yill shop us all," muttered Harry.

"Drink up an' we'll go down till the Sportsman's an' watch the horse racin' on the TV," whispered Andy, lying low across the table in an effort to avoid Henry's enquiring gaze.

Henry waited until they reached the door. "What about youse lazy bastards ... Have yis anythin' for me?" he asked stonily.

Harry shook his head negatively. Andy walked to the table. "I got two half-crowns from a Cullybackey man."

Henry swept the coins disdainfully from the table where Andy had set them. He watched silently as the carrier stooped to pick them up.

"Git me an' Chiseller a drink before yis go," were his only words.

Jim watched as Andy placed two more whiskeys on the drink-littered table. He could see Henry was reasonably drunk. His eight-piecer clung to the side of his head, covering his left ear.

He leaned over the table and locked eyes with the youngster.

"Don't be messin with them idjits. Go home an' git yer ma ta put the whites of two raw eggs ontil yer shoulder an' then git ta bed. Don't know why yer shoulder shud be sore, for I've ate more spuds the day than yiv carried."

Jim blushed as the men in the bar laughed derisively. Andy and Harry waited for Henry's contemptous dismissal before leaving the bar and crossing into Fleet Street.

Andy grinned at Jim. "Don't let it git ye down. Hey," he added quickly, "is yer back still sore?"

"Aye," muttered the lad.

"C'mon then," he winked knowingly at Harry. "We'll call inta the Stalingrad. Aw c'mon," he coaxed, as Harry faltered.

They had just ordered the first round when Andy approached one of the females sitting round the fire. The American ship had left the port and business was slack. "Diamond," he said like a client discussing a deal. "Jim's got Potato Shoulder. Cud ye cure it the way ye did with the rest of us?" Jim was barely listening as his attention was focused fearfully on the door in case Crozier arrived.

The woman measured the lad with her heavily mascaraed eyes, then pursed her smeared lips thoughtfully. "It'll cost ya," she said.

Andy dismissed this with a smile. "There'll be a bottle and a glass a wine when yiv finished, nurse."

She turned haughtily to Jim and beckoned him into the darkened backroom. He followed her suspiciously. When they were both inside the dank room which smelt of perspiration and stale beer, she closed the door tightly and turned on the single light. Jim watched curiously as she took off her imitation fur coat and rolled up the sleeves of a faded sweater which she wore over a faded polka-dot patterned short-hemmed skirt.

Looking sharply at the lad, she spoke curtly in the manner of an overbearing hospital matron. "Take yer shirt aff. Git up on that table an' lie on yer belly." The no-nonsense manner allayed his fears of a set-up. He knew there were woman in the district with certain unexplained gifts that could cure things like warts and whooping cough. Lizzie Stenson in the lane had more than once cured him of a dropped palate by putting the end of a spoon sprinkled with pepper into the back of his throat.

He climbed obediently onto the table top, trembling a little as his hairless chest met the cold surface. Kicking off her high heel shoes, she clambered shakily onto the chair beside the table, then after a moment's hesitation onto the table top. He closed his eyes, thinking that she was about to perform some magic with his wound.

He looked up after a moment when he heard her breath coming harshly. To his horror he saw her crouched over him. Her skirt was tucked into her waist band and she was holding one leg of her pink bloomers to the side exposing a clump of pubic hair.

Her eyes were closed and he knew by the contented look on her features that she was about to urinate.

Wriggling furiously, in an effort not to send her crashing to the floor, he managed to roll from the table. Grabbing his shirt and coat, he opened the door and ran into the bar, leaving her cackling uproariously and peeing all over the table.

An audience had gathered and all eyes were on him as he emerged ashen-faced. Andy's forage cap was on the back of his head as he leaned against the bar buckled in mirth. Beside himself with anger Jim lashed out and felled his tormentor with a swinging right hook to the jaw. Andy fell between the barstools as Harry and other drinkers grabbed the young man before he could do any more damage.

"Cool down, Jim," yelled Harry. He looked at Andy who had scuttled into a corner, ruefully rubbing his jaw. "I toul ye yid act the idjit someday till yer cost!"

Jim was breathless with anger. "Imagine gittin' thet poxy oul bitch ta piss on me wound ... " he snarled at the frightened Andy who had risen shakily to his feet. Harry spoke directly to the lad.

"It was his idea of a joke," he explained grinning at the rueful Andy. "But it backfired an' I don't think he'll be playin' anymore on ye." His tone changed to respect. "That was a fair punch, Jim ... Yill be makin' a name for yerself wid a dig like that."

"Yer not kiddin'," agreed Andy with a grimace. "Only a greedy person wud want two slices a that."

He was pulled roughly around by Diamond. "If ye don't supply that drink ye promised, I'll hit ye such a kick in the balls, yill be talkin' like a fruit for a week," she screeched. As he ordered the drink she looked slyly at Jim. "Ye shuda stayed," she purred through stained teeth, "it really wurks y'know!"

The Sportsman's Arms was a large two-storied house on the corner of York Street and Fleet Street with an entrance in each street.

Most of the regulars used the side door in Fleet Street and some had given the bar over forty years' custom without using the other entrance. The outside of the building was brightly painted with the owner's name in large lettering stretching acoss the front door and the two expansive windows on either side of it.

Inside, the tiled floor was cracked and uneven. Heavy wrought-iron tables and stiff-backed chairs filled the space between the bar and the windows that looked out into Fleet Street. The windows let in plenty of natural light which reflected in the large mirrors behind the well-stocked bar. On each side of the York Street entrance sat two snugs with high wooden partitions for privacy. These were known as 'loose-boxes' to the locals. Like most bars in the area it had only a gents' toilet, as the majority of its clientele was of the male sex.

When Jim entered the bar from the side door he noticed many of the casuals he worked with at the cement boat. This was not unusual as the cement stevedore's office was just around the corner.

A large red-haired man with a soft country accent welcomed them from behind the bar.

"What about yis boys?" he grinned. "What'll yis be havin'?" as he scooped some empty pint tumblers from the bar-top and wiped away a few puddles of Guinness.

Jim began to order but Andy stopped him. "C'mon poultice," he said admonishingly to Harry, "it's your hook-on." He turned to wink at Jim. "It's like drawing a tooth gittin' him ta buy a drink," he grinned.

"Three bottles, Paddy," called Harry, taking the hint with a scowl. The barman drew the corks from the bottles and threw them expertly into half-pint tumblers. Lifting their drinks they found an empty table and exchanged greetings with the men around them. Jim watched as other men filtered into the pub from the bookmaker's office in the lane around the corner.

Harry took a sip and spoke to a tall but extremely gaunt young man slouched dejectedly at the bar. "Did ye not git a lie-on at the wee spud boat this mornin', Sandy?" he asked in a friendly tone.

"Naw," answered another man before Sandy could reply, "a load of lorry-drivers from Fenton's Haulage came round to the schoolin' pen flashin' their union cards and got all the checks."

"That's desperate," scowled Andy. "Youse do the dirty wurk all week and they get a handy wee turn at time-and-a-half."

"Aye," muttered Sandy looking morosely into his half-finished pint, "it's bad enough havin till ball-lick dockers without havin' lorrymen shovin' our noses intil it."

"You didn't help yerself walkin' outa the houl of that boat last week because it was rainin'," said another man.

"Aye, an' he brought us out with 'im. That's why we didn't git a job this mornin'," said another man bitterly.

"Shure it was peltin' so hard weda got our deaths," replied Sandy defensively, remembering how Ned had humiliated the men by making them stand in the centre of the potato shed like criminals until the rain stopped. "Registered dockers wud have been allowed to sit in the heat of a public house," he argued.

111

"Ye can't really blame Ned or any of the bosses. The rules have always been a man with a union card gets work before them that hasn't," said another man quietly.

"But them rules weren't meant for lorrymen workin' all week in their own firm comin' down and takin' the bread outa our mouths at the weekend. I blame that bastard Ned. Him an' all them other first preference men. They hate our guts an' wud love ta see us chased off the quay altogether."

"Aye," said Harry, "that's because we cud wurk better wid our eyes closed than they cud. But they got the cards," he added sadly.

"But yid need to be in a constant job till to git a union card so how kin we git cards if we can't git wurk," snarled one man.

"Aye, it's a bloody vicious circle," muttered Sandy into his empty tumbler.

Paddy had been listening to the conversation and thought it was taking an ugly turn. He noticed one or two registered dockers in the bar who were sipping their drinks or reading the sports pages in embarrassed silence.

"Andy," he called out in an effort to ease the growing tension, "what do you reckin 'ill win the big one today?"

At that moment the York Street door opened and Ned entered with a group of men. The ganger paused for a moment, grinning sardonically at the silent drinkers before moving into one of the snugs. His companions followed obediently.

"Fuckin' bastard," whispered Sandy, but Ned heard him. The black pig-like eyes hardened like concrete as he sat down heavily.

Sandy couldn't conceal his anger. "Them's the bastards he schooled in front of us this mornin'. It's only drink money till them," he added angrily.

His voice was loud enough to carry into the box and Andy tried to defuse the situation. "Take it easy, Sandy," he pleaded. "The Blackpool Clipper is due on Monday an' yill git two weeks wurk if ye keep yer nose clean. The reds an' blues steer clear of the timber so there'll be wurk for everybody."

Jim sat self-consciously quiet during the exchanges. When

silence descended he rose from the table. "What do yis want?" he asked quietly.

"Whiskey," snapped the opportunist Harry, whilst Andy, shaking his head pitifully, ordered a bottle of stout.

Paddy had just finished serving Ned's company through a hatch in the box when he noticed Jim standing at the counter.

"What'll it be, young fella?" he roared cheerfully, casting a worried glance at the morose Sandy who was still mumbling obscenities under his breath.

Sandy looked round with glazed eyes at the youngster. "You're the wee buck got the cement boat the other day, aren't ye," he laughed, slapping Jim hard on the back and raising a cloud of potato dust. Fortunately for Jim it was his left side and he felt no pain. "Fair play till ye son," continued Sandy moving from the crutch of the bar and staggering slightly. There was no malice in his tone as he added, "Least yer an Arab like the rest of us an' not a parasite like them bastards in there." He pointed an accusing finger at the snug.

The box door creaked open and Jim watched as the ganger loosed his fly buttons and walked towards the toilet. He saw Jim and paused. "Still fuckin' about wid troublemakers, eh Aggie," he sneered. He looked at Sandy who had fallen silent.

"At least when yer with Kelly, yer with a man. Not like this yap who blames the world because he got overlooked this mornin'."

Sandy knew he had gone too far. His eyes were pleading as he spoke. "I shovelled shit for you all week, Ned. I wus dependin' ..."

Ned broke in savagely. "Never depend on nuthin', son. Nobody owes you a livin' on the quay, today or any day. Yis are fuck all to me ... All of yis. I kin school whoever I like an' if ye don't like it fuck aff till the spinnin' mill down the road. They're lukin' for doffers an' spinners. Them's jobs that 'ill suit a bunch of oul dolls like yerselves."

He pointed at the snug. "Them men in there pay union dues every week. As a fella union man I am duty bound to take them after the blues an' the reds."

113

"But what happens when yer men short in the middle of the week for a boat the reds or blues won't go to?" wailed Sandy.

"It kin lie till the next mornin'," roared the ganger, "before I wud let youse bastards hold me till ransom." His black eyes turned viciously on Jim.

"Well, are ye goin' ta buy me a drink for services rendered?"

Jim blanched, wishing for the courage to say no. "Aye, Ned. What'll it be?" came out instead as he dipped his hand in his pocket.

"Glass of Black Bush, an' send it into the box," came the curt reply as he moved off to the toilet, adding for Sandy's benefit, "I'm particular who I drink wid."

The lad looked at Sandy's empty glass. He wanted to buy him a drink but feared offending the ganger. Lifting his order he sat down wearily between Harry and Andy.

"What'll happen till yer man nigh?" he said pointing at Sandy.

"He's a baten docket," replied Harry without lifting his eyes from the racing form, "He'll niver wurk for Ned again."

"Can't he wurk for others?" asked Jim.

"Not if Big Ned blackballs him," stated Harry.

Sandy continued to mumble about recent events but he was ignored by the customers who didn't want to run foul of the ganger. He glared after Ned when he returned from the toilet. His muddled mind told him he had gone too far. He vaguely remembered getting a loan of money from the barman on the strength of the work on the Blackpool Clipper would have brought him. He searched for Paddy's friendly face. "Wud ye givus another pint on the slate an' wud ye send Ned in a Black Bush?" he whispered with lowered eyes. Paddy began the pint then moved to the snug hatch with the whiskey. His eyes were grim as he returned. "He doesn't want a drink from ye," he said quietly. Sandy sighed and nodded in resignation.

As Paddy set up his pint two men left the snug for the toilet.

Harry gripped Andy's leg tightly. "There's Red Ennis," he whispered.

"Oh fuck," sighed Andy, "there'll be trouble nigh."

Both men stopped beside Sandy and looked him over disdainfully. The bigger one was about five feet ten. He had short cropped red hair and prominent ears. His eyes were blue and a stubble of beard surrounded small even teeth.

He was built like a fairground wrestler with shoulders and arms like a gorilla. His fearsome reputation as a streetfighter had preceeded him over the Queen's Bridge into York Street. Luckless opponents who had tangled with him nicknamed him 'The Pig' because of his fondness for biting off pieces of their ears during combat. He was employed as a driver for Fenton's Haulage, and, it was rumoured, doubled as Fenton's bodyguard after business hours.

He sized up the drunken casual. "Bit of a mouthpiece, aren't ye, son?" he said patronisingly. Sandy kept his eyes on the floor and didn't answer.

Jim looked around the bar at the unconcerned faces. "There's two of 'em—is nobody goin' ta help him?" he asked.

"He talked hisself intil it," replied Andy tersely, his eyes focussed firmly on the racing sheet. "Sandy's too cute ta fight. He'll take a dig in the gub an' lap it. Besides," he added, "Big Paddy won't stan' for any acrobatin' in here."

Their eyes went to the door as a jacketless man carrying a bicycle on his shoulder entered the bar-room. He placed it against a table and straightened up with a wide grin. Jim laughed as he recognised Billy Kelly.

"How's the boys?" nodded Kelly as he stepped up to the bar. "Pint an' a Black Bush, Paddy, an' give Sandy his pleasure," he shouted.

Paddy flashed him a warning smile. "I think Sandy's had enough for the day," he said adding, "What in Heaven's name is that all over ye?"

"Suki flour," grinned Kelly. "I got a spell at a boat at the mill."

He turned to the assorted faces and saw Jim. "What about ye, wee Harvey?" He motioned with his hands besides his private

115

parts, "still toughenin' 'em up?" Jim replied with an embarrassed grin.

Kelly's face grew serious as he saw the tense situation between Sandy and Ennis. He walked forward into Ennis' gaze.

"Somethin' wrong, Sandy?" he asked without taking his eyes from the lorry-driver's face.

"Fuck off," said the Eastender tonelessly.

Paddy rounded the bar instantly and put his considerable bulk between the two men. He looked sternly at Ennis. "I don't know you," he said, "but if you want to drink in my bar you stay with your own company or out you go."

Kelly grinned. "Let me introduce you, Paddy. This yers Red Ennis, from the Eastend of the city. Some people call him the Pig. Personally he looks more like a rat to me. Oh aye, he's supposed to be a tough guy."

Ennis stepped forward menacingly, causing Kelly to grin tightly. Sandy lurched up to him "Watch yerself pig or rat or whatever yer name is. Billy Kelly's mashed bigger peas than you in his soup."

The redhead ignored him but grinned at Kelly.

"Are you Billy Kelly, the first preference man?"

"I'm under suspension!" retorted Kelly, "So technically I'm an Arab."

"The lowest of the low," muttered Sandy, striving to stay upright.

"But yer still a union man an' you should side with me your brother in union instead of this scum."

The bar was silent as Kelly pushed his cap to the back of his head. The front door creaked eerily and an old man ambled in from the street. The sound of a trolley-bus moving away from the stop outside was cut off as the door closed behind him. He ordered a pint and a worried Paddy edged to the other end of the bar to pull it.

Kelly took in Ennis' physique. "There's no such thing as scum," he said, "Scum is part of the whole portion and is created by the portion and is equal to the portion." His eyes laughed at Ennis' baffled look. "They aren't scum an' neither are you. You're shit. I've bin three hours knee deep in rotting flour yet you smell worse than I do."

The driver took the insult without rancour. He looked at the tightly knit men listening to Kelly's every word.

"Playin' to the gallery," he grinned. "I kin see I'm outa my own territory an' there'd be no chance of a fair go as we're well outnumbered." His eyes took on a hardened glint. "I ain't afeared of you," he finished.

"I hear you're fond of eatin' ears," continued Kelly relentlessly. The lorry-driver allowed a slight smile to cross his features. "Some other time, Willie," he answered, turning to the snug.

Kelly's voice followed him. "Put yer hands on Sandy an' I'll take out all yer teeth, Pig." The driver entered the snug closing the door tightly on the jeers of the clientele.

Kelly turned to Paddy. His eyes were soft and his voice was pleading. "Wud ya give Sandy just one more then I'll take him home?"

He turned his head and searched for Jim. "C'mon up an' have a drink," he called. The lad rose proudly and went forward to be embraced against the docker's dusty chest.

The bar erupted as the tension lifted. Andy turned his forage cap back to front. He rose from the table and folded his arms. Putting one leg in the air he lowered himself to the floor by bending the other. "Hi Kelly, kin ye do this?" he cried remaining in the position for a few moments before straightening up. The drinkers roared and clapped as Kelly took his cap off and scratched his head in mock bewilderment. He raised his hands for silence. "Listen," he shouted through cupped hands. "Does anybody wanta buy a good second-hand bike with three speed gears an' a dynamo lamp?"

A man came forward and looked the bike over. At Kelly's request he rode the length of the bar on it.

"How much?" he queried.

"Thirty bob to you, Albert," grinned Kelly.

"It's a deal," came the terse reply as he slapped the money into Kelly's open palm.

"C'mon Sandy an' I'll take ye home," said Kelly. Sandy pushed his long hair out of his eyes and gazed blearily at his protector. "Away ye go Billy," he muttered dejectedly, "I'll be alright."

Kelly shrugged, hitched his trousers, and moved out the door.

"Billy Kelly's a good man," said Andy drunkenly.

"What about this bet?" wailed Harry, ever the businessman. "We'll pick 'em now an' the kid kin run round to the bookies before the off. So givus yer rent," he finished.

Andy looked up in surprise as a small, crabit faced man tapped his shoulder irritably. "Have ye seen Billy Kelly?" he muttered impatiently. "I lent him my bike to go for a drink at lunchtime. I need it to go home till Castlereagh," he added.

A roar of laughter drowned out his pleas for information and he left the bar in disgust.

The laughing voices floated into the snug and made Ned grimace. "They'll be laughin' on the other side of their faces when I school the Clipper on Monday," he scowled, setting his empty tumbler down with a bang that caused one of his company to run to the hatch and order him another drink.

"What's the cargo?" asked Ennis, unruffled by Kelly's taunts.

"Timber," stated the ganger, pulling a crumpled packet of Woodbines from his pocket, he extracted a cigarette and waited for someone to light it. "Oregon pine," he continued, "Twelve inches by three inches wide and forty foot long. She starts eight o'clock in the mornin' an' finishes at twenty to midnight ... an' I mean midnight."

"How long will that last?" asked someone.

"Two weeks," retorted Ned proudly. "Takes 'im six weeks till load her in the States but I turn her round an' have her back on the high seas in two. Know why?" he continued with a smug smile. No one spoke.

"Because I niver let them lazy bastards lift their heads," he

118

snarled. "Most of 'em have already borrowed on the strength of it an' give the proceeds till the bookies or the publicans, so they do what they're tole. They know I can sack anyone who steps outa line. There's not a bastard among them that I cudn't replace just like that," he finished, snapping his fingers in contempt.

"Aye," agreed Ennis, glad he was a driver, "Shure they're just so much dirt under yer feet."

Ned ignored him. His mouth was a thin line as he continued. "I know the names they call me—animal, pig-eyes, beast. Next week," he said with what passed for a grin, "they'll be dreamin' about me. I'll invade their sleep like a divil from hell. They'll be tossin' an' turnin' all night ... makin' up heaves in their slumber an' kickin' their wives or their fancy-wimmin outa bed. They'll git up sweatin' wid fear knowin' I'm standin' over the hatch watchin' their every move. They'll waken in the mornin' tireder than they went ta bed with hands fulla timber splinters an' blistered by their hook-handles an' sawdust stickin' till their grimy useless bodies."

"Do they git any breaks?" asked Ennis to fill the embarrased silence. "Aye," answered Ned disapprovingly. "But the wurk doesn't stop! They go two at a time. The hard men take twice as long as the meek fellas, but I don't care as long as there's six men constantly slingin' out the sticks."

"Sounds rough," muttered another man, placing a pint to his lips and downing it with a shudder.

"It's rough as hell," roared Ned, "but it's all there is for non-union labour at the cross-channel on Monday an' once they start wid me they havta stay to the death no matter what other handy jobs comes up later in the week. Hi," he said changing the subject, "Does any of yis wanta buy a good fishin' rod for three quid?" The men looked at each other blankly as he continued slyly, "There's a brave handy wee spudder due in next Sar'day."

"I'll take it," snapped a low-set cloth-capped man who immediately produced the cash. "Come out to me as soon as the reds are schooled," said Ned airily, as he pocketed the money. Squinting at his watch he rose from the table.

"Luk intil our office on Monday an' someone 'ill give ye the rod," he muttered with a belch. "I'm movin' on."

"Are ye away, Ned?" shouted Barney over the din of a horse race on the television.

"Aye," snorted Ned adjusting his overcoat and nodding at Sandy who was now fast asleep in a corner. "Yer not a bit particular who you sell drink to."

Paddy roared with laughter that only an expert would know was fake. "Shure Sandy's no trouble if he's left alone an' that wasn't exactly Saint Christoper you brought in."

He turned from the ganger who slouched unsteadily out to his car.

"Bastard," said Andy savagely as the door closed. "He was tryin' till git Sandy barred."

"Aye," agreed Harry, "But this is one place his rule doesn't apply. Paddy's his own man an' answers to no one but hisself."

Jim looked approvingly at the barman as Harry continued.

"That's why Kelly didn't knock that redheaded bastard dead on the spot. He's got too much respect for the big man to fight in his bar."

The mention of Kelly caused Jim to laugh drunkenly. "Imagine Billy sellin' oul Soda's bike"

"I didn't see the joke in that, kid," said Harry soberly. He looked at Jim, "Don't git too fond of him kid, some people say he's not the full deck."

"Ack, he wudn't do the kid any harm," said Andy defensively, "an' he'll probably buy Soda's bike back on Monday."

The drivers emerged from the snug and laughed at Sandy's sleeping figure. "Youse York Street shits cudn't drink tea," jeered Ennis. "Ball-lickers," replied the locals as the door slammed shut.

Henry opened one eye groggily and peered at the clock on the littered mantlepiece. "Four o'clock," he gasped disbelievingly.

He sat up and immediately fell down again. "Ghost to ghost, I'm dyin'," he moaned. He eyed the floor and made another effort to rise and fell off the narrow settee. Rolling onto his back, he rested for a moment and then pulled himself upwards using the table leg as an aid.

His feet were bare and he was stripped to his underclothes.

He couldn't remember undressing and knew he generally didn't when he slept on the sofa. Scratching his head absently, he tried to marshall his thoughts. Stiff with dried sweat and caked potato dust he staggered out to the backyard.

"Ma ... are ye in?" he called in a little boy whimper. Receiving no answer, he pulled off his long johns and began to wash in cold water at a stone coloured sink. He dried himself and lifted a pair of clean drawers from the top of the mangle and walked into the kitchen. Stopping at a long and narrow mirror, decorated with insignias from his late father's regiment, he proceeded to pull on the combinations. He noticed a note on the fireboard and lifted it. It was scrawled in his mother's spidery handwriting. Focusing his eyes, he read 'Gone with Aggie on the bus to Carrick. Go to bed and sober up. Will see you at supper-time.'

He threw the note into the fire and rubbed vigorously at his hair to dry it. "Where's me clothes?" he mumbled suspiciously as he gazed around the room. Going out to the hall he climbed the stairs slowly and went to his wardrobe. It was locked and the key had been removed. He shook the door furiously, but was reluctant to break the lock, as it was the only thing that kept Jack and Sam from stealing his clothes and pawning them for a lark. He moved downstairs with the idea of borrowing a shirt and trousers from Sam, but found the front and back door locked from the outside. "The bastards," he roared furiously. "They know I can't stand being locked in since I went to jail."

He went to the first flight of stairs. The house was an end one and his father had built a small window into the gable wall to allow the natural light to filter onto the landing. Rubbing his pencil moustache thoughtfully, he went into his mother's bedroom and opened her wardrobe. He took out her best Sunday coat and pulled it on him. Buttoning it with difficulty, he rummaged around until he found a pair of red backless carpet slippers with large blue pom-poms on each foot.

He slipped them onto his bare feet and hobbled down to the backyard. Approaching the mangle he bent and lifted one end clear of the tiled floor. Grunting a little with the effort, he searched below it with one hand until he located and brought forth a large waterproof envelope. Taking some paper money from the envelope he was about to replace it when a large black and very shiny cockroach scurried out from under the mangle and over his foot.

Henry screamed with terror. Throwing the envelope and the money into the air he raced to the safety of the kitchen. He closed the yard door quickly then opened it a fraction to watch with fast beating heart as the insect crawled back under the mangle. He waited a full minute before venturing back into the yard and retrieving the envelope and the money.

He decided on a new hiding place and opted for the high steel cistern above the toilet. Taking the lid off the cistern he placed the envelope inside. Insects and vermin were Henry's Achilles' heel.

The sight or sound of them filled him with horror and revulsion. This fear was well-known to his friends and foes alike and many of them took great delight in putting dead mice or live insects in the pockets of his clothes. Discovery of such objects in his pockets sent him rolling to the floor and screaming in abject terror until the creatures were removed from his person by some kindly onlooker.

Going back into the kitchen he sat down on the sofa to get his breath back and shock faded from his ashen features. He found the need for a drink more compelling than ever and went to the landing where he climbed cautiously through the small window and dropped the few feet remaining into the street.

Weaving drunkenly, he made his way up North Thomas Street

past the decaying Unionist Hall and turned right into York Street. Oblivious of the curiosity his female attire was arousing in those who passed, he continued resolutely until he reached the Sportsman's Arms.

Not a word was spoken as he limped up to the bar and climbed thankfully onto a stool. "Givus me usual an' hurry Paddy, for I'm at death's door," he moaned.

The barman took one look at the figure before him and burst into uncontrollable mirth. "That's a brave lukin' new coat yer wearin' an' is trousers outa fashion nigh?" he roared, setting up a large whiskey. He continued laughing as Henry lifted the glass with two hands that were shaking violently and poured the contents into a large water jug sitting on the bar-top. Setting the glass down he lifted the jug to his head with both hands and didn't set it down until it was bone dry. "Same again, Paddy," he gasped, but with less urgency.

He reached for the bottle of Guinness that had accompanied the whiskey and tried to pour it into the tumbler provided. The neck of the bottle rattled against the glass like a jackhammer against a nail.

Unable to control the shaking he looked at Paddy for help. The bartender took the glass and bottle gently and poured the liquid smoothly into the glass.

Jim Harvey had returned from the bookmakers and stared incredously at his uncle. He recognised the mauve-coloured coat with the astrakhan fur collar and matching hem as his Granny Harvey's favourite which she wore when she went to the meetings in the Co-operative Guild in the Husband Memorial Hall. The legs of his spotless white drawers contrasted vividly with the red mules.

Curiosity drove Jim to the bar to question his uncle.

"Why are ye not wearin' yer trousers, Uncle Henry?" he asked in a puzzled tone.

If Henry heard him he didn't answer but continued to stare gravely at his own reflection in the mirror at the back of the bar.

After a moment or two Jim gave up and went back to his table. "How'd the bet go?" slurred Harry.

"Two winners an' one bate," spat Jim.

"I'm goin' home," said Harry rising. "I've one ta see tha night an' I wanta git my head down for a minute or two."

"Aye," muttered Andy, "I'm starvin' so I am."

All in agreement they moved unsteadily to the back door to yells of farewell from Paddy and their cronies.

Reaching home eventually, Jim hung his cap and coat on the back of the kitchen door and grinned impishly at his sister's loud clucks of disapproval.

"Nuthin' wrong wid yer back now," she scolded, rising to get his supper. He lurched across the room and turned on the radio.

"Where's me ma?" he giggled slumping heavily onto the settee. "She's away till Sally Johnston's wee country house in Carrick with me Granny Harvey. Henry came in poleaxed at lunchtime so me granny hid his clothes an' locked him in."

Jim took an uncontrollable fit of laughter at this news. His sister looked at him with undisguised contempt as she sat down a plate filled with pork chops, peas and potatoes in front of him.

"Suppose yer goin' out the night as well?" she asked.

Jim fell back beaming broadly at her. "Aye, Lizzie, I'm goin' to the wee Orange Hall."

"Luk at ye," she scolded. "Hardly a week workin wid them hallians an' yer turnin' into a drunken pig just like the rest of 'em. Watch ye don' spill yer milk," she warned, as he reached over the shaky table for a knife and fork. Steadying the table she sat down to her book.

A pleasant melody floated from the radio and Jim began to sing along, ignoring his supper. Lizzie looked over at him and shook her head sadly. A few moments later he was fast asleep, his dinner untouched. The girl rose wearily from her book and placed it back in the oven before lifting the collapsible card table and putting it into the scullery. She took off his heavy boots and loosened the scarf tied tightly around his thin neck. Lifting an overcoat from the bannister rail in the hall she placed it tenderly over his body.

The ganger had to lower his head slightly to enter the small kitchen house. His bulk filled the hallway as he swung on the handle of the kitchen door. The room was empty. "Are ye there?" he called.

The woman peeling potatoes in the squat back scullery grimaced. Putting the knife into the basin she dried her hands and walked out through the curtain that served as a door. She was young with a pretty snub-nose and a heartshaped face. Premature lines at her eyes and throat were faint and had so far failed to mar her beauty. She ran a hand quickly through her copper coloured hair to take it out of her large dark brown eyes. Catching him as he staggered against the staircase, she led him gently to the sofa and sat down beside him. Her short brown skirt rode over her thighs showing the tops of her stockings but she made no attempt to adjust it.

He rubbed roughly at her knees and tried clumsily to put his hand between her legs. "Where's yer man?" he slurred, looking at her with a smile on his glazed features.

"Out in some of the pubs I suppose. I haven't seen him from this mornin'," she replied.

"Aye, he wus wurkin' for me. I put him in the big hatch so he'll be a while yet," he remembered with a leer.

The woman nodded silently and began to unbutton his heavy overcoat. The door opened and three youngsters between the ages of five and ten years raced into the centre of the room. The first two stopped suddenly when they saw the ganger, causing the youngest, a girl, to slip on the linoleum and fall on her backside.

He watched until she rose shakily, then beckoned the children to him. They stood expressionless as he foraged deeply in his trouser pocket and dug out a handful of silver.

"Away till Madgie Walshe's an' git some sweets," he mumbled, giving each child a shilling as the woman ushered them out.

"Here," she said to the oldest boy, as she reached him an empty polish tin, "Go an' play some hopscotch an' don't come back till yer sweets are ate or yer man'll take them off ye." She didn't bar the door in the hall, praying that her husband wouldn't come home until suppertime.

Sitting down beside her visitor, she summoned up a smile.

"Yiv a brave mouthful in ye the day big fella. Yill niver git till yer wee country house in that condition. Have a lie down there," she added, deftly loosing his belt and opening his fly buttons.

He fell back rolling his eyes and she placed a cushion behind his head. His cap had fallen to the floor and she saw for the first time how grey and sparse his hair was. "Dirty oul ballocks," she muttered distastefully as his groping hands unbuttoned her food-stained blouse and fondled her breasts. Her own hands were also busy as she took loose money from his jacket pocket and stuffed it silently under the cushion of the settee.

Suddenly the shadow of a man loomed in the hall through the half glass of the interior door. She disengaged herself and ran terror-stricken to reach the door before it was opened. Three swift knocks set her thumping heart at rest. "Prudential," shouted the collector.

"Kin ye come back at five?" she called. "He's nat in from wurk yit." Her hands were trembling as she moved back to the settee. The inert ganger came to life again reaching for her breasts as she lowered her head to his lap, sweating each time someone passed the window.

Moments later she rearranged his clothes and sent him on his way. As his car left the street her husband rounded the corner. He brushed past her without a word as she stood at the front door watching the car disappear. She returned to the room and found him seated at the crumb-littered table in front of the window.

"He come round to tell ya to stan' him on Monday mornin'," she explained, "an' as usual he fell asleep on the settee." The

126

children returned from the street and stood around her clasping tightly the end of her apron and skirt.

"He gave us money for sweets," shouted the youngest, her bright little face smudged with chocolate.

"Are ye givin' me anything till ate?" said her husband dourly, ignoring the children.

She moved into the scullery and ladled soup from a large black enamelled pot into a bowl. Placing some boiled potatoes into it she carried it to her husband.

Lifting a large carving knife he cut a thick wedge from a white loaf lying on the table. The children watched silently as he dipped the bread into the soup and then wolfed it down hungrily.

"Will ye be able till take me till the Gibraltar Bar the night?" she smiled.

He flicked away a fly that came close to his bread. "Naw," he replied tersely, without feeling or warmth, "I got skint the day but I'm takin' a run up till Dunmore ... I gota tip for a dog." He lifted the bowl to his head and emptied it. "Have ye ten bob about ye," he asked gruffly, without looking at her. "Not for you to put on a stupid dog," she bristled.

He rose and pushing through the children, went to the fireboard and lifted the lid of a tarnished silver teapot and took what cash there was in it.

"That's all there is till feed us till next week," she cried, grasping his arm to restrain him. He shoved her forcefully across the room and her back hit the handle of the coalhole door causing her to gasp in agony.

Looking at her with contempt written all over his sallow unshaven features, he snarled—"Did yer fancy man nat give ye anything fer lettin' him fuck ye?"

"Mind the childer," she screamed, forgetting the pain in her back. She rose groggily to her feet. "Shure he's an' oul man, an' wudn't I have the door locked if we were up till somethin'?"

"There's more than one way till skin a cat," he leered, looking at her with unconcealed disgust.

"I didn't do anything," she shouted as the children ran to her side. "It's you he comes ta see."

"Aye," he laughed bitterly, "that's why it all over the quay about you an' him. But I close my ears. If he didn't fancy you I wudn't git any wurk an' nobody misses a slice from a sliced loaf." He looked contemptously at the children. "Which of them's mine, if any?" he added, his face black with anger. She didn't reply as he lifted his overcoat and stormed into the street.

As the door closed behind him, she wearily cleared his dishes from the table. Scooping the bread crumbs in her cupped hands she walked out to the front door and flung them onto the street for the birds that nestled on the roof tops. Returning, she folded the soiled newspaper pages that served as a table cloth and replaced them with fresh ones.

With the departure of their father, the children began to scramble around the tiny kitchen. She grabbed the little girl and held her tightly. "Right," she smiled through her tears, "Hands up for a bath an' a bottle of syrup of figs."

When they were safely in bed she hoked out the money from below the sofa cushion and placed it with the rest in her sewing bag. Half-an-hour later the door opened and the insurance man came in and sat down beside her. He put his arms around her as she forced a smile. "Did I come at a bad time love?" he asked.

Mrs. Harvey raised her head from the *Belfast Telegraph* and snorted as Henry stumbled up the long hall and fell into the kitchen. He rose on one elbow and looked drunkenly at the group of women of various ages who occupied the room.

"Yid think youse 'un had no homes of yer own the way yis congregate here every night," he wailed.

"She's our ma as well as yours, an' we're entitled to come an' see her when we like," replied the eldest.

Pulling off the astrakhan coat he lurched to the yard door

mumbling under his breath. Pushing it open a fraction, he wedged the front of his body into the aperture and began urinating noisily onto the backyard tiles. The women eyed the ceiling in disgusted silence as he adjusted the fly of his long johns and threw the flip-flops into a corner.

"I'm away till my bed," he slurred, leaning on the fireboard for support. "Waken me at half-eight an' don't fergit till git me ten Woodbine."

"Aye, son," demurred the white-haired old pacifist. Henry turned at the door and glared at his sisters. "Why don't yis sit in some nights with yer husbands instead of clockin' here?" he complained before clambering up the stairs and falling into his neatly made bed.

Making a mental note of the amount of money in his wallet, he placed it into the pillow slip and rested his aching head firmly on it. He narrowed his eyes at the disapproving features of his father imposed on a large framed photograph on the opposite wall.

He stuck his tongue out. "Goodnight, ye oul cunt ye ... " he chuckled before falling into a drunken sleep.

His mother waited until the overhead noises ceased and then continued reading aloud the stories of interest in the pages of the nightly newspaper.

It was a ritual began when the family was young and continued over the years. They listened intently until she finally folded the newspaper before putting it on the kitchen table.

"So the big pig got out after all," said her youngest daughter, a well-endowed girl who had most of the local lads lusting after her.

"An' wearin' my best coat," said the mother to herself, searching thoughtfully but vainly through the pockets.

The daughter continued teasingly—"Suppose nigh yer gonna wait till we go, an' then yill run over till the shop an' git him his fags an' bring them uptil him along wid a wee cuppa tea."

"Aye an' have a good search at his pockets," laughed another.

Aggie Harvey rose from the gathering and lifted her coat.

"Our wee Jim wasn't home when I left till go to Carrick. I hope he's alright," she said worriedly.

"Aggie," replied her mother-in-law, reaching her a pinch from her snuff box, "he'll be like the rest. He'll only come home when he's nowhere better to go."

"Ack, I worry about him," answered Aggie, dutifully kissing her before running through the narrow lane that led to her home. She smiled with relief when she saw him sleeping blissfully on the sofa.

Kelly walked through the friendly noisy throng that littered the brightly lit hallway of the large house in Nelson Street. The parlour and kitchen was packed to capacity with people with drinks in their hands and the noise of their conversations spread out into the street. He eased his way into the kitchen, being careful not to jostle anyone and handed a paper bag containing six bottles of Guinness and a half-bottle of Black Bush over the table set across the door of the kitchen to serve as a bar.

A plump girl with flaming red lipstick took it from him. She was wearing a yellow smock which clashed with her red hair.

"Billy Kelly special, eh," she grinned showing broken discoloured teeth which caused him to grimace. He waited until she poured him a drink from the bag and looked around for a vacant seat.

Everyone in the room was known to him, some more than others. He decided to sit beside Sandy Carstairs, who was more than a little drunk.

"What about ye?" he grinned, nudging his shoulder. Sandy stared at him blankly for a moment, then recognition filled his eyes with laughter.

"Dead on, Wullie," he slurred through numb lips. "I wanta sing a wee song ... Will ye call a bita order?"

Kelly laughed. "Order for the singer," he roared.

The room fell silent for a moment, then resumed talking in muted tones.

"Luk at yer man," jeered a calloused-faced casual good-naturedly, running an appraising eye over Kelly's white shirt, dark striped tie and neatly pressed blue serge double-breasted suit. His black leather shoes were spit polished and shone like beacons against the worn orange oilcloth that took the bad look of the uneven floor tiles.

"Billy, wud ye risk it for a biscuit?" roared a chubby middle-aged woman with long white hair and a fluffy cardigan that hid floppy breasts that fell to her waist

"No," countered Kelly, "But I'd rump it for a crumpet, if you didn't tell yer oul fella." Her husband, a carter winked broadly at Kelly before changing his wad of tobacco to the other side of his mouth and spitting unerringly into the centre of the fire.

This drew an embarrassed yelp from his wife. "Stap that. Yer nat in yer own house." At that moment Sandy launched into a wailing lament and the room fell dutifully silent.

Kelly watched with amusement as a girl seated opposite him silently fought off an unwanted admirer who was trying to put his hand up the back of her blouse. She was modestly dressed, dark-haired and quite attractive, and looked to be in her early twenties.

She caught his amused glance and smiled tightly with a mixture of tension and determination. Sandy's song finished on a loud plaintive note and he immediately slaked his thirst in anticipation of the roisterous applause which dutifully followed.

As Kelly searched the eager faces for another volunteer singer, the room door opened with a bang and Henry Harvey landed on his hands and knees in the middle of the floor.

The party-goers roared with laughter at his sudden entrance. He remained on all fours and the end of his broad hand-painted yellow and green tie trailed the grimy oilcloth as he moved like a dog towards a plate of sandwiches which he proceeded to eat, whilst barking and yelping like a hungry puppy.

Kelly waited until the laughter subsided before lifting Henry to his feet. Like most of the men he was neatly dressed. A bottle green suit and tan boots complimented his gaudy neckwear. As usual he was not as drunk as he appeared to be and moved easily as Kelly guided him towards the dark-haired girl.

"Peter," he said smilingly to the bald-headed man who had been forcing his attention on the girl. "Wud ye be a good lad an' let this oul idjit sit down?" Peter smiled grimly, and moved to another room.

A woman's voice lifted in song and instantly the crowd muted. Harvey put his finger against his lips and smiled at the girl beside him. No one spoke as the singer, nervously knotting her fingers through a small printed handkerchief on her lap, sang sadly of a lost love who had perished in the war when his ship was torpedoed. When she finished, she acknowledged the warm applause with flushed cheeks and downcast eyes that were full of tears.

Seizing the moment, Henry rose shakily and took the centre of the floor, singing meaningfully, but totally out of tune, a bittter ballad outlining the hardships of prison life in the Crumlin Road jail. Most of the listeners knew Harvey had served time out of loyalty to another man and applauded loudly when he finished with bowed head. Not all were taken in by his tale of self-sacrifice.

"He's some actor," scowled one man well out of hearing.

Kelly watched as the dark-haired girl used the break in the singing to make a beeline for the outside toilet.

"Anybody out?" he heard her asking the girl who was pouring the drink. "It's all yer own, but the seat'll be soakin' with them beagles pissing all over it," came the cheerful reply.

She opened the latchdoor and disappeared into the darkness of the long backyard. Kelly turned his eyes to Harvey and watched as he pulled a large ornate silver hip flask from his pocket. Removing, with exaggerated difficulty, the top which also served as a cup he brought the two together and vainly tried to pour himself a drink. The crowd roared as the neck of the flask beat a staccato rhythm against the rim of the cup. He gazed frustratedly as his hands continued to shake until a sympathetic woman took them from him and poured the drink.

Kelly noticed the girl had not returned from the yard and moved to the backdoor.

"Anybody out, Ella?" he called to the barmaid.

"Give her time till git dacent," scolded the girl with an impish grin.

He smiled and stepped out into the darkness. Walking slowly he allowed his eyes to become accustomed to the gloom. Seeing her framed against the door leading to the entry he spoke softly. "Are ye okay?"

She recognised his voice immediately. "Yis," she called with relief, "Thanks for gittin' rid of Peter the groper for me."

He nodded, taking closer inspection of her trim body in the dull light that shone from an upper bedroom. She was wearing a red sweater which immediately took his mind back to the woman he had insulted in Dubarry's. Although her breasts were not as full, they were ample, accentuated by her waist which was minute. He noted disappointingly that her legs were somewhat on the thin side.

She seemed to read his mind. "They called me Minnie with the skinny legs, at school," she smiled.

"Legs niver worried me," he teased, "Shure they're the first things y' throw away." Moving closer, he pulled her into him. She felt the hardness of his arms and body as he gripped her tightly, yet no so tight that she couldn't break free if she'd wanted to. She returned his caress, raising her face to meet his.

His eyes were wide open as they stared down at her. They were challenging, judging, awaiting her response. They were about to kiss when the door to the kitchen opened and a shadowy figure began to urinate noisily into the small drain which served the downpipe from the kitchen sink. Adjusting his buttons, he broke wind contentedly before moving back into the house.

"Lissen Minnie," said Kelly urgently as the door closed on the noise from the kitchen, "Do you know where the attic is in this house?"

"Aye," she replied guardedly.

"Good," he grinned. "Go there an' I'll see you in five minutes."

"I'm not a good thing," she chided, gripping his arm as he made to move off.

He kissed her, not roughly or harshly, but with a gentleness that caused her to hold him tighter.

"If ye were a good thing, I wudn't be askin' ye," he smiled as he walked to the door.

He spoke to the owner of the house to assure they wouldn't be disturbed then made his way up the long narrow staircase into the roomy attic. She was seated close to a large window that looked out into the street when he entered the room. Picking his way through the old and broken furniture, he sat down on the floor beside her.

She did not look at him but continued to stare out the window with a horrified look on her features.

"Ack, that wud make ye sick!" she said bitterly. Kelly, puzzled, moved closer to the large window and found himself looking into the bedroom of the house opposite.

"That's Sadie Mackle's house," he explained, "She does it for a livin'."

"With black men!" screamed Minnie. "An' three at a time? Luk at that big buck nigger on top of her an', nat a stitch on 'im ... "

Kelly laughed. "Well ye know what they say. Red an' yella, black an' white ... they all like it when it's tight."

Minnie turned on him savagely. "How cud yis allow her to bring them fellas intil her house. Heaven knows what diseases she'll be handin' roun' the locals in a month or two."

"Not to us," shuddered Kelly. "She's off limits till us. None of the lads wud touch her wid a barge pole. Those are the only men she kin git, an' it'll be them goin' home with a dirty rifle."

She looked at him disgustedly. "When yis are drunk yis wud try it with a barber's floor."

He continued to grin. "Shure ye know us York Street men. Don't we git up every mornin' with the horn ... I mean Gallaher's horn," he added hastily as she took her shoe to him. He held her tightly and looked over her shoulder as the woman entertained the three men simultaneously on the large double bed that rocked like a storm-tossed ship.

Minnie turned from the scene and buried her head in his chest. She wept bitterly. Kelly's eyes hardened. "Wait here," he said tersely, "I'll be back shortly."

"Black men," sniffed Henry as they stood in the hall. "If the oul dolls hear about it, they'll tar an' feather her."

"I think the woman needs a good wash," said Kelly with a grin. Harvey looked at him. "The big hose!" he whispered.

Both men left the house quietly and moved quickly towards the back gate of the Fire Brigade Station, a few yards up the street.

Henry kept watch as Kelly scaled the large wooden gates and silently stalked across the station yard towards a large, neatly rolled red fire hose. Checking the handle at the nozzle of the hose was in the off position, he quickly played it out and placed the brass nozzle under the gate and into Henry's waiting hands.

When the hose was stretched to its limit, he went back and turned the water on full at the main. The hose filled quickly, wriggling like a snake as Kelly vaulted the gate and dropped into the street.

Sadie's door was open. She was a large, sad-faced woman in her late thirties with bleached hair. Unmarried and living alone, she was both despised and pitied by the women of the area.

As they crept up the narrow stairs the sense of danger seemed to transport Kelly back to his service days. To his drunken mind the heavy nozzle of the hose held tightly in his hands became a Lee Enfield rifle with the working parts forward.

He turned blank eyes to his colleague, "Stay close till the wall an' keep a grenade handy," he whispered to Harvey who gave him a puzzled look.

Reaching the darkened landing, they lined up with the door

135

of the bedroom and with an ear-piercing scream kicked it completely off its hinges.

Kelly leapt into the middle of the room and dropped into a crouch. "German bastards," he screamed and pushed the hose handle forward. The power of the jet almost knocked him off his feet as it hit the black man astride Sadie squarely in the buttocks with a force that smashed him against the bed room wall.

Henry leapt forward and used his weight to steady Kelly, who quickly aimed at a second man clad only in a pair of yellow socks. He screamed in terror as the blast knocked him to the floor. The jet followed him down and literally swept him under the bed in a rush of swirling water.

The third man fell to his knees in a praying position as the grim-faced Kelly turned to him. Harvey released his hold on the hose and lifted the unfortunate woman's mattress, tossing her naked flabby body to the floor. Kelly slipped and the surge of water crashed into the rotting window frame and smashed it to pieces. The negro with the yellow socks clambered from below the bed and jumped through the gap into the street.

He was followed quickly by his companions. Kelly leaned nonchalantly out of the window and pushed them down the street with a long jet of water.

Sadie had been washed up into a corner and lay with a pillow over her head and her white flaccid backside in the air.

"Give her a coupla blasts afore we go," yelled Harvey. "It's been a long time since she's had the barnacles scraped off her arse."

He sluiced her a few times, then dropped the hose and ran down the stairs into the street. The prostitute screamed in terror as the hose spun about the room like a live thing, until the station yard man, aroused by the noise, turned it off at the main and retrieved it.

Both men ran back to the house party pushing their way through the crowds of watchers who cheered them as they climbed the stairs quickly to the attic.

Minnie grasped Kelly tightly as he and Henry collapsed with

laughter on the floor. "Billy, I seen it all. I seen it all," she roared. "Yis went in there like Buck Rogers and Flash Gordon. The Rocket Men wudn't be in it."

Regaining his breath Harvey took out his flask and reached it to Kelly who took a slug before handing it back. Harvey also put it to his mouth disregarding the cup. Returning it to his pocket, he moaned, "Luk at my suit. It's ruined."

Kelly moved to the window and carefully looked out. "Poor oul cow's still lyin' in the corner," he laughed.

"Yis shuda horsewhipped her," snapped the affronted Minnie.

Kelly put his hand on her shoulder. "Go down an' git us a drink girl, an' pass the word, if the cops come, nobody saw nothin'."

"Aye," nodded Harvey thoughtfully. "If McKinstry's on he'll give us a medal for clearin' them sambos out of his area."

"Where's the big fella, ma?" growled Sam as his mother opened the front door to his belligerent knock.

"He's away till a party somewhere," she muttered, shuffling back to the large soup pot simmering on the stove.

"Boys, that soup smells lovely," he grinned, moving past her and into the backyard. The old woman watched narrow-eyed as her eldest son closed the door firmly behind him.

"Out searchin' for my Henry's hard-earned money," she scowled. The front door knocked again. She sighed as she walked down the long hall, turning the light on as she went.

"My goodness," she screamed as she looked out and saw by the light of a street-lamp, her favourite son, Henry, lying flat on the back of a handcart being pushed by Billy Kelly.

"It's alright, Mrs. Harvey," said Minnie comfortingly, "He collapsed at Annie Mitchell's party an' as we cudn't carry him, wee Johnny MacDermott lent us his cart till bring him home."

Kelly lifted the giggling red button man to his feet and frog-marched him into the house.

137

Once inside Henry straightened up. "I'm alright nigh, Billy," he said with dignity. "Away ye go wid yer woman."

In the light of the room Mrs. Harvey saw both men were soaked to the skin.

"Yis are sappin'," she wailed. "Yis 'ill git yer death of coul."

She looked worriedly at Minnie. "Did they fall intil the dock or somethin?" she asked.

All three began to giggle as Minnie and Kelly moved unsteadily out to the street.

Mrs. Harvey suppressed her fright as Henry walked straight to the yard door. Sam hid quickly behind the mangle when he heard his brother fumbling at the door latch. Holding his breath, he watched as Henry stopped facing him and, weaving unsteadily, began to urinate against the mangle. He clenched his teeth as he felt the heat of the water as it soaked his trouser legs and cascaded into his unlaced boots.

Unable to move, he stood cursing silently to himself, until Henry's bedroom light lit the window above him. Mrs. Harvey roared with laughter when Sam strode sullen faced and dripping through the kitchen and into the hall, almost taking the front door off its hinges.

Minnie jumped with fright as the heavy door slammed shut. Kelly held her tightly as the darkened figure of Sam ran down the street blaspheming loudly to the stars. Moments later another bang punctuated the silence as Sam entered his own house.

"Wonder what that was all about?" muttered Kelly running his hand down Minnie's thigh. "Heaven knows," she replied, grabbing his hand and dragging him away from the darkened doorway he had pulled her into. He offered no resistance and they walked slowly along Earl Lane.

She looked up into his face. "Are ye married, Billy?" she asked softly.

He looked at her teasingly. "Who wud marry a drunken troublemaker like me?"

"Don't givus that," she laughed, taking his hand on an impulse.

They continued to walk, passing through Earl Lane and into Little York Street. The street-lamps had gone out and only the lit windows of the little kitchen houses marked their path.

"Aye," he muttered softly, "I'm married, but I haven't seen her in ten years. It was a whirlwind romance and a wartime wedding. We were in married quarters in England when I wus posted overseas leavin' her pregnant." He returned Minnie's curious glance with a drop of his head. "Aye, that's why I married her ... Did the decent thing. When I returned she had scarpered, baby boy an' all. I haven't seen them since."

"Couldn't the army have traced her?" she asked.

"I didn't ask them to, 'cause I didn't want her. Didn't know her anyway. I wus drunk when I met her, drunk when I married her an' drunk when I left her at the boat-train. Where do ye live anyway?" he scowled with a finality which said that the subject was closed.

"Just off Henry Street," she answered, squeezing his arm consolingly.

They crossed York Street and saw the formidable silhouette of Head Constable McKinstry bearing down. He stopped directly in front of them and waited until a trolley-bus heading for Greencastle swished by them before he spoke.

"Well Mr. Kelly, I see you've changed mounts. What have you been up to tonight?" he asked pointedly.

"We were at a wee party, Head," answered Minnie quickly, as Kelly grinned sardonically.

"No trouble?"

"No trouble, Head."

He turned his baleful glare to her companion. "Hope you learned your lesson in court."

"Yis, Head," grinned Kelly.

McKinstry turned his attention to Minnie. "This is a rare jewel Missus, or is it Miss?" he said apologetically. "Almost a child when he enlisted in the Rifles during the war. Won a battlefield commision during the Normandy landings and was mentioned in dispatches during the fighting at Monte Cassino." He looked at her blank face. "Just names to you girl, but places where boys like him were tempered into the finest fighting machine in the world. Incidentally, he was in the Airborne where he learned all the tricks of dirty fighting, courtesy of the British army." He looked at Kelly's downcast head and continued. "Then he made his worst mistake. Gave up being a colour sergeant in Ireland's greatest regiment and returned to Belfast to become a shiftless well-paid docker like his daddy."

Kelly's eyes glinted as he looked into McKinstry's face. "It's better than being a black bastard," he grinned without mirth.

Minnie trembled as the Head brought his blackthorn from behind his back and fingered it thoughtfully.

"If you were just an ordinary dockie, Billy, I'd split you from arse hole to breakfast time and run you in so fast you'd be in a cell before your shit hit the street. But you're not. Behind that stupid and facile front I know there is a first-class man hiding. I've studied your record and it fascinates me. You're an army man. A twenty-four year man. Get back in. You don't belong here. You're a square peg in a round hole."

"Head, I need to go for a widdle," said Minnie, her eyes on Kelly as McKinstrey's words landed on him like blows from the blackthorn.

"Away you go," smiled the Head with a mock salute. "I shouldn't have held you anyway. You'll get your death of cold in those wet clothes. And don't worry," he added reassuringly. "Mr. Kelly won't attack me. He knows I have too many brothers, and that light never goes out." He turned and pointed the blackthorn in the direction of the beacon shining brightly above the door of the police station. "In other words missus ... the law never sleeps."

Kelly was strangely muted as they moved off. Minnie clung protectively to him. "Did he hit a weak spot, Billy?" she asked softly. He ignored her question.

"C'mon," he grinned "I kin git my clothes off in your house."

The street they turned into was narrow and cobblestoned. A

two-wheeled cart similar to the one they had brought Henry home in was the only vehicle in the street. Kelly leaned her against it and put his arms around her waist, but she motioned towards the house she lived in and produced the key of the door. Turning the latch key, she banged the door twice before opening it. "Chasin the mice an' the creepy crawlies," she whispered.

She led him into the tiny kitchen and giggled abruptly as he hit his head on the cross member of the room door. He stood in the darkness until she ignited a gas mantle above the fireboard.

They looked at each other in the bright light. Suddenly she remembered his wet clothes and her face lit with an impish grin. "Git them off ... yer on next," she laughed, making an exaggerated grab for his trousers.

He looked at her curiously as he began to strip. "Where did ye learn all that docker slang?"

"Shure my da's a docker," she laughed.

"Ye tell me now!" he yelped, struggling to put his coat back on. She laughed even louder at the consternation on his face as he made for the door looking sideways at the stairs as if expecting her father to leap down them at any minute.

"It's alright Billy. He's a cow-walloper. He's away on the Ardrossan boat an' won't be back till the marra night."

"An' yer ma?" he said, still looking at the staircase.

"Somethin' like yerself. He returned from Ardrossan one night an' found she had left me with an aunt an' skedaddled."

It was his turn to feel embarrased. "That's a quare smell comin' from the scullery," he muttered.

"Pork ribs," she answered, throwing her coat onto a chair. She straightened her hair in a long mirror over the fireboard before turning to him.

"Wud ye like some?" she asked.

"Aye," he leered, "warm an' on a plate"

He was surprised to see her blush. "Some ribs I mean."

He feigned innocence with a spread of his arms. "Why? What else is goin'?"

141

"Luk," she said, "stop the doubletalk. I'll git ye a pair of me da's oul trousers and one of his shirts an' if yer good to me ... " She saw his eyes light up expectantly. "Nigh none of that," she countered. "If ye behave yerself there's three or four bottles of cold Guinness in the backyard that'll help wash down the ribs.

She busied herself with a wind-up gramophone that sat at the window as he ate the food with the dignity and discipline of a drunk man.

"Got a coupla new records yesterday," she said. "Seein' as yer an ex-soldier, ye might like this one." He nodded and rose, taking his empty plate into the kitchen. She was pleasantly surprised to hear him running the water as he washed the plate along with his hands and face.

As the introduction began she held out her hands inviting him to dance with her. He moved willingly into her arms and held her tightly as the voice of the female singer wafted across the room.

See the pyramids along the Nile,
Watch the sunrise on a tropic Isle,
Just remember darling, all the while,
You belong to me ...

Kelly held her tightly and closed his eyes and she was content to let him dance with his memories until a prolonged scratching told her the record had finished.

His eyes remained closed and she saw a small tear trickle down his cheek. She left him standing in the centre of the floor and quickly turned off the gramophone. She blew out the mantle and turned off the gas before taking his hand and leading him gently up the stairs and into her bedroom.

Hours later he gingerly extracted himself from her warm and naked body and made his way warily down the narrow staircase

142

to the kitchen where he gathered up his clothes from the front of the glowing fire. Dressing in the firelight, he threw two pounds onto the floor before letting himself quietly out into the street.

As he walked briskly under the shadow of the recently rebuilt Henry Street Flax Spinning Mill he thought of McKinstry's hard-hitting speech.

"Big bastard doesn't need a blackthorn to draw blood," he scowled, making a quick dash across York Street and into the lane.

It was dawn when he entered his own home. His father's snores greeted him as he went into his bedroom and located his working clothes. Going downstairs again he stood naked in a small bath at the sink and sluiced his body and particularly his private parts with cold water and carbolic soap.

After dressing, he went out into the small backyard where a large bull mastiff growled a sleepy welcome.

"C'mon Soldier, it's time for yer usual," he grinned cheerfully as he attached a short leather lead to the dog's studded collar. Opening the backdoor, he allowed the powerful animal to pull him out into the grey-lit entry.

Soldier reached hungrily for a bone lying beside an empty dustbin and growled as Kelly pulled his head back with a snap.

"No time ta waste, Soldier. Cavehill an' back then we'll have our breakfast," he murmured as the dog practically dragged him up Brougham Street.

Henry Harvey was wakened by the sound of the pealing bells of Sinclair Seamen's church. The mattress of his single bed squeaked in protest as he raised himself to a sitting position and rubbed his head wearily. His clothes lay scattered across the room and he realised he was still wearing his shirt and socks.

"Ma," he roared in the direction of the room door. The stairs rattled instantly as the old lady wheezed her way into the room.

"Is Maggie McGaw's open yet?" he roared as she entered.

"Aye, son," she answered, stooping dutifully to pick up his discarded clothing. He reached her a crumpled ten shilling note.

"Away over an' git me some ice-cream an' chocolate an' two bottles a lemonade an' git yerself a box of Carroll's peppermint snuff," he added grudgingly as she puffed her way down stairs.

He turned on his side and looked at the bottle of whiskey fastened by adhesive tape to the leg of the bed closest to his head. After a moment of hesitation, he pulled a length of narrow rubber tubing from below his pillow and blew through it before inserting it into a hole in the cork.

Closing his eyes he sucked a long draught through the tube and savoured its flavour, before burping appreciatively. When his mother returned he put the chocolate and the ice-cream into an enamel bucket which he pulled from under the bed. Pouring the lemonade in, he proceed to stir the concoction with a large wooden spoon already in the bucket. When it was mixed to his satisfaction, he lifted a cup from his bedside table and dipping it into the bucket, downed the contents in one long swallow. Finding it to his taste, he filled the cup again.

His headache was receding when the room was filled with a short sharp tapping which he recognised as one of his sisters cleaning the stairs with a handbrush. He was incensed as his head started throbbing again.

"Wud yis git away roun' till yer own houses an' give my splittin' head a bita pace," he roared angrily.

The tapping stopped immediately and he lay back and sampled another sip from the whiskey bottle. Putting the tube down he reached below his mattress and pulled out a bulky notebook.

He touched the lead of a small pencil to his tongue and began writing the names of the men working with him and the names of the potato cargoes they were detailed to. The union rules stated each cargo had to have at least one man on it to unload the lorries that brought the potatoes into the sheds. Most of the transit sheds could hold five or six cargoes and the carriers and checkers were paid a day's pay for each until the designated tonnage had been stacked. The drivers were always in a hurry and preferred to carry their own loads off rather than wait for a carrier. Henry often left some of the cargoes unmanned and claimed the pay with fictitious names.

Sometimes a load or two would come in days before the cargo was to officially start. The stevedore would pay for this to be off-loaded by the men in the sheds. Henry would however tell the men it was classed as storage and they wouldn't be paid until it officially started. He then told them if they didn't off-load it the stevedore would send it to another team who would, and thus be guaranteed the rest of the cargo. He also juggled and changed the envelopes, taking the money from original envelopes and putting it into others he had lifted from a drawer in the stevedore's office. Thus paying the workers not what they had earned but what he thought they were worth. The lion's share went into the plastic envelope hidden in the backyard.

With beginners like Jim Harvey he paid them a stable wage, no matter how hard they worked or how many cargoes they worked on. Some of the men muttered darkly, but they knew they were not represented by any union, and the wages they got, boosted by the ready cash tips on a daily basis from the drivers and owners of the lorries, gave them a reasonable week's pay. And, as Henry would say, there was always plenty of men willing to take their place if they weren't happy.

Jack and Sam were a different story. Sam got a percentage more than Jack because Henry was more afraid of Sam than he was of Jack. Such simple but cunning economics kept Sam reasonably happy. He knew something underhand was going on but hadn't as yet been able to prove it.

When the paperwork was finished, he took off his shirt and rolled contentedly onto his back, reaching for the end of the tube and took a long swig from the whiskey.

The drink relaxed him and he felt ready for another snooze. He generally stayed in bed all day Sunday to get his strength up for the hard week ahead, but he remembered Jack had mentioned a card school in the afternoon.

"Ma," he shouted and waited until the old woman popped her head around the door. "Waken me at one o'clock," he ordered, "There's a card school round in Jack's."

His mother nodded diligently and made her way slowly back to the kitchen.

"You shudn't tend that big fella han' an' foot they way ye do. He's forty bloody years old nigh," scowled her youngest daughter.

"Wheesh," was the only reply she got as her mother sat down with her knitting.

The group of men lounging at Dock Street corner were unaware of the car approaching until it stopped beside them. With something of an effort Ned removed his considerable bulk from behind the steering wheel. The men had stopped talking and viewed his approach with apprehension.

He greeted them with an exaggerated warmth. "How's the boys?" he said chummily. "I wus wonderin' if yis cud come roun' an' givus a han' till unload a lorry full a mortar that's arrived unexpectedly at the new store we're buildin' in Marine Street. Y'know the Clipper's due the marra an' I'll not fergit yis." Most of the men groaned inwardly but nodded with feigned enthusiasm.

"Thanks a lot boys, I'll be waitin' for yis," he continued, taking a note of the faces in front of him. His features tightened when he saw Sandy Carstairs in the group. "You needn't bother," he said impassively.

The veiled threat showed the others what happened to those who didn't co-operate, and the message was not lost. They moved off quickly in the direction of the new store.

"We shuda put a luk-out for him" said Reilly disappointedly. "I wus all set for the card school."

"Aye, we shuda knowed he'd pull a stroke with the Clipper due

146

tomarra, but it's two weeks wurk an' we'll be favourites if we git roun' there an' help him out."

Ned couldn't help grinning as he drove along Nelson Street.

The men wandered morosely into Marine Street.

"Hope he buys snowballs instead of them stale Paris buns," growled one man. "I heard he gits them on Friday at half price an' keeps them for us on Sunday," snorted another causing a ripple of subdued laughter.

"Who says he buys them?" answered Reilly. "Yer woman in O'Hara's gives him them for free till git her man a lie on."

"Aye, an' that's nat all she gives him accordin' till the oul dolls who go intil the pawn when I'm there," said another.

Reilly looked at him with scorn. "Don' be sayin nuthin ye can't prove. Her husband's a dacent fella an' he wud punch the gub off ye if ye were man enuff till say it till his face."

The man refused to be silent. "It's the talk of the street," he insisted. "I wudn't like my wife be seen with a ganger," he added.

"Frankenstein wud'nt be seen with your wife. It's as well ye don't depend on her looks gittin' ye a job or yid be in the poor house nigh," laughed Reilly.

"Shure Reilly's must be right or ye wudn't be asked till the floor-layin' ceremony, Hackles," laughed another as they stopped and ducked in throught the wicker gate.

Ned detailed them and watched as they gouged out the earthen floor with picks and shovels before levelling out the reinforcing wire and stone screenings that would make the foundation for the concrete.

He felt the need for a drink and explained to Reilly what exactly was wanted before driving off in the direction of Nelson Street to a pub that opened discreetly a few hours every Sunday.

Parking the car in an adjacent street, he walked to the bar window and rapped it with a half-crown. The door opened silently and he entered the bar. He paid no attention to the familiar faces that littered the darkened bar-room and walked quickly into the snug.

147

He nodded at the barman's inquiring features before he closed the door. "Black Bush an' a bottle a Guinness, Johnny," he ordered.

Jack Harvey nudged his brother Sam knowingly. "He musta got his volunteers."

Sam took a swig from his pint and sighed heavily. "It's bad enuff goin' till work all week without gittin' caught on the Sabbath for free *gratis*," he said lighting a Park Drive and blowing the smoke across the room. "There must be an easier way of gittin' a few bob," he added wistfully.

"Ye shud thank yer lucky stars yiv got a job," countered his brother slowly.

Sam glared at him. "I wud be happy if we were gittin' what we earned. If ye think I'm gonna knock my ballocks in carrying bags of spuds all day an' every day while that big bastard pockets half the money, yiv got another think comin'. They say hard wurk niver killed anybody, well I've went till too many funerals of guys who grafted themselves intil Carnmoney by workin' all day in pourin' rain. There's nobody gonna pat me in the face wid a shovel if I kin help it," he snapped irritably.

Jack played with his half-empty glass. "I don't think he's fiddlin' us. Shure how cud he?" he murmured.

Sam looked at him pityingly. "Know your problem? You've tuk too many digs till the napper." He lowered his head and continued in a whisper. "That stuff he calls storage. He gits paid for it," he declared fiercely.

"Ye can't prove that," argued Jack.

"I know," replied his brother with an exasperated shrug of his shoulders, "but the other day when he give me my pay packet in the pub, he pulled out an envelope with Slice Bar Christie's name on it an' anyone'll tell ye Slice Bar has been on a tramp-steamer in the Pacific for the last three years."

"Maybe it's somebody doin' the double and usin' Slice Bar's name ... " replied Jack loyally.

"He's gittin' more than we are," persisted his brother. "Luk at them suits an' shirts he has in his wardrobe. He's better dressed than some film stars."

"Shure everybody knows he gives Jack Barton the harbour watchman a few pounds till stale them outa the Heysham cargo shed."

"That might be," snarled Sam, "but someday he's gonna slip up an' I'll git 'im."

"Aye," smirked Jack, "like ye got him yisterday. Mi ma tole me how he pissed all over yer trousers." Despite his anger Sam couldn't dispel the embarrassed grin that floated across his stubbled face.

"Niver min' that," he countered. "I'm empty an' it's yer hookon." Jack glanced warily in the direction of the snug. "Mebbe we shud go elsewhere ... Ned's liable till capture us."

Sam patted his brother's head affectionately. "We've got jobs—remember? So we don't haveta ball-lick Ned or anyone else," he explained slowly as if he was speaking to a child. "Now go up an' git me a drink," he added with a shake of his head.

Ned sat quietly in the snug. He could hear the muted exodus as men drank up and headed elsewhere. He grinned as he heard the front door opening and closing. How were they to know he had all the men he needed? The new store would soon have a freshly laid concrete floor and the money the stevedore had given him to hire honest labour lay in his wallet. The only outlay was the Paris buns purchased yesterday in O'Hara's Bakery.

Reaching for the Black Bush he sipped it slowly, savouring the taste. He loved the quietness and privacy of the Sunday morning drink. The only thing about the solitude was that he had to pay for the drink himself.

He heard the window being tinkled discreetly, but didn't see Sandy Carstairs ambling in white as a sheet. "Johnny," he muttered almost inaudibly, "Givus a Monk an' a glass of Mundies." He carried the drinks to a vacant table and, using both hands to lift the glass, polished the wine off in one go. He shook himself like a dog and then laughed at the Harvey brothers.

149

"The animal caught all the flymen at the corner a Dock Street and sentenced them all till hard labour wi' picks an' shovels. He wudn't take me, even for nuthin'," he laughed dismally. "Mebbe it's as well. They'd a bin buryin' me below the floor."

He lowered his voice fearfully as Sam and Jack signalled silently that the enemy was in the snug. He tactfully raised his voice. "Like, I'm sorry he didn't want me, because Big Ned is good till us Arabs an' we shud be glad till give him all the help we can," he finished, making a fierce two-fingered gesture in the direction of the snug.

"Were ye at the party last night?" asked Jack in an effort to change the subject.

"A was," replied Sandy forlornly, "but I flaked out near the end. Fell asleep wid me mouth open and somebody used it for an ashtray."

"I hear Kelly an' Henry played themselves."

Sandy laughed. "Niver seen anything like it. Three big niggers as naked as the day they were born runnin' down the street shoutin' 'Mercy mercy'. Kelly was leanin' out Sadie's windy like it was a blitzed-out buildin' in Berlin, houlin' a hosepipe like it was a machine gun." His face crinkled in thought as he continued, "But what puzzled me was Kelly was shoutin abuse after them an' callin' them German bastards ... Shure everybody knows German's aren't black," he muttered sadly.

Jack grinned at the thought. "Kelly musta bin blitzed outa his mind."

"Maybe just outa his mind," said the weary-faced barman who had sat down to read the *News of the World*. "I think he's crackin' up. He shud niver have left the army."

"That's true," agreed a thin-faced drinker, wearing a red and black striped cap and drawing on a hand-rolled cigarette that gave off a sweet odour as the smoke curled into the rafters. "I served with him during the best part of the war. He was wild then but disciplined. Now he's just wild. He's bin worse since he got suspended. His oul fella's give up on him."

150

"Aye, he's foolish for himself, Freddie," commented Jack, "but the animal wuda chased our Jim if Kelly hadn't volunteered till carry the lad."

"There's nat a bad bone in his body," said the ex-soldier, "but the divil's lukin' outa him."

"He musta had somethin'," argued Sam "or he wudn't a reached the rank he did an' collected all those commendations."

"I wus tole he killed more Germans than we've had hot dinners," said the barman. "No! It's true," he persisted. "There's a Harbour Peeler comes in here an' he tole me he met Kelly in the town one night. Him an' his wife were goin' till the Plaza dancehall. He says Kelly went for a drink with them an' while they were sittin' Kelly tole his wife about the times he wud call the peeler to go wid him behin' the German lines. The peeler said they only carried knives and used them till cut the throats of the German sentries. Kelly tuk great delight in tellin' hor how many Germans the Harbour peeler killed an' when he went home that night his wife wudn't sleep wid him. She said he was a murderer," finished the barman seriously. He paused for a moment. "But before he went out the Peeler said Kelly done twice as many as him," he added soberly.

"Aye," said Freddie, his face a mask of remembrance, "He wus a good 'un, but I remember hearin' how he made a decision, near the end of the war that resulted in some of his close comrades bein' killed ... "

"I remember that," interupted Sam. "Their position wus overrun an' quite a few of his platoon were seriously wounded. He withdrew without them as they were unable to walk. He left them in a field ambulance with a couple of stretcher-bearers thinking the Gerries wud ship them behind the lines to a hospital. I believe he almost went crazy when he heard the Gerries set fire to the ambulance killing everyone in it."

"Sounds like he made the right decision," said the barman, "but then I'm no soldier."

"It was a textbook decision," said Freddie "The wounded

151

would have slowed the rest of the platoon down and they'd probably have been shot out of hand. Those were the dyin' days of the war an' the Gerries were takin' no prisoners. The saddest part was that one of the wounded was Kelly's closest friend. I don't think he ever got over that," he concluded, taking another swig from his drink.

"He's a good frien' to me," said Sandy, breaking the brief silence that followed. "Red Ennis wuda made mincemeat of me if Kelly hadn't marked his cards."

The barman looked up from his paper. "Is that the lorry-driver with the red hair from over the bridge?" he asked.

"Aye," chorused the drinkers.

The barman scowled. "Nasty piece a wurk. Fractured Frankie Johnston's jaw here a week ago and then bit a lump outa his ear. It tuk four peelers till git him outa here. I think he's tryin till make a name for himself," he added huffily.

Sandy shivered and ordered another wine.

"He'd haveta be good till give Kelly any trouble. Most guys only fight when they haveta, but he's different. He loves it. An' he niver stops smilin'. Y'cud hit him wid the Queen's Bridge an' he'd still keep comin'."

"As I said," repeated the barman, "he shuda stayed in the for.:es."

"He come out because his oul fella got him a docker's button. I've bin on this quay for nearly twenty-five years an' I can't even git a second preference button," growled Sam.

Freddy swirled the remains of his drink slowly around the glass before answering. "No disrespect Sam, but as an ex-serviceman he wus entitled to wurk."

"I had eleven childer an' wuda joined up for the peace an' quiet but the wife wudn't let me go," replied Sam defensively. "An' what about yerself an' men like ye? Shure yer ex-service, but y'didn't git a button."

"But my da's not a docker," said Freddie with a shrug of resignation.

"What about Kipper Devlin's son? He served his time as a butcher an' had his own shop when his da heard the books were openin'. He's a first preference man an' he's not ex-service."

"Aye," agreed Sam "An' us men with families to feed haveta stan' an' wait till a wee buck like him, who hasn't quit shitin' yella yet, gits a job in fronta us."

"Keep yer voices down," whispered Jack, gazing at the snug.

Sandy, speaking low agreed with Sam. "There wus a wee buck over the hatch at the Heysham boat last week an' he luked as if he was just outa short trousers, but he got a handy job while oul Billy Withers who's near seventy was in the shafts of a truck."

"Shure," replied Sam with a tight grin, "if Billy Withers was six months dead he'd still be a better man than any of 'im." He rose and looked around the sparsely populated bar. "If anyone's interested, there's a card-school in Jack's startin' about one o'clock."

"An' two bucket's a wellicks," added Jack as they shuffled out into the grey sunlight.

Jim Harvey was awakened by his mother's voice as she shouted from the bottom of the stairs. He looked sleepily at his watch and was shocked to see it was twelve noon. He loved Sunday mornings. The deep dreamless sleep had refreshed him and he stretched contentedly, reluctant to leave the warmth and security of his single bed.

The dance had been good the previous night and Maureen had agreed to let him walk her home. They'd stood a while in the doorway of a shop at the top of her street and he'd found himself confused because he hadn't tried to take advantage of her. He'd been a proper gentleman and was surprised to find he couldn't get her out of his mind.

His mother knocked on the bedroom door, interrupting his reverie. "It's okay," he called and she entered the room carrying

153

a large bowl of milky porridge, a plate of toast and melted cheese, and a mug of hot sweet tea.

"Thought ye were niver gonna git up," she smiled as she placed the tray on his bedside table. "Do ye want the Sunday papers?" she asked.

"Naw, I'll be down later," he replied.

She nodded and shuffled silently out of the room.

"Ma," he said some time later as he rocked lazily on his chair in front of the fire. The radio was playing loudly and he raised his voice as he continued, "Do ye know a woman called Jeanne McGivern?"

"Yis," replied his mother, raising her eyes from the pages of the *Sunday Pictorial*. Her voice became firm. "She's a money-lender. I hope ye haven't ... "

"I didn't borrow anythin'," he said laughingly. "I left her daughter home last night an' I've till see her tonight down at Fortwilliam."

"I'm glad till hear that," laughed his mother grimly.

"Perhaps it'll keep ye away from Kelly an' all them other alcoholics. Nigh get yer shirt aff till I have a look at that back."

His mother beat up the whites of two eggs in a cup and rubbed the mixture gently into his wound. She was glad to see it had dried up considerably as had the broken skin on his hands.

He smiled as the music from the radio became familiar to him although it was being played as an instrumental. He recognised it as the song he had heard when he first saw Maureen at the dance. The words sung by the bandsinger returned to him, and he found himself humming them as he put his shirt on.

Once you have found her,
Never let her go.
Once you have found her,
Ne—ver let her go ...

Her face seemed to swim before him and he realised he was

154

looking forward to seeing her again. He lifted his jacket from the back of the door. "I'm away up till the corner for a bita crack, mum," he said.

When he reached the shop doorway at the junction of Earl Street and Nelson Street he saw a poker school in progress. A group of men knelt around a piece of newspaper on which playing cards and money was scattered around. He nodded at a small boy who was being paid to watch for the police.

A game had just finished and cigarette smoke wafted in the air as the cards were being dealt out. He noticed the game was stud poker and the players were betting on the turn of their first card.

Pennies, brown threepenny pieces, silver shillings, sixpences, florins and half-crowns littered the newspaper as the game progressed to the last card. The winner scooped up the pool and a fierce discussion erupted as the cards were picked up, shuffled and dealt out by the next dealer.

"Nat many about today, Napper," said Jim to a heavily built man clad in a long tan coloured burburry with a thick woolen scarf tied around his throat.

"Big Ned made a raid this mornin' an' caught the cream of the crop." He nodded at the boy peeping into Nelson Street. "He's bin tole ta keep an eye open for Big Ned as well as the Bert Wheelers," he laughed.

Napper was a boilermaker and had worked in the Belfast shipyard all his life. It amused him to see the consternation Ned's car or one that resembled it brought to the men who frequented the corners.

Jim nodded at the card school. "Are ye not indulgin'?" he asked.

"I'll wait till the pontoon starts in Jack's house, it's safer. Must be near time now," he added, looking at his wrist-watch, "There's yer Uncle Sam away in."

As Sam entered, Jack was counting the chairs. Satisfied he had enough he began placing sheets of newspaper on the top of the large mahogany table that sat in the centre of the parlour. The aroma of boiling whelks permeated the house. He poked the parlour fire until its embers glowed then placed a hefty shovel of coal into the heart of it. Closing the room doors to keep the heat in, he made his way to the kitchen where two large galvanised buckets bubbled on top of the hob of the black range.

Siphoning off the frothy water, he emptied the cooked seafood into a small bath his wife used to bathe the children on a Saturday night.

Sam pulled a safety pin from the lapel of his coat and selected a whelk from the bath. "Have ye got the new deck?" he asked, skilfully hooking the cooked snail from it shell and placing it in his mouth.

"Aye, it's on the fireboard in the parlour."

"I see wee Jim out there—I'll git him ta come in an' lift your entitlement seein' as you an' me will be playin'," said Sam.

Sam called his nephew and explained his role in the game. "Jack's entitled to lift a threepenny piece each time there's a hand played. He's entitled to this because it's his house an' his electricity an' his whelks, understand?"

Jim nodded earnestly. He'd played the game many times himself in alleys and shop doorways and knew the rules backward, but he didn't want his uncle to know.

One by one the prospective players drifted in. When the chairs were filled, the latecomers stood behind them and waited their chance to sit in when some of the others were skint. The cards were thrown around to select a banker. Jack dealt himself an ace and proceedeed to take the bank.

As Jim positioned himself, he looked around the players. Uncle, the ganger, was seated with his back to the window, still wearing his navy-blue duffel coat despite the heat building up in the room. Harry and Andy, the two potato carriers were facing Sandy Carstairs, who was slightly drunk and eating whelks hungrily. Billy Kelly was leaning back on his chair, with his hands jammed in his trouser pockets and smiling vaguely at the fireplace.

Freddie, the ex-soldier, had positioned himself beside the

door and was filling the room with the haze from his chain-smoking. Napper was absently piling silver coins in front of him on the table. Henry Harvey was deep in thought with his chin clamped in his hands as his elbows rested on the table. He wore a thick piled Russian fur hat which sat at a rakish angle on his head. His kiss-curl had been dipped in a sugar and water mixture before he came out and he imagined he looked like Douglas Fairbanks, the celebrated star of the silent movies his mother had taken him to see.

He had purchased the hat from a Polish seaman and was especially proud of it.

The game began briskly and Jim at the end of each game leaned respectfully over the table and lifted out a threepenny piece which he then deposited into a child's money-box that resembled a post-office pillar-box.

Jack dealt quickly, whilst Sam, working over his brother's shoulder, handled the money end, covering each bet from a shilling upwards. Most men did the dealing and banking themselves, but Jack, being a little uncertain of his arithmetic, preferred help in that area.

As the bank began to win heavily, Jim's eyes were drawn to the strange behaviour of his Uncle Sam, who now and again would poke at his dentures as if trying to remove some irritant. A closer watch showed Sam was folding ten-shilling notes into minute squares the size of postage stamps and pushing them into his mouth between gum and cheek whilst his brother was dealing. The other men were watching their cards intently and kept their eyes on the table. No one noticed except Jim who promptly averted his eyes in another direction.

Their good fortune came to an end when Henry turned an ace and a king back to back and took over the bank.

"How'd we do?" asked Jack, somewhat disappointed at the size of his winnings. "Ack, they caught ye a couple a times a few han's ago," lied Sam. He winked knowingly at Jim. "I'm away till the bogs, catch me han' till I come back," he ordered.

They played on through the day whilst the bank changed hands frequently. Men moved out and others took their places. Some paid a ritual visit to a nearby money-lender and returned to try again. The room was thick with tobacco smoke and empty whelk shells littered the floor and glowed in the fire. The betting had increased and quite a lot of paper money lay on the table. The action was fast and furious and Jim, taking a leaf out of Sam's book, was now and again pocketing a threepenny piece.

Sam took over the bank and was dealing and backing out confidently. His blue eyes were narrowed to avoid the smoke that drifted from a cigarette butt that simmered close to the side of his mouth threatening to incinerate an ugly hairy mole that grew above his upper lip.

He stopped suspiciously at Henry's bet. "A fiver?" he snarled eying the crumpled bank note that lay on top of his brother's card. "Hope it's not an ace," he growled.

"It's a picture card. I'm entitled to back the limit on it an' the limit's a fiver."

Sam paused for a moment. "How do I know it's not an ace? Turn it up," he repeated.

Henry sat back on his chair. "Don't haveta!" he replied stubbornly. The atmosphere in the room turned from joviality to silent tension. The players watched apprehensively as the two brothers eyed each other warily. Money was being lifted slowly and discreetly from the table top. Both were behaving with their usual stubborness and no one cared to adjudicate, knowing it was a family matter.

Sam blew smoke into Henry's face and covered the bet with a dissatisfied grunt.

Henry held the cards close to his chest and thumbed back the one he had just drawn. With a self-satisfied smirk he put an ace and a queen face up on the table signifying pontoon. Taking over the bank he threw the first round of cards across the table and waited pensively as the stakes went down. He paused suspiciously as Sam placed a five pound note on top of his card.

"Is it a facer?" he growled

"Yis," snorted Sam.

"Let's see it," challenged Henry, straightening in the chair and pursing his lips.

"No chance," snapped Sam.

"I'm nat coverin' it!" declared Henry, moving swiftly to the next man. Sam spun him back again and snapped the deck of cards from his hands. "I covered you," he yelled, rising to his feet and knocking a chair over.

"Sit down, Sam," said Henry quietly, "The blood's gone over yer eyes."

Sam's temper flared. Reaching upward he grabbed Henry's hat and threw it into the heart of the fire. Henry's reflex action was to slap Sam across the mouth causing the cigarette end to fly into the whelk basin and Sam to collide with an ancient upright piano immediately behind him.

The occupants of the room began to panic as Henry hurled the table out of his path—men fell to their hands and knees as money rolled all over the floor. Henry clawed off his jacket and shirt while Jack vainly tried to hold back Sam who was literally foaming at the mouth with anger.

Some men helped Jack bundle Sam into the kitchen whilst others fought to restrain Henry who had torn off all his clothes with the exception of his trousers and shoes and socks. He was roaring like a castrated bull.

Jim shielded himself behind the piano whilst Kelly, feet up on the sofa, calmly dug into a whelk. He watched as Henry dragged the men who were trying to hold him all over the parlour. Eventually breaking loose he gave the door handle such a wrench that it came off in his hand. Screaming with frustration, he smashed it against the room wall causing everyone to hit the floor as it bounced all over the place.

His eyes fell on the window and before anyone could stop him he was through it with a mighty leap. He landed on his hands and knees in the street amidst a shower of broken glass and window frame. Rising to his feet he ran to the side of the house and into the entry. He was almost at Jack's back door when he saw Sam's leg straddle the yard wall. Crouching behind a rubbish bin, he waited until his brother's feet hit the ground, before running forward with a roar of defiance that petered out when Sam turned to face him. His shirt was torn to ribbons and his face was caked with dirt, but it was his right hand that claimed Henry's undivided attention. It was above his head and was holding a small but lethal hatchet.

Henry lifted the bin in desperation and threw it at his crazed brother before running for his life from the entry. Word of the battle had spread through the side streets and the children of the area were racing to the scene. Running just as fast but moving in a tight group were Sam's children who had heard their father was being murdered.

They hit Henry in a bunch as he emerged from the entry. He roared in pain as sharp teeth bit into his hands and legs and little boots stung his shins. He fell to the ground and rolled himself into a ball as the children swarmed over the top of him pulling at his hair and punching him in the face.

He heard an ear-piercing scream that turned his blood cold and caused the children to stop their attack. Sam stood at the mouth of the entry. He was waving the hatchet like a demented Indian and was covered in potato skins and egg shells.

Henry rose and his strength carried half of the children into the air as they continued to cling fiercely to him. He relaxed when he saw Jack move behind Sam and quickly disarm him

"Leave it or the cops'll raid the house, Sam," urged Jack as he held his brother tightly in a neck lock. The older man did not answer, neither did he resist as Jack lead him back into the entry.

Nipper smiled ruefully at Jim. "An' here's me sayin' it wud be safer in there. Yer granny shuda called them two dynamite an' detonater. 'Cause there's always an explosion when they git together."

Henry, reluctantly freed by the children, cautiously entered the parlour and began collecting his clothes. A sudden thought struck him and he fumbled fearfully in his jacket pocket.

"It's gone! It's gone!" he wailed balling his fists and preparing for action. Kelly's friendly hand containing the bulging wallet stayed him. "I removed it before someone else did," he said quietly.

Henry was visibly relieved. "Thanks Billy," he gasped.

Kelly threw an empty whelk shell into the remains of Henry's cossack hat causing the embers to erupt briefly.

"At least I've got you figgerd out, Harvey," he smiled, "You actually hate yer brother more than you like money."

Henry readjusted his silk cravat in the mirror above the piano. "You said a mouthful," he growled.

FIVE

THE table and chairs were reassembled and then Jack apologised for the fracas. "Shure, things were gittin' dull an' it livened the day up," laughed Napper.

"I'm sorry about the hole in the wall but my brother has peculiar ideas about enterin' an' leavin' a room. But from now on," his voice took on a steely edge, "there'll be no limit on a face card but the dealer has a right to see it if he wishes ... All agreed?"

Most of the men nodded or raised their hands and the game restarted. Kelly had the bank and was dealing when Red Ennis and two of his cronies entered the room. Jim felt the atmosphere in the parlour become distinctly hostile as the three men gathered behind Sandy.

"Any chance of a hand?" asked Ennis in a friendly tone. He was wearing a russet-coloured double-breasted Crombie overcoat with padded shoulders than made him even broader than he was. The cold weather had beaten his ruddy features until they were rough and raw looking. Despite his smile, his eyes bore a cruel glint.

"No seats at the minit," said Jack without looking up.

"Alright if I wait?" he continued politely.

"No problem, but there's two or three in front of ye."

"Can I bet on the side?" asked Ennis.

"Suit yerself. No law agin it, as long as ye stick till the rules," answered Jack as he studied his cards.

The Eastender was directly behind Sandy and was able to see the man's cards as he received and studied them before betting.

162

Some moments later he watched as Sandy drew a king and bet five shillings on it. "A fiver wid him," stated Ennis, dropping the money onto the table. Sandy dutifully turned up the card exposing its face value. Kelly covered the two bets without a word and continued to the other players.

Ennis smirked when the other card dropped in front of Sandy was another king. Kelly began with the first man in rotation.

"Twist or bet?" he asked, holding the top card at the ready.

"Sittin'," replied the man nervously.

The dealer continued until he reached Sandy. "Twist or bet?" he asked. "He's sittin'," declared Ennis before Sandy could answer.

Sandy turned in his chair and regarded him angrily. "I'm playin' this han'," he snarled. Turning to Kelly he yelled, "Twist!"

Kelly flipped the card into the air.

"Busted," yelled Sandy triumphantly as the seven of clubs fell on the table.

Ennis grabbed him savagely by the back of the neck and aimed a huge fist at his face.

"Do it," said Kelly soberly, "an' you an' yer cronies 'ill end up at the bottom of the Dock."

"But he didn't play fair," growled Ennis, "He twisted on twenty. You needed twenty or twenty-one to beat him."

"We know the rules," replied Kelly, "but it's his han'. Nobody asked you to play on it." He smiled wickedly and fingered the two five pound notes. "We usually give little boys their money back when they start to cry. Do you want yours?" he asked.

Jack rose and walked slowly around the table. The normally placid brother whom many shrewd observers thought to be the best man of the Harveys had been vexed by his brothers' earlier antics and was now in an aggressive mood.

"Mister," he said softly and tiredly, "we've just had World War III in here an' I don't want ta see World War IV in the same day. This is my house," he continued evenly. "I don't want ye in here an' I'm askin' ye nicely to leave."

163

Ennis glared at the small scrub-haired man over whom he towered and seemed about to make a fight of it.

"Yiv two ways of goin'," continued Jack softly, "either through the door or through the windy."

Ennis looked past Jack and surveyed the hostile faces around the table. Wisely judging the odds were against him he turned to his cronies. "Too many, boys ... " he said with a flippant smile. "Maybe some other time."

He looked over at the white-faced Sandy as he left.

"I suppose yill be stuck till Kelly like shit to a blanket," he said with a mocking grin.

Sandy remained silent.

"You'd need till be," concluded Ennis before closing the door and leaving the room.

Mesmerised by the dramatic situation, Jim lifted a threepenny piece from the pool and put it into his pocket. He looked guiltily at the players and saw Sam gazing straight at him. He relaxed when his uncle's face broke into an amused grin that said his secret was safe.

Henry Harvey regained the bank and eventually took the school with three clear boards in a row. He counted his winnings and grudgingly threw Jack three pounds to help fix the damage to the window.

Kelly stood up and smiled wryly at Jim. He pulled the lining out of his trouser pockets to signify he was skint. Moving to the door he was almost out when Henry stopped him. "Are ye stannin' the Clipper the marra?" he asked. Kelly nodded.

"If I send wee Jim wud ye mate wid him?" said Henry.

Kelly looked across the room at the lad. "Why not?" he asked before leaving the parlour.

Henry turned to Jim. "We kin git along wi'out ye an' whatever dough ye git at the end of the spell 'ill go intil the hat. It'll be extra dough for ye. Kelly 'ill mate ye an' show ye the ropes."

Jim was uncertain. "What if Ned doesn't take me?" he asked.

"Ned'll need all the men he kin git," answered Henry. "The

blues 'ill shun it like the plague an' there'll be few reds, but they'll go for the handy jobs anyway. Git there early" were his last words as he left the house counting his winnings.

Jim followed him out and walked slowly home. Once again tomorrow was uncertain and his stomach began to throb with the fear of the unknown. He had begun to enjoy working with Harry and Andy and more than that he knew he and his mother would miss the daily tips given by the kindly country drivers. He brightened up considerably when he discovered seventeen shillings and ninepence in threepenny pieces in his trouser pocket. Jack had also given him ten shillings for doing the job.

The set-to between Henry and Sam dominated the conversation later that night when Jim and his friends dandered slowly along York Street towards the Shore Road. Their ultimate destination was Fortwilliam, a sparsely populated area with avenues of leafy trees and green fields. The young folk of the various districts of the city made their way there in groups every Sunday night, foul weather or fair.

They used the occasion to show off their new clothes or flirt with each other as they gathered beside a long stone wall made of huge slabs of granite. The boys were dressed almost uniformly, and wore vaseline on their hair to give it a sheen and keep it from being tossed in the wind.

Almost without exception they wore spear-pointed shirt collars and no ties, a fashion copied from a recent gangster film. Single-breasted suits with one button and cut square at the front with drain pipe trousers that clung to their legs was the current style. Socks were worn short and the favoured hues were yellow, pink and white. Thick-sponged wedge soled shoes in a variety of colours made no sound as the boys walked all the way.

They sang snatches of popular songs and indulged in horseplay to assert their masculinity. Only the appearance of a police officer on foot or riding a bicycle spurred them to walk in an orderly fashion.

Jim was watching intently for Maureen. The tune they had

danced to had not left his head and more than once he found himself unwittingly humming snatches from it.

Once you have found her,
Never let her go.
Once you have found her,
Never let her go ...

They had reached the Troxy cinema when he saw her standing alone on the stone steps that led to the balcony. She was gazing intently at a collection of still photographs which advertised the features for the coming week.

Jim's colleagues began to banter as he strolled towards her. She was bare-headed and carrying the customary handbag and rolled-up multi-coloured umbrella. A fawn-coloured loose fitting coat stretched almost to her ankles and flat-heeled shoes matching the colour of her coat made her look petite beside the tall gangling youth.

Her cheeks glowed with a warmth that showed her embarrasment as she smiled up at him, ignoring the wolf whistles from his friends. They engaged in small talk before walking off together towards Fortwilliam. Passing a phone booth packed with girls they were subjected to an unladylike display of good humoured cat-calls.

Jim smiled broadly as the blush returned to her cheeks. His shyness had been knocked out of him in the gyms and clubs he had boxed in. They continued in silence and occasionally she would look up at him with fawn-like eyes that were large and blue.

Later that night as he walked her home, he took her hand gently and led her towards an entry at the top of her street. At first she hesitated before surrendering to his impatience. When he judged they were far enough into the darkness he stopped her beside a back door and took her in his arms. Leaning down he smiled and kissed her gently on the lips.

She was pleasantly surprised by his tenderness and put her

arms around him. He found he had to bend almost double to caress her even though she co-operated by raising herself on tip-toe. Chuckling, he lifted her in his arms and carried her to another door that boasted a large concrete step. "That's better," he whispered as he placed her feet gently onto the step.

When they kissed again she was able to encircle his neck with her arms and pleased him by holding herself close to his body. He found to his amazement, a lack of sexual desire and was content to cuddle and kiss her in the darkness until she told him reluctantly that she would have to go.

"Will ye go out with me some night?" he asked her awkwardly, looking into her eyes, his face barely inches from her own.

"If you want me to," she murmured.

He suddenly remembered the Blackpool Clipper. "It wouldn't be till next week. I'm workin' overtime this week," he said embarrased.

"What about Saturday?" she asked.

He hesitated. Much as he wanted to be with her, he still preferred Saturday night with his pals. She realised this and smiled. "Okay, we'll make it next Sunday."

He loved her for that. Laughing at her thoughtful compromise, he took her hand and led her out into the light of the street-lamp. Stopping short of her front door, he was giving her a brief goodbye kiss when the door opened.

A small thin faced woman wearing a white blouse and a dark skirt with a coloured pinney over it stood in a patch of light and looked over at them. "Is that you Maureen?" she called.

The girl released herself and moved away from him. "Yes mum," she answered. Her mother looked over her head at Jim.

"An' who's this?" she asked icily.

He waved and smiled warmly. "Jim Harvey, missus," he called, suddenly realising he had not told Maureen his name.

The woman looked at him anxiously. "Nat one of the Harveys from York Street," she continued.

"Yis, missus."

As Maureen walked placidly past her mother and into the house, Mrs. McGivern left him in no doubt as to what she thought of his pedigree. She glared stonily at him before stepping back and slamming the door almost in his face.

Jim gazed for a moment at the closed door then walked dejectedly into the Shore Road. He brightened up considerably when he remembered Nora would probably be still sitting in the Moyola Cafe sipping coffee. He moved quickly in the direction of North Queen Street.

Entering the cafe his ears were immediately assailed by the loud rocking sound of Bill Haley coming from the jukebox. His friend John was seated in a booth surrounded by a few other girls and fellows who were listening to the music. Ordering a coffee he joined them.

Nora was in another booth and her dark eyes flashed disdainfully as he smiled in her direction. It was almost closing time and the youngsters rose and headed reluctantly for the door when the cafe owner dimmed the lights and turned off the jukebox.

Falling confidently into step with Nora, he encountered no resistance when he cuddled up to her in the shadow of one of the tobbacco factory's spacious gates, a few yards from her home.

Cold at first to his caresses, she quickly surrendered, and kissed him hungrily as he held her tightly. She was deeply in love with him and the fact was lost on no one but himself. She refused his futher advances knowing if she permitted him his ultimate goal he would be lost forever to her. Tired of coaxing her to obey his sexual demands and angry at her defiant refusals, he left her quickly and in a huff.

Tears filled her eyes as she walked quietly to the home she shared with her parents and five sisters. Her mother looked up from her knitting as she ran quickly past her and up to bed.

Ned stood mutely in his usual position the following morning, with a small semi-circle of casuals around him at a respectable distance. His number one and two assistant foremen were at either side of him and also surrounded by men.

Union men were scarce and many of the faces were young and unknown to him. Most of Dock ward knew about the timber boat and he guessed rightly that the youngsters were absent from their jobs in the local spinning mills or timber yards in an effort to secure a turn at the timber boat and earn good money.

"Git away over till Johnny Robinson's boat. He's loadenin' empty beer bottles," he growled at the youngsters, "Yis wudn't be able for this boat."

The work was hard and back-breaking with the men toiling in stooped positions most of the day. The timber was in different sizes and these were denoted by paint marks which distinguished the various lengths. The different sizes had to be kept strictly apart and this was difficult to do under the inadequate lighting system that came from the ship's generator when the darkness fell. The holdsmen examined each heave closely before they sent it ashore knowing a mixed bundle meant the shoremen who received it would have to go to more than one pile thus slowing down the speed of discharging.

This would bring the foreman over the hatch to berate the guilty pair and send the heave back in to be separated.

Ned dreaded the first two hours and knew he'd be unable to leave the ship until at least ten o'clock. He needed twenty-four men for each hatch and wasn't confident of getting them. If he was short he would treble up his own responsibilities and spread himself to a job at each hatch. This unselfish gesture would triple his daily wages.

His main problem was a lack of good winchmen. The blues were going to the handy potato cargoes his two colleagues were schooling. They were small boats and would be finished before lunch.

Good winch-drivers were essential in guiding the forty foot

lengths out of the narrow hatches without damage to the ship or the men handling the cargo. The Clipper had a deck cargo that would be piled above the winches and restrict the driver's vision. The thought of inexperienced operators and untried casuals working above the dangerous steam-driven barrel winches made him feel uncomfortable, yet the ship had to be manned and Ned would make do with what was in front of him.

He looked to the sky, thankful for the dry start to the day and began schooling as the Albert Clock began to chime the hour. He selected his men quickly, judging those he didn't know on their height and weight. Four regulars were sent to the store to collect a two-wheeled handcart filled with the equipment needed to unload the timber.

After the flurry of movement, the school disappeared with the exception of two youths standing white-faced and fidgeting before him. He turned his eyes to the centre of the compound and noticed the entire workforce had been employed. Against his better judgement he reached the two of the three remaining checks to the boys who grabbed them before he could change his mind.

Turning the remaining disk in his hand he watched with a cruel grin as Sandy ran into the schooling compound and looked all around him dejectedly as he saw the gangers depart. He was capless and his hair was uncombed. He saw Ned still standing and approached him haltingly. His face was drawn and pinched with the cold as he looked pleadingly at the ganger.

"I slept in, Ned," he whispered hoarsly. "Do ye need any men?"

The ganger answered without a trace of humour. "Aye ... Do ye know where I cud git any?" Sandy wilted at the insult and was glad no one was around to hear it.

Ned looked him over. He was an experienced and willing worker but was inclined to shoot his mouth off. He remembered how he had been out of order in the bar and decided he should be punished.

He held out his hand palm upwards with the silver job-check

resting in its centre. "There it is," he grinned, "When yiv got it yiv got a job on the Clipper." Sandy gasped with relief and reached for the disk. Ned swung his arm in an arc and the circle of metal flew high into the air.

Both men watched as it glided like a sea bird before falling with a plop into the deep and murky waters of the Clarendon Dock.

"When yiv got the check, report to the Clipper," repeated Ned with a laugh before joining the other foremen and driving off.

Sandy was so desperate he contemplated diving into the water but knew he would never be able to locate the disk. As the car moved off he stuck his hands deep into his overcoat pockets and trudged through the empty compound toward the gates at Dock Street. His mind raced as he tried to think of what he would tell his wife. She had warned him the previous night to check the alarm clock and stay sober. Needless to say he had done neither.

Ned stopped the car at a group of men standing outside the American Bar. He rolled down the car window. "Job goin' at the Blackpool Clipper at the Pollock Dock," he shouted.

A small rheumy-eyed man with bandy legs that caused him to move sideways when he walked stepped to the car. "I'll take it," he yelled.

"Beat it," snarled the ganger to the amusement of the others. "It's a slinger I want, not a singer. What about you?" he called to a younger man who ran forward and took the check.

Reaching the boat Ned climbed the gangplank wearily and surveyed the men who stood on the highly stacked deck cargo. The experienced men had already teamed up and groaned out loud as he split them and paired them with rookies. He saw Jim Harvey with Kelly and allowed them to remain together as Harvey was also a learner. "I'll be watchin' ye, Aggie," he growled cheerlessly.

The two youngsters he had schooled last remained together as he had no one to put with them. "Watch the other men an' yill git the hang of it," he snarled. "If yis haven't got it by lunchtime I'll bring down yer stamp an' yer insurance cards an' yis kin lick 'em, stick 'em an' fuck aff," he finished, placing them as far away from the winch as he could.

The men detailed to the store arrived with the rubber-wheeled handcart. It was packed with six by six inch wooden battens each three feet long and a set of nipper-chains for each hatch. They were quickly hoisted onto the deck cargo as the men began to unload the timber.

Kelly beckoned Jim to lift a heelstick and follow him, as he walked aft slowly, eyes down, studying the timber lengths. The ship's hatches were fully loaded but the deck cargo obviously had to come off first. Ned was still apprehensive and walked toward the winch.

"If ye can't see the men, Hawkins, shout out an' they'll direct ye. I've gotta check out the other hatches. Don't be heavin' too quickly till ye kin see the men an' I don't want ye damaging any ship's property. If ye do I'll take it outa yer earnins. Is that clear?"

"Yo," shouted Hawkins from the ship's deck.

Kelly motioned Jim to him. The two lads had taken long hooks from their coats and were trying to pick up the timber.

When Jim produced a hook borrowed from his Uncle Jack, Kelly told him to put it away.

"Wait till ye learn how ta use it," he said quietly adding, "One's enough in the right hands." Jim put the hook away as Kelly continued to move around. Finding two of the planks with their ends almost level, he spaced his legs and stood over them. Sinking the point of his hook into the plank at his right foot he put both hands to the handle of the hook and hoisted the end of the forty foot long plank as high as he could. Gripping it with both hands between his knees for more support he called to Jim.

"Slip the heelstick below this length as far back from this end as you can. Make sure it doesn't foul the one I'm gonna lift next."

Jim quickly obeyed. Getting down onto his knees he slipped the piece of wood at an angle into the space Kelly had created.

Kelly slowly released the length down onto the skid which served as a trestle. "Yev got the idea," he said warmly. "Now I'm

172

gonna lift the same plank with my bare hand and the one next to it with the hook. When I yell, straighten the heel stick so that it fits in the space left by the two sticks an' it'll cradle both planks. An' go back as far as ye can to allow us till git the nipper-chain close till the middle of the heave. Got it?"

Jim nodded and knelt down so that he could see the space when Kelly lifted the other length. Kelly sunk the point of the hook deeply into the end of the second plank and pulled it level with the first one. Jim rolled onto his stomach and pushed the heelstick into the gap left by the two planks. Kelly lowered the ends only when he saw Jim's hands were clear. It was a dangerous moment to be repeated many times during the unloading. The plank in Kelly's hand was reasonably safe but there was always a chance the hook could slip from the other and crush the boy's hands. Releasing the hook, Kelly straightened and turned to face Jim. He pointed to the opposite ends of the planks he had just lifted onto the batten.

"Go down there," he said, speaking slowly, giving the lad time to savour his instructions. He stabbed with his right foot at three planks. "We'll toss these three one at a time on to this one." He pointed to the length of timber on the heelstick nearest the three. "Then the three on the other side plus an extra one for the ditty an' we've got a heave made up." He gave Jim a tight grin. "Now one or two words of warnin'," he said grimly. "Don't touch a plank until I give ye the nod otherwise yer fingers 'ill be lyin' all over the place. I remember a fella gittin' two cut aff at a boat fulla railway sleepers an' before we cud pick 'em up a bloody big seagull made off with them in his beak."

Unsure as to whether or not Kelly was joking, Jim nodded obediently and trotted the forty feet to the end of the planks. He watched as his mate buried the hook savagely into the side of the first plank and lifted it knee high before grabbing it with his free hand and putting it against his stomach for support. He leaned left and then right causing the opposite end of the plank to force the ones on either side of it away thus leaving hand room on each

173

side of the plank. Using all his strength he turned the stick almost on its edge to give Jim a clean lift at the other end.

"Pick it up," yelled Kelly, "and watch for it bellyin' in the middle." Jim spaced his legs and stood directly over the end of the plank. Taking a deep breath he stooped and grasped the plank with both hands. Sure enough it bent in the middle like a bow. Yelling in unison they swung the plank squarely onto the other.

"Right," yelled Kelly with a grin. "Keep that up an' we're home in a boat." They used the same procedure to lift the rest and their first heave was ready to go ashore.

"Git a nipper-chain an' measure what ye think is the middle an' fire one end of the chain under the heave. Throw it far enuff under for me to reach an' haul it up my side. Give me the end with the hook on," he added sliding the large hand-hook into his belt to leave both hands free.

The chain slid clear with a rattle and Kelly lifted it and put the hook around the other end of the chain, pulling down on it as tightly as he could. He sat down on the made-up heave and beckoned Jim to him. "We don't sink a cargo like this, we skin it layer by layer. That means we'll be movin' all over the stack. "Yill be concentratin' hard an' that's only natural, but don't go inta a trance. Keep yer eyes open an' watch the heaves an' the hook as it comes intil the hatch an' don't stan' in a space or a hole. When the winch lifts a heave it will slide an' the timber below it will slide until it meets the end of another plank. That's what we call a butt, an' if yer feet's in that space, they'll be cut off at the ankles.

Kelly felt for the lad as he saw him digesting the information knowing his life and limbs might depend on it. He patted Jim's head affectionately. "An' if yer gonna fall off the cargo," he grinned, "fall that way." he pointed to the seaward side. His face hardened as he pointed to the winch wire as it trailed along the cargo. "An' always run a mile from that," he ordered.

They watched as the hook drifted toward them. It was a double derrick and there was no need for a bull-rope man. Jim grabbed the large ship's hook and pulled it to the heave. Kelly hooked it

174

into the eye of the nipper. "Always make sure the back of the nipper-chain hook is in the direction the winch is gonna drag otherwise it cud come undone an' send the heave back in on top of us," he shouted over the roar of the donkey engine.

Jim nodded grimly as the driver on the starboard winch positioned his derrick and under Kelly's instructions lifted the load clear of the floor. When it was clear the winch man on the portside of the ship whipped it to the shore.

"Okay," commanded Kelly, "let's git another one, but don't fergit my words. Keep yer eyes on the hook an' on the heave. Watch where yer puttin' yer feet an' always leave yerself room for escape an' don't git trapped between heaves. Those two drivers are pretty good but when they git a drop of jungle juice later on, yill be divin' for cover more than once."

They stooped to the task and within minutes had another heave stacked and ready to go. The two young lads were finding it difficult. One of them whom Jim knew as Sammy Robinson was angry at not being able to get a heave built and was venting his frustration on his workmate. Both insisted on using large hand-hooks but were unable to pick the first plank from its bed.

Robinson refused advice from the other slingers and continued to verbally abuse his partner. The ganger was drawn to the hatch when he saw the hook swinging idly above the cargo. He watched for a moment then rushed across the cargo and grabbed Robinson roughly by the shirt front.

"If yer nat able, fuck off," he snarled.

The lad lost all his aggressiveness and began to sob. "It's him," he cried, pointing his hook at his crestfallen mate, "He won't do what I tell 'im."

The ganger laughed savagely. "Won't do what you tell him," he snarled. "What do you know about it? Go on home the pair of yis. I've seen better men in the children's hospital. Yis are too young. I niver shuda schooled yis."

Robinson pointed vindictively at Jim who was watching quietly. "I'm as oul as he is," he declared.

"Aye, but the difference between him an' you," thundered the ganger, "is that he keeps his trap shut an' does what he's tole. Away down till our office an' git yer cards. Tell them to give yis two half-crowns each. Yis are finished."

He dismissed them and turned to the other men. "Wurk on till I scour the corners for another two men." He looked with contempt after the departing figures of the two boys. "Ben White has better men than them lying in his parlour," he roared before moving down the gangplank.

The men laughed at the reference to Ben White, who was the local undertaker with a funeral parlour in York Street.

Kelly stepped forward and hooked on. "We'll just havta go a bit faster, kid," he muttered dryly.

Half-an-hour later the ganger returned with two men. He instructed them briefly and left them to their task. They knew the procedure but were quite elderly. Jim marvelled how the same task done in minutes by him and Kelly could take so long when done by the others.

"Maybe Ned got them outa Ben White's backroom after all," muttered Kelly causing Jim to grin for the first time that day. They continued to enjoy breaks of five and ten minutes whilst the others scarcely got their heads lifted and the hook seemed to be constantly hanging over them.

He realised Kelly's strength and knowledge was making life easy for him. His confidence grew with each heave and soon he found himself anticipating Kelly's every move.

Things were not going as smoothly in the Chapel Sheds. Andy and Harry were bogged down doing most of the work whilst Henry and Sam skulked around the lorries sulking and scowling at each other. The depot was packed with traffic and Henry, still smarting over the loss of his hat, was eating the face off anyone who spoke to him.

The checkers ignored them and hoped things would soon return to normal. Henry's squad was related either through blood or marriage and would leave en bloc if anyone interfered in what they saw as a family affair. Sam had not smiled all morning. His head was sore from the Sunday drinking and his jaw still ached from Henry's backhander.

He watched as his brother sidled up to a Ministry Inspector who was keeping a close eye on the treatment of the potatoes being off-loaded. He decided to make a move for a curer, and was tip-toeing towards the shed door when Henry spotted him.

"Git back till yer wurk or yer sacked," he roared, smiling triumphantly as his brother moved sullenly back to the lorry. The potato inspector watched as he took a bag onto his back. Instead of tossing it to the cobbles as he usually did, Sam cradled it like a baby and put it carefully on the floor.

"Gud mon," said the civil servant approvingly, "That's the proper way to handle the tubers. That way you won't smash them."

"Aye, sor," replied Sam courteously.

Whilst the inspectors were in the depot the men were warned to handle the potatoes gently as a load could be rejected and sent home if the officials thought it had been damaged during off-loading. When they left it was a different story. The bags were thrown straight from the men's back and onto the ground as they emptied the lorries as quickly as possible.

Despite the cold Henry was coatless. An armless leather jerkin covered a dirty brown army shirt with rolled up sleeves as he stood on the cobbles and surveyed all around him.

Each time a bag landed on Sam's back he felt a spasm of pain shoot through his jaw. The inspector had returned to speak to his brother and because of this Sam had to hold the bag longer than usual. Bending also sent a shiver of pain across the small of his back which had been bruised when he collided with the corner of the piano in Jack's house.

He decided on another tack. Smoking was illegal in the transit shed so he decided to go out one of the many gates to light up. Henry had other ideas. As Sam left the lorry his brother beckoned him over.

"Where are ye goin'?" he asked politely for the benefit of the inspector.

Sam held his rising temper in check. "I'm goin' for a smoke," he answered civilly.

Henry turned slightly away from the inspector. "Excuse me a moment, sor," he purred, then raising his voice he snarled in Sam's direction. "Git back till yer work an' stop botherin' me."

Turning to the impressed inspector he said primly, "I don't tolerate skiving." Sam's right arm came up like a flash at the insult and his fist crashed into Henry's unprotected head just below his right ear.

His brother's body hit the square-setts with a thud and lay in a crumpled heap as still and as silent as death. Without even looking down Sam turned on his heels and strode out of the shed.

Three double whiskeys later Jack hurried into the pub. His cap was back to front on his bullet-shaped head with the peak resting on the nape of his neck in an effort to keep the dust and soil from going down the back of his shirt.

"Sam ... Sam," he whispered, "they've tuk Henry till the Mater."

Sam poured a drop of water into his whiskey. "Shuda bin the morgue," he growled.

Jack drew up a bar-stool. "They reckon he's got a broken jaw," he continued anxiously.

"I didn't hit him that hard," answered the unconcerned Sam.

"Ye hit him when he was talkin' an' his mouth was open. They tuk the inspector away in the same ambulance," he added

Sam looked sharply over his glass. "I niver touched him," he stated.

"He fainted after ye hit Henry," explained Jack. His face was creased with worry. "What are we gonna tell ma?" he asked desperately.

"Say nuthin'," advised his elder brother. The drink had warmed him and eased the pain in his jaw and body. "Shure it's near the male-hour nigh. We'll say he's away off on the tear somewhere."

He patted Jack's shoulder reassuringly and was almost choked by the dust he raised. "Say nuthin' ... I'll handle it," he added.

At twenty minutes to twelve they left the bar and sauntered down to their mother's house for lunch, actually passing their own homes on the way. Mrs. Harvey said nothing at first and attended them dutifully, carrying the boiled potatoes and the slices of bread wrapped up in the folds of her apron. She laid the food quietly on the table beside the meat and soup.

She poured the third glass of buttermilk and put it down with a bang that caused the knives and forks to bounce into the air. "Where's my Henry?" she screamed suddenly into Jack's ear.

"I don't know ma," he almost sobbed, spilling buttermilk all over the tablecloth. She spaced her feet and glared from son to son. "There's somethin wrong," she hissed.

Sam lifted his fork to his mouth and she knocked it to the floor. "Nobody's eatin' another bite until I know where my Henry is?" she thundered.

Sam glared nervously at Jack who was wilting visibly. "We don't know ma. He's probably out likkerin' somewhere."

His mother put her hands on her hips and stared at both men aggressively.

"If I don't git an answer in five seconds ... " she muttered, lifting a large wooden spoon from the table.

"He's in the Mater, ma," whined Jack.

"Ach, ghost ta ghost," sobbed the old woman, rushing to a chair and lifting her shawl. "Is he hurt bad?" she whimpered, wrapping the shawl around her and rushing to the door.

"Sam hit him," explained Jack with the innocent air of a choirboy.

"Oh," she said, stopping in mid-stride. Her face wrinkled with disgust as she dropped the shawl back onto the chair and walked towards Sam.

179

"Hit him, did ye? Hit the brother what give ye a job an' puts a loaf a bread on yer table for yer wife an' yer wee 'uns, an' sits here an' worries until the wee hours of every mornin' thinkin' up ways till keep yis all in a job that allows yis to run to the pubs every day an' puts the food on this table that feeds yis every day. Well yis won't git another bite in this house until I see my Henry home an' well again. So git away up there an' find out what's happenin'."

"But ma, it's dinner-hour," wailed Sam, whose appetite had been sharpened by the whiskey.

His mother wrapped him none too gently across the knuckles with the spoon. "It might be dinner-hour for dacent men, but not youse two. So git away up there an' see what's wrong an' remember," she finished with a frosty edge to her voice, "No Henry ... No Dinner."

Both men rose obediently and left the table. Sam berated the hapless Jack all the way to the bus stop at the corner of Trafalgar Street. Moments later they entered the casualty ward of the Mater Hospital. Removing their caps they stood awkwardly in the middle of the room until an orderly approached them.

"Can I help you?" he asked pleasantly.

At that moment the lift doors opened and a trolley was wheeled out. Henry lay on it wearing a white smock and propped up on one elbow. His face contorted with rage as he saw them. "Jack," he snarled through jaws that were obviously unbroken, "Git away back till yer wurk an' tell that Judas bastard he's sacked."

Before Jack could restrain him Sam raced forward and aimed a blow at Henry's head. It caught him on the side of the neck throwing him from the trolley onto the tiled floor.

Both men raced from the hospital chased by the porter and with the screams of abuse from the outraged Henry ringing in their ears. "Yiv done it now," gasped Jack as they reached the Antrim Road and quickly lost the porter in the maze of little streets.

Sandy watched dejectedly as the workers moved away from the corner. The dinner-hour was over and they were drifting back to the various sheds and boats.

Taking a crumpled daily paper from his overcoat pocket, he lowered himself to the pavement and began to study the racing.

Fumbling in another pocket he selected a small wrinkled cigarette butt and put it between his lips. He had not gone home that morning, unable to face his wife. Now she would assume he had got a job at the Clipper, despite having slept in, and would have a substantial dinner waiting in the stove for him.

The thought of the food made him capitulate. Rising wearily he trudged the short distance to his home in Nelson Street. She was in her usual place in the scullery when he entered. Her thin frame was hunched over a brown wash basin filled with soapy water as she rubbed a nappy on a glass ribbed scrubbing board. A pile of grimy clothing lay in and around a tin bath at her feet.

"It's in the oven," she said, casting a quick glance at a small clock sitting on the scullery window. "What kept ye?" she asked quizzically.

"Ack, Billy Kelly ast me in for a drink," he lied.

She laughed with relief. "You an' that Kelly. Where does he git the bloody money from?"

"Shure his da gits a fortune at the Liverpool boat. Billy wants fer nuthin' an' don't fergit he's got an army pension." He lifted the hot plate of potatoes and flour dumplings and sat down at the table.

"I suppose everybody's workin'," said his wife, interupting her toil to bring him in a cup of freshly made tea.

"Aye," he mumbled through a mouthful of food.

She was a slight shadow of a woman, wearing a beige pinny over a flowered dress. Her eyes were slits of pain set in a pallid face and dulled by nights of sleeplesness as she tended her frail babies who cried either from sickness or hunger or both. She was in her early thirties, but her hair was grey and frizzled, the aftermath of a botched home perm. The lips of her toothless mouth were

181

pursed tightly together as she hated to smile when she wasn't wearing her dentures. The rest of her face was pinched and lined with worry.

"Is that gum-boil still hurtin' ye, Sally?" asked Sandy sympathetically.

"Aye," she replied like a ventriloquist through pursed lips. "An' I hate goin' out without me false teeth."

Sandy gazed at her bent figure as she went back to the scullery.

"Why cudn't ye a bin a good lookin' bit like Bertie Millar's wife? He gits more work than some of the first preference men," he thought selfishly, rubbing the stubble on his face with the handle of his fork. Deep down however he was grateful that his woman was not attractive enough for the gangers to take an interest in her.

"But it isn't only the dock gangers," he thought wearily. He knew of men who spent a lifetime on the nightshift in the Belfast shipyard blissfully unaware that the foreman was in his bed sleeping with his wife. He looked at a picture of two of his childen. "At least yis are all mine," he reflected as Sally entered the kitchen carrying a bundle of nappies. He watched her as she lowered the pulleys from the ceiling and folded the nappies over the narrow wooden battens.

Gazing at her boyish bottom and thin white legs, he chuckled to himself despite his problems "No chance a me gittin' a lie-on on the nightshift."

"Yid be as well gittin' that intil ye before the cubs come home from school," she called, arousing him from his reverie.

He cleaned the plate with a piece of bread and walked to the door.

"Will ye be late tanight?" she called after him.

"Yis," he lied, groaning inwardly. She knew the Clipper worked every night until midnight, weather permitting. Swallowing the urge to tell her the truth, he rushed out into the street.

Unable to think constructively and feeling the need of a drink, he made his way to Dock Street corner. After an hour's deliberation, he walked quickly to a pawn shop at the corner of the New Lodge Road and pledged his jacket and pullover for eight shillings.

His next stop was the unemployment centre in Great Patrick Street where he was obliged to report every day between one-thirty and three-thirty when unable to find a job. He approached the mahogany-grained counter of box forty-six to the surprise of the clerk.

"Not workin', Carstairs?" he said sarcastically, digging out Sandy's bulky file and placing it in front of him for the signature that entitled him to a day's unemployment pay. He leaned on the counter and watched as Sandy scrawled his name on the sheet. "You're the only one in the day. They tell me the lame and the blind are employed. I heard there was so much work they had to put a woman over the hatch at the Bristol boat." He shook his head negatively. "I don't think you'll be paid. Did you sleep in perhaps?" he added.

"Mind yer own business," snarled Sandy throwing the pencil on top of his file and walking out. He moved despondently along Corporation Street fingering the silver coins in his overcoat pocket, and decided to go to Barney Vallery's for a few hot wines. Perhaps they would supply him with the courage to tell his wife the truth.

Entering the sidedoor, he walked across the sawdust-covered floor to the small, but well-stocked, bar.

"Givus a glass a hot Bannerman's, Barney—that day wud skin ye," he muttered, rubbing his hands together.

"Aye," agreed the large, white-haired owner as he turned on the geyser and reached for the Bannerman bottle. Moments later Sandy was seated on a small wine cask beside a large wine cask that served as a table, sipping the hot and delicious drink that was spiced with a piece of lemon and a handful of cloves. He closed his eyes gratefully as the liquid warmed his frozen body.

He was down to his last mouthful when the door opened and Billy Kelly walked in, closely followed by Jim Harvey. They moved straight to the bar. As Kelly ordered Jim gazed around the bar. A middle wall had been knocked down to make the room larger. Quite a few men and a surprising number of women sat around in groups or stood at the bar. There was a collection of seamen and dockers. Other customers wore boiler-suits beneath their overcoats and black caps with shiny peaks. The caps bore a red hand emblem which identified them as drivers and labourers from the nearby Ulster Transport Depot.

The elderly man behind the bar was extremely tall and wore a long white apron which stretched to his ankles. Jim marvelled as he stood in the centre of the space behind the counter and reached every optic at the back of the bar without moving his feet.

Kelly noticed Sandy and brought a hot wine over to the table. The downhearted casual accepted it gratefully. Sitting down beside him, Kelly lowered a hot Irish whiskey as quick as his throat would accept the scalding liquid. Jim, sipping at a Wee Willie Dark, moved to buy another round but Kelly's hand stopped him.

"No more nigh, Jim. We've a long way till go an' we need clear heads." He turned to Sandy and smiled sympathetically. "Bad luk this mornin'," he said.

Carstairs shook his head in disgust. "Ack, if I hadn't a slept in I'd a touched for a job wid Uncle, but the youngest un's teethin' an' I niver got my eyes closed last night. An' ta make matters worse I think the buroo ill be cancelled."

Kelly sighed. "I think it wud. Ned had ta go to the low-dock corner for a coupla men."

"That cowyard," roared Sandy angrily, "I hope the hairs on his arse turn till drumsticks an' bate the balls of 'im." Jim and Kelly laughed in unison, causing Sandy to giggle despite his problems.

"Cud ye not go to the Assistance?" asked Jim.

"What for?" scoffed Sandy wearily, "To be shunted from pillar till post an' gittin' the third degree for about four or five hours wid oul dolls askin' ye what ye had fer breakfast an' where ye shit last, an' then, if yer lucky, givin' ye a pittance that wudn't buy ye

184

five fags?" His voice tailed off as his chin dropped onto his chest.

Jim took a shallow sip from his glass, feeling ashamed that he, a young single man should be working whilst a capable and experienced man with six children went unemployed.

"Why don't ye take yer overcoat off Sandy, yill feel the better of it when ye go out 'cause that's a day wud skin ye," said Kelly.

Sandy grinned. The wine was beginning to mellow him. "I've no jacket or jersey on beneath. I pawned them. Needed the price of a drink," he replied.

Kelly sighed in mock disgust and pulled a crumpled ten shilling note from his pocket. "Take that an' git yer stuff out. That's no weather to be without it."

Jim rose and looked for the toilet. He walked to the only other door in the room and opened it. He was greeted with the overpowering smell of stale urine which a daily sluicing of bleach could not eradicate. Seeing no urinals, he went to a whitewashed wall and began to relieve himself.

He turned his head in the direction of the door as it squealed open and was amazed to see an elderly woman enter. He watched as she nodded politely to him before hitching her dress up over her waist and sitting down to pass water. Leaning on a rubbish bin to steady herself, she grinned sweetly at Jim as he hastily buttoned his fly and returned to his seat.

Both men laughed at his shocked features. "It's like that in here," grinned Sandy, forgetting his troubles. "See that chalk-line there?" he guffawed, pointing to a thin shaky line that cut the room in half." Jim nodded. "The other side a that's the lounge—walk over it an' yer drink costs another penny."

When the laughter subsided, Kelly nudged the lad with his elbow. "Nip you home an' get a wee tightener. Call for me on yer way back."

Jim drank up and moved out. Trotting along Nelson Street he passed his old school house feeling very grown up. His mother gave him a fried egg between two slices of toasted wheaten bread which he washed down with a mug of tea. After which he went dutifully to the toilet and performed his daily operation on his hands hoping they would hold out until the end of the day. He was thankful the skin on his back was getting a respite.

He arrived at the pub and was surprised to see Sandy playing a piano-keyed accordian whilst two men solemnly danced a jig. Kelly rose when he saw him. Dropping his mask of hilarity, he quickly moved out to the street. "It's hard ta leave when the music starts," he muttered as they crossed Whitla Street, "But yev gotta keep yer wits about ye when yer in the houl. It's different from wurkin' ashore" he added thoughtfully. "Got to be always watchin'—watchin' where ye put yer feet, watchin' the swing of the hook, watchin' ye don't fall or git knocked off the cargo on to the concrete or inta the dock." He slapped the youngster playfully on the arm as they entered the dock gates with the Clipper in full view. "Keep on the way yer goin' an' yill be able ta put in for a docker's button," he added.

They climbed the gangplank under the baleful eye of the ganger who then ordered another two men to leave. "Tuk yer time Aggie," he growled. "Goin' ashore wid the hard men an' learnin' all the bad habits."

Jim said nothing as he walked behind Kelly onto the timber which was getting closer to deck level. They moved quickly and had a heave up in record time. As he sat on the timber he looked down the Pollock dock towards the sea and watched as other boats loaded or unloaded their various cargoes into or out of the sheds. A flock of seagulls screamed hungrily overhead as a seaman tipped a bucket of refuse over the side. As the gulls swooped quickly on it Jim automatically put his hands in his pockets, remembering Kelly's story.

Lunchtime came quickly and he left Kelly with an assurance that he would call for him at ten minutes to one.

Henry strode angrily from the casualty ward of the Mater Hospital.

The staff had sent for the police who quizzed him about the incident at the lift. He insisted the men were strangers and was eventually allowed to leave. Reaching the street he quickly tore off the large white bandage the nurse had tied around his head, and threw it at his feet. Boarding a trolley-bus, he jumped off at Gallaher's and walked down North Thomas Street.

"Are ye alright?" cried his mother, taking his arm and leading him to the sofa.

He shook her away irritably. "Where's them other bastards?" he snarled.

They're away back till their wurk ... but without any dinner," she added triumphantly.

"Ma, I'll haveta sack that fella Sam," he said worriedly, sitting down heavily at the table and putting his injured head in his hands.

"Ack nigh, son," she said defensively hovering over him as she put his favourite dish of food in front of him. "Ye wudn't wanta git the name of deprivin' all them wee childer of a loaf of bread just because their da is an ungrateful whelp.

He thought about the kicks and bites he had received from them during the fight. "Wisht to hell he wud feed them. They nearly ate me alive the other day," he replied.

He looked into her sad eyes. "Alright ... I'll give him another chance," he said.

He rose from the table. "I'm gonna take the rest of the day off an' give them a coolin'," he decided. "That'll leave them a bit more to do. Sort of a punshment to fit the crime," he added smugly.

"Aye son," she replied, glad she had gained Sam a reprieve.

After changing his clothes he walked thoughtfully to the Stalingrad. One of the woman approached him immediately, but he rebuffed her. "Maybe later, Maggie," he smiled, "I'm only lukin' for a drink at the moment."

He joined a group of lorry-drivers from Ballymena who bought him a drink.

Soon he had forgotten his sore ear as he swopped anecdotes with the men, some of whom he had known over a long period of time.

The drink was beginning to loosen him up when a medium-sized, heavily-built man wearing a tweed-coloured eight piece cap, shouldered his way into the company and lifted a glass of whiskey from the bar-top. He gazed fiercely at the man who owned the drink.

"Is this yours, kulshemuck?" he growled in a thick gutteral voice. The man nodded mutely, sensing the aroma of danger.

"Well I'm gonna drink it," continued the stranger. "Any objections?"

The driver was a long way from home. He gazed fearfully at the man's massive jaw and barrel-like chest, hid below a khaki shirt and a tweed jacket with frayed sleeves. "No," he muttered through lips that had turned to chalk.

The intruder lifted the glass to his lips and smiled thinly at Henry. "Any objections, Harvey?"

"As long as it's not my drink, Bull." The words were out of Henry before he knew it.

Bull swallowed the whiskey and looked around the bar-top. "Which one is yours?" he grunted, fixing his steely-blue eyes on Henry's face.

"Don't do it, Bull," he whispered. "I've had enough fightin' to do me for a while."

Bull grinned. "Aye, I heard yer brother's childer give ye a hammerin'. You ain't got the heart to be a fightin' man, Harvey, an' ye ain't gonna git yer hair wrecked for a lousy whiskey," he growled as his eyes located Henry's drink. He placed it to his lips.

Henry looked at the beefy fist holding his drink. It had fingers the size of pork sausages and was covered with faded tatooes. He switched his gaze to the drivers and the other customers around him who were watching the situation intently. For the tenth time in as many minutes, he wished he had gone to bed. It seemed everyone in the world had an interest in rearranging his face.

Bull Murphy was long past his prime and about ten years older than Henry.

He was the toughest son York Street had ever sired. Hard as nails and utterly ruthless, he had the ideal build for a fighting man. Almost neckless, his bullet-head sat on wide shoulders and his short arms were corded by heavy muscle developed by hard work on the Belfast dock.

Unpredictable when drinking, he sometimes felt the need to assert his authority on the men of the district. His intimidation of the man in Henry's company had been a direct challenge to Harvey. Henry knew this and equally knew scorn and ridicule would follow him for the rest of his life if he allowed another man to drink his drink.

"Put it down, Bull," he pleaded, softly and cajolingly, "an' I'll buy ye a double."

He felt sweat breaking on his forehead and knew every eye in the bar was on him. Even the bartender had ceased to serve, waiting for the explosion or the capitulation.

Bull continued to smile. "Some people say if ye let a man drink yer drink yid let him sleep wid yer woman." He raised the glass to his lips and emptied it.

Smacking his lips in satisfaction, he looked at the perspiring Henry. "The ball's at yer toe, Harvey," he muttered with a cynical smile.

Amid muted laughter Henry turned abruptly and walked into the toilet. Holding onto the cistern pipe he forced his body to stop shaking and then began to take off his clothes with the exception of his trousers. He rolled his shoes and socks into a bundle along with his shirt and vest and pulled the sleeves tightly to secure it.

Emerging from the toilet he placed the clothes on the counter. "Luk after them for me, Alf," he whispered to the barman before throwing himself through the drinkers and grabbing a surprised Bull in a bear hug.

As a tactical move it was wrong. As Bull propelled across the bar

189

he drew back his head and Henry saw stars as it jerked forward and forcibly collided with the bridge of his nose.

Instinctively he stuck his knee into his opponent's groin and both men fell to the floor rolling under tables and toppling chairs as each fought to climb on top of the other. Blood coursed thickly from Henry's nose into Bull's eyes and momentarily blinded the streetfighter. It was enough time for Henry to unlease a powerful right cross which caught Bull flush on the chin and caused him to roar like the animal he was named after. Harvey was thrown from the outraged chest and rolled quickly onto his knees. Both men rose from the debris and glass and circled each other warily. Henry saw a glimmer of respect in Bull's eyes and breathed a little easier as he watched for the man's next move.

"Take it outside," screamed the irate barman, from the safety of the high counter. Bull threw his coat and cap to the floor and launched himself at Henry. The impact took both bodies through the swing doors and into Dock Street, where they rolled punching and kicking until they hit the kerb on the other side of the street. A horse, drawing a cart laden with bags of flour, reared on its hind legs with a frightened whinny as the pair rose to their feet and circled each other.

Henry tried to unscramble the basic course of self-defence he had learned from his father many years ago in the backyard of their home, whilst Bull, breathing heavily, decided the younger man was too strong and too fit for him to chase around a wide street. He moved backwards into a narrow alley that served as an emergency exit from from a bookmaker's office and beckoned to Henry to follow.

Harvey needed no coaxing, and he raced forward and rained body punches on Bull who moved back under their force until he collided with the light hard-board door into the bookmaker's office. It gave under his weight and the punters scattered as Henry chased Bull across the terrazzo-tiled floor of the betting shop.

Bull had gathered his wind and waited until Henry's stubbled chin came into range. Squaring his feet he connected with a hard left followed by a crushing right hook and grimaced as the potato carrier kept coming. Henry, remembering his father's instructions, lashed out with a succession of straight lefts that bounced off Bull's nose and mouth and forced him out of the main door and into Earl Lane.

Realising he was in danger of being stopped in his track by the heavy duty left that was smashing his face, he let out a wild roar and ran in below the jab wrapping his arms around Henry's waist. The force sent Henry careening backwards and through the parlour window of a house on the opposite side of the street.

Bull retained his vice-like grip as they fell onto the parlour floor, and Henry felt his hot gasping breath in his ear as he tried to break the hold that was threatening to crush his ribs. Lowering his head he sunk his teeth into Bull's shoulder.

Both lost their concentration as the owner of the house, a heavily built widow in her sixties attacked both of them with a broom handle. Bull released his grip as she harried them into the street.

Henry was beginning to enjoy the combat, finding that Bull, like many other fighting men, was not as good as the reputation that preceeded him. They fought their way into York Street which was crowded with doffers and workers from the tobacco factory. The women screamed as the two pot-bellied men brawled through a pavement fruit display sending apples, oranges and tomatoes rolling all over the road.

A mutual need for a respite caused them to circle, flicking blood at each other whist the women continued to mill around them screaming and crying at the brutality.

Henry decided to finish it. He rushed forward throwing open-handed punches at Bull's grey head. The older man ducked under the onslaught and delivered a heavy right to Henry's unguarded ribs which forced the wind from his body. As he doubled up in pain he instinctively unleased a hard upper-cut which miraculously found Bull's tucked-in chin. He fell under the impact and Henry felt the end was close. As Bull raised himself groggily onto one knee his opponent rushed forward and grabbed his belt in an effort to raise him to his feet for the final onslaught.

The belt broke under the savage wrench and the blank-eyed Bull fell against the railway station wall as his baggy trousers flapped to his ankles. He wore no underwear and Henry was momentarily shocked by the sight of Bull's private parts peeking through a forest of pubic hair.

His first reaction was to move forward and help Bull cover up. For one stupefying moment he thought the roof of the railway station had landed on his head as Bull's avenging right hook exploded on his chin. He legs turned to water and he threw his arms around Bull dragging both of them back onto the pavement.

Although his head was spinning from the force of the blow, he realised the cheering of the watchers had stopped and they were now chanting one word. "Peelers ... Peelers ... Peelers ... "

"It's the peelers, Bull. Every man for hisself," he shouted. Rising shakily he ran through a gap as the crowd opened up to let him through. Looking over his shoulder he saw four grim-faced cops being hampered by the crowd as they came after him. Bull, unable to move because of his trousers, was not as fortunate and was wrestled all the way along York Street to the Police station where he was charged with disorderly conduct and released on bail.

Henry ran into the home of a fellow second preference man where he was allowed to wash up whilst a young lad was dispatched to the Stalingrad to pick up his clothes.

Jim Harvey ate a full supper and drank two pints of milk straight from the bottles. His hands were peppered with minute splinters of wood but were not as sore as he thought they would have been.

Looking at the clock on the mantlepiece he set down the evening newspaper and rose to return to the Clipper. The next session would be overtime or as Kelly had stated, every plank was 'a plank an' a half.'

Further advice from the experienced dockworker caused him to put a heavy pullover with a rollneck over his shirt. Kelly said the weather would get colder and there was no shelter from the wind and rain until the deck cargo was cleared and they entered the ship's hatches, probably the next day.

Leaving home fifteen minutes early, he sped to Barney's and sat down beside his mate. The bar was almost deserted and Sandy was sleeping peacefully on long wooden seat which stretched the length of the pub. His overcoat was over his legs and upper body like a blanket. Two giggling women were gleefully blacking his face with burnt corks.

Kelly was finishing a cup of coffee laced with a glass of rum and handed the remains to Jim. He accepted it gratefully.

"Did ye eat anythin'?" asked Jim.

"Aye, a coupla Barney's hot pies. They'll see me through till I git home the night."

The deck cargo was in semi-darkness as they began to build a heave. The tide was at its highest point and they were over sixty feet from the surface of the open berth. The Pollock Dock was lit up by the navigation lights on the vessels moored on its quays and the huge gantries of the nearby shipyard towered over the transit sheds and blackened the skyline. Inadequate lighting on the ship itself was casting long shadows across the cargo which had been rendered slippery by a fall of rain. Some of the winchmen were feeling their liquor and more than one heave had to be restacked as the drivers misjudged the lift.

Backs were beginning to ache and bodies were soaked with perspiration despite a heavy frost which was forming on the planks they stood on. The nipper-chain numbed Jim's hands as he fastened it around each heave. They moved steadily across the cargo skinning the layers of timber one by one. The most difficult bit was opening a new layer and making sure fingers and feet didn't go where they shouldn't.

By now the work had become second nature to Jim and Kelly's calls of warning or instruction became rarer as they toiled silently almost always apart under the constant grinding of the winch and the screech of the guy ropes.

During a lull Jim noticed a woman being hurried up the gangplank by two men. Kelly sat down beside him and answered the unspoken question. "Sailors have urges the same as the rest of us," he grinned.

At exactly fifteen minutes to midnight the last bundle was winched to the shore-gang. As they made their way to the quay Kelly noticed one of the older men was limping badly. "Ketch a butt Mack?" he asked softly.

"Aye," gasped the man, leaning for a moment on the ship's rail, his face wrinkled with pain. "Did ye report it?" continued Kelly.

The slinger gave him an old-fashioned look. "I'll be alright in the mornin'—I'll sleep wid me boot on the night. I need the money," he added wryly.

"Don't we all," muttered Kelly before moving off in the direction of the harbour gates that opened out into Garmoyle street.

As they strode through the dark and deserted streets Jim's curiosity got the better of him.

"Will he really sleep wid his boot on?" he asked.

"Yeah," muttered Kelly, "'cause if he takes it off, he'll niver git it on in the mornin'."

"But surely they'll see he's in pain," said Jim.

"That's his business," retorted Kelly, almost sharply. "He needs the job. Long as he does his wurk, no one will bother him."

"An' if he doesn't?" persisted the lad.

"He'll be up the road. Need the money or not!"

"Shure there's no men," countered Jim.

Kelly stopped and looked at the lad's earnest face. "There's always men to man boats, but there's not always boats for men to man. That's the biggest pity."

They walked on in silence until Kelly crossed toward Henry Street. Jim watched him as he disappeared into the darkness before entering his own home.

The bright light almost blinded him as he walked into the kitchen. Dance music drifted from the radio as his mother rose from her seat at the fire. She beckoned to the the hearth where a plate of toast with cheese melted on it sat, as she went to make him tea.

His body felt as if all the liquid had been squeezed out of it. Finishing his tea, he drank the contents of a full bottle of lemonade and carried another one up to his bedroom. He called the cat with a click of his fingers, and it padded behind him. He smelt of stale sweat and his whole body ached as he undressed and clambered gratefully between the sheets.

He slept fitfully, tossing and turning, making up heaves and running for his life as planks showered down on his head. Ned's twisted features swam before him as he snarled oaths in his direction. More than once he woke up exhausted and trembling.

His mother called him at seven fifteen the next morning. As he started to climb out of bed he found he was unable to open his eyes as particles of sawdust had gummed his eyelashes together whilst he slept. Because of the slivers of wood in his hands he was unable to close them properly and every muscle in his back ached with pain.

A hot wash at the geyser cleared his eyelids and eased the pain in his hands, and within an hour he was throwing up the first heave of the day. After two or three heaves the pain left his back and hands as the work warmed the muscles and flesh.

A carpet of white hoar frost had settled on the cargo overnight and crowbars were employed to prise the planks apart.

All the holdsmen had returned and on a rare occasion when they had to wait for the hook, Kelly commented on the stubbornness of the man whose foot had been crushed. "It's alright for wee slips of fellas like yerself to throw in the towel when the goin' gits tuff. Mack's got a family to provide for an' he's nat in the inner circle when it comes ta gittin' somethin' regular."

"Yer nat in the inner circle, but ye git plenty of wurk," probed Jim.

"That's true," agreed his companion. "I don't need to ball-lick or bribe anybody. Although I'm under suspension, I'm still a first preference man an' blood's thicker than water. My oul fella helped form the cross-channel union an' he's bin on the committee since its inception, so that makes him a pretty powerful man in anybody's language."

"If he's so powerful why did you git suspended?" asked Jim.

"I hit a foreman," said Kelly simply. "They had no other option."

"How long will you be suspended?"

"Until I apologise an' return to the ranks of the privileged. My oul fella an' a lot of the bosses drink together an' they keep him informed of my doin's. They don't like us to mix wid the Arabs," he pointed at Jim, "that's what they call guys like you. There's dockers wudn't even drink wid their own brothers after they got their buttons. It's like an exclusive club. A licence to print money, but yer nat allowed to mix with the riff-raff."

The hook glided towards them and Jim hooked on. They made up another heave and sat down for a breather. Kelly looked seriously at his young co-worker.

"Jim, don't fall in love with the image of a docker. It's not what ye think it is. It's a hard, stinkin' game an' yid be better away from it. Git a trade or somethin'. Better still, join the army. Yill niver be anythin' but used an' trampled on an' when yiv served yer purpose, or speak up for yerself, yill be dumped. There's nuthin' but fear an' degradation here. I've seen men take a crack from a cargo hook that wuda killed lesser men an' go on wurkin' because they knew if they left the boat there'd be another man in their place."

He pointed with his hook across the shadows to a pair of older

196

men slinging silently in the gloom. "There's Charlie Stanley, the oul guy in the army greatcoat an' no cap. Know what I saw him doin' at seven-thirty this mornin' when I was comin' down till the boat?" he asked grimly.

Jim shook his head and Kelly continued. "He was takin' tallow outa a grease box of a railway wagon an' rubbin' it down in between his legs to ease the pain of the chaffin' in n' aroun' his private parts. He's too old for this kinda wurk but Ned tuk him because he needed him. He may niver need him again, but Charlie can't afford till take that chance, so he'll wurk till he drops."

The lad shuddered and moved for a heelstick as Kelly, tired of talking, picked up two planks after forcing them apart with a crowbar.

It was shortly after the noon break when Kelly nudged him abrubtly. "Have ye any buroo to git?" he asked.

"Two days," replied Jim, "What about you?"

"Like I said, when there's wurk I git it, but ye kin nip down on the afternoon break," he replied.

Dinner time in the Harvey household began quietly. Henry's nose was swollen from his bout with Bull and his jaw still ached from the savage blow by Sam. He was having trouble chewing and picked listlessly at his food with his fork. Suddenly the silence was split by a roar of terror as he fell backwards off his chair and onto the sofa.

"What is it, son? Have ye tuk a seizure," screamed his mother, throwing her knitting to the floor and rushing to him.

"My dinner ... My dinner," he roared fearfully, getting as far away from the table as he could.

Mrs. Harvey poked suspiciously through the potatoes and peas and uncovered a large black cockroach. Pushing it to the edge of the plate, she examined closely it before glaring grimly at Sam

197

and Jack. Sam's pent-up laughter which burst at that instant quickly turned to a roar of pain as his mother hit him squarely on the forehead with the soup ladle.

She turned to Henry who was watching fearfully. "Go back till yer supper, son, it's one of them joke things"

Henry didn't move. Joke or no joke, there was no way he would touch anything on the plate.

The old woman rounded furiously on her eldest son. "Why do ye have ta be so cruel? Ye know he's bin terrified since he foun' a nest of them things all over him when he slept all night on the floor." She was plainly distressed and wiped her eyes with a dish towel.

"Henry's bloody good till youse an' yer families an' whot does he git for it? If ye hadn't a hit him when his back wus turned he'd a bin at his wurk instead a brawlin' wid that scoundrel Bull Murphy. If it wasn't for my Henry yis wudn't be on a good tidy sum every week," she whimpered.

Sam threw his knife and fork across the table. "Aye an' if it wasn't for your Henry we'd be gittin' a bloody sight more."

Henry bounded from the sofa and grabbed Sam's throat. "Just you start," he snarled. Jack and the mother prised them apart.

Henry shook himself huffily and gazed at the clock. "It's time yis were back at yer wurk," he declared

"Are ye goin'?" queried Sam suspiciously.

"I've other things till do," answered his brother primly

"Aye," roared Sam, "Like fuckin' about while we git murdered."

He moved backwards angrily as Jack dragged him into the hall. Henry sat down and held his aching head.

"It'll be worse the marra," he moaned. "There's a cargo startin' in the Pollock an' I'll haveta put Jack on it an' that'll leave only four of us ta man the other sheds."

"Why don't ye give Sandy Carstairs a turn?" suggested his mother.

"That idjit," rounded Henry scornfully. I passed him this mornin' in Dock Street an' I thought he was a coolie off one of the Clan boats. His face is as black as a nigger minstrel. Besides he's nat family."

"Is he nat wurkin'?" asked the woman as she tidied away the dinner dishes.

"Naw, he slobbered at Big Ned an' missed the timber boat," said Henry.

"Does his wife know?" gasped Mrs. Harvey.

"Everybody knows except her," replied her son, writing out a horse bet with the stub of a pencil he carried in his shirt pocket.

"Ack, may Heaven forgive him," sighed Mrs. Harvey, placing a hand to the side of her face in genuine concern. "She was in McCormick's this mornin' and got a big boilin' chicken and a lega lamb on tick on the strength of his spell at the timber."

Henry laughed as he went upstairs and changed into his drinking clothes.

SIX

JIM and Kelly left the Clipper shortly after the one o'clock start. The lad continued along Garmoyle Street as Kelly turned into the London House Public Bar. Jim moved quickly past the Bunch of Grapes and decided against nipping home for a quick cup of tea as the unemployment centre closed at three-thirty and some of the other slingers had money coming to them.

Reaching Great Patrick Street, he moaned inwardly as he saw the crowd waiting outside the door of the government building. Slowing his pace he dawdled to the end of the queue.

"Hiya kid. How's it goin'?" said a man he quickly recognised as Snowy, the casual Uncle had lashed to the truck at the spud boat.

"Wurkin' away," he replied with a nod.

"I'm at the spuds wi' Uncle," snapped Snowy edgily, hopping nervously from toe to toe, "An' the big bastard say's he'll sack me if I'm late back."

Jim grinned. He was used to waiting. Waiting to sign, then waiting to be paid.

"I tole the Right Honourable Brian Faulkner about this the last time I had lunch with him an' the Governor," complained Snowy.

"What's he gonna do? Build a bigger buroo?" laughed another man. Snowy turned on him furiously. "Brian Faulkner tole me last week when I met him in Stormont Castle that he'd tole the Harbour Commisioners till git the Chapel Sheds tarmacadamed or else."

"Aye," yelled his tormentor, "an' Brookborough tole me at a poker school last night that he wus puttin' in for a red button."

The queue shuffled forward a fraction amid more laughter as Snowy shouted down his persecutors. "The red buttons are on their way out," he revealed mysteriously, "I got that from the top."

"They wudn't be missed. Shure the blues hate them an' they hate the blues n' everybody hates us," muttered a man close by.

"Mark my wurds," repeated Snowy, narrowing his eyes.

Jim took a closer inspection of the man as they moved nearer to the door. One of his legs was shorter than the other causing him to walk with an exaggerated limp. His face bore a perpetual snarl and lank dark hair hung in a donkey fringe over his left eye. Bib and brace overalls with a daily paper portruding from the breast pocket covered a khaki working shirt. A checkered cap, faded with the dust of many cargoes, clung to the side of his head.

"Has he really got money?" asked Jim of another casual. The man took his eyes from a newspaper and grinned warmly. "I'm sure he has for he's one of them foolish bein's that go inta a bank wid his wages an' come out wid nothin'." Jim laughed as the man returned to his reading.

The crowd braced as a uniformed porter who could be seen through the large glass windows stepped forward to open the doors. The men surged through like runners in a marathon heading quickly for the individual signing boxes. Jim reached his box and found himself abreast of Reilly. The little trucker seemed glad to see him.

"Toilin' along wid Kelly, I hear," he grinned.

"Aye, he's a good teacher."

"Fair enuff," agreed Reilly, "but don't fall inta his ways son. Hard drinkin' an' fightin's only for mugs."

Jim didn't answer. Twenty minutes later he was at the head of the queue. "Wurkin'," he replied to the question from the stone-faced civil servant who dug out his file.

The man pursed his lips and grunted. He produced a small slip of paper bearing Jim's signatures for the previous days. Setting them in front of the lad, he said tersely, "Sign there."

Jim obeyed and the man stamped the paper and handed it to

him without another word. He went over to the queue at the payout which was single file and stretched back to the door. He walked to the end and found Sandy standing deep in thought.

"What's happened till yer face?" he blurted quickly as he saw the man's dark brown complexion.

"Somebody blacked it up when I fell asleep in Barney's last night. Nobody tole me an' the wife near tuka heart attack when I walked up the hall. I've washed it till it 's raw but it won't come aff." He answered with a pained expression.

"Are ye wurkin'?" asked Jim, trying hard not to laugh.

"Naw. Uncle wuda tuk me but he had all his regulars an' them bastards up the coast take ye only if yer da's a docker or yer ma's a good thing," he sighed.

"Everybody else's is wurkin'," said Jim helpfully.

"Don't rub it in," groaned Sandy, "My wife thinks I'm at the Clipper."

As both men lapsed into an uncomfortable silence, Jim looked idly around the large room. Hundreds of men sat on hard wooden forms waiting their turn to sign on. Others had lost their jobs and were signing for the first time. Unlike the casuals they attended twice a week and were paid out on Fridays.

The casuals signed every day and had to produce their insurance cards with each signature. They were also responsible for seeing their first employer of the week provided them with an insurance stamp. They were paid on Tuesdays.

Sometimes there were two pay-out windows, but today, as with most days, there was only one. Some of the men cursed inwardly at the prospect of missing the first race. As they moved forward at a snail's pace Jim recognised quite a few of the men he'd worked with over the past week.

Reilly had fallen in behind him and was talking to Bob the quiet man he had worked at the potato boat with. All acknowledged him and he felt grown-up. Some of the men were covered with cement dust, others had flecks of maize meal or china clay embedded in their clothes, faces and hair. Their bantering good humour vied sharply with the jobless men who sat sad-eyed and silent.

Two bored but very attractive girls were conducting the pay-out behind a grilled cage. "Chit forty-seven, number eighty-three ... Pay fourteen and threepence," droned one, her eyes firmly fixed on the piece of paper. Her counterpart lifted coins from a pile of silver in front of her and pushed them through a slit in the grill. "Fourteen shillings and thrupence paid," she replied in the same bored tone.

Jim was four places from the front when a tall broad-shouldered man with thick grey bushy hair walked confidently to the head of the queue. Sizing the lad up, he squeezed in between him and the man in front. He looked in his middle thirties and was about six feet two inches tall and weighed about sixteen stones. His face was cratered like a dug-up street and his right hand, lying on the counter close to Jim's shoulder resembled a side of beef.

"Hi," said Jim indignantly. "This is the front of the queue."

The big man turned slowly and Jim gulped as his watery blue eyes fixed on his features. "Do you know who I am?" he asked with a growl.

He felt a dig in his ribs and looked around to see Snowy. "Say nuthin'," he whispered in the boy's ear. No one else spoke and the man was paid out. Placing the money carefully into his pocket, he turned his attention to Jim.

"If I ever see ye again ... I'll knock sixteen different colours of shit outa ye," he promised before moving off.

Jim remained silent. As he gave his chit to the sullen-faced girl he was ashamed to see his hand was shaking. He scooped up his money quickly and backed away.

He walked through the doorway and caught up with the dejected figure of Sandy. On an impulse he separated two half-crowns.

"Here," he muttered self-consciously, "have a drink on me."

"Tryin' till act Kelly nigh," sneered Sandy, taking the money grudgingly. "That was a wrong thing ye did in there," he added.

"That was Sammy Gibson," he continued, "an' yer lucky he's kind till dum' animals an' childer."

"He'd no right to ... "

Sandy interupted. "Luk son, yer in a man's world nigh. Don't git carried away because yev wurked a boat or two or boxed a roun' or two. Yer about nine stone soakin' wet. Gibson cud put ye in his arse-pocket an' suffocate ye with farts. Wise up son or people will think yer gittin' cheeky on Kelly's reputation."

Jim's face turned crimson under the verbal attack. He bent his head and muttered "Hope ye git fixed up soon," and moved off before Sandy could see the tears in his eyes.

Sandy stopped for a moment and then ran after him. He put his arm affectionately around his neck and grinned sheepishly.

"Sorry kid," he mumbled. "Yer a genuine lad an' I don't wanna see ye gittin hurt."

They plodded along in silence until they reached the London House.

Kelly did not see them enter. He was watching another man who was throwing darts at a board close to the toilet. Jim's heart almost stopped beating when he recognised the man who had threatened him at the pay-out.

He moved to the bar. "They're playin' nearest the bull for a pound a time," whispered a grizzled old timer wearing an black overcoat that stretched down to his wellington boots.

They watched as Kelly moved to the chalk line and threw a dart which landed on the other side of the wire around the bull's eye. Gibson concentrated before tossing his dart which landed an inch to the right of the bull. He passed a pound note to Kelly as both men retrieved their darts.

"Heard yer an ex-squaddie," said Gibson loudly as Kelly aimed at the board. Kelly smiled, knowing it was an effort to break his concentration. He hit the bull dead centre before answering.

"That's right," he said putting his hand out for another pound as Gibson's dart landed two inches from the target.

"What regiment?" asked Gibson as he reached the pound.

"What does it matter?" said Kelly, lining up.

"Para myself ... sergeant ... " continued Gibson.

Kelly grinned. "Super-dooper, yer a paratrooper," he mocked.

"Best outfit in the army," said Gibson proudly.

Kelly looked at him squarely with eyes that were devoid of humour. "How wud ye know?" he asked flatly.

Gibson turned away from the board and looked at Kelly's lean build. "Are ye callin' me a liar?" he said menacingly, before letting the dart fly.

Kelly stepped forward and aimed at the bull eye. He was about to throw, but paused and turned to Gibson with an amused grin. "Ye were a two year man in the Skins' an' spent most of it in the glasshouse cryin' for yer mammy. The only action ye seen was the night ye bate the hell's gates outa an oul age pensioner outside the Plaza. So don't talk ta me about soldierin' ... I wus longer in a drunken sleep." The dart left his hand in a furious flight and smashed into the dartboard almost level with Gibson's.

"I wus regimental Heavyweight champion in 1950," persisted Gibson.

"Two walk-overs an' a bye into the final," jeered Kelly.

"Wait a minit, yer outa order," snarled Gibson, moving forward menacingly.

Kelly's hand shot up and grabbed him by the shirt front.

"Wait fuck all," he snapped. "I know all about ye, but ye don't know about me ... So wrap up," he finished. Loosening his grip on Gibson's shirt slowly, he looked down at the dartboard. "They're kinda close," he mused walking away from the other man to examine the darts.

They were indistinguishable. He looked around for an impartial witness and was amused, but not surprised to see that every man's eyes had dropped to his paper or his pint. Those without either stared fixedly in front of them.

Gibson's eyes fell on Jim. "Hi big mouth," he ordered, "git up here an' judge whose dart's nearest the bull."

"Don't go son," warned the old man through pursed lips, "yer on a hidin' till nuthin'." Jim's stomach knotted with tension as Gibson lifted him from his seat and dragged him to the dartboard.

"Mine has the blue flight," he whispered.

Jim found his eyes wouldn't focus. He gazed at both darts for a moment. "I don't know," he whimpered, keeping his eyes on the darts, fearful to glance at Gibson's furious features.

He felt a hard blow to the back of his head which knocked him to the floor and drew a frightened sob from his body. He grasped the end of a table and tried to rise but his trembling legs would not support him.

Kelly's reaction was swift and brutal. Reaching down he grabbed a handful of Gibson's ample testicles and twisted them savagely. The big man gasped with pain and dropped his hands to the offended parts. Kelly leapt into the air and whipped his head forward hitting Gibson savagely on the mouth. He forgot the pain in his groin and fell to his knees as blood gushed from his ripped lips.

His opponent's right boot connected with his chin and sent him head over heels into a table knocking glasses and bottles to the floor.

The bar-room was silent as he lay still for a moment then climbed shakily to his feet and swayed drunkenly as blood spouted from his mouth and nose. Kelly dropped into a boxing crouch.

"Come an' git me champ ... " he jeered.

Gibson stayed where he was, rubbing gingerly at his bruised face. He had risen on impulse but had no heart for further combat.

Kelly dropped his hands in disgust. "I wudn't feed you," he said scathingly before moving to lift Jim off the floor.

He nodded to the barman. "Sorry Joe, but he started it."

When they left Gibson walked to the toilet. Flushing the stone coloured lavatory bowl, he scooped some water from it onto his bleeding face. He glared angrily at his swollen features in a blurred mirror, as he daubed the wounds with wet toilet paper. Examining his mouth he found two teeth being held by a sliver of gum. Bracing himself he jerked them free and threw them down the toilet bowl.

He was about to leave when an elderly man entered sheepishly. Fumbling at his fly buttons, he moved slowly towards a urinal. Feeling Gibson's eyes on him he looked up. "Tough luck, son," he muttered apologetically.

"Aye," nodded Gibson, moving forward and hitting him twice. The first blow landed on the side of his head, spinning his body to the left. The second punch crunched against his cheek-bone splitting the flesh like a surgeon's knife. He dropped without a sound, but his head hit the tiles with a thud that spilled his dentures from his gaping mouth. They settled in a deep channel filled with urine and yellowed cigarette ends. Gibson left him where he lay and strode out of the bar by the side exit.

Jim had controlled his boyish tears when they arrived at the dock gates. Sandy was about to leave them when the burly overcoated figure of Ned's second-in-command called to him.

"Are ye sober, Carstairs?" he asked. Sandy nodded. "Git away down till the number two hatch at the beg boat down at the Silo an' mate wid Matchett," he ordered.

"Thanks Bill," yelled Sandy breaking into a run.

The ganger walked through the gates with Kelly and Jim. "Maxwell was knocked inta the water by a heave. He nearly froze till death before we got him out. I've haunted them pubs for a sober man who wasn't wurkin'," he muttered.

They climbed the gangplank and stacked a heave.

"What'll Ned do when he finds Sandy's at the beg boat?" asked Jim as they waited on the hook floating to them.

"Chase him!" replied Kelly flatly, adding, "Come on now. Keep yer eye on the hook."

A drizzle of rain started to fall and brought blue smoke from the winch wires as they rolled around the barrel. Kelly allowed him to use the hand hook and select the heaves and they worked without incident until the ganger called them up at twelve minutes to midnight.

Jim went straight to his bedroom and examined the back of his head in the wardrobe mirror. There was no visible damage but he felt a large lump that was covered by his hair. He shrugged off the incident with Gibson and climbed into bed and fell into a fitful sleep. Like the previous night he was haunted by Ned's ghoulish face as he tossed and turned, dodging runaway heaves and swinging cargo hooks. He rose groggily when his mother called him the next morning. Before he left he gave her a portion of his unemployment money.

The second ganger told Ned about Sandy as they left the stevedore's office. He explained how no one else was available at the time. "There'll be plenty available nigh, so git rid of the slabber," advised Ned. Sandy was broken-hearted when the second ganger met him and gave him the bad news.

"He won't have ye at any price," added the man sadly.

Sandy understood. "Thanks anyway Bill." He was overjoyed when the man insisted on paying him the previous night's spell out of his own pocket.

"We're nat all bad bastards," he said apologetically before moving off to the schooling pen. Sandy stood a moment outside Cullen's Bar and watched as the crowds of men walked through the dock gates to the various boats.

On an impulse he turned in the direction of the Queen's Bridge and kept walking until he came to the Bakers', a licensed club that catered for nightworkers from the baking industry. He knew the fellow on the door slightly and was signed in after pressing a half-crown into the man's grateful hand. Wearily climbing the stairs, he entered the smoke-filled room which opened every morning at six and was already packed with coal dockers, carters, shipyard men and off-duty police officers. Ordering a hot whiskey and a bottle of Guinness, he found a vacant seat and unbuttoned his overcoat, feeling calmer and more relaxed than he had for days.

When Henry woke at half-past eight he was unable to rise from his bed. His body ached all over and it took a moment or two for him to remember the pain was from his tussle with Bull. He recalled doing his bet and having a few drinks in the Sportsman's Arms, but didn't remember anything else.

Looking around the room he was relieved to find he was in his own bed. "At least I'm nat in jail," he grunted as he pulled the rubber tube from below his pillow and inserted it into the whiskey bottle. He began choking and coughing as the raw liquid touched his dry throat.

He dressed in his working clothes and staggered down the stairs and into the kitchen. Despite his mother's protests, he left without breakfast and lurched off in the direction of the York Branch dock. Reaching the American Bar he stopped and rapped hopefully at the window and breathed a sigh of relief when Joe's silver head looked down at him with a quizzical stare.

He motioned with his shaking hands that a drink was needed and presently the door creaked open wide enough to admit his frame.

He emerged later feeling somewhat better with a half-bottle of whiskey sticking out of his overcoat pocket and three glasses of the same liquid settling in his stomach. He staggered over the road and into the Chapel Sheds and went straight to the checker.

"Tell them parcel a bastards I'm goin' till the Pollock till start a new cargo," he ordered. The man nodded and grinned as Henry turned on his heels.

Two lorries were already in the shed when he stumbled in. The drivers and helpers who were in the process of unloading the potatoes laughed at his condition. Henry had lost all interest. The whiskey in his empty stomach was hitting him harder than Bull had.

He gazed with heavy eyes around the shed until his glance fell on the checker. "Hi Johnny," he called to the dimunitive man with long dark hair that was plastered with brylcreem. He had a handlebar moustace and was dressed neatly in a suit and tie.

The man came forward reluctantly and Henry instantly threw his arm around his shoulder and his knees almost buckled under the weight. Henry tried to focus his eyes on the man's face. "Hol' the fort for me son, I'm gonna have a wee sleep."

Johnny nodded and helped him to the rear of the shed where a pile of loose straw and hay lay from a previous cargo. Henry dropped in a heap and stretched out as if in his own bed. Pulling the bottle from his pocket he put it to his lips and lay contentedly as Johnny obediently covered him with straw to keep the cold out. Moments later he was snoring contentedly with the bottle resting on his heaving chest.

"Is he alright?" inquired one of the drivers with a soft Derry accent.

Johnny laughed. "Him an' one of the local tough guys knocked the hell outa each other the day before yisterday. He wus just outa the hospital after being sent there by his brother."

"He'll niver change," laughed the driver as he continued to throw the sacks of potatoes into the pile. Other lorries drove into the shed and the drivers off-loaded themselves whilst Henry lay in a drunken sleep.

The checker in the Chapel Shed relayed Henry's message to Sam and Jack. When he returned to his desk Sam winked at his brother. "Right," he chortled, rubbing his hands gleefully, "That means we kin spend a few hours in the heat of the pub."

"What about the loads?" asked Jack.

"The farmers 'ill be glad till throw their own loads off. They'll think we're away till another job". replied Sam

Jack hesitated. The interior shed was bitterly cold with no heating facilities. He shuddered as he remembered the last load he had carried off earlier that morning. It had been exposed to a cloudburst of hailstones whilst awaiting inspection and the rain held in the sacks had soaked him through to his skin. He shook his head however and decided to stay in the shed.

"Suit yerself," said his brother, flashing him a grin he reserved for imbeciles. As he sauntered over to the bar Jack walked to a lorry that had just entered the shed. Rain water was dripping from the cover onto the shed floor as the young helper climbed to the top of the load and started to remove the tarpaulin. The driver released the straps holding it to the bed of the lorry and the lad rolled it to the back of the load and kicked it to the ground.

The stripped cover revealed a load of two hundred bags. Each row contained three tiers at six high with two bags on the joint making twenty bags a row. Selecting a bag, the lad held it by one lug and slipped it down the side of the load as far as his arm would stretch. Jack put his hands above his head to steady the jute bag before placing it on his shoulder. As he did so a stream of ice-cold water ran from the bottom of the sack, straight down his sleeve and into the cosy heat of the hair under his armpit. He shuddered but held the bag and tossed it deftly into the pile.

"I'm away till the toilet," he scowled.

Taking off his sodden overcoat and jacket, he placed them in front of the pub's roaring fire before ordering a hot rum. He shivered a little as he sat down beside Sam.

"Why don't ye go away home an' git them wet clothes aff ye," snorted Sam. "I tole ye nat to go near any wet loads."

"Ack, the driver wus under pressure, he'd only a slip of a wee lad wid him," said Jack.

"An' ye'll be under pressure too if ye git pleurisy an' yer aff a month or two," answered Sam reproachfully.

Jack sipped gratefully at his hot drink and remained silent.

Sam changed the subject. "Bet the big fella's gittin' it rough," he gloated. "There's a brave lot a lorries headin' in the direction of the Pollock. I hope he gits his bollocks knocked in."

Jack refused to be drawn, content to sip the hot nectar and appreciate the warmth of the bar-room.

Sam glared suspiciously as Harry entered the bar. "What's wrong wid you?" he growled as his nephew sidled up to the fire and warmed his hands gratefully.

"Wee Johnny's round from the Pollock. Big Henry's bin flaked out at the back of the shed since half-past nine this mornin' an' the piles are fallin' down all over the place," he explained, edging towards the bar.

"Right," snapped Sam immediately assuming the mantle of command. "Git you an' Andy roun' there nigh an' straighten up any piles that have fallen so the wee checker kin count them. Stay till yis rid up whatever traffic there is. Me an' Jack 'ill cover this end."

"Kin I have a quick one before I go?" asked Harry.

"Yis," grunted Sam. "Ye kin git me an' Jack one as well, an' no slopin' intil Cullens on yer way roun', ye hear?"

Harry and Andy stopped at the door of the Pollock Shed.

"It's like a bloody battlefield," gasped Andy.

The inside of the shed was packed with lorries and a long line of vehicles waited outside as well. Both men took off their overcoats knowing nothing but hard work for the next two or three hours would clear up the backlog.

At half-past six o'clock that evening the last lorry drove into the Pollock Shed and stopped at the pile where it was to be unloaded. It was carrying two hundred bags of Arran Banner ware potatoes from the townland of Kilkeel in the county of Down. On top of the load and secured by a light piece of rope was a new brass-handled coffin. The lorry was owned by a firm which also specialised in the undertaking business and the coffin was being transported back to the firm after being picked up in Belfast.

"Somebody git away?" asked Andy respectfully as a tall cadaverous man wearing a long black over coat and a flat charcoal grey cap emerged slowly from the cab.

"Aye, the local publican expired yesterday and I had to come to Belfast for that quality casket. I'll be preparing him tonight," he answered in a dry professional tone as he rubbed his hands together mournfully and looked Andy up and down.

"He's measurin' ye up," laughed the driver, carefully reaching the coffin down from the truck to the floor. When the lorry was emptied Andy grinned wickedly at Harry.

"Givus a han'," he muttered. They lifted the coffin carefully and carried it quietly to where Henry was snoring. The Kilkeel men watched as Andy quickly manufactured a makeshift shroud by cutting two arm holes and a head hole from in an empty flour sack. Taking some flour dust from the bag he slapped it onto his face and hands. Harry removed the lid from the coffin and placed it out of harms way before creeping toward the sleeping Henry and placing a noose of thin cord over the toe of his boot.

He began to giggle, but was reproached by the serious faced Andy who lay down at the side of the coffin farthest away from his uncle. Harry tugged vigorously at the string until Henry aroused and sat up. He gazed drowsily at his boot moving slowly from side to side but was unable to see the cord in the half light. Unaware of his surroundings he looked around vaguely until his eyes fell on the lidless coffin with its brass handles shining eerily in the weak glow of the shed light. A shiver of terror coursed through his body as he struggled to get to his feet.

At that moment Andy sat bolt upright and screamed like a tortured ghost. His face and hair whitened by the flour, he stretched his arms stiffly in front of him and proceeded to rise slowly. From Henry's horrified viewpoint, it seemed as if a corpse was trying to leave its last resting place.

With an ear-splitting yell as loud and as shrill as a banshee's wail, he scrambled through the straw on his hands and knees. Free from the pile he rose to his feet and sprinted through the shed doors and into the street. He didn't hear the loud burst of hilarity that emerged from the dock shed.

When he was able to stop laughing Andy lifted the discarded whiskey bottle and shared the contents among them.

Henry crashed through the doors of Cullen's Bar at the corner of Whitla Street and Garmoyle Street with a bang that caused the customers to turn in their seats. He sat down at the fire and lifted a double whiskey belonging to a luckless carter who watched with astonishment as the white-faced Henry emptied the tumbler with one gulp. He reached for another glass and a row was only averted when after a moment's composure, he rose and replaced the carter's drink.

Sandy, having been ejected from the Bakers' Club at ten in the morning, pub-crawled his way back to York Street. He had just under half the money the ganger had given him and decided to do a bet.

Entering the bookmaker's office at Dock Street he tried to study the horses but found he was in need of another drink. He plumped for three horses selected as likely winners by the *News Letter* tipster called John O'Connell.

"Ten bob treble, John O'Connell three," he mutterd to a bored clerk trapped in a pigeon hole. Moving slowly round to Paddy's Bar he kept a wary eye open for Sally. "Givus a pint an' tramp it well down," he shouted as he entered the door and draped himself on a barstool.

"Ack, it's yer worthy self, Sandy," cried the ever-cheerful barman as he moved to the barrels to pull the pint. "How'd ye git so much drink at this hour a the day? Not wurkin' in that condition are ye?" he added.

Sandy smiled drunkenly. "I've missed the boat in more ways than one. Cud ye put that on the slate?" he asked slyly as the drink was set in front of him.

"No sooner said than done," roared the owner, moving swiftly off to serve another customer. Sandy watched him with a feeling of guilt. Shrugging his shoulders helplessly, he reflected dryly. "Shure if I don't see ye through the week, I'll see ye through the windy," he chortled stupidly.

He leaned against the snug wall and sipped the pint contentedly. His eyes closed and he was about to doze when an elbow dug viciously into his ribs. His anger mellowed when he saw Sammy Gibson towering over him. "Mine's a wee one," hissed Gibson.

"Mine's not so big either," grinned Sandy.

"Set me up a half-in or I'll tear the thraple outa ye."

Sandy looked ruefully at the barman. "Cud ye set up a whiskey Paddy?" he muttered.

Gibson downed it in one go. "Same again," he called to the barman. "Me mate's buyin'"

Paddy looked at the crestfallen Sandy. "Are ye okay? I kin phone the peelers."

"Naw," replied Sandy quickly. "Keep them outa it. Give him another an' give me a coupla pies. I haven't cut corn since yisterday."

"I'll have a pie as well," shouted Gibson.

The pies were heated and placed on the bar. "Where's mine?" asked Gibson as Barney set a knife and fork beside Sandy.

The bar-owner's smile vanished. "Ye aren't gittin' any, panhandler," he said before turning abruptly and walking to the other end of the bar, his ruddy features encased in a seldom seen frown. Gibson headed to the toilet to consider his next move. Paddy returned. "Do ye know that guy?" he asked Sandy.

"Naw," replied Sandy. "He's bin down tryin till git a lie-on at the boats, but he cudn't wurk in convulsions."

"Where's he from?" asked the owner.

"Dunno," replied Sandy, "Shure the world an' his uncle comes till Sailortown till git a job at the quay. Y'know Paddy, this is the only area where ye cud git a Shankill Road man drinkin' with a Falls Road man an' ——"

"I know well enough," sighed the barman, "I had a boat loada Russian sailors in the other night and a crowd of American sailors came in behind them."

"Did they fight the cold war?" laughed Sandy.

"Naw," grinned Barney, "They had a vodka drinkin' contest an' I didn't git them out till twenty till twelve. It was as well McKinstry wasn't on that night."

Paddy moved off still laughing and Sandy tucked into his pies. As he raised his fork a lightly-built elderly man with a large bulbous nose sprayed his ear with spittle as he whispered excitedly into it. "Yiv got a winnin' bet. John O'Connell's treble is up."

Sandy looked into his vacant eyes. "How'd ye know I backed it, Dinny?" he asked curiously.

"I wus behin' ye in the queue," said the old man impatiently. "Luk," he added as Gibson came out out of the tiolet, "Yer nat gonna git rid a that hardshaw ... Do ye want me till lift it for ye?"

Sandy hesitated, then slipped Dinny the docket as Gibson decided his next move. "When ye git the money, don't give it ta me. Take two pounds for yerself an' slip the rest intil that pocket." He jabbed his overcoat pocket on the side closest to the wall he was leaning against.

The oldster touched his cap obediently and was off as quick as his legs would take him. The total winnings came to forty-eight pounds and he was obliged to wait until betting was confirmed before he was reluctantly paid out by the owner who had the reputation of being a sore loser.

"Did ye ever try walkin' on water?" he sneered as he threw the bank notes across the counter. The sarcasm was lost as the messenger lifted the money and walked quickly into the toilet.

Counting out five single pound notes he placed them in his shirt pocket which nestled below two pullovers and a waistcoat. A further two pounds he placed in his hip pocket and soon the bulk of the money was burning a hole in Sandy's coat.

Gibson had finished another pint and tapped the empty tumbler meaningfully. Sandy adjusted his overcoat and stood up.

"That's me credit finished, mate," he said apologetically, walking gloomily out of the side door.

Gibson took one look at the unsympathetic Paddy and strode out behind Carstairs almost knocking him down.

Sandy stopped at the pub corner and watched Gibson walk off in the direction of the railway station. When he disappeared from sight the happy casual took the wad of notes from his pocket and danced into the bar.

"Give everybody their pleasure," he roared to the astonished barman. "Whatever they want, an' take what I owe ye," he continued happily counting out ten single notes and placing them on the bar-top.

Paddy looked disbelievingly at the money. "Are ye sure nigh?" he asked uncertainly.

"Yis," beamed Sandy, "and don't fergit one fer yerself."

Paddy set up each man's order, and Sandy, overjoyed at his luck promptly ordered another for everyone.

"Yer nat on," said Paddy evenly. "There's fellas there drinkin' doubles a whiskey who niver bought a single in their lives. Some of them had the cheek till ask for cigarettes as well. Here's yer change, nigh take my advice an' go home till yer wee woman with what yiv got left. It's comin close till Christmas an' it'll come in handy," advised the friendly barman.

"Aye," agreed Sandy. "I'll go home this minute." He held out his hand and the barman solemnly shook it. "Yer a grate man Paddy, there's nat enuff talk about ye," he concluded before walking shakily up the street.

Reaching the Stalingrad, he was unable to resist the urge for another drink. "Give everybody their pleasure," he roared as he fell throught the doors and into the public bar. Space was quickly made for him as he produced his money to back up his words.

"Everybody?" queried the barman.

"The lot," roared Sandy as the resident ladies descended on him like pigeons on an open-topped grain lorry. Diamond Lil cooed in his ear, whilst viciously kicking the Duchess who was

217

trying to rifle his pockets. Soon every table was littered with glasses of spirits as the wily old waiter fulfilled Sandy's orders to the last detail. Those unable to drink anymore were supplied with a double packet of their favourite cigarettes.

Sandy was the centre of attraction and enjoyed every moment. A persistent seaman persuaded him to buy three gold watches which he promptly gave to the ladies. They showered him with kisses and later sold them back to the sailor.

He lifted a tumbler filled with whiskey and tried to guide it to his mouth whilst Diamond kissed his cheek and the Dutchess fondled him under the table. Through a drunken haze he saw Billy Kelly standing over him grinning.

"Billy ... Billy ... " he yelled in genuine delight. He rose unsteadily to embrace the slender docker. "C'mon ... C'mon," he roared impatiently at the barman. "A glass a Black Bush fer my frien' Billy Kelly."

"Fergit it," said Kelly to the barman, "an' no more for you," he said tersely. "Yer goin' home with whatever yiv got left," he added.

Word had spread of Sandy's win. Kelly had heard it whilst lazing on a break in Barney's. Gibson had also been informed and entered the bar brashly, but slowed down when he saw Kelly look questioningly in his direction.

He decided to bluff it out. "I went halfers on that bet?" he stated. Kelly ignored him as he guided the hapless Sandy out.

Gibson squared his feet menacingly. Kelly noticed the threatening stance and set Sandy on a chair.

"Did ye not git enuff the day?" he asked bluntly.

"I wus drunk the day," said Gibson defiantly.

Kelly shook his head sadly. "Drunk or sober son," he explained patiently, "Ye just can't fight."

"Will ye fight me clean?" stuttered Gibson. "Will ye box me?"

"No fightin' in here Billy," pleaded the barman, "I've just restocked the tumblers after yer last episode."

"That's okay, we'll take it outside," replied Kelly calmly. The pub emptied as the men stepped out into the twilight.

218

They moved under a solitary lamp standard and were bathed in its blue glare. Kelly removed his jacket and cap and spat grimly on his hands. He looked balefully at his opponent who outweighed him by about three stones.

"Napper," he called to the shipyardman lolling against the lamp-post. "You're the referee. First man to use anything other than his fists, turn the crowd on him."

"Aye," replied Napper grimly.

Gibson removed his jacket and rolled up his shirt sleeves before beckoning his readiness. They circled warily in the spluttering light. Gibson had his two hands held high, defending his head and jaw, whilst Kelly moved almost lazily, holding his right fist close to his temple and his left hand casually extended waist high in front of his body.

His was the first punch as they closed. A sizzling straight left which struck at Gibson's head with the speed of a snake and missed by a whisker.

"That wus a good 'un," acknowledged Gibson, playing to the crowd.

"Here's a better one," grunted Kelly stepping forward and placing all his weight behind a short right jab which sunk into his opponent's body just below the breast bone. He watched as Gibson's eyes glazed with pain and moved quickly aside as the man's lips burst open and a stream of vomit cascaded from his mouth.

Still conscious, he collapsed without a sound and gazed up in astonishment at Kelly, who resisted the urge to finish it with his boots.

"Count him out, Napper," he said before turning on his heels and striding into the bar. The crowd followed, back-slapping and roaring their approval.

Sandy's wife had entered the bar by the front door accompanied by Henry Harvey's youngest sister. She had heard of his win and was vainly trying to raise his limp body from the chair he had collapsed into. Unable to waken him she searched his pockets and cried with frustration when she found four half-crowns and seven pennies.

She had heard about the watches and approached the two prostitutes who sat staring stonily into the fire.

"Know fuck all about it," snarled Diamond as Sally tearfully confronted her. Sally's frustration turned to anger and she lifted a pint and slashed its contents into Diamond's face. The force of the deluge tore her false eyelashes from their moorings and sent them rippling under the table.

Lil rose with a howl of fury and grabbed Sally's thin hair. The men roared in appreciation as both women fell gouging and scratching to the floor. Kelly grinned silently as a sailor quietly pulled the telephone wire from its housing. "This is too good to spoil," he chuckled.

The Duchess joined in the fray by leaping onto Sally's unprotected back. Jean Harvey raced forward and threw a neck lock around the woman's scrawny throat. Pulling her from Sally's back she waited until the prostitute rose to her feet before she started raining punches on her head. In desperation, she grabbed a handful of Jean's emerald green smock which was fastened up the front by large green buttons. The inevitable happened and the bar held its collective breath, as two magnificent breasts, a taut belly with a tantalising whisp of body hair and a pair of massive but shapely thighs were exposed to the appreciative audience. Wolf whistles rent the air as Jean wrapped the buttonless smock around her exposed body and knocked the Duchess senseless with a blow to the chin, before running out the door weeping with embarrassment. Sally disposed of Diamond with a bottle across the head, and stood over her she screamed at the top of her voice.

"Someday the decent wimmin in this area are gonna see youse poxy bastards for what for what yis are and kick yis intil the dock. Although yis 'ud probably contaminate whatever fish there is in it." She turned to the men. "What do yis see in these washed-out oul bags a shit," she screamed. They watched passively as she turned her attention to Sandy. "If I thought ye had anythin' till do with hoores I'd geld ye," she snapped slapping him until he took to his heels and ran into the street.

Jim Harvey entered the bar as Sally left holding her head high. The Duchess remained dazed, sitting on her rump on the drink-stained floor. Her dress had ridden to her waist revealing pink cami-knickers which bit into her fleshy thighs. She sat in a pool of spilt drink and urine and gazed stupidly at the senseless body of Diamond Lil lying across the front door.

Kelly looked at Jim with a distant grin. "Is that aunt of yours married?" he asked.

"Yis," replied Jim.

"That's a shame," said Kelly wistfully. "She's some looker!"

He groaned as Gibson re-entered the bar and walked shakily towards him. His face was the colour of chalk. Someone had wiped the vomit from his face but his shirt was caked with blood.

"Cud ye do that again?" he shouted hysterically.

"Go on home whilst ye kin still walk!" advised Kelly.

"It wus a lucky punch—I want a return," he screamed.

"I'm gettin' the peelers," yelled the barman, "This is a pub, not a boxin' ring."

Gibson ignored him. "Outside big man ... Outside. Round two ... You an' me ... Step out. Step out an' I'll take ye apart," he continued, backing through the front doors and into the main street. Waiting for Kelly to follow he continued to move backwards onto the road and was knocked into the air by a car whose driver had spent the previous four hours in Pat's Bar. He drove on singing along with his radio as Gibson rolled in agony with two broken legs and a fractured spleen. A passing police officer heard his moans and cautiously entered the Stalingrad to use the telephone to call an ambulance.

The barman produced the hand-set with the torn out wires. "It's broken," he said apologetically.

Henry Harvey rose early, his night's sleep ruined by horrific dreams of corpses and coffins and blood-spattered furniture. Lighting his tenth Woodbine with shaking hands he walked listlessly down the stairs and into the yard. He was heartily sick of the constant bickering and fighting, but worse than that, a few men in Cullen's had told him Bull Murphy was looking for him.

Although not afraid of Murphy, he saw no use in premediated violence and decided to get out of town for a while. Under circumstances such as this he generally went to Liverpool with his friend Captain Sweet, a Cornishman who owned the flour boat that berthed once a week at the Clarendon Dock. He made the trip twice a year and stayed with friends of Sweet until he or his money was exhausted.

Finding a new hiding place for his waterproof envelope he visited the potato sheds making sure every carrier was at his post. He exchanged small talk with the workers but made no mention of the coffin firmly believing it to be a part of a horrible nightmare brought on by too much alcohol. Leaving the last shed, he entered the American Bar by an unlocked side door and enjoyed two hot whiskeys which put the glow back into his cheeks and dulled the pain in his stomach.

At half-past ten he went to the Stevedore's office and had his paybook stamped for the week. He received a white pay card for every man working for him and plodded along Corporation Street to the Central Wages Office at the corner of Great George's Street and Corporation Street.

Exchanging the white cards for pay envelopes he went straight to his bedroom and locked the door. Opening the packets he took money from each one and put it into fresh envelopes he lifted from his bedroom cabinet. He then wrote the worker's name and the amount he had put in the envelope on it before sealing it. He had marked considerably more into Sam's original envelope. This was because his eldest brother had many children and paid no income tax. Taking another new envelope he wrote Sam's name and insurance number on it and put a generous amount into it, before sealing it. He was tiring of Sam's arguments and hoped the extra cash would keep him quiet. Three original envelopes bearing fictitious names were locked in the bedroom cabinet and the rest of the money was placed in his cap.

He looked again at Sam's bulky envelope. "Maybe that'll make the cryin' bastard laugh," he thought mirthlessly before descending the stairs.

He was seated at the dinner table when Sam and Jack entered at lunchtime. Mrs. Harvey had ladled out the dinner before moving to the comparative safety of the sofa. Sam said nothing as Henry slipped him an envelope beneath the table. He signed a treaty with his eyes as he stuffed the money into his pocket.

The cap was placed in the middle of the table and Henry was about to divide up the contents when Jim Harvey arrived. He stood quietly until Henry looked at him quizzically.

"I've come for me wages, Uncle Henry," said the boy.

Henry grunted and searched his pocket. "That's good money boy," he grunted, throwing the envelope across the table.

There was silence as Jim opened the envelope and counted the money. His young face was pale and hurt. "Shud there not be more than that?" he asked quietly

Henry stared at his dinner. "I pay ye what I think yer worth," he stated flatly, adding, "That's a good wage for a sixteen year oul boy."

Jim was incensed. "Shure I made most of that at the cement. Yer only payin' me buttons."

Henry flung his dinner across the table and glared at his mother. "See what I mane?" he snarled, "Another sea-lawyer, as if I hadn't enuff to contend with. There's many a man on the buroo would be content to be wurkin' for them buttons as ye call them. An' don't fergit the tips ye git. Some fella's 'ud wurk for the tips alone"

"Who asked ye ta wurk wid us anyway?" shouted Sam savagely. "If ye don't like it ye kin always sign on as a doffer in the mill."

Jim felt tears of frustration and bitterness fill his eyes. He turned blindly and ran from the room. Henry rounded on his mother as the front door slammed. "There's gratitude for ye. Two or three days on the quay an' he wants till run the place. Yid better let him an' Aggie know if he wants till stay wid me, he'll take what I give him. He's only an apprentice ... A pup ... An' ye don't give a pup a man's wages."

Jack and Sam nodded wholeheartedly. The rest of the money was divided without the usual rancour. Andy and Harry called a few moments later and took their envelopes without any comment.

Jim Harvey returned to the timber boat sullen and withdrawn.

Kelly sensed it was a family matter and didn't press for an explanation. During the supper break at six o'clock he accompanied Kelly as he visited the numerous pubs in the area paying off the drink-debts he had accumulated over the past week. Jim said little during the journey but his anger began to recede as he realised the money he had received was a lot more than many men with families to provide for had lifted that week.

He almost blurted out the problem to Kelly. He had grown to like the unpredictable docker but knew the problem was between him and his Uncle Henry.

He worked automatically, paying little attention to his torn hands and sweating body. He was glad when the mid-evening break came about half-past eight. A cold wind tugged at their scarves and overcoats as they walked down the gangplank. The heat in Barney's was warm and comforting as they set down to meat pies and coffee laced with rum.

"We'll haveta take it easy Jim," said Kelly, worried at the lad's mood. If that frost persists it'll stop all potato movements. There'll be no wurk elsewhere an' Big Ned'll have all the men he wants, so he'll be settlin' a few scores by findin' excuses ta pay off anyone who doesn't toe the line. An' ta make matters worse," he added, leaning across the table and looking into the young man's eyes, "there'll be red button men outa wurk who'll come down an' claim the jobs of the non-union men."

Jim felt betrayed. "Can they do that?" he asked bitterly.

Kelly nodded tiredly. "It's the system ... They're second preference an' if they turn up at the boat before a quarter-past eight tomorrow morning Ned'll haveta put them in a job an' pay off Arabs. It's as simple as that," he finished softly.

"Ye were right when ye said this was no place to be," muttered the lad grimly. "I'd be as well gittin' a job in the mill or a timber yard, at least I'd be treated like a human being."

"Kid," whispered Kelly seriously. "There's only two things ye kin do about it. Ye kin swim above it or sink under it, because there's no way ye kin change it, savvy?"

The bar had begun to pack up as they rose from the table and buttoned their overcoats. Jim pondered his future as they walked silently through the darkness towards the lights of the Blackpool Clipper. Kelly had marked his cards. Ned didn't need him and Henry could do without him. His mood changed as he fingered the money in his pocket. Better half a loaf, he figured, than no bread at all.

The following morning he rose, bitter, strong and resentful. He refused to feel the pain as he washed his face with his bruised and calloused hands. True to Kelly's prophecy, six red button men arrived at the boat looking a start. Ned reluctantly fired the man with the bruised foot along with his mate. They left without rancour as the second preference took their places and Ned moved off with the remainder of the reds to put them in another hatch.

Jim knuckled down striving to look competent and resourceful and praying he wouldn't be selected to be replaced.

The decision of the Ministry of Agriculture for Northern Ireland to place a ban on the movement of all potato shipments until the Arctic conditions lifted, helped Henry decide about Liverpool.

Informing no one except his mother about his plans he

arranged to board the S.S. Normanby Hall the following night and travel to Liverpool in the company of Captain Sweet. The carriers would be working every other day as the stevedores would not pay full rates during this time. Only the checkers would be fully employed, staying with the heavily strawed cargoes until the night watchman relieved them at five o'clock in the evening.

Henry decided to make a day of it before he sailed. Dressed in a navy double-breasted pinstripe suit with a flashy hand-painted tie at his throat he ambled quietly into the bar of the Stalingrad. Picking a table away from the crowd he sat down with a newspaper and a drink, keeping one eye on the door in case Bull showed up.

He looked to the bar and saw Stanley Case, a taxi-driver studying a racing paper. "Nat toilin' today?" asked Henry.

Stanley took a Park Drive from between his lips and placed it in an ashtray before answering. "Not much happenin'."

Henry looked to another table where a group of old men sat nursing half-empty pints. He rose and walked over to them.

"Fancy a trip along the coast road boys?" he asked.

The men nodded in excited agreement. Henry walked over to Stanley. "Get the hack, Stan," he said, "yer hired for the day."

As the car pulled out into York Street and headed countrywards the old men all seated in the back began singing and clapping their hands like children embarking on a Sunday school trip.

Henry ordered the taxi man to stop when he noticed a forlorn Sandy Carstairs huddling in the doorway of the Gibraltar. Stanley jumped out and opened the door as Henry left the car like royalty. He pulled a ten shilling note from his pocket and gave it to Carstairs. "Away and git yerself drunk ye silly oul fool ye," snorted Henry before returning to the cab. Sandy stared numbly at the note before slipping it quickly into an inner pocket.

Sandy had steered clear of the Stalingrad since the horseracing catastrophe. His wife had forgiven him everything except the wrist-watch presentation to the prostitutes. She was not originally from York Street and could not understand how the local women tolerated them in their midst. She was aware that few of the local men entertained them and most of their custom came from the foreign seamen that infested the pub. She told Sandy he should hang his head in shame for destroying the money that would have given them a happy Christmas. He held back tears as these thoughts passed through his mixed-up mind. Shuffling into the warmth and friendliness of the Gibraltar Bar he climbed gratefully onto a bar-stool.

"Givus a big hot wine an' a Monk, missus," he called to the grey-haired lady owner who was still trying to get over the trauma of the madman who had rode into the bar on a motor cycle.

The wine came up steaming and he rubbed his hands around the hot tumbler in an effort to warm them. As he sipped slowly, he listened appreciatively as two men began singing a soft lullaby in close harmony. The patrons remained silent until the singers finished to a ripple of applause.

Ordering another drink he waited for a break in the singing and tiptoed to the toilet. Standing at the urinal deep in thought, he paid no attention to the bulky figure that entered the dimly-lit lavatory and stood at the next urinal. A damp feeling in his left trouser leg caused him to turn indignantly to the man beside him.

"Stop pissin' down my leg!" he started to shout, but tailed off to a frightened whisper when he looked into the features of Red Ennis, who continued to urinate freely against his thigh.

Sandy looked fearfully for an escape route but there was none. Even if he bawled his head off no one one hear him above the voices of the singers. He rushed to the door, but Ennis moving with surprising agility blocked him.

"Well ... Well," he leered, "here's the man who twists on twenty."

"Billy offered ye yer money back," wailed Sandy defensively.

"Kelly didn't lose it," came the sinister reply that made Sandy's blood crawl as Ennis tightened the grip on his throat.

"Where's my fiver?" he snarled as Sandy gasped for breath.

"Where wud I git a fiver?" he stammered.

"Then I'll just haveta take it in instalments," growled his tormentor bringing his knee up into Sandy's crotch with a force that brought tears to his eyes. He sagged at the knees but Ennis held him upright and leaned forward as if to caress him. Sandy braced himself as Red's teeth closed over the lobe of his ear, but the lorry-driver released it after licking it playfully with his warm and wet tongue.

Relaxing his grip on Sandy's throat he slapped him viciously about the head before tossing him like a bundle of dirty washing into a darkened corner of the toilet.

"Next time I see ye have my fiver or I'll bite yer ears off an' shove 'em up yer arse," he growled. Despite the terrible odour Sandy remained where he was panting with fear. Some time later he rose slowly and limped from the toilet into the side street. Ennis' howls of laughter drowned the voices of the singers as he relayed the episode to his companions in the bar.

Kelly gazed at Jim's morose features as they relaxed on an afternoon break in Barney's. The lad had drank virtually nothing from his tumbler which he now and again twirled vaguely with his fingers as his eyes stared absently into space.

"Why don't ye take the night off?" suggested Kelly.

Jim was immediately interested. "Kin ye do that?" he asked. His hands were calloused and he dearly wanted a break from the hard repetitive work that left him with time only to sleep.

Kelly smiled. "There's any amount of guys who'll stan' in for ye for a night if yer prepared to pay 'em the spell."

"That wud be great," grinned the lad. "But regardin' the dough ... "

"I'm gonna do a bit a chasin' meself the night so I'll arrange for two good men to replace us. I'll pay 'em an' ye kin square me up later," he said with a wink.

"That's great," beamed Jim feeling better.

"The deck cargo's almost cleared so we'll be in the hatch the marra. It'll give us a bit a shelter from the wind an' the rain," continued Kelly. He phoned the Sportsman's Arms for two stand-ins. They returned to the ship and worked until half-past five when they were relieved for the night.

"Don't be gittin' drunk an' sleepin' in!" was Kelly's last word as they parted at Jim's corner. Continuing into Nelson Street he stopped on an impulse at Sandy's door.

Walking the long dark hall he knocked at the door before entering into the kitchen. Sally Carstairs sat on a well-worn leather sofa with her thin legs tucked underneath her. Her knitting needles stopped clicking as she looked up first in surprise then in pleasure as she saw Kelly framed in the doorway.

"Is he home yit?" he grinned taking off his cap and squashing it into his pocket.

She dropped her head sadly. "Haven't seen him all day. He's bin out since the crack a dawn without a bite in 'im, Billy," she sobbed, "I cud forgive him anythin', but buyin' watches for them whores has tore the heart outa me every time I think of it."

Kelly sat down and held her hand. "Sally," he said solemnly, "When are youse wimmin gonna learn that guys like us aren't worth two dee? Where else wud ye git grown men drinkin' an' fightin' an' makin' public spectacles outa themselves? An' we'll niver change Sally ... 'cause we're too oul an' too stupid an' too set in our ways an' besides, there's somethin' in the air outside that door that turns us inta savage thoughtless bastards." He sighed heavily. "Ack, Sally wudn't it be grate if we didn't haveta go out the bloody door an' down till that slave market till sell our flesh till any bidder. Us men go till the corner, and the likes a Diamond till the Stalingrad till be pawed over the Yanks."

He released her hand and rose abruptly. "But I'm nat here till

229

make speeches." He burrowed in his trouser pocket and produced a five pound note. "Here," he continued, "I borrowed that from yer man when he touched for his bet. Wud ye give it till him for me?"

She knew he was lying and wept at his decency. "Deed I won't give it till him," she cried, "It'll pay for the chicken and roast I ordered for Christmas when he tole me he was at the Clipper."

"Where's the childer?" he asked reaching in his pocket for change. "They're at the children's Christmas party roun' at Maguire's Mission Hall in Great George's Street," she said, her thin worn out features creased in a nostalgic smile. "Member we used till go Billy? They showed us an oul film, give us a cup a tea an' a bag a sticky buns ... Sore heads we used till call them—an' we were so ungrateful we used to throw them at the man who showed the pictures."

"Aye," interupted Kelly "an' don't fergit the wee bag a apples an' oranges an' the wee silver sixpence we got on the way out."

She sighed and looked at the five pound note crumpled on her lap. "Hand-outs Billy—that's the story of our lives," she murmured.

"I'll luk out fer him," said Kelly tenderly. He walked respectfully to the mantlepiece. "There's a few bob for the kids," he muttered, adding, "Goodnight, Sally."

Outside he donned his cap with a tired tug and walked grimly along the unlit street. He gazed at the clear night sky and wondered who'd be giving out handouts to his wife and child.

Henry Harvey, some sixty miles away in the Country Antrim town of Portrush had no such problems. He was seated along with the taxi-driver and the group of old men in the spacious dining room of a luxurious hotel close to the seafront.

The old fellows were in buoyant mood. Having shifted all the drink they could handle, they were now tucking into a five course meal and enjoying every mouth-watering moment of it. They

230

chatted among themselves and took little or no notice when their benefactor rose and said he was going to the toilet. Had they been less relaxed and more observant, they would have seen his covert glance in the direction of the taxi-driver who also rose and left the room.

Minutes later, the driver sat at the wheel of his car with Henry beside him. "Yer jokin'?" he gasped. "Yer gonna drive off an' leave them poor ould devils here in Portrush? Shure they haven't a penny between them."

"I know," said Harvey gleefully. "I left the price of the meal and their bus fare home with the head waiter, but I tole him not till tell them till the last minit. They wanted a day till remember an' they've got it." His tone changed as he glanced at his watch. "C'mon get her movin', I'll need to be at the Flour Shed before Captain Sweet sails."

The driver looked at him for a moment in baffled silence before starting the car and moving off in the direction of Belfast.

On the Ballymoney Road Henry spotted a lorry loaded with potatoes heading towards them. He told the taxi-driver to stop and ran towards the lorry and flagged it down. Despite his well-dressed appearance, the driver recognised him and stopped. Henry jumped onto the running board.

"What's wrong yer havin' to take 'em home again, Brendan?" he asked. The driver pulled a long face. "The inspection shed's closed, so I'll haveta take 'em back when the frost lifts," he said glumly.

"What cargo are they for?" asked Henry with narrowed eyes.

"The one yer settin' down in the Pollock," replied Brendan.

"Are they yer own taties?"

"Aye."

"Okay," snapped Henry. "Have ye twenty pounds on ye?"

"I have me cheque book," answered the puzzled driver.

"Right," commanded Henry, pulling out his pencil stub. "Givus the dockets ... I'll keep the one that shuda got the Ministry stamp and conveniently lose it. You hold the one with my signature an' as far as yer concerned this load was dropped in my shed yisterday."

"Fair enuff," grinned Brendan. He drove happily off minutes later as Henry entered the taxi twenty pounds richer.

"Drop me off at my ma's house till I git a bag packed, Stanley," he said, "Git a pint an' come back for me."

He groaned when he opened the kitchen door and saw the house was filled with his female relatives.

"I'll soon haveta book a bloody seat in my own house," he snarled, making for the back door and ignoring the catcalls that followed him. "I'm goin' till Liverpool the night for a while ma. Will ye pack me a bag an' make me somethin' till ate?" he called before going out to the yard and stripping down for a wash.

The old woman rose and walked stiff-legged to the stove. "I'll haveta go till Maggie McGaw's till git some eggs," she said, more to herself than anyone else, as she lifted a slice of raw steak and put it in the frying pan.

The moment she left the room the eldest daughter lifted the steak and pushed it up under her skirt. The others roared with muffled glee as she rubbed it vigorously between her thighs before tossing it to the youngest girl who rose with a grin and stuffed it into her knickers. She walked around the room with an exaggerated limp until she heard her mother coming up the hall. She drew the steak out and threw it on the pan just as her mother opened the door. Mrs. Harvey glared suspiciously at her daughters before cracking the eggs into the pan. The gas ignited with a bang and a frightened cockroach scurried from under the grill. She lifted it and threw it into the fire.

Henry returned to the room and sat down to his meal. The girls giggled uncontrollably as he tucked hungrily into his steak and eggs. "Silly bastards," he muttered.

The taxi was punctual. "Pull over till the Rotterdam Bar till I git a cheque cashed," instructed Henry as they approached the flour shed.

SEVEN

AFTER picking at his supper Jim rose and washed himself in an effort to fight off the fatigue that threatened to put him to sleep. His childish features were scorched by the wind and rain during his time on the deck cargo and no amount of scrubbing would remove the syrupy substance that weeped from the timber and clung to his hands.

He dressed quickly and joined his friends who were waiting at the street corner. After a moment or two of horseplay they crossed the road and waited at a trolley-bus stop until one for the Shore Road arrived. They climbed noisily aboard ignoring the pointed glance of the conductor. "Behave yerselves!" he ordered as he collected their fares.

Jim fell asleep on his seat and has to be shaken when the bus stopped outside the Times Bar on York Road. They all piled into the lounge bar and began drinking whiskey and chasers in an effort to emulate their elders.

"There's a dance in the North," said his pal John, "fancy goin' up later?"

"Aye," replied Jim sinking a pint greedily in an effort to quench the thirst that had stayed with him since his first day at the cement boat. He was finding it hard to keep his eyes open as the alcohol invaded his weary system.

Later in the dancehall he downed the best part of a smuggled-in bottle of cream sherry. After combing his hair and adjusting his tie he made his way into the ballroom. The heat of the dancehall hit him immediately and caused him to stagger.

233

Grabbing the girl nearest to him and ignoring her protests, he dragged her onto the dance floor. When the music finished she broke away from his limp grip and disappeared into the crowd.

He staggered off the floor and bumped into Maureen, who had come to help him. Rolling slightly, he grabbed at her wrist. "Let's dance," he slurred, trying to drag her onto the floor. She cringed with embarrassment. "Wait until the music starts ... " she implored, desperately trying to lead him to a seat.

As he stared tiredly at her he realised he was behaving badly. He tried to hold her tenderly but the alcohol in his system caused his hand to slip from her shoulder and onto her breast. Before he could find the words to apologise he was pulled roughly away by another young man.

"Leave her alone," he ordered in a voice that contained a nervous tremor.

"Fuck aff mate, or my boots 'ill play tennis with yer balls," he scowled angrily. He could have cut off his tongue when he saw Maureen hang her head in embarrassment.

Her saviour smiled grimly. "Empty vessels make the most noise," he observed, "What about you an' me outside?"

Jim was flabbergasted at the affrontery of this insult. He eyed the slightly built lad with undisguised scorn.

"Ye wudn't wake me if I wus sleepin'," he snarled, throwing a punch that took him off balance and caused him to fall. In an instant his colleagues surrounded the other man and grabbed him roughly.

"Please don't hurt him," wailed Maureen. "Don't hurt my brother." Harvey found the room was spinning violently as he tried to haul himself to his feet. "Let him be," he roared. He put his hands out in a friendly gesture to Maureen who pushed him from her.

"Suit yerself," he snapped, walking away.

Her brother put a comforting arm around her. "Yer better off away from that drunken ignoramus," he whispered.

"How could anyone be so horrible, David?" she cried, wiping

her tears with a dainty handkerchief laced with red roses. She watched sadly as Jim forced his way through the crowd pushing people out of his path. Getting as far away from her as he possibly could he sat indignantly down on a straight-backed chair and promptly fell asleep.

The music began to play and Maureen's brother danced with her to comfort her. As they waltzed to the other end of the room she saw him, mouth agape, snoring loudly with his hands clenched in fists across his chest. The small pretty girl with long dark hair whom she had watched him jiving with the night they met was gently holding a wet cloth to his forehead.

Kelly allowed Soldier to pull him vigorously until they reached the white-washed cottages at the foot of the Cavehill Road. He slipped the chain from its neck and as the powerful bull terrier surged up the steep gravel hill, he sprinted along behind it.

More than once his heavy leather-soled boots slipped on the pebbles as he pushed himself relentlessly until he and the dog reached the summit.

He sat down beside the dog who was nuzzling the damp grass and looked at the bright lights that twinkled all over Belfast city and beyond. Regaining his breath, he glanced at his watch.

"Must be gittin' oul Soldier," he grunted, "Tuk us an extra minute." The dog licked his hand affectionately as he rubbed it briskly.

Rising slowly, he looked at the winding path that led to the foot of the hill. "Let's go," he roared, pulling his cap firmly onto his head.

Arriving home he spoke to his father who was huddled in an armchair with a copy of the *Belfast Telegraph*. He didn't expect an answer and got none. The old man had not spoken to him since the day he was suspended from the dockers' union. Smiling tightly to himself he went to the scullery and watered and fed the dog before pulling some clean underwear from the overhead pulley lines and dropping them into a bag.

"I'm goin' to Peter's Hill for a bath, do ye want anything brought in?"

A puff of grey pipe smoke rose in a cloud over the newspaper as his father leaned forward, and taking deliberate aim, spat into the heart of the fire. The paper rattled as he settled back in the armchair. Pausing only to collect his shaving gear, Billy left without another word.

He made his way to North Queen Street and up Peter's Hill to the site of the Public Baths. Paying for his ticket he climbed the stairs and entered a steam-covered room where he searched for a chair. There was quite a crowd already there waiting their turn. He could easily have washed in the small scullery of his home but every Friday he preferred the luxury of a soak in one the private bathrooms in the building. The constant toil of the timber boat and the long run with the dog had left him grimy with stale perspiration.

"Heard ye broke Gibson's two legs the other night Billy," called an old docker from two rows behind him.

"Not me," grinned Kelly, "Some guy in a motor car ran over him."

"Did he not stop?" continued the man.

"Dunno," replied Kelly.

"So he'll niver know the service he did till the community putin' that big bastard outa action," called another man who was reading a daily paper. "It'll be a long time before he bates up another oul age pensioner," he finished, grinning with gratitude at Kelly.

Another man stood up and called across the room. "Did ye hear about that other cowboy from the Eastend givin' oul Sandy a sore pair a clappers?"

"When did that happen, Fred?" asked Kelly

"Supposed to be in the Gib earlier the day. He's another bastard needs a pin in his nose," scowled Fred

Before Kelly could answer his turn came and he went to his cubicle. Stripping, he settled gratefully into the warm water and began scrubbing vigorously at his body. He had just time for a moment's relaxation when the attendant hammered noisily at the room door. Climbing reluctantly from the bath he shaved and combed his hair in the misty reflection of a tarnished mirror hanging on the wall, before dressing and heading for home.

After a hasty supper he made his way to the White Lion Bar at the corner of York Street and Henry Street. The bar had an upstairs lounge which operated a sing-song at the weekends. The talent was excellent and the proceeding were kept in order by a master of ceremonies who mixed good humour with no nonsense.

Kelly attended in the vague hope of seeing Minnie. He'd been ashamed at the way he left her the night they had been together and wanted to make amends. He'd thought quite a bit about her since their meeting and had enjoyed her company very much. He had declined calling at the house in case he embarrassed her.

Climbing the stairs he opened the lounge door during a lull in the singing and found a space at the crowded bar. He ordered a Black Bush and a Guinness and edged onto a barstool as the chairman called order for the next singer.

"An' now ladies an' gentlemen, flown all the way from Gallaher's Tobacco factory in the heart of Belfast, I ast ye to put yer hands together for Miss Minnie Renwick, a young lady with a beautiful voice who needs no introduction whatever."

The accordion player ran his fingers appreciatively along the keys as Minnie rose from a table surrounded by young women.

"She says she will," roared the MC before sitting down heavily and taking a large swig of porter. Minnie stopped beside the musican and whispered her choice of song in his ear. Climbing onto the rostrum, she looked out into the crowd and blushed when she saw Billy Kelly. Her smile disappeared and she became subdued, almost embarrassed.

With her eyes glued to the floor, she waited nervously as the accordionist led her gently into the song.

See the pyramids along the Nile,
Watch the sunrise on a tropic Isle,
Just remember darling all the while,
You belong to me.

Her voice was sweet and melodious, and although soft, it reached every corner of the room. As she finished to thunderous applause she lifted her eyes and searched for Kelly's face and found him to be handsomer than she'd remembered.

"No doubt, no doubt. With a wee bita coaxin' I'm sure the same singer will oblige," yelled the chairman when the din had subsided. She called out another tune to the musician who nodded his knowledge of the air. As she sang again to the appreciative audience she looked closely at Kelly who was grinning broadly at her.

He was wearing a Harris tweed sports jacket and a pair of tan coloured trousers and dark brown brogues. The collar of his white shirt was out over the collar of his coat and accentuated his tan caused by the wind and weather.

When she finished he gave her a quizzical nod and she crossed the room to wolf whistles and cat-calls from her company.

"Didn't expect till see ye again," she said softly, looking into his eyes for any sign of guilt.

"Oh," he replied with a grin that showed clean even teeth.

"Yis," she answered with a bitter tone in her voice. "When ye skedaddled in the middle of the night I tuk ye ta be a hit an' run merchant. Hit an' run's right," she mused almost to herself, "I don't remember nuthin' after we left the Harvey house."

"Don't ye remember singin' for me?" he teased.

"That wusn't all I did for ye," she scolded bitterly. "By the way," she continued, "I foun' two pounds lyin' on our floor on Sunday mornin', an' I hope it wasn't for services rendered."

She was hushed by the drinkers as another singer took to the rostrum after a great introduction by the silver-tongued chairman. The break gave Kelly time to think. "So that's where it went," he whispered, "I thought I'd lost it in the raid on oul Sadie's house. I'll have it now," he added with a prim smile, putting his hand out palm upwards.

"No chance," she grinned, warming to his company. "I bought this blouse with it. Put it down to a gift in honour of my beauty and my company."

"C'mon git yer coat an' we'll go somewhere where we kin talk," urged Kelly as the chairman gazed disparagingly at them.

She hesitated for a moment. "I don't really know ye," she said, looking towards her friends. Turning to look at him she almost melted at his smile. "Okay," she whispered, "I'll meet ye outside."

Some moments later they walked slowly along York Street. "Where are ye takin' me, Billy Kelly?" she asked

"We'll go to the Sportsman's an' have a few in peace an' quiet," he said.

"That's a man's bar," she gasped. "My da wud take rickets if he knew I wus in there wid a strange fella."

"Nuthin' wrong wid it," he defended, "an' only decent wimmin go there with their husbands or boyfriends. Paddy wudn't let any of that other scum across the door."

Reaching the bar, she entered warily and was immediately treated like royalty by the ever-bubbling owner.

"Heaven take care of us, Billy," he yelled across the crowded bar. "I heard ye had the night off from the timber boat, but I didn't think yid the time till go to Hollywud and bring back a film star. Shure there's niver been a beauty like her in here since Betty Grable stopped off on her way till the Hippodrome durin' the war."

Minnie grinned uncertainly at this welcome. "Here Billy," she mutttered frightfully as she looked around the bar filled with men. "My da wud kill me if he thought I wus sittin' at the bar like a fella"

"It's alright," he said softly, guiding her into a small private cubicle. "Gin an' tonic an' a Black Bush for me, Paddy," he called as he sat down beside her.

"Comin' up sir Billy," roared the owner. "Shure that's the best place," he added with a wink. "I'll turn down the light an' make sure yer nat disturbed, for that one luks a bit too classy fer this oul joint."

Minnie was completely taken by him. "Is he always like that?" she grinned, as they sat down at the table.

"Niver knew him till be any different," replied Kelly.

Shouldering his way through the narrow doors of the cubicle Paddy placed the drinks and refused to accept payment.

"Them's on the house on account of ye bringin' in the prettiest girl I've seen in a long time," he backed out still laughing.

Minnie fingered the glass and stared straight ahead. "Niver though I'd see ye again, Billy Kelly."

He remained silent, not knowing what to say, as she continued. "Hope ye didn't put it roun' the docks that Johnny Renwick's daughter is a good thing," she stammered. "It wud break his heart because I really am a princess till him. He's bin calling me that since I wus four."

The cubicle was small and narrow and painted grey. He stretched his legs and put his feet on a chair, feeling like a priest in a confessional as she continued. "I musta bin stoned outa my mind lettin' a married man intil my bed. That's the last house party I'll ever attend without a chaperone. You were the first, did ye know that?" she added bitterly.

"Aye," he answered pensively, "I noticed when I wus doin' the washin'."

She gazed quizzically at his deadpan expression. "Ye do the washin'?"

"No woman in the house, remember?" he added innocently.

She resisted the urge to scream. "Here I'm talkin' about the loss of the most precious possesion a girl kin have, an' yer tellin' me about yer laundry."

He grinned impishly. "Shure ye niver miss what ye give till a friend."

She looked at him for a moment, taking in his boyish grin and his lack of respect for the occasion. "There's no seriousness in ye, is there?"

He shook his head like a lovable juvenile deliquent. "Minnie," he said rising to his feet, "Drink that up an' we'll go along till the Edinburgh Castle. I want till see the Christmas tree gittin' lit in the Railway station, an' if ye haven't got yer knickers in yer handbag, I'll be lukin' for me two quid back."

Her anger and frustration exploded into infectious laughter. He felt suddenly possesive and pulled her to him. Close enough to smell his aftershave, she reached impulsively for his hand as they walked out of the bar to the sound of Paddy's colourful farewell.

As they passed Lipton's grocery store, Kelly peeered through the gloom at a shadowy figure huddled in the doorway.

"Is that you, Sandy?" he asked moving closer.

"Aye, Billy," came the toneless reply.

Kelly sighed as he saw Sandy crouched over like an old man, with his coat collar turned up and his hands jammed in his overcoat pockets. "Yill git yer death stannin' there. C'mon wid us an' git a drink in the hate," he whispered.

"Naw," replied Sandy, wallowing in self-pity. "Yer too good till me as it is."

"Walk on a bit will ye, Minnie? I'll catch up." Minnie nodded knowingly and moved out of hearing range.

"Sandy," scowled Kelly, "Yill haveta pull yerself together. The money's gone an' there's no good 'ill come of tearin' yerself apart."

"I still can't fathom it out," cried Sandy. "Forty-eight poun's disappeared in nearly as many minutes. I've tried desperately to remember where the hell it went until I've nearly drive meself crackers. I've searched me pockets a hundred times, thinkin' maybe some of it fell through a hole. I've torn the bloody pockets out thinkin' I might find a poun' or two in the linin' ... " he finished desperately.

"C'mon wid me an' Minnie," muttered the embarrassed docker. Sandy lurched out of the gloom and threw his arms around Kelly's neck. "God bless ye Billy, yiv always time for an' oul idjit like me." He looked at the figure of Minnie waiting at the corner of Ship Street casually watching the people moving towards the Railway station for the traditional lighting of the Christmas tree. "Go away with yer wee girl an' enjoy yerself," he muttered thickly. "I'm the road till no town," he added darkly.

Kelly pulled out a pound note and placed it in his hand. "Away an' git yerself a coupla hot whiskeys in Paddy's an' then git roun' home. Sally's not worried about the money, but she's mad worried about you."

Sandy made no reply. He took the money silently and walked stiffly in the direction of the Sportsman's welcoming lights.

"Givus a double hot wine, Paddy," he sighed, oblivious to the cries of welcome from the bar-owner.

"Hurry up Paddy, that's Sandy Carstairs, the last of the big spenders," shouted someone from the back of the bar.

"Away an' fuck yerself," he snarled defensively over his shoulder. The men roared at his predictable response.

Paddy set up the drink and returned to the Christmas tree he was decorating for the coming festive season. The dingy wooden ceiling had earlier been hung with brightly-coloured paper decorations.

Paddy looked over to Sandy. "Yer man says he'll be down till see ye shortly, Sandy."

Sandy felt a tremor of hope rise in his chest. Maybe he dropped some of the money and someone had picked it up.

"Who'll be down shortly, Paddy?" he asked barely concealing his excitement.

"Daddy Christmas," roared the barman, doubling with laughter. Despite himself Sandy smiled forlornly at being caught by such a hoary old joke.

"Shure he was down last week, Paddy. Didn't ye hear about him bein' in the Stalingrad buyin' double glasses of spirits and double packets of cigarettes an' spoilin' the hoores by buyin' them gold-plated wrist-watches," yelled a wag behind him.

Sandy sank lower into his stool with embarrassment and lowered his wine in one long gulp. "Paddy, the same again," he called wearily.

"I can't give ye the same again," roared Paddy, "but I kin give ye somethin' similar."

Sandy smiled tiredly and wondered if the barman ever got tired telling the same old jokes and sayings day in and day out.

"Ack, some are born till laugh, others are born till cry," he whispered mawkishly to himself. He felt a tear begin to trickle down one of his cheeks and his face contorted as he tried to hide a sob that came from his chest. He grabbed the fresh glass of wine and forced it down his throat as he rubbed the teardrop from his cheek. A feeling was beginning to form in his mind that he was coming to the end of his tether. He couldn't remember when he had last eaten and the wine was making his stomach rumble painfully.

A titter of scathing laughter rose behind him and made up his mind. He finished the wine and turned to face his tormentors.

"A soldier's farewell—goodbye an' fuck yis," he snarled with a two fingered gesture, as he stormed from the bar. Once outside in the cold he regretted his impulsive move and slowed to the pace of a man with nowhere to go.

He made his way to the Stalingrad and stood outside for fifteen minutes before he screwed up the courage to enter. Then with a swagger bordering on bravado he pushed open the doors and walked into the bar-room. Ignoring the jeers that greeted his arrival, he sidled to the end of the crowded counter and waited until one of the barmen found time to speak to him.

"What are ye havin?" he asked quickly, wiping the bar with his apron edge.

Sandy looked to his left and right before speaking "Cud ye give me two bottles a Mundies wine an' put it on the slate till next week?" he pleaded quietly.

The barman's eyes narrowed through the smoke that belched from the cigarette gripped firmly between his lips.

"Don't know ye," he scowled.

"Don't know me?" gasped Sandy, "I spent over forty quid in here last night."

The barman laughed scornfully. "Where wud ye git forty quid?" he said, as he moved off.

Another waiter heard the end of the conversation. "It's alright," he called, "Give him the pitch-pine, I'll vouch for him. Don't let me down nigh," he added glaring at Sandy's grateful grin.

When the two bottles were bagged and threw on the counter, Sandy threw forward a two shilling piece. "Cud ye givus twenty-four pennies for that?" he asked.

The barman returned and tossed the coins at him. "Thinkin' a gassin' yerself?" he grinned.

"Aye," answered Sandy, to the man's quickly vanishing back.

He was about to leave when he heard his name being called over the noise of the customers. He turned and saw Ned laughing in his direction.

"I wus good till ye, but ye niver bought me a watch, Sandy," yelled the ganger as the bar erupted with noisy laughter.

A mixture of sadness, remorse and futility left Sandy unable to answer. He snarled an obscenity and shouldered his way into the street. Taking a bottle from the bag he stood in the barber shop doorway and drank hungrily from its neck until it was finished.

Gathering his composure, he pushed away the dejection that was threatening to engulf him and forced himself to think positively.

The money-lender's wife opened the front door slightly and peered around it suspiciously. Her hard frozen eyes were devoid of pity as she looked Sandy up and down.

"Yis?" she barked.

"Cud I spake till Mr. Andrews?" asked Sandy politely.

She stared distastefully at his shabby overcoat and unshaven features.

"C'min till the parlour till I see if he's in. Who are ye anyway?" she scowled, looking suspiciously at the brown paper bag clutched under his armpit.

"Sandy Carstairs," he replied respectfully. "He knows me from when he worked on the dock, before he got his claim," he added as she ushered him into the parlour.

He lowered himself gratefully into a settee that was too big for the over-furnished room. A large walnut coloured radiogram sat mutely in a corner alongside a cocktail cabinet made entirely of mirrored glass and filled with bottles of spirits. Sandy was paying this item of furniture a great deal of attention when the door opened and a young lad about nine years old entered the room and stood watching him sheepishly.

Now and again he poked a finger furitively into his nose, but never took his eyes from the visitor. Sandy knew he'd been sent in to make sure he didn't pocket anything of value. A moment later the boy's mother entered the parlour. "He's nat in," she said primly, "He says till come back the marra."

"Tell him I only want fifty bob," pleaded Sandy.

"He's nat in, come back the marra," she reiterated, taking Sandy's arm and leading him to the front door. "Bring some security," she added before slamming the door in his face.

The youngster pulled back the curtains and stuck out his tongue. Sandy glared angrily at him. "Away an' do that at yer da, if ye know who he is, ye wee bastard ye," he roared angrily.

Staggering a little, he walked into Earl Lane and stopped at a house with a green door and drawn curtains on the downstairs windows. He thumped the heavy knocker until the door was opened by a dumpy middle-aged woman wearing large spectacles. She gazed at him with the expression of a puzzled starling as she swung the door open wider.

"I've an oul one till see, Maggie," he explained. "If I give ye five bob fer a drink cud ye let me have the house for an hour?"

She immediately discarded her apron and reached for her shawl. As she took the money, she looked at him seriously. "Wud

245

I not do?" she whispered, putting her arms around him. "Shure I'm every bit as good as any young thing. Henry Harvey 'ill vouch for me. He says I'm a sex machine an' I only charge half af what them young 'uns do."

Sandy gazed at her. Although over sixty, she carried a sexual aura that was rare in an elderly woman. She had never been married as far as Sandy knew and subsidized her pension by bringing home the odd sailor.

"There's many a good tune played on a oul fiddle," she finished coyly.

"It's nuthin' personal, Maggie," he answered lamely, "I've bin after this one for a long time."

She shrugged and pulled her dark shawl around her. "It's yur dick, but remember—all women are fair when the candle is out." She put a large latch key down between her breasts and closed the door firmly behind her.

Sandy drew back the curtain on a box cupboard beneath the window which housed the gas meter and placed the twenty-four pennies into its slot. Moving like a man in a trance, he lifted two cushions from the sofa and carried them into the small scullery.

Closing the door tightly, he uncorked the remaining bottle and took a swig from it before opening the stove to examine its interior.

Like the rest of the house it was spotlessly clean. He removed a roasting dish and two frying pans before placing the cushions inside.

Lying on his back he put his aching head on top of the cushions and sipped at the bottle. His last thoughts were of Sally and the children as he reached drunkenly for the knob that would send gas flowing into the oven.

"What about takin' me to the Silver Slipper, Billy?" smiled Minnie as he sat her down another drink.

"I thought ye wanted till see them lightin' the tree at the railway?" he said.

"Yill be wantin' me till sing carols next," she sniffed.

"Okay," he agreed reluctantly, emptying his tumbler with a flourish. She looked at him admiringly. "Yer insides must be made a blottin' paper," she said, finishing her drink a great deal slower.

"How is it ye niver seem to be drunk?" she asked him.

He grinned. "It's all in the mind," he said, "Don't think about it an' ye won't git drunk."

She looked at him earnestly. "What does Billy Kelly think about these days?" she asked coyly.

"When's yer da's next trip?" he grinned, as she rose and took his arm.

They walked along York Street citywards and crossed the road when they saw the figure of Head McKinstry bearing down on them. The policeman tilted his head and touched his cap to Minnie as he passed.

Entering the dancehall at the corner of Great Patrick Street, Kelly paid the entrance fee and waited until Minnie shed her coat in the cloakroom. A Latin-American tune wafted from the four piece band as he took her into his arms and glided onto the floor. A slow foxtrot followed and Minnie clung blissfully to him as he led her faultlessly around the ballroom.

Kelly buried his face in her long auburn hair and was enjoying the close contact. He turned his head irritably when his shoulder was tapped.

A small but powerfully built man with red curly hair and the petulant features of a schoolboy, dancing with a tall girl the shape of a pipe cleaner, whispered harshly in his ear.

"Stan' by, Billy. We're throwin' the niggers out durin' the next black-out waltz."

"How are ye gonna tell the difference?" grinned Kelly. The joke was lost on the red-haired man as he continued bitterly. "One of them felt Joannie's arse. We're sick of these bastards

247

comin' in here an' thinkin' every woman's a good thing. Lights out in two minutes," he finished before dancing away.

When the music stopped, Kelly unwrapped Minnie's arms from his neck. "Git yer coat," he ordered in a tone that forbade discussion. She obeyed mutely, but once outside allowed her frustration to show.

"I wus enjoyin' that," she said.

"Gonna be a murderin' match," he grunted, "an' we're better away from it."

"The niggers?" she asked.

"Aye, there's a Clan boat in and the coloured gentlemen can't tell the good girls from the bad ones an' the lads are gittin' angry about it."

"Thought ye liked a fight?" she laughed.

"Not my kinda fight," he answered grimly.

She watched as a woman emerged from the hall with a smiling black man. "Some girls 'ud stan' for anything," she sniffed.

"Aye, an' some things 'ud stan for any girl!" he replied with a rejoinder that earned him a hefty thump from her handbag.

"Wanta go roun' till my house," she asked coyly as they approached Henry Street .

"Too apt," he answered quickly.

"Me da's in," she replied with an impish smile as his enthusiasm quickly waned.

"Aw," she said grabbing his hand, "He'll nat bite ye an' besides he goes till bed at eleven."

"What about a carry-out?" he asked as they passed the White Lion.

She frowned. "McKinstry's on the prowl, so they'll nat open the door. Besides, my da always has a drop of scotch an' some Guinness lyin' down in the backyard."

Her father looked up quizzically from his rocking chair when they entered the kitchen house. A large black and white cat lazed at his feet. He did not rise or speak when Minnie introduced them to each other. Kelly stood until the girl told him to sit down.

Her father eyed him sombrely until he settled into the chair.

"Is yer da Rabby Kelly?" the old man asked quickly.

"Yis, Mr. Renwick," said Kelly civilly.

"Aye," nodded Renwick, "I kin see the resemblance. Are ye the buck idjit that hit Capper Quinn?"

Minnie blanched, but remained silent as her father leaned forward in his chair waiting for an answer. He looked every inch a docker, with a large mane of undisciplined white hair that never saw sunlight as his cap never left his head until he entered his or someone else's home.

Thick arms bulged in the sleeves of a khaki working shirt which was tucked neatly into heavy corduroy trousers held up by broad braces and a wide belt with a large silver buckle. A grey silk scarf decorated his bull-like neck. The cat was lapped fondly around his heavy woolen socks and a pair of tartan carpet slippers added a domestic touch to his outdoor appearance.

"Aye," repeated Kelly. "Guilty on both counts."

"At least yer honest," growled the old man. He nodded at Minnie. "Git him a drink," he ordered.

She returned from the yard with a glass of whiskey and a bottle of Guinness which she poured for the grateful Kelly. He looked up to thank her and found her father's hostile eyes boring into him.

"Why'd ye take a docker's button if ye were gonna degrade it?" he asked with the air of an interrogator.

Kelly waved aside Minnie's protests with a sleepy smile. He poured the remains of the stout into his glass before replying slowly. "I didn't degrade it. It degraded me. I hid behin' it an' wus able till git a job in front of men who were slingin' an' stowin' when I wus nuthin' but a twinkle in me da's eyes."

"What men?" exploded Renwick. "They're nat men, they're parasites paraded every day by the bosses an' encouraged till come down an' take whatever we can't do. An' whilst they continue to be there we'll find it hard to get constant employment an' good conditions for ourselves."

"Shure we've got all the conditions we ever dreamed of. We turn up every mornin' an' cream off the handy wurk an' leave the dross and low paying jobs to the reds an' the Arabs. That's as close to Paradise in workin' conditions as yill ever git."

"An' who created those conditions?" exploded Renwick, kicking the cat away from his feet and rising from the chair. "We did," he continued, "Men like yer da an' me who organised the union an' suffered at the han's of the employers until we got solidarity and the closed shop."

"My da tortured me till leave the army an' take a button. I done it to please him an' came on the docks along wid a lot of other privileged sons who didn't know their arse from their elbow, an' got the cream of the wurk. There's families of first preference men with each one taking home wages every week that wud keep a family for a fortnight. Where's the justice in that?" asked Kelly, his eyes blazing.

"They're entitled till it," thundered the old fellow. "As I said, we built the industry up from nuthin'. We didn't ask outsiders or the reds to come on the stones. They don't go roun' till the shipyard or Mackie's lukin' a lie on. No! They git their arses kicked an' toul to take themselves off. So why shud we tolerate them here? Their proportion of numbers eats up all the extra wurk an' gives us nuthin' to bargain with. Did ye know there's a scheme afloat in Britain to register all first preference dock-labourers and git rid of all the other parasites?"

"An' how wud that git the wurk done?" asked Kelly.

"Like in every other industry," said Renwick, settling back into his chair. "If we can't do it today, we'll do it tomorrow."

"The employers will want a sizeable wurkforce to give them a chance to compete. It costs money for a ship to lie overnight," argued Kelly.

"We'll fill the ranks wid our off-springs, an' their off-springs. That 'ill ensure solidarity and discipline an' satisfy the masters," replied the old man.

"Surely ye can't do away wid experienced dock han's an' then

250

bring in raw kids," protested Kelly wearily. "Wudn't it be better till allow some of the long servin' red button men, who are nat family, till be promoted till our section, thus leavin' a hole that cud be filled by non-union men. That's how it's done in every other field. Had your system prevailed in the British army, I wud niver have risen above the rank of private."

"Willie Kelly," sighed the old man, shaking his head repeatedly in a negative fashion, "The quay is like a feudal kingdom. Some are born to rule, others to serve. Whilst I don't agree wid Ned Semple's brutal an' heavy-handed methods, he rules his square wid a rod of steel an' has turned many a lie-about intil a first-class wurker. There's a sayin' on the quay an' even the Arabs agree wid it. If ye kin wurk fer Big Ned, ye kin wurk for anybody."

"Ned Semple's a twenty-four carat bastard," said Kelly evenly. "He's destroyed better men than he'll ever be. All done from the height of privilege an' wid no fear of retribution. The only people who cud bring him down are men like you an' me da. Men who are nat afraid of him and the power he wields. Power that decides whether or nat childer go hungry. Power that kin humilate a man till he turns till drink, or eats the insides outa him."

Minnie had sat down completely forgotten by the two men.

"Ned's nat the worst," said Renwick defensively.

"No," agreed Kelly sarcastically, "He's nat as bad as the ganger who hands out the jobs till the men with the prettiest wives an' then calls to the house when the men are stuck in the ship's houl an' the childer oul enuff to catch on are at school."

"I don't believe a wurd a that," gasped Minnie.

Kelly smiled grimly. "It's true," he argued. "Just like yer da says, it's a medieval kingdom where all the damsels are fair game. The gangers rule it an' then at the end of the day they head off in their big cars till their bungalows in the country or their semi-detached in the suburbs." He turned to the old man. "Yer talkin' of buttons for docker's sons. I'm sure there's many an Arab unwittingly rearin' one of yer royal brood. As Shakespeare or somebody like him once said, it's a wise child knows its own father."

251

Renwick was angered by the ex-soldier's ability to turn his argument against him. He decided to change the subject as Kelly took a sip from his drink.

"Why did ye hit Capper Quinn?" he spat.

The question was thrown with the air of a prosecuting council and Kelly thought for a moment that he was in the dock of the Crumlin Road courthouse.

"Because he sacked a non-union man who was drinkin' wid me," he replied truthfully.

"Because he sacked an Arab who was drinkin' wid ye," echoed Renwick in an incredulous tone. "Why didn't the Arab hit him?" he added.

"Because Capper wuda had him arrested an' blackballed from the quay," came the curt reply.

"So ye became a hero an' fought for the poor under-privileged outsider an' hit a man who is yer father's best friend," sneered Renwick.

Kelly looked apologetically at Minnie and then at the door. He swallowed his whiskey and rose.

"There ye are, Minnie," grinned her father, sensing victory, "The hard man's runnin' away from the oul fella's logic."

Kelly turned and looked down at him. "I hit Capper because he shuda sacked me along wid the outsider," he said evenly.

The old man rose and looked straight into his eyes. He spoke slowly and deliberately.

"I tole ye it's a Kingdom an' in that Kingdom yer superior to the red button an' the outsider. Just as a sergeant-major is superior to a private. In yer army days were ye allowed to mix wid ranks inferior till yer own? Ye don't havta answer that! I did a bita solderin' myself. But back to the point. First preference buttons are handed down, they are not apprenticed or journeyed. Ye got the callin' an' accepted. But instead of being a good member an' knucklin' down, an' enjoyin' the benefits, ye choose to attack the system instead of its enemies who niver cease in their efforts to undermine everything we have fought for.

"But thank God yer a minority of one. Any other young man who stepped outa line in the past has come till his senses quickly. As I've said, we had to wurk an' fight for anything we have an' we're nat prepared till give it away till anyone except those comin' behin' us who are of our flesh an' blood an' whom we kin trust. If we get the decasualisation that's talked of, then we can build a workforce comprisin' of our members only an' control our own destiny."

Kelly remained sceptical. "What wud the employers say to that?" he asked pointedly.

"What wud they say?" grinned Renwick, "They'd have till like it or lump it. With the closed shop operatin' we wud do the dictatin'. Certainly we'll unload their ship for 'em, but at our price an' on our terms. Think of it," he continued, "Work for all our people. Every day of the week for life. That's nat a bad future for any lad." He reached to the mantlepiece and lifted his pipe. Tearing a piece from a page of the *Telegraph* he lit it at the fire and put it to his pipe.

"Aye," he continued, between puffs, "Many's the lad wud give his eye teeth for a future like that, so fall inta line Kelly. Apologise till Capper an' there's nuthin' but security for ye an' if ye sire any sons, well, their future's secured as well. If ye don't ye'll waken up some day an' find that even yer oul fella has disowned ye."

He sat back in silence, concentrating on his pipe as the grey smoke curled lazily to the ceiling. After a moment or two he rose and looked at Minnie. "I'm for bed," he said. "Give him another drink," he added, "I think there's a bita air gittin' intil him."

He walked to the bottom of the stairs. "An' don't fergit what I told ye," he scowled, "Keep yer knickers up an' yer legs crossed." He proceeded slowly up the stairs as Kelly almost choked on his drink.

Minnie waited until the noise overhead stopped. "What in Heaven's name was that all about?" she asked as Kelly sipped pensively.

"He's markin' my cards—tellin' me the hierarchy is gittin'

tired of my antics, an' he's right. My da an' his da before him spent all their days on the quay. There wus no unions in them days an' they wurked from dawn till dusk till turn the boats round as quickly as possible so there'd be more profit for the masters. They used ta git a break at half-past-six an' I remember runnin' all the way till the boat wid a can fulla hot tea." He grinned at the fond recollection. "The points peeler at Corporation Street used to see me comin' an' stop the traffic till I got across the road."

Minnie filled his glass. "That's what's eatin' me da—havin' no wee lad till pass his button down till. I suppose if I'd bin born a boy I'd be travellin' with the beasts on the Ardrossan boat an' smellin' a cow-dung, instead a tobacca."

He grinned sympathetically. "Put on a coupla records," he said.

"Okay," she agreed, "but we'll haveta keep it low or he'll come down in his underwear an' turf ye out, hardman or not."

"I don't doubt it," sighed Kelly, casting a sidelong glance up the darkened staircase. "He's from an era when the boats were wood an' the men were steel."

"Billy," she asked anxiously as they danced to the music wafting from the gramophone. "Will ye lose yer button, an' if ye do lose it will ye ever git it back?"

He smiled at her concern and held her tighter to him. "I haven't lost it yet," he answered softly. "I wus drinkin' durin' a dinner-break wid an outsider I'd served wid in the Rifles. The crack wus good an' we came back fifteen minutes late. Quinn pushed an' shoved my mucker all over the shed, humiliatin' him in front of the rest of the gang before he sacked him. I tole Quinn it wus my fault, an' it wus, because the poor guy had pleaded with me to let him go back to the boat, but I'd got the taste of the jungle juice. So I blew up an' asked Capper till sack me as well, but he just muttered an' tole me to go away an' catch meself on an' think how much I wus hurtin' my father wid my antics. The guy had five kids an' naturally I felt bitter. So I chinned Capper an' said sack me now. He did. I wus fined an' suspended for four weeks, after which if I went back to the green table an' aplogised, I'd git me button back."

"But ye didn't," surmised Minnie. He shook his head. "An' ye won't," continued Minnie. He shook his head again—slowly this time and to the beat of the waltz that was drifting from the record player.

"My mate hasn't got an hour's work since that day," he sighed.

Sandy opened his eyes quickly and fearfully. The slamming of the front door had wakened him. His head was bursting and he looked vaguely around him trying to gauge his surroundings. Rising slowly, he wondered why his head was inside the gas stove. Almost immediately it all came back to him, crowding his horrified mind and causing him to move quickly away from the stove.

He shivered when he realised he'd fallen asleep before he had time to turn the knob on. As he sat contemplating his next move he heard the sound of voices in the next room. Rising silently, he peeked through a knot hole in the scullery door.

He saw Maggie, still wrapped in her shawl, holding earnest conversation with a giant of a man who was seated on the sofa beside her. Shaped like a massive pear, he wore a white fisherman's turtle-neck sweater with baggy tweed trousers tucked into long black sea boots. His cheeks were bloated and his black hair was plastered to his skull with oil. A small goatee beard gave him the decadent look of a Roman emperor.

They went into an embrace and Sandy almost laughed out loud as he watched Maggie vainly trying to encircle his huge bulk with her arms. After a moment or two the man began to speak in a thick foreign accent.

Maggie's face was a picture of intense concentration as he outlined what he wanted her to do. Nodding seriously, she disengaged herself and began stripping off her clothes.

The sailor began to disrobe, braying like a donkey.

255

"Be a little quieter, dear," she chastised, "or the neighbours 'ill call the peelers."

The man grunted agreement as he stood clad only in a pair of socks and a navy blue canvas money belt which stretched his ample waist biting into his skin, giving him the shape of a sack of potatoes tied in the middle.

He leaned forward and whispered in Maggie's ear, bringing a puzzled expression to her face. She listened again to his instructions and then put her hand out.

"Money first Captain, then we'll give it a go," she purred.

The seaman was puzzled until she rubbed her forefinger and thumb together in a gesture that was international. He laughed and removed the money belt, giving her some coins from it before tossing it away from him. It hit the scullery door with a thud that caused Sandy to jump with fright.

He returned his eye to the knothole and watched in amazement as Maggie, obviously following the sailor's instructions went to the furthest corner of the room. She lay down cautiously on her back and faced him with her legs in the air and open wide. Wearing nothing but a pair of pink laced stays, she watched apprehensively over her spectacles as the sailor removed himself to the opposite corner of the room.

He pawed at the faded linoleum with his stockinged feet and bayed like a rampant stallion. She screamed in fright as he fixed his staring eyes on her and ran forward suddenly. Sandy almost betrayed himself with a cackle of laughter as the seaman threw himself into the air and landed with a thud on top of the frightened woman.

She sighed with relief as he rose muttering to himself and walked back to the other corner. When it became clear he was about to try again, she re-opened her legs and closed her eyes.

This time he landed with a bang that sent the brass ornaments crashing from the mantlepiece to the floor. It was a successful copulation and soon they were grunting and growling like two animals in heat.

Sandy eased the door open a fraction, praying it would not squeak. Grasping the canvas money-belt, he pulled it silently around the bottom of the door and into the scullery. Holding his breath he opened one of the compartments and saw it was filled with paper money. He was delighted to discover it was British currency. He removed it quietly and was about to place the belt back on the floor when he realised the consequences for Maggie.

He found a newspaper and using a pair of scissors from a cupboard drawer he cut a wad of paper about the same thickness and breadth as the money and put one note over it before placing it into the pocket of the belt, and easing it back to where it was.

His heart was thumping so loudly against his chest he was afraid he would be discovered. He pulled the door back and then scurried to the yard door on his hands and knees. He eased up the latch and entered the yard on his hands and knees.

It was pitch black. He groped his way silently to the entry door but found a ladder Maggie had placed against the yard wall to facilitate quick getaways. Holding his breath he climbed to the top and dropped silently into the darkness of the entry.

The Stalingrad door was closed when he reached it. He banged heavily on it with his fist, feeling washed-out and in need of a cure. When the door eventually opened he stumbled through it and ran to the toilet. "Givus a bottle a whiskey an' a bottle a egg-flip," he cried to the astonished barman who tried to halt him.

"Do ye know what time it is?" screamed the barman. "I thought ye were McKinstry."

Sandy stopped in mid-flight. "Am I too late?" he gasped, having lost all track of time.

"It's bloody eleven o'clock an' McKinstry's on the prowl," growled the frightened man.

"Sorry," said Sandy apologetically. "All I want is a bottle a Haig an' a bottle a egg-flip."

The barman gave him an old-fashioned look. "Yill git that when I see the colour of yer money," he growled, closing the door with a bang.

"Just set it up an' I'll pay ye when I come outa the bogs," shouted Sandy.

Inside the safety of a cubicle, he counted the money and almost fell to his knees when he found it came to sixty pounds in ten pound notes. Taking one note, he folded the rest and pushed the wad down the side of his boot before entering the bar. The waiter gazed suspiciously at the bank note.

"Is that real?" he asked, holding it up to the light.

"Aye," replied Sandy hoarsely, "It's one youse bastards didn't fleece me outa when I got my big bet up."

"Tuk ye long enuff till present it. Didn't ye git a drink here on tick earlier on?"

"Aye," retorted Sandy grimly, "Ye kin take for that too."

When the barman handed over his change he counted every penny before shoving the white five pound note down his stocking and the pound notes into his trouser pocket.

"Yer nat thinkin' yill be robbed?" asked the barman sarcastically as he moved to open the door.

"I wus, last night, in here," replied Sandy grabbing his drink. He selected a florin from his change and gave it to the barman.

"Thanks fer yer help," he whispered as the door closed behind him.

His own home was in darkness when he arrived. He banged heavily on the large knocker and sighed with relief when the hall light lit and Sally pulled open the front door.

She blinked in the darkness for a moment before recognising him and throwing her arms tightly around his scrawny neck.

"Oh, thank God," she whispered tearfully. "Oh, thank God yer safe."

He felt the wetness of her tears on his cheek. "Hurry outa the street," he muttered with embarassment, adding, "I've bought ye a wee drink."

"Sandy," she began as he ran up the hall and into the scullery and brought out two glasses. Her eyes widened as he produced the bottles. "Whiskey! Dear God, what have ye done?" she cried.

"Nuthin'," he grinned soothingly, looking with contentment at the roaring fire. He popped the cork off the Haig and poured himself a stiff drink. He threw off his overcoat and she screamed. "My goodness, where's yer jacket an' pull-over? Ye cuda got yer end out there."

"Don't worry. Tomorra it's a new suit for me an' a new outfit for yerself. Sally," he beamed, "I know it sounds corny, but there's no place like home."

She pulled her faded nightdress tightly around her and sat down with a worried frown as he poured her a drink from the egg-flip bottle. He finished his drink and knelt down in front of her. His eyes were bleary with lack of sleep and his features were red and raw with the weather. A grey stubble made his face look even thinner than it was.

"Sally," he asked, "How long is it till Christmas?"

"Two weeks—as if ye didn't know," she answered sadly.

He reached into his boot and pulled the money from it, resisting the temptation to slip off another note for himself, he handed her the cash. "Happy Christmas," he roared joyfully, grabbing her roughly and kising her.

She fought off his attack and sat up straight. He saw her eyes were red-rimmed from crying. "I'm glad of the money an' I don't care where ye got it," she sobbed. "I thought yid left us when ye didn't come back for yer supper. The childer did nothin' but cry all night for ye."

He put his arms around her and cradled her with a tenderness he had not felt for a long time. "I've learned my lesson, Sally," he murmured into her ear. "God mixed goodness with mercy. I've bin till the gates a hell an' back again, but I'm finished nigh wid messin' about. Uncle's got a wee puffer the marra an' what with the boys havin' a good week or tied up at the timber, I'm in we a chance."

259

Sally wasn't listening. She was opening the ten pound notes and pressing them flat on the arm of the settee, rubbing each one slowly and lovingly with the palm of her hand before placing another on top of it.

EIGHT

THE schooling corner was almost deserted the following morning. A small group of men had arrived about a quarter to eight and were stamping their feet and blowing into their hands in an effort to ward off the biting cold wind that blew in from the water.

A few minutes before eight, Uncle walked briskly to his schooling point. The men immediately shuffled forward and formed an untidy semi-circle around him. Sandy got as close as he could to the ganger and began counting the union men in the school.

A cross-channel ganger entered at the opposite end and many of the men raced to him. "No blues an' only two reds. I'm in wid a chance," thought Sandy triumphantly. He also knew if Uncle was pressed he would allow him to work under a false name and pay him in his hand. That way he would save his employers the price of an insurance stamp.

His spirits sagged when Red Ennis and a half-dozen other men rounded the corner and moved to the school. He looked to the other ganger, but he had already schooled and left. Uncle was about to select his gang when Ennis produced a union card.

"We're all union men," he shouted to the ganger.

"Not my union," grunted the foreman, his eyes on the men he wanted.

Ennis pushed forward. "The committee man says we've got to be schooled in front a this non-union dirt," he persisted.

Uncle hesitated. The docks committee was all powerful and he

261

didn't want any trouble with them. He looked at the grim-faced casuals before addressing Ennis contemptuously.

"Some of these men have followed me for years. They've forgot more about dockwork than you'll ever know."

"We pay union, they don't," explained Ennis.

"That's 'cause we can't git intil a union," snarled an outsider.

Uncle saw the situation was getting ugly as the men began to push and shove each other. He schooled the two red button men. "Git away over till the Liverpool boat an' git me a committee man over here as quick as yis can" he shouted. Turning to the crowd he spoke softly. "Settle down boys, we'll let the committee settle this. They're the only ones who'll tell me what till do," he added, giving Ennis a withering look.

Moments later a small but dapper man approached quickly accompanied by the two reds. He held the peak of his cap firmly as the wind tried to blow it from his head. Uncle left the centre of the school to meet him and both men spoke quietly until Uncle turned away disgustedly without speaking.

The union official spread his hands in a sympathetic gesture and turned to the outsiders. "I'm sorry lads, but they pay society so they'll haveta be taken in front of yis."

"Bollocks," shouted someone. As the drivers tried to push their way to the front of the school they were shouldered back by the casuals. Uncle was forced back against the Harbour Office railings.

"This is outa order," he shouted to the committee man. "I shud be able till pick my men. They're experienced beg-wurkers who know the game. If I take them other men we'll be there all day."

The committee man stood his ground.

"Rules is rules," he stated obstinately.

"Well fuck the rules! I'll nat be dictated till by a lot a blow-ins," he snarled, taking an impulsive leap and throwing the job-checks into the air. "Whoever gits them, report to the Spencer Dock as quick as yis can," he snorted before moving off.

The pieces of aluminium were caught by the wind and floated

yards down the schooling pen, before hitting the square-setts and rolling in all direcrtions. They were followed by the men who rushed forward pushing, shoving and snarling in their efforts to pick up one of the discs.

Others who were not prepared to sell their dignity stood back and watched with disgust as the men brawled with each other. Sandy was the quickest away—before the checks left the ganger's hand he was off and running in the direction they would fall.

He dropped to his knees and was about to pick one up when a heavy hobnailed boot squashed into his hand. Suppressing a scream he leaned forward and sank his teeth through the greasy denim and into a well-muscled calf. The man gasped with pain and lifted his foot quickly before hitting Sandy a savage blow on the side of his head with his fist. He ignored it and scooped up the check with his nail marked fingers.

Protecting it with both hands, he rose and shouldered his way through the mob and ran towards the Spencer Dock.

Fierce fighting continued and only ceased when the union delegate threatened to take the names of all present and have them blackballed from the quay.

The previous night's work on the timber boat had, as Kelly predicted, cleared the remainder of the deck cargo. They spent the first half hour stripping the sodden hatch covers before removing the hatch boards and the beams.

Jim had not spoken all morning except in answer to Kelly's orders. He was capless and his dark uncombed hair contrasted with his pallid features. Kelly suspected rightly that he had drank too much the previous night and slept in. He said nothing, knowing that sooner or later the boy would break his silence.

He was also concentrating on the new hazards created by their entry into the hatch. The timber lengths were longer than the hatch-opening and the heaves had to be coaxed out by the winch-drivers. It was a risky procedure and every man needed to be on his guard.

They built their first heave and Kelly put down his hook. "Place the nipper further up the lift this time," he instructed. "Don't go for the middle. The winch-driver will pull the dipped end astern as far as he can, until he kin turn the raised end outa the hatch an' onta the shore. Keep yer eye on the heave, kid," he warned, "an' watch fer the butts."

The load was eventually coaxed over the side and onto the breast of the quay. They made up another and Jim moved up to sit beside his companion. "Made a right mug a meself last night," he confessed in a voice that was cracked and hoarse.

"Shure wait till we go for our break an' ye kin tell me all about it," replied Kelly softly. Jim nodded—he knew the situation was too dangerous at the moment for Kelly to relax his guard.

Leaving the ship, they knocked at Barney's door for admittance. Once inside Kelly ordered tersely. "Two hot whiskeys an' a hot meat pie." Jim almost threw up as Kelly pushed the meat pie in his direction. "I cudn't ate that," he groaned.

Kelly was adamant. "If ye don't ate the pie, ye don't drink the whiskey," he growled.

"Aw come on, Billy," pleaded Jim, "I only want the half-in till straighten me up."

Kelly looked to the ceiling in mock amazement. "Yer hardly two weeks on the quay an' yer wantin' till drink whiskey on an empty stomach at nine o'clock in the mornin'," he stated with disbelief.

"Shure ye do it yerself," countered the boy.

Kelly heaved an exaggerated sigh. "I have two fried eggs, four sausages an' three pieces a dipped bread in me before I came out. What had yerself?" he asked.

Jim dropped his head. "I thought so," grinned Kelly. "Nigh ate that pie," he finished with a roar that caused the boy to lift the round shaped meat pie and stuff it into his mouth.

Supressing a smile, Kelly turned to the man sitting beside him.

"Nothin' doin' this mornin, Jackie?" he asked.

The man sighed ruefully. "The Clyde ganger tuk a few men for shadin' an' Uncle had a wee beg-boat, but some big red-haired bastard brought a lotta lorrymen roun' flashin' their union cards. Uncle ended up firin' the checks intil the air."

Kelly shook his head in disgust. "Did ye nat git one?" he asked.

Jackie grimaced and turned his head. The hair above his ear was wet with blood. "I had one, but somebody hit me a kick in the nut an' when I came roun', they were all away," he muttered.

Jim had managed to finish the meat pie and reached greedily for the whiskey. Kelly said nothing until he emptied the glass.

"Feelin' better nigh?" he asked with a knowing smile.

Jim was about to reply when he felt the meat and the spirit start a riot in his stomach. His features took on a greyish hue and he felt as if his insides had caught fire. Putting his hand across his mouth he rose quickly and ran to the toilet.

"Now what brought all this on?" asked Kelly when the lad returned.

Jim put his arms on the table and laid his head across them. "Last night," he mumbled, "too much drink, an ' it made me insult a wee girl I'd bin lukin' forward till seein'." He lifted his head and his young voice was filled with uncertainty. "What'll I do, Willie?"

"Yill just haveta go back an' apologise if she means that much till ya," answered Kelly, putting his feet up on a chair. "In the meantime, go an' git yerself a double tomata juice, it'll settle yer stummick."

"I'd be afeared till go back till her. I kin only remember up till a point, so I don't know what I've done," he groaned.

"Well, it's Sar'day, so we'll only go till noon the day. When we finish git away home an' put yer head down till supper-time. Yer bound till be knackered," said Kelly, lifting a newspaper and turning to the racing section.

"Aye," grimaced Jim, as he lifted the tomato juice, "I'm as sick as a dog," Kelly grinned as Jim drank sparingly. When the glass was empty they rose and walked back to the boat. As they gradually worked their way down the hatch Jim found himself bent double in the shadowy recess of the hold and working almost blind. Kelly had volunteered to go in but Jim had insisted on pulling his weight. He was working immediately below the winch and the noise from the donkey engine exacerbated an already agonising headache.

The perspiration poured from him despite the cold and his shirt was saturated with sweat when they hooked on their last heave.

He decided to accompany Kelly into Paddy's. After a few drinks Kelly saw he had no intention of leaving. Sandy entered an hour later covered from head to toe in yellow dust. He insisted on buying a drink, causing Kelly to look strangely at him.

"Touched for Uncle's maize meal boat," explained the casual with a wide grin. "Paid me in me han'. I'm only havin' a couple till slake me thirst Billy, then I'm goin' home."

"Aye," muttered Kelly in a disbelieving voice as Sandy took off his overcoat and muffler and threw them on a chair. "Then I'm goin' up till the pawn an' git me jacket an' pullover out."

"Good man," said Kelly approvingly.

Sandy returned with the drinks. "Did ye hear about that bastard Ennis an' his gang?" he asked as he sat down.

Kelly was about to answer, when Jim lifted his head from his drink. "Aye," he shouted, his eyes ablaze, "Somebody shud kick his ballocks in."

"I thought ye were goin' home," grunted Kelly.

"I'm alright nigh, Billy," he answered with a laugh. "I'm flyin'! An' shure ye niver go home if yev anywhere better till go. Do ye want a bowl a soup?" he added, "I'm starvin'."

Sandy watched as Jim weaved his way to the bar. "Another week or two an' he'll be as big a juice-head as me," he whispered.

"Leave him alone," said Kelly thoughtfully. "He's had the stuffin' knocked outa him in more ways than one this past fortnight."

266

His eyes automatically went to the door as a group of men entered noisily. "Red Ennis," snarled Sandy softly. "He's got a neck a brass comin' in here." They watched as the group moved to the bar and began to speak to the owner.

"Tryin till sell their white cards," he whispered. They watched as Paddy listened for a moment then shook his head.

"He didn't buy them," said Sandy laughing. "Maybe they'll go elsewhere."

Ennis took the refusal good-naturedly and sat down at an empty table whilst one of his cronies bought a drink. He saw Kelly and grinned warmly at him. "Heard ye were defendin' yer title," he called, referring to the fight outside the Stalingrad with Gibson. He glanced in Sandy's direction. "See yiv still got yer number one ball-licker wid ye," he growled.

"Get stuffed," snarled Sandy, thankful for Kelly's company. His testicles were still sore from his last encounter with the lorry-driver. The Eastender was unruffled. "I'll git that fiver one way or the other," he stated flatly.

"What fiver?" asked Kelly.

"He give me a beefin' in the Gib the other night because I cost him a fiver at the pontoon," answered Sandy, all in one breath.

Kelly grinned wickedly at Ennis. "He doesn't owe ye a fiver. Ye had yer chance till get it when I tole ye we give little boys their money back when they girn. Yill niver git it nigh. Not while yer arse luks down."

Red looked at him with a pained expression. "No need for us till fall out, Billy," he purred. "Why don't ye come over here an' drink wid real men." He spread his hands on the table in a gesture of peace, "Shure I've always given ye yer place," he added benevolently.

The docker looked at him with undisguised scorn. "Yer givin' me my place?" he echoed. "Nobody gave me my place," he continued angrily. "Any place or respect I've got was earned by deckin' big slabbers like yerself who use their strength and animal cunning to beat up lesser men."

Ennis was unafraid. "Kelly, the king a the underdogs," he laughed softly. "Yer a big sprick in a wee pool. At least I come outa my territory. Do ye ever leave York Street?" he taunted. The bar noise dropped to a quiet hum as the anger in his voice deepened.

"I've bin more than polite till ye, an' I'm well outnumbered, but personally I think yer a bit light for heavy wurk ... So if yid like till go somewhere, sometime, on yer own ... " he stopped for a moment as Jim staggered between them carrying a bowl of soup. Ennis stared at him for few seconds before continuing, "Maybe some day we'll meet where ye won't have too many backers."

Kelly rose slowly from the chair and placed his cap on the table. He looked across the bar at Ennis. "What's wrong wid nigh?" he asked softly.

Paddy rushed around the bar. "Billy," he cried worriedly.

Kelly spoke without removing his eyes from Ennis. "Don't worry Pat, we're takin' it outside."

"No chance," scowled Ennis, showing no fear. "There's no way I'd git a fair go."

"Nobody will interfere," promised Kelly.

Ennis realised there was no backing out. He was unafraid and more than fancied his chances of beating the smaller and lighter man. Removing his overcoat and jacket he threw them to one of his cronies and moved to the front door which Kelly held open for him.

The moment the doors closed the occupants of the bar rushed to the two large windows that looked out into York Street.

Passers-by and a queue at a nearby bus stop were astounded when the two men, bare-headed and in their shirt sleeves, dropped into fighting crouches and began circling each other.

Kelly stepped back quickly as the heavier man threw a fast right and left, both of which missed. He noted instantly that Ennis carried his guard low and didn't bother to protect his granite shaped jaw.

Kelly moved tactically into range. Ennis grinned wickedly. That was where he wanted him. As he stretched to grab the slim docker by the shoulders, Kelly moved back a pace and feinted with a straight left. Ennis leaned forward to block it and didn't see the right fist which exploded on his Adam's apple. The air was cut from his lungs and he immediately fell into a kneeling position, his eyes wide with fear and his hands clawing at his throat.

Kelly was about to wade in with his boots and finish it when he was struck lightly from behind. Spinning with a snarl he was surprised to find himself confronted by an elderly woman who hit him repeatedly across his back with a rolled-up umbrella.

"Leave that poor man alone," she screamed as Kelly took her gently by the shoulders and tried to restrain her. The break in concentration and discipline was disastrous. He took his eyes off his opponent and did not hear the muffled warnings from behind the glass windows as his friends tried to warn him that Ennis had risen and was lumbering towards his unprotected back.

A brutal roundhouse right landed on the nape of his neck causing him to stagger forward under its impact. Out on his feet he shook his head desperately trying to dislodge the veil of pain that momentarily blinded him. The right hand landed again, smashing against the side of his jaw causing the other side of his head to crash against the pub's brick wall. He grabbed vainly at the pub window sill in an effort to remain on his feet before crashing heavily to the ground and rolling onto his back.

Ennis roared in triumph and knelt down beside the fallen man. He was about to sink his teeth when Sandy burst from the bar and attacked him with a bottle. The victor quickly disarmed him and, grabbing his shirt front, pulled him into a savage embrace.

Sandy screamed as he was separated from his ear lobe by the razor-like teeth. He hit out desperately and was smashed to the ground. Ennis spat the piece of flesh contemptuously from his mouth and ran triumphantly into the bar-room.

His path was blocked by an ashen-faced Jim Harvey who threw the remains of his soup into the streetfighter's face. He gasped in terror as Ennis roared with rage and flung him across two tables causing the glasses and bottles to crash to the floor.

Ennis threw tables and chairs out of his path as he moved in to finish the lad. He stopped when a crowd of casuals circled him menacingly. "Clear out," snarled a short man he recognised as Jack Harvey. "Yiv got the victory wid a Judas punch an' the help of an oul interferin' bastard wid an umbrella, but if I wus you I'd git away back over the bridge before Kelly comes roun'," he added with a conviction he did not feel.

"Kelly's finished ... All washed up, " declared Ennis as he took his coat and cap from his fawning henchmen. "He's a baten docket, but if he wants more tell him I'll be down in Brennan's Bar until closin' time."

Paddy had rung for an ambulance whilst Sandy, one hand over his injured ear, was trying to revive Kelly.

"Give 'im air ... Let 'im breathe," he snarled as the men crowded around the fallen champion. The ambulance arrived and the driver examined the injured man briefly. "No broken bones," he said to his colleague as they placed Kelly on a stretcher. He looked at Sandy's torn ear. "You'd better come along as well till we see what can be done wid that," he said.

The doors were closed and the ambulance moved quickly down York Street towards the Mater Hospital. A solitary policeman who had witnessed the brief battle from the far side of the road, took out his notebook and scrawled a few details into it before replacing it in his tunic pocket. "No sense in me interferin' in the like a that," he muttered to himself as he slowly continued into Brougham Street.

The male nurse was tending Sandy's ear when Kelly began to stir. The nurse moved to him and spoke comfortingly. "You're gonna be alright, mister?" he turned inquiringly to Sandy. "What's his name?" he asked.

270

"No idea," said Sandy blandly, "I'm just a innocent bystander."

Kelly opened his eyes and gazed at his surroundings. His eyes widened when he saw the khaki blanket across his chest.

"Jock! Jock! "Where are ye?" he screamed loudly, rising from the stretcher. It was the first time Sandy had seen terror in his face. The male nurse moved to restrain him and was grabbed by the throat and thrown against the side of the vehicle.

Kelly's eyes were wild as he gazed fearfully at Sandy. "Git the bren Jock ... Git the bren. These bastards 'ill murder us. Get the bren or they'll burn us alive," he screamed. Staggering to the door he tried to open it. Sandy grabbed the nurse. "Stay clear mate," he warned grimly, "He's outa his head."

Kelly smashed into the rear door with his shoulder. Moving back he began to kick at it with his boots until the lock broke and the door flew open. He turned to Sandy: "Shoot the driver, Jock ... Shoot the fuckin' driver or we'll be roasted alive." Sandy and the driver's mate cowered in the corner. Kelly looked at them disdainfully, and was moving towards the front of the ambulance when it skidded to a halt at the side of the road. He turned quickly and leapt out. "That's a fuckin' madman," stuttered the driver as he ran to the back of the vehicle and examined the smashed door handle. "C'mon," he said to his mate, "We're nat insured for this."

"I think I'll git out here too," smiled Sandy apologetically, "This is sumpthin' I've gotta see."

Kelly took to the backstreets. Apart from a dull pain at the side of his head, he felt alright. The moments of panic in the ambulance had taken him back to a nightmare from another time. His head was clearer now. He paused for breath at the corner of Great George's Street and Nelson Street and sat on a window ledge. The years of hill-climbing and hard work had given him a fitness and durability that enabled him to shake off quickly the results of the two savage blows.

He was surprised to be joined by Sandy who sat down exhausted beside him. "Billy," he gasped, holding his chest and struggling to breath. "Billy," he repeated, "It wus a sucker punch. Ye shuda knocked the oul doll out an' went about yer business."

Kelly grinned ruefully. "There'll be no more sucker punches," he said grimly as he rose and strode forward. Sandy jumped up quickly and barred his path, hugging him affectionately.

"Billy, yer nat right," he protested. "C'mon roun' till my house an' have a wee rest until yiv fully recovered."

"No chance," snarled Kelly, pushing him aside. "First things first."

Sandy ran along beside him, speaking between breaths. "Billy— he's goin' nowhere. He's down in Brennan's havin' a victory parade. C'mon till my house an' have a good wash and Sally'll luk at yer head. Ye kin have a few hours sleep an' in the meantime I'll arrange till feed the big bastard a bit of misinformation till make him relax."

Kelly stopped in mid-stride and grinned at the logic. "Aye we'll do that," he said falling into step with his relieved companion.

Jim Harvey rose from the table and took a long deep breath before walking unsteadily towards the counter. Reaching it he held tightly onto its bevelled edges to support himself as he tried to focus on Paddy's amused features.

"Givus another scotch," he slurred.

The barman refused good-naturedly. "Shure yiv had enough, Jim. Go on away home an' git yer head down."

"But I've got money, Paddy," said the boy, totally misunderstanding. He reached into his jeans and pulled out the linings of the pockets, spilling coins all over the bar-room floor.

He stared mutely at the ground as laughing patrons gathered up the money and put it in his hands.

"Alright," he conceded as the bar-room began to spin rapidly before his eyes, "I'm away." Pausing at the door he tipped the back of his cap forward causing the peak to slip over his unseeing eyes. Stepping gingerly outside he clung to the sill of the pub window and began to sing.

Once you have found her,
Never let her go.
Once you have found her,
Nev—er let her go!

The impromptu chorus was warmly applauded by a group standing at the bus stop. Jim was oblivious to his amused audience. The song reminded him of Maureen and he suddenly felt a burning desire to see her again.

"Must see Maureen. Must see Maureen," he repeated drunkenly as he walked off in the direction of York Road.

Inching his way forward he collided with a display of fruit outside the Anchor stores. Steadying himself, he moved on and walked into a brace of turkeys hanging from the shop's awning.

He paused for a moment looking stupidly at the birds, and suddenly decided to buy one for Maureen's mother. "Comin' up till Christmas," he reasoned. "Might make the oul bastard like me," he muttered slyly to the assistant as he paid for the bird.

Without waiting for it to be wrapped, he trudged forward holding his purchase by its feet, causing the neck and head to drag along the pavement behind him.

Maureen was pensively smoothing a dress she had selected to wear at the the dance later on that night, when their front door was almost dislodged from its hinges by loud and heavy banging.

"What the hell's that?" cried her mother rising in alarm. Opening the door she screamed as Jim and the turkey collapsed in a heap on the hall floor. He smiled stupidly up at her. "I've brought ye a wee present missus ... Merry Christmas," he said struggling to his feet as the woman glared angrily at him.

"If my husband was here he'd take a horse whip to you," she snarled. Maureen began to sob as she watched him trying to remain upright. His shirt tails were out over his trousers and his fly buttons were undone.

"I'll take him home," cried Maureen.

"Yill do no such thing," screamed her mother. Grabbing the turkey from Jim's limp fingers, she threw it as far out into the street as she could. "An' you git out along with it," she yelled, sending him sprawling into the street. He heard the door slam and shook his head sadly. With a superhuman effort he raised himself to his feet and staggered to the other side of the road where he found a lamp post to cling to. Holding on tightly he closed his eyes and began to sing at the top of his voice: "I'm dreamin' of a white Christmas,/Just like the ones we used to know.."

"What in heaven's name did ye ever see in a lie-about like that?" she asked grimly as they watched the spectacle through the widow. Other neighbours had been drawn to their doors by the noise and stood in silent amusement, watching the display.

Her mother pulled the curtains closed. "If I hear of ye associatin' with that fella yill nat git out fer a month," she stated grimly, as Jim slid down the lamp post and vomited all over his shirt front.

Brennan's Bar was empty except for Ennis, his companions and a few casuals. It was a bar that was busiest during the day when it was packed with dockers, sailors and railway workers. The custom began to tail off about half-past six at night when the men reluctantly made their way home.

Situated on the dockside of Prince's Dock Street it was close to the grey gates that closed to traffic at seven o'clock each night, turning the busy street into a deserted cul-de-sac. Facing it were the grey wooden walls of the Chapel Sheds.

Gerry Mullan walked in and ordered a drink. Paying with the

pound note Sandy had given him he turned and sat down at a table beside the fire. "Kelly's in a bad way," he said to the young barman. Red Ennis looked up from the shandy he'd been nursing.

"What was that?" he asked Mullen.

The old man took a pipe from his overcoat pocket and drew out a slab of Warhorse tobacco. "I said Kelly's about finished," he repeated, using a pocket knife to slice thin wafers of tobacco off the slab. "A fractured skull an' a broken jaw. No turkey for him this year," he added sadly, "an' it'll be a long time before he drinks another pint."

"When he does it'll be through a straw," guffawed Ennis to the amusement of his henchmen. The rest of the clientele remained stony-faced. The barman was more than fond of the likeable docker who had spent some time in his pub.

He moved slowly and reluctantly when Ennis came up to order. "Gimme a ball a whiskey, Sean," he growled. Despite his sneer the barman could see he was visibly relieved. When he'd heard of the row between Kelly and the Eastender, Sean had watched the man every time the pub door opened. Now his smug grin said Kelly wouldn't be back tonight or maybe ever again.

He set up the drink and gave him his change without a word. Ennis returned to his seat and gulped hungrily at the spirit. He'd heard about Kelly's reputation and refrained from heavy drinking, knowing that fighting men usually returned to avenge a defeat as soon as possible. Every time the door opened he had expected to see the docker framed in it.

"Get me another," he snarled triumphantly to his colleagues. "Kelly won't be back the day or the marra."

Three hours later, he lolled on his chair singing loudly and lustily. His jacket lay in a corner and his shirt was unbuttoned to the waist revealing heavy body hair all over his chest and stomach.

When the song finished, he looked around the room at the other customers, and began to giggle. "Kelly's finished," he roared, flinging his arms in the air. "I'm the King a the dockside nigh." Turning to one of his companions, he nudged him playfully with his elbow, and began to sing.

Where's oul Kelly nigh,
Where's oul Kelly nigh,
The poor oul cratur's
Lyin' in the Mater ...
Where's oul Kelly nigh!

He closed his eyes in merriment and was about to repeat the chorus when he heard the door open slowly. The bar-room fell silent and he opened his eyes to see Kelly sauntering towards his table. Freshly washed and shaved, he was jacketless; wearing a pair of light blue jeans and a denim shirt with the sleeves rolled up. On his feet were the shiniest pair of hobnail boots Ennis had ever seen. There was no evidence of the punches that had felled him and he looked supremely confident as he grinned down at the astonished lorry-driver.

"Round two," he stated quietly, pointing with his thumb to the door.

Ennis realised he had been outwitted. "Shure I'm drunk," he wailed.

Kelly's smile grew even wider. "I know," he replied.

The man beside Ennis lifted a bottle and wielded it at the docker's head. Kelly pivoted quickly, pushing his hip into the man's crotch in an almost obscene gesture. He caught the arm holding the bottle and stopped it in mid air. At the same time the index finger of his other hand was forced unerringly into and up the startled man's nostril. Pushing viciously until his finger would go no further he hauled the agonised man by the nose over his shoulder and onto the stone floor in front of the fire. He lay where he fell, moaning loudly as blood cascaded from his ruptured nostril.

Ennis threw the table aside and launched himself at Kelly's throat. The docker swung his right arm like a scythe. The heel of

276

his open hand hit Ennis on the bridge of his nose at its highest point. He fell back onto his seat. "I can't see," he screamed, groping around and trying to get back on his feet.

"Have ye blinded him?" asked Sean conversationally.

Kelly nodded, watching his opponent, "Temporarily," he said.

"Pity," reflected the barman.

"Where's oul Ennis nigh?" screamed Sandy with delight as the driver staggered unseeing around the floor.

Kelly threw a quick glance at the barman, as Ennis's sight began to return and the man prepared to come after him. "Will I take it outside?" he asked.

"Yis please, just in case the boss comes in an' spoils it." Leaning on the safe side, the barman was enjoying the conflict.

Kelly raced forward, head down and grabbed Ennis by the testicles. With a violent jerk upwards that caused the man to howl with anguish, he turned his enemy in a tight circle. When Ennis' back was in line with the front door, Kelly easily averted the fumbling hands that searched for his throat. Fixing a cold eye on his target he swung his head in a vicious butt that opened his opponent's cheek to the bone.

Unknown to the brawlers, a group of Salvation Army carol singers had stopped outside the bar and were about to serenade the customers when Ennis' huge frame was propelled through the bar doors by the ferocity of Kelly's head-butt. He cannoned into a portly drum-major and both men crashed to the ground.

"Silent Night! Holy Night!/All is calm, all is bright!" sang the rest of the choir nervously as Ennis rose wearily and squared up to his tormentor. Kelly moved forward, deliberately throwing light lefts that peppered the man's face, whilst he steered him respectfully away from the ranks of the dedicated singers.

The straight lefts pushed Ennis backwards until he hit the grey wooden wall of the Chapel Shed. Feeling the reassurance of the wall against his back Ennis lashed out with a roundhouse right that skidded off Kelly's shoulder and spun the lighter man off balance.

Encouraged by his first solid punch of the fight Ennis used the wall to propel himself forward, only to scream in agony as the docker leapt into the air and met him half-way. He was momentarily blinded again as the point of Kelly's elbow smashed against his left eye. A split second later the docker's knee collided with his aching crotch.

Kelly moved in to finish it but stopped when he saw the stricken face of Sandy in front of him. He was pointing down the street. "Cows, Billy—cows!" screamed the little man, taking care to stay well clear of the lethal hands and feet. "Stan' aside Billy, or they'll be on top of ye."

Kelly's eyes left the stricken Ennis for a brief second to look in the direction Sandy was pointing, and saw a herd of steaming cattle bearing down on them at a dangerous pace. The dock gates were opened swiftly by a harbour constable and Kelly stepped aside quickly as the drovers beat the animals onto the quay in the direction of the Ardrossan boat.

He stood among the silent carollers who gazed at him with a mixture of awe and fright. Ennis had been bowled over two or three times by the frightened beasts, but when the street cleared he was on his feet brandishing a long and lethal bamboo cane he had wrestled from one of the passing drovers.

"C'mon ye bastard, I'm nat finished yit," he snarled across the road to Kelly. His face was laid open like a raw piece of flesh, and Sandy felt a sudden stab of pity for him when Kelly moved forward cautiously. As they closed, the cudgel whistled through the air and thudded against Kelly's lower ribs, knocking the wind from him. Catching it between his elbow and body he wrestled it from his opponent's feeble grip and threw it across the street.

Clenching his teeth and narrowing his eyes, he stepped forward to finish it. He saw Ennis' defence had all but crumbled and got as close as he needed to be before unleashing a powerful left and right combination that slammed almost simultaneously, and with sickening accuracy into the man's injured face.

No one could have shipped the devastating double punch and

remained upright. He fell without a whimper, his arms outstretched and his legs bent.

Kelly stood over him. "Just one more thing Pig, to insure there'll be no more ear-bitin'," he muttered.

Sandy grasped his own ear instinctively as the heel of Kelly's boot dug into Ennis' gaping mouth and smashed his front teeth. The injured man whimpered and rolled onto a pile of cow dung dropped by one of the passing beasts.

Kelly, white-faced and hands clenched, looked over at the spectators. "Where's his mates?" he snarled.

The men came forward slowly looking anxiously at their fallen leader. "Git him ta fuck outa here an' tell him if he likes livin', niver come near me again," he snarled.

None of the men replied. Lifting Ennis gently, they placed him on the back of a nearby lorry, close to the headboard. Two men sat with him, eyes downcast, refusing to meet Kelly's malevolent gaze, as the engine started and the vehicle roared off at high speed down past the Chapel and into Garmoyle Street.

"C'mon back in, Billy," shouted Sean. "Ye kin wash up at the sink. The men were already re-living the fight blow by blow as the barman set up a drink on the house.

Their joy was short-lived as the closed door was hammered with a ferocity that caused them to stop speaking and look at each other with alarm.

"Open this door in the name of the law," shouted a voice oozing with authority.

"Who are ye?" retorted Sean, reaching for a bung-starter.

"Harbour Constable Harold McFetridge, an' yis are all under arrest for disorderly behaviour an' drinkin' after hours."

"Ye've no jurisdiction on this side of the gate," growled the unconcerned barman, "Now go away or there'll be no free beer for ye the marra."

The drinkers were astonished to see the man's outraged features appear at the pub window, as he climbed onto its narrow sill.

"I've put a bolt in the outside keeper, so yis are all locked in," he screamed. "Nigh I'm goin' till my hut to ring the RUC an' git yis all lifted."

"Hell roast it," grimaced one of the men angrily as the grinning constable jumped down from the window ledge, "We're all for the high jump the night. McKinstry 'ill throw the book at us."

"Not necessarily," said Sean smugly as he washed a tumbler and polished it meticulously. The men looked at him blankly as he explained.

"There's only one way in here sure enough, but what a whole lotta people, incuding that blirt out there doesn't know is that I have a fire exit that leads out till the back entry beside the Rotterdam Bar in Pilot Street. So away yis go quietly an' I hope till see yis all on Monday." He lifted another tumbler and polished it pensively as the men filed quietly to the end of the long backyard and out through the fire door. When he heard the door quietly closing, he went out into the yard and hastily covered its existence with crates of empty bottles, before turning off a concealed light switch and throwing the area into complete darkness.

Head McKinstry was out of the police car before it stopped. The harbour constable stuck out his chest and saluted as the senior police officer approached him.

"I've got them all, sor, fightin' an' brawlin' they were, sor, like a pack a animals in the middle of the street. Real murderin' match it wus, sor," he concluded.

"Did ye know any of 'im, son?" rasped the Head.

"No, sor, I'm new here, sor. I wus sent over to let the cattle through an' I saw them out in the street beatin the hell outa each other. Too many for me ta apprehend, but when they all went back intil the premises, I locked them all in till await yer arrival." He nodded with pride at the bolt on the keeper.

"Good man," roared McKinstry, pulling out the bolt and banging on the door with his blackthorn. Pushing the door open he turned to six policemen behind him. "Draw batons and advance," he yelled, following the men into the empty bar-room.

Sean looked at him with mild amusement. "Kin I help ye, Head?" he asked, "Git ye a drink or sumpthin'?"

McKinstry glared daggers at the harbour constable who had followed in triumphantly behind them. "Search the toilets," he barked at one officer who sprinted in the direction the blackthorn was pointing. "You, the back lounge; you, the upstairs lounge and you the store out the back." As the officers ran to obey his commands, he sat down on a bar-stool and placed his cap on the counter.

"Givus a Black Bush," he said rubbing his forehead wearily. The police men returned empty-handed and Sean sat each one of them up a drink with the exception of the harbour constable.

"Don't suppose you'd know any of them?" purred the Head patronisingly.

"Hasn't bin a sinner in here since eight o'clock," replied the barman smoothly.

"That's a lie," shouted the harbour policeman angrily.

"Get back to your post!" screamed McKinstry, "And the next time you imagine anything, bring out one of your own mobile patrols, if you can task one that isn't lying blutered somewhere."

The constable's face contorted with rage as he turned on his heels and left the pub. McKinstry savoured the last of the Black Bush. "Thanks very much for your co-operation, Sean," he said sarcastically, before leaving the bar, hurriedly followed by the other constables.

Sandy was demonstrating the fight punch for punch as Sally rubbed methylated spirits on Kelly's bruised ribs. The children had been brought out of bed by their father's noise and were now watching wide-eyed as he demonstrated to their mother.

"First off Billy stuck his finger up one guy's nose an' fired him

281

over his shoder. Then he spun like a balley dancer an' hit Ennis with the heel of his han' an' blinded him—jist like that." Sandy demonstrated the movement to the delight of his children. "He staggered about like a bull in a china shop an' at that point Billy got the big bugger by the balls and blattered him with his head. He's a one man demolitition team Sally, an' it did my heart good till see Ennis gittin' what he give me in the Gib. Shure," he added proudly, smiling at his children, "it was no contest."

Sally wasn't listening. She was looking intently at Kelly. "When are ye gonna stop all this, Billy? Minnie Renwick was over here distracted about ten minutes after yis went out again. She'd bin toul yid bin tuk away in an ambulance an' she sobbed her eyes out here on my sofa. She's mad about ye! I tole her it was all nonsense. But she wudn't lissen. She's away till the Mater on a trolley-bus till see if yer there."

Kelly said nothing. He was thinking of his father's reaction and knew the start of the episode would have been carried to the old man. He decided to go home and let his father know he was alright.

Sally kissed his cheek as he left the house and Sandy hugged him. He walked along the darkened pavement deep in thought, hoping he hadn't seriously injured Ennis. Most of York Street was asleep and only a few lights shone through the blinds as he moved past Trafalgar Street. Some front doors were open and courting couples called to him from the darkness of the long halls as he passed. He acknowledged with a lazy wave of his hand. A soldier and sailor, obviously good friends, staggered past him, with their arms around each others shoulders. He felt a touch of envy at the men in uniform. "Will ye be home for Christmas, Tommy?" he asked the soldier. "Dunno, Billy. Depends on this business in Kenya. We might be goin' out till take on the Mau Mau shortly," came the reply as they disappeared into the darkness.

Reaching the corner of Nelson Street, he stood for a moment, breathing deeply. Through the gloom he saw a figure huddled on the Harveys' window sill. Moving closer he heard a drunken wail and realised it was Jim. The hall light was on and he knocked at the door before reviving Jim by slapping gently the boy's pale strained face.

Mrs. Harvey opened the door and peered into the darkness as Kelly hoisted the lad from the window sill. "He's bin out there for hours, singin' his head off," she muttered. "Four wee bucks carried him home, said they'd found him sleepin' on the pavement outside the railway station. He wudn't come in—just sat there, singin' his head off."

"Will I put him till bed for ye?" asked Kelly gently.

"No," replied the little woman firmly. "I'll take off his boots an' he kin lie on the sofa, in case he's sick." As Kelly put him down, the lad opened his eyes slowly and blinked unseeing. A serious look filtered across his young features. "Don't fergit till waken me early tamarra ma—I'm goin' lukin' for that bastard that filled in my mate, Billy."

She turned to Kelly and tried to grin through her tears. "That's the first time I ever heard him use bad language," she muttered sadly, as she sat down at the fire and picked up a toasting fork with a piece of bread stuck to its prongs.

"Yer welcome to a cup a tea Mr. Kelly," she said, nodding to the tea pot sitting on the hob. "I'm doin' Jimmy some toast and yer welcome to a plate of it."

Kelly sat down and took off his cap. "I have a lot to answer for," he murmured softly.

She looked at him with a smile. "No more than anyone else," she replied. "At least ye helped him when his own uncles did the dirt on him, despite tellin' me at the funeral of his father that they wud luk after him. Some lukin' after ... " she sniffed. "Barely sixteen an' he's lyin' there like an oul man."

"His dad was navy durin' the war, wasn't he?" asked Kelly.

"Aye," she replied warmly, looking at her late husband's photograph on the wall. "Jimmy's gittin' till luk just like him. Did ye know him?" she asked conversationally.

"I only met him once," said Kelly, "but he made a man outa me." She looked at him strangely as he continued.

"I wus just a wee buck when I joined the army, Mrs. Harvey. I went till the Recruiting Office in Clifton Street an' lied about my age. I hated the trainin' an' when I got home leave I decided I wasn't goin' back. My da was in hospital with a leg injury he'd got at the docks an' I went in an' out through the back door of our house in Michael Street. I wus three days absent when the front door knocked. I gathered up a few bits an' went out the back door an' yer husband was stannin' there in civvies. He ushered me back intil the house and sat me down."

He twisted the cap in his hands as he continued. "He tole me the Military Police had come to him about me. He said if I went back of my own accord, he wud tell them I'd stayed over because I wus worried about my father. He explained if I stayed home another two days I'd be classed as officially absent without leave and sent to prison as a deserter. I was afraid, Mrs. Harvey. Confused and frightened. Your husband tole me to think of the worry I wud bring till my father if I decided to run away again. He said he couldn't and wouldn't try to stop me, an' said the MPs were sittin' in his home waitin' to take me back, no questions asked.

He said if I wud promise to go back that night he wud send them away. I did, an' he tuk me down till the boat himself an' bought me a san'wich an' a pint a beer in the Liverpool Bar before takin' me over to the Provost Marshall."

He smiled grimly. "I returned a hero an' niver even bought him a drink. I always meant till call over when I wus on leave but he wus the only man who'd ever seen me weep an' I cud niver git up the courage till face him. I attended his funeral and saw wee Jim cryin' an' lukin' lost an' confused the same as I wus. The next time I saw him was at the cement boat when the Animal wus gonna send him home. I tuk him under my wing an' I guess I've made a mess of it."

She leaned over and held his hand. "I'm glad ye tole me that story. It musta tuk a lot a courage. My husband wus a lot older than most of youse lads that went till the war. An' ye weren't the only one." She smiled at the recollection. "Many's the time the MPs cum up that hall an' threw their rifles under that sofa an' ate me outa house an' home while Tommy went roun' an' talked till young lads just as confused an' frightened as ye were yerself. Nine times outa ten they went back, just as yerself did." He rose to leave and she stood up. "I'm glad ye tuk him under yer wing an' I know yill turn him intil a decent man like yerself." He nodded silently and waited until she closed the door before walking into York Street and crossing the deserted road.

He hoped his father wouldn't be asleep as there were many, many things he wanted to say to him.